PORT DANBY COZY MYSTERY SERIES

BOOKS 7-9

LONDON LOVETT

LONDON LOVETT

PEONIES AND POISON

Peonies and Poison

Copyright © 2018 by London Lovett

All rights reserved.

CHAPTER 1

So much blinding white heat reflected off the sidewalk, I half expected my sandal to get mired in sticky cement. A heat wave had roared into town two days earlier and it seemed even the cooling ocean breeze had given up trying to compete with the determined sun.

I took another sip of the strawberry, banana and yogurt smoothie I'd blended for breakfast and plodded toward the shop. Cooking anything on the stove or in the oven had been out of the question in my tiny house. I'd resorted to salads, sandwiches and all things that were refreshing and blend-worthy.

Kingston flew ahead but arced quickly to the ground when he spotted Elsie standing out at her sidewalk tables. My bird knew the small, fast moving woman with the gray and toffee hair was always a sure bet for a cookie or muffin crumb. To Kinston's disappointment, the box Elsie carried contained batteries and mini handheld fans.

Elsie glanced toward Kingston as he paced anxiously on the hot cement, still holding out hope that there were scones buried beneath the batteries. She placed the box on one of her tables and scanned the sidewalk.

Her white smile flashed my direction. "I saw the crow and figured the owner wasn't far behind."

I pressed the smoothie cup against my cheek. "I can't believe it's this hot already."

"Never felt anything like it. It's actually cooler in my kitchen, with four convection ovens blasting baked goods, then it is out here on the sidewalk. Smart that you left your bike at home today." Elsie pulled a tiny fan from the box and started putting batteries into its base.

"I tried to convince myself I was tough enough to handle the bike ride to town but the second I stepped outside, I raced back in for my keys."

Elsie shrugged. "You've got to get out before the sun comes up. I ran five miles before I opened up at dawn and the temperature was lovely."

"Yes, well, you are super woman and I'm the mild mannered florist who doesn't rise from bed until I can see sunlight peeping around the drapes."

Kingston waddled under the table we were standing at but even the shade of the table top wasn't enough to cool the cement. He danced back and forth impatiently, waiting to get inside to his perch.

"That poor bird is stuck wearing head to toe black." Elsie turned the fan on. I closed my eyes as a small blast of air hit my face." What do you think?"

"I guess the Great Table War is back on. I thought you two had grown bored of competing." Elsie and Les had taken sibling rivalry to a whole new level with their sidewalk sitting areas, but I doubted the fancy furniture and even the small handheld fans would convince people to sit out on the blistering sidewalk. Even the trees lining Harbor Lane looked as if they wanted to be anywhere but standing on the city street.

"I've told you before, it's not a competition." Elsie scoffed. "Clearly, people prefer to sit in front of the bakery. Who can resist sitting in the swirl of cinnamon, sugar and spice drifting out from my shop?"

I tapped my chin. "Hmm, maybe people who prefer to sit in the swirl of rich roasted coffee aroma. I don't think anything will entice people to sit on either side this week. At least not until the sweltering temperatures are gone."

Ignoring my prediction, Elsie went right on dropping batteries into the fans.

Footsteps grabbed both our attentions. Ryder strolled past staring at his phone and looking more than a little distracted. His sunglasses were shoved on his head and his mouth was set in a firm line. He didn't notice us, or the crow who immediately trotted his direction.

"Kids and their phones." Elsie clucked her tongue. "The entire world could be burning down around them and they wouldn't notice because they'd be too focused on their friend's latest Instagram picture of the world going up in flames."

I watched as my normally astute and dialed in assistant continued on without even a glance our direction. "That's strange. I know a lot of people are glued to their phones but it's not like Ryder. Something must be up." I turned to Elsie. "Anyhow, I need to get inside. I've got a future bride coming in this morning to pick flowers for the bridal bouquets. I'll see you later. And good luck with the fans."

"Thanks."

Kingston startled Ryder as he unlocked the flower shop. The crow flew past him and headed straight for his perch beneath the air conditioning vent.

"You'll have to excuse his rude behavior," I said from behind, startling Ryder again.

"Hey, boss," he said with mild enthusiasm. Something was definitely up and I was certain it had to do with my capricious best friend. Lola seemed pleased about their relationship. At the same time, she occasionally had that nervous deer look on her face as if she was just waiting for one sign of danger so she could run for the hills.

I followed him inside and walked straight to the thermostat on the back wall. "It's already eighty degrees in here." I flicked the switch on. The drumming sound of the air conditioner rumbled through ducts over head. "I have a feeling the electric bill is going to surpass my profits this week, but I have to keep the shop cool for the flowers and customers."

"Or you could turn it into a big greenhouse." Even his usual smile was weak. "Has the bride picked the kind of flower she wants?"

"Yes, she wants peonies. I created a few examples last night before I closed up. Hopefully, one of them will work."

Ryder followed me down the short hallway to the office. His footsteps didn't have the usual bounce.

I put my purse away and turned on my computer. Ryder glanced at his phone once more before pushing it into his pocket.

"Anything wrong?" I asked hesitantly. I knew having my best friend and my coworker in a relationship was going to add a layer of trouble to my close knit social circle but I had only myself to blame. I'd pushed and prodded and hinted about them getting together so much, I could easily have earned the title of meddling matchmaker.

"Everything is just peachy," Ryder said dryly.

"Since you're throwing around words like peachy, I'm going to assume things are anything but peachy." I walked out behind him.

"Lola is going to France," he blurted the words quickly, as if they left a bitter taste in his mouth.

Lola's parents had rented a cottage in France. They told her they would pay for her plane ticket if she wanted to join them. The last time she'd mentioned it to me, she seemed dead set against it. She must have changed her mind.

"I'm sure she won't be gone long." It was a lame response to make him feel better, but it was the only thing that popped into my head.

Ryder swung around. "So you knew about her trip?"

"Huh? No, not really. She mentioned that her parents offered to fly her to France but last we spoke, she'd decided not to go." My words rushed out as if I was making them up as I went but they were true. I smiled weakly at him. "She won't stay long, Ryder. Besides, you know the old saying—"

"If you're going to say absence makes the heart grow fonder, I should warn you that my mom already threw that pearl of wisdom my way and it bounced right off my hard head. Lola will forget all about me when she's dashing around the dazzling French coastline and traveling the countryside. And I wouldn't blame her either. What am I compared to the sights, smells and sounds of France?"

I put my hand on his arm. "As far as I'm concerned the sights, smells and sounds of Ryder Kirkland are just as exciting." His bunched brows mirrored mine. "Yes, now that I've heard that aloud, it didn't quite work the way I expected."

A smile finally broke on his face. It seemed I'd temporarily humored him out of his moment of self-doubt. "I'll get started on the bouquets for the Woman's Club luncheon," Ryder said. "And I promise not to sulk. Not too much, anyhow."

"That's the spirit." I headed to the refrigerator and pulled out the four bridal bouquet samples I'd created. One was a simple bouquet of pale pink peony buds mixed in with full white blooms. I left the stems long and bare and wrapped them with burlap. A second bouquet was a more formal mix of pink peonies and yellow roses. White baby's breath sprigs lent a whimsical touch. I'd pulled together a striking monochromatic bouquet of double pink peonies and tied them off with a white satin ribbon. It was vibrant with color and fragrance. The last bouquet was a country charm mix of pale pink peonies and yellow buttercups framed by lacy green fern. With any luck, the bride would know exactly which one would fit seamlessly into the occasion.

CHAPTER 2

A baby blue Fiat parked in front of the shop. I'd only spoken to Jazmin, the bride-to-be, on the phone once, but she struck me as decisive and confident. She knew she wanted peonies in her bouquets because they were her grandmother's favorite.

The door swung open and two young women were chatting away as they walked inside. It was easy to spot the future bride. She had that radiant glow of a woman immersed in a fantasy world of satin and lace and everything bridal. Or it might have been the brutal hot streaks of sunlight pouring down from the sky. She was clutching a bottle of vitamin water in one hand and an oversized designer handbag in the other. A tiny head of gray curls popped up from inside the bag. The teacup poodle had a quick look around the store, sneezed twice and then dropped back into its hiding place. The second woman, who appeared much closer to her teens than to adulthood, skittered across the floor in her sandals and white cut off shorts.

"Look, Jazzy! I heard they had a crow inside this shop." The girl had hair the color of caramel. Long fringy bangs hung close to her blue eyes. She looked across the store at me. "Is he friendly?" she asked.

I'd found it best practice to not let strangers touch Kingston. As domesticated as he was, I never knew exactly how he was going to react to someone new. And most people tended to just shoot their hand straight at him, not considering that it might startle him.

"Kingston loves people," I said. "But he prefers to be admired from a distance."

"Come on, Trinity. We don't have time to dawdle. I'm meeting Bradley for lunch in Mayfield." The bride walked directly to the peony bouquets on the work island and placed her handbag on the floor next to her feet.

"Hello." I reached my hand out. "I'm Lacey, the shop owner. You must be Jazmin."

She took my hand. Her nails had tiny flowers painted across the tips. "Yes, I'm the one you spoke to on the phone." The younger girl had lost her interest in Kingston and joined us at the island. She hopped up on a stool. "This is my sister, Trinity. She's supposed to be helping me, but, well . . ." Jazmin scowled at her sister, who responded with an eye roll.

"Whatever, Jazzy. It's just that you can't make up your mind about anything. We spent like three years in the print shop picking out her invitations. Then she changed her mind ten minutes after we left the store."

Jazmin had dark, expressive brows. They were showing frustration. "Sure, three years. It was two hours at the most."

"Nope, nope, nope." Trinity shook her head. She shot me a serious glance. "I walked into the shop with short bangs and left with these." She pointed to her overlong bangs and then swept them away from her forehead. Her blue eyes landed on the peonies. "These are so pretty. Grammie is going to love them."

Jazmin seemed less enamored with the bouquets. She pursed her lips and tilted her head from side to side. She backed up and squinted at the bouquets.

Trinity blew a puff of air straight up, ruffling her long bangs. "Why are you backing away from the flowers and doing this?" Trinity squished up her nose and squinted her eyes. She laughed and fished for her phone. "I should get a picture of you with that goofy face."

Jazmin shook her head and sighed audibly. "Do you see what I mean?" she asked me.

I didn't respond. I already spent my entire workday between the king and queen of sibling rivalry. I certainly didn't need to step between two sisters.

"If you must know, Trini, I'm trying to see how the flowers will look from a distance. It's a big church. I want the people in the back to see them. I should take a few pictures to send to Mom." Jazmin's tiny dog squeaked and stuck his nose out of the purse while she searched for her phone. She set to work taking pictures of the bouquets from every angle as if she were doing a photo shoot for a florist instead of picking her wedding bouquets.

I patted the counter. "I'll let you decide then. Just let me know if there's a combination you like or would prefer to see."

Ryder came out from the store room with a large bag of potting soil draped over his shoulder. Trinity sat up perkily on the stool. "Hello," she chirped across the store.

"Good morning," he said politely back.

Trinity leaned forward and dropped her voice to a whisper. "He's cute. Does he work here?"

Before I could answer, Jazmin piped up with a short laugh. "No, she just pulled him in off the street to carry dirt around the store." As hard as Jazmin was trying to be the mature, soon to be married, older sister it seemed she couldn't resist a sarcastic sisterly barb.

"Ryder does work here," I added. "He's a great assistant."

Trinity repositioned herself on the stool. "He's cute but too old. I only just turned eighteen. Besides, I have a boyfriend." She quickly swiped through the photos on her phone and showed me a picture. A pillbox style red usher's hat squashed down the teen's curly sun bleached hair. He had his thumb and pinky raised in the hang loose gesture. "His name is Justin. He doesn't usually wear that stupid looking theater usher uniform. I mean he dresses cool, like a surfer, when he's not stuck in the uniform." She lowered the phone. "We both work at the Mayfield Four Movie Theater. Have you been there?"

I couldn't remember the last time I'd been to the movies. Briggs had suggested it a few times but then we always had a hard time agreeing on a movie. "I haven't seen a movie in a long time," I said. "But in this heat wave, I'll bet it's a great place to hang out for a few hours."

"For sure." Trinity kicked her suntanned legs back and forth. "Especially because we have the best slush making machine for miles. We just added a new flavor too. Lemon-lime. It's super tasty."

"Hmm, lemon-lime sounds good." I flicked my attention her sister's direction. She was still taking pictures. "I'll have to check out the movie listings to see if there's anything my boyfriend—" I paused. I suddenly realized I had yet to call Briggs my boyfriend. It sounded strange to my ear.

Trinity's laugh pulled me from my thoughts. "I know what you mean. Justin and I can't ever decide on a movie. I like horror movies and he likes superhero flicks."

"But I'll bet you get to see them all for free so you can see anything you want."

She shook her head and her long bangs fell over her eyes. She brushed them aside. "I wish. Our boss, Mr. Samuels, is *soo* stingy. He only gives us a ten percent discount on the snack bar. Even then, he watches us like crazy to make sure we're not eating or drinking too much. The only time we see the movies for free is when we have to walk in and tell some bratty kids to be quiet or ask someone to stop throwing popcorn at the screen."

"That's too bad. It seems like a free movie, or at the very least, a free box of licorice should be one of the perks of the job."

"All right." Jazmin finally put down her phone. "I really like this one." She pointed out the bouquet with pink peonies and yellow buttercups.

"Great. The buttercups are hard to come by at this time of year, but I'm sure I can track some down. They might be a little more money though."

Jazmin waved off the mention of money. "Daddy said I could pick whatever I like."

Trinity clucked her tongue and hopped off the stool. "Oh brother.

I ask for a new phone and he throws a fit." She wandered across the room to the work area where Ryder was cutting flowers for bouquets. He didn't seem to mind the company. Apparently there was nothing like a cute girl to take your mind off relationship problems.

Jazmin picked up the bouquet and moved it around, circling it through the air. She was a very thorough flower shopper. The dance act caught her sister's attention. Trinity's giggles filled the shop. "Are you going to be walking down the aisle like that?" She stuck one hand on her hip and performed an exaggerated bridal walk across the shop waving her invisible bouquet around as she went.

Jazmin ignored her sister's antics. "I wonder if it's a little heavy."

"I could lighten it up by putting in more greenery and leaving out some of the peonies."

Her mouth swished back and forth in thought. "No, I think maybe less of the yellow flowers. I want the peonies to stay the star of the show." She laughed lightly and pointed to herself. "Other than the bride, of course."

"Naturally. And you'll make a very beautiful bride at that."

My comment earned a scoffing sound from Trinity, who had joined us at the counter.

I circled around to the back side of the work island and pulled out my order book. "Great. I'll keep the peonies for your bouquet at ten and reduce the yellow buttercups to four. How many bridesmaids will there be?"

"She doesn't know because her two best friends have been fighting over the maid of honor spot." Trinity said with a spoonful of derision added on top. "Doesn't it seem right that her only sister should be the maid of honor?" she asked me.

Jazmin elbowed her aside. "No, it isn't right. But it's true. I have two best friends and I'm having a hard time deciding. But there will be six altogether, including the little sister that my parents insisted had to be part of the bridal party—"Jazmin curled a scowl Trinity's way.

Trinity picked up one of the bouquets and ran her fingers over the soft petals. "She's just worried I'll outshine her on her wedding day."

Jazmin plucked the bouquet from Trinity and placed it on the counter. "Why don't you go talk to the bird while we finish the order."

Trinity's phone buzzed. "That's probably Justin. He's looking for another job because of horrible Mr. Samuels," she said to no one in particular.

Jazmin sighed in relief as her sister walked away with the phone. "Teenagers are always such big shots. I don't think I ever acted like her."

I smiled and glanced across the store at Trinity. She was rocking back and forth on her heels while she texted on her phone. "I think I acted a lot like your sister. She's fun but then I'm not her big sister. I'm sure my opinion would be different in that circumstance." I continued with the order. The wedding was in early fall so I'd have to contact my supplier right away to get in my order. Neither flower was easy to come by at that time of year but I'd partnered up with a number of hothouse suppliers who could get me virtually any bloom I wanted. Even in fall and winter.

Trinity's sandals slapped the floor dejectedly. "Poor Justin didn't get the job at the warehouse. They wanted someone with experience."

"Too bad surfing doesn't come in handy for job skills," Jazmin sniped before walking away to answer her phone.

"Just because Bradley is a computer nerd doesn't mean I can't date someone cool," Trinity said to her sister's back. She climbed back on the stool, stuck her elbows on the island and her chin on her hands. "I guess he's stuck working at the theater. Mr. Samuels really hates Justin. He yells at him about everything." Trinity went on with her one-sided conversation. I politely nodded but I was concentrating on writing the order. She slapped the counter suddenly, startling me into a mistake. I crossed out the nine that should have been a six.

"Sorry about that," Trinity said. "But I just thought I'd let you know about vintage movie night. It's tomorrow night at seven. We're screening Casablanca. I've never seen it but I've heard it's one of those cool old black and white flicks."

"Here's looking at you kid," I muttered absently.

Trinity blinked at me. "Huh?"

"Oh, that's from the movie. It's a classic. And that line is probably the most famous movie quote of all time." I stopped and tapped my pen on the order pad. "Did you say it starts at seven?"

She straightened her posture, excited that she'd caught my interest. "Sally Applegate, the assistant manager sets up cool events like vintage movie night. She does an awesome job. You'd think Mr. Samuels would pat her on the back and tell her good job, or at least give her a free soda for her effort, but nope. He's as stingy and mean as they come."

"He does sound like a terrible man to work for."

"Do you think you might come? Ask your boyfriend. It's nice and cool inside the theater and don't forget to try the lemon-lime slush."

"Actually, that does sound fun. Thanks for letting me know."

CHAPTER 3

*T*he sweltering temperatures of the morning had amped up to the blistering, searing heat of mid afternoon. The air was thick and gooey as I headed along Harbor Lane to the Port Danby Police Station. It felt like I was wading through a viscous vat of syrup. The high temperature had burned off any coastal breeze. The usual odors wafting up from the marina, including the fishing boats, were extra pungent. Kingston hadn't left his perch inside the air conditioned shop all day and I could hardly blame him. If I hadn't been invited to lunch by my favorite local detective, I might have stayed huddled inside too.

The door to the police station opened a good twenty feet before I reached it. Briggs' dog, Bear, came galumphing out. It seemed every time the pup's body finally grew into his long legs and massive ears, his limbs and ears grew again, leaving him more room to catch up. He was in the silly, gangly teenager stage.

I stooped down and let him lick my chin as I rubbed his soft fur. His owner's shadow loomed over us, providing us with a much needed touch of shade for our greeting.

I stood up straight. "Don't take this the wrong way, but I think your dog might be part cartoon. Sometimes he looks more like an animated character in a kid's movie than an actual dog."

Briggs laughed. He always looked extra sharp with his shirt sleeves rolled up. He was still dressed for work but a tie and coat were out of the question today. "I have to agree. I had to bring him to work today because the air conditioner overheated in my house last night and it's like an oven."

"That's terrible. What a time for the thing to overheat. Although, I guess that wouldn't happen unless it was running nonstop."

"Since I've got my animated nuisance along for lunch, I thought we'd just pick up a hot dog on the pier. Maybe walk down to the water. It has to be at least a few degrees cooler near the ocean."

"Sounds good to me. I'm starved. My house has no air conditioner to overheat, so I've been relying solely on the rare breeze to blow through. I haven't turned on the oven or stove for a few days and I've been mostly drinking my meals. Sinking my teeth into solid food is just what I need."

"Jeez, and here I am complaining about my broken air conditioner."

"Yes but I can feel the ocean breeze at my house." I was tempted to take his arm but it was too hot even for that. "Although, it seems the afternoon breeze has hightailed it for cooler shores. Which reminds me, I've got an idea for a movie date."

We reached the pier. Bear galloped enthusiastically up the steps ahead of us.

"Bear, sit," Briggs called. The dog reached the landing and sat down obediently. But his tail swished excitedly from side to side at the prospect of terrifying pigeons and gulls.

"Impressive," I noted. "He's come a long way." I glanced over at Briggs. The faint lines on the side of his mouth seemed to indicate he was holding back a proud grin.

"I have to admit, it's nice having a dog again."

This time, hot or not, I reached over and curled my arm around his. "It suits you. You look even better with a big furry pal strutting next to you."

His brown eyes flicked sideways at me. "Even better? I like that. I'll have to bring him to work more often." Right as he said it, Bear loped ahead scattering a group of industrious pigeons into the air, which, in turn, caused a woman to startle and drop her ice cream cone, scoop first, onto the pier.

Briggs reached for his wallet. "Or maybe not." He hurried ahead and quickly apologized for the dog as he handed her money for another cone. Bear *sacrificed* his pigeon chase to clean up the ice cream mess.

The heat wave had given everyone the same idea as us. The pier was crowded with people looking for a cooler spot to have lunch. But without the breeze, there wouldn't be much of a reprieve.

I crinkled my nose in an attempt to tamp down my extra acute sense of smell. Most of the time, the coastline was ripe with the fresh, salty scent of the ocean. Today, the mix of aromas and odors was overwhelming. As hungry as I was, even a hot dog didn't sound appetizing.

Bear finished lapping up the ice cream and was busy flicking his tongue across his wet, black nose to get the last drops as Briggs finished his apology.

"Bear, here." He pointed to his side. For the first time since the ice cream calamity, the dog seemed to gather that he was in trouble. He dropped his head and tail and wiggled his hips as he shuffled over to us. "I should have brought his leash."

"He's fine," I assured Briggs. "Besides, I think you made that woman's day with your chivalrous apology. I'm sure she wasn't expecting it. However, the ice cream fiasco has sort of made me change my mind about the hot dog. I think I'll lick my lunch."

"You're going to eat ice cream for lunch?" he asked.

I twitched my nose. "Samantha can't seem to switch off all the pungent odors on the pier today. The hot air has magnified every-thing. It has sort of ruined my appetite." Briggs had come up with the nickname Samantha for my nose since I moved it like the character in the vintage television show Bewitched.

"I'm sorry, Lacey. I shouldn't have suggested the beach for lunch."

He wore concern so genuinely (and handsomely) on his face it made me smile.

"Nonsense. I'll enjoy lunch no matter where we are as long as I'm with two of my favorite guys." I patted Bear's head to let him know he was included in the list. "I think super nose or not, I'd still be craving ice cream. It's just too hot for anything else. Go buy your hot dog and get me a scoop of that lemon gelato. In fact, make it a double. Bear and I will wait for you."

"Right. Double scoop of lemon gelato." He instructed Bear to stay. The dog sat down next to me but his tail wagged with frustration. He badly wanted to follow Briggs. It was a true friendship. Or it might have been because Briggs was heading to the hot dog stand.

A few minutes later, Briggs had his hot dog and I had my bowl of gelato. The creamy treat was tart and lush and refreshing in my mouth. And the strong citrus scent was doing an admirable job competing with the strong odors circulating around my nose.

We headed down the end of the pier and toward the sandy path to Pickford Beach. School was several weeks away and the sand was dotted with kids playing volleyball and hanging out with friends. The water was more crowded than I'd seen it all summer with people splashing, swimming and keeping cool in the waves.

"So you mentioned a movie date?" Briggs led me to a bench near the path and we sat down to eat. Bear crawled beneath the shade of the bench but I was certain he was keeping a close eye on the group of seagulls strutting around the sand in front of us.

I swallowed another bite of the silky gelato. "Yes. I had a bridal order this morning and the bride's sister mentioned that she worked at Mayfield Four Movie Theater. Hates her boss, by the way, but that's another story. Anyhow, they are having a special screening of Casablanca tomorrow night. Are you interested?"

"Are you asking me out on a date, Miss Pinkerton?" he teased.

"As a matter of fact, yes, I am, Detective Briggs. My treat. I'll even spring for the lemon-lime slush drinks, which I've been assured are delicious. I'm mostly drawn to the idea that theaters are always just a touch too cold. In any case, it'll be much cooler than my house."

"A little Bogie in the air conditioning. Sounds good." Briggs wiped some mustard off the corner of his mouth. Now that we were clear of the unpleasant aromas on the pier, the hot dog looked pretty tasty. Apparently he caught me gazing longingly at his relish and mustard topped bun. He lifted it for me to take a bite. Which I did.

"Hmm, yep, should have gotten a hot dog."

Briggs scooted forward. "I'll go up and get you one."

"No, don't worry about it. So it's a date. The movie starts at seven tomorrow."

"Great. I'll pick you up at half past six. Should I wear a fedora and trench coat?"

"Only if you want me to keep favoring you with my Ingrid Bergman smoldering, starry-eyed gaze."

"I could put up with a little smolder and stars." Briggs handed Bear the last bite of hot dog and took a drink of soda. "Interestingly enough, last fall I had to deal with a theater feud between the owner of Mayfield Four and the owner of Starlight Movie Theater across town. Apparently, there's always been a good dose of rivalry between the theaters. Then one night, after closing thankfully, the Starlight Theater had a fire. The source was determined to be a faulty plug on the pretzel warmer. No one was hurt but the damage was significant. The owner, Connie Wilkerson, had to close up the theater for months. She nearly lost everything in the process, but she's back up and running. From what I've heard, it's been nearly impossible for her to compete now. Which brings me to the trouble. Miss Wilkerson came to me alleging that Ronald Samuels, the owner of Mayfield Four, had started the fire or at least hired someone to start it. There wasn't any evidence to support her claim so she had to drop the matter. She wasn't happy."

"I'll bet. I know Trinity, the girl who told me about the Casablanca screening, had nothing but terrible things to say about Mr. Samuels. He sounds like a hard man to work for."

Briggs carried our trash to the nearest can, and we started our walk back to work. It seemed the whole world was moving in slow motion due to the heat. Three boys on bicycles pedaled along the planks of the pier as if they were dragging wagons of bricks behind their bikes. People strolled slowly and closely to the railing trying hard to catch a cooling mist from the water below. Most of the pigeons and gulls that milled about the food stands had taken off to shady trees or the cool grass beneath the lighthouse. Even Bear's earlier exuberant prance had been replaced with a sluggish, plodding trot.

"My phone says the heat wave might break this weekend," I said. "I'll be ready for it."

"Me too. One good thing, the excessive heat always seems to tamp down crime. Guess people are too hot to get into trouble."

"Really? Interesting. Well, if we're going to be murder and crime free in our fair town for awhile, then I should get back to the Hawksworth case. I want to keep my detective skills sharp and ready for the next moment of mayhem."

"Have you learned anything new?" Briggs took my hand. I loved the protective way he squeezed my fingers. My heart skipped a beat or two. I let it get back to normal before focusing on his question.

"Did I tell you about the letters I found in the trunk inside the gardener's shed?"

"You mean the Hawksworth Museum you break into every chance you get?"

Bear insisted on pushing between us, making it impossible to continue holding hands. We parted as we turned the corner onto Harbor Lane.

"Yes, but I don't think you can call it a break in when the lock just slides open. Anyhow, are you interested in my very interesting find, or not?"

Briggs smiled my direction. I wondered if he knew the power behind that grin. "Yes, I'm interested. Continue."

"First of all, the trunk is not a hope chest. It's filled with a man's ascots and straw boaters. I'm sure the items belonged to Bertram Hawksworth. In fact, his business ledgers are stored inside."

"Really? Anything of note inside the ledgers?" Bear trotted ahead and sat in front of the police station door, apparently anxious to get back into the air conditioning.

"Lots of numbers in columns. Just what you'd expect. But I did discover something. I'm just not sure if it's anything important." We stopped in front of the station. Briggs opened the door and Bear darted inside.

"Pampered pooch," I mused.

"Said the woman whose pet crow has his own collection of treats, custom perches and gets to decide the day's agenda."

"Touché. Back to the ledgers. I'll talk fast because I need to get back to the shop. According to the signatures in the account ledgers, it seemed Jane Price, Mayor Harvard Price's daughter from his first marriage, worked as Bertram Hawkworth's accountant for a short time."

Briggs stared at me expectantly, apparently waiting for a bigger shoe to drop.

"That's the interesting part," I said, hesitantly. "Mayor Harvard Price, great-grandfather of the current Mayor price," I added.

"Yes, I made the connection. We detectives are good at things like that. But what does it have to do with the murder?"

I raised a dramatic brow. "Yes. What indeed?"

"So you found a connection?"

"Well, no. Not exactly."

Hilda poked her head outside. "Dear me, it's like sticking my head in the oven to check if the roast is done," she quipped.

"Oh, it's done," I said. "In fact, I'd say it's well done. How are you, Hilda?"

"Aside from being sticky from head to toe, I'm fine. Thank you."

I nodded. "This weather makes everything sticky."

Hilda's round cheeks turned to apples. "No, I'm sticky because that big, slobbery dog just licked me from head to toe as if we'd been parted for weeks." She looked over at Briggs. "I've finished typing those reports. I was going to take off early. My sister is having a pool party."

"Absolutely, Hilda. Enjoy yourself. Uh, Hilda," Briggs said quickly before she closed the door.

She popped her head back out. This time Bear's head came with it. "Yes?"

"Is Officer Chinmoor on the schedule tomorrow night?"

"I'll double check but I think so."

"Great. Thanks."

Hilda and Bear withdrew their faces from the hot outside air. Briggs turned to me. He had that sparkle in his brown eyes that tended to make my knees turn to gelatin. "Then I guess the date is on for sure." He clipped me lightly on the chin. "Here's lookin' at you, kid." It was an impressive impersonation of Bogart and it added to the wobble in my knees.

"We'll always have Paris," I replied. "But I guess we'd have to go to Paris first for that line to have meaning."

"Maybe someday. Have a nice afternoon, Miss Pinkerton."

"You too, Detective Briggs."

CHAPTER 4

*R*yder had moped around most of the afternoon. He left early for a swim at the beach and I finished with my paperwork. The shop had been close to deserted most of the day. My offer of free air conditioning and flowery fragrances wasn't enough to entice people out for a day of flower shopping. It was just too hot to think about anything except staying cool.

Kingston had finished his lunch and was sleeping soundly on his perch. Something told me he was dreaming of swooping through red and gold trees on a blustery fall day. He was not a summer lover. Like Elsie had noted—the poor guy was clad head to toe in black.

I left him to his bird dreams and locked up for a few minutes to walk across the street. Lola's shop looked as deserted as mine, so it seemed we'd have an opportunity to chat. I had more than a few questions to ask.

Lola was stooped down below the counter. Her red hair peeked up over the display of vintage lighters. "When were you going to let your best friend know that you were flying halfway across the world to France?" I asked as I headed toward the counter.

The thick red hair emerged and a face came with it, only it wasn't the one I was expecting. The red haired girl behind the counter looked to be in her early twenties. Her skin was paler than Lola's and her eyes were blue instead of brown. But there was something about her expression that reminded me of Lola. She found her tongue before me.

"Oh, you're the pretty lady who runs the flower shop. I saw you this morning with your crow. Lo-lo told me all about your pet crow, Kingston. I can't wait to meet him." Before I could say hello, she scrambled on about my bird. "Although, if I'm being honest, they kind of scare me with those long sharp beaks and beady black eyes. Is he really as friendly as Lo-lo says?" Sleuth that I was, I quickly determined the loving nickname Lo-lo, the red hair and the similar expressions meant I was talking to Lola's relative.

"I'm Lacey, owner of Pink's Flowers. You must be—" I paused for her to fill in the name. It took her a second to understand.

"Oh right, I'm Shauna. I'm Lo-lo's cousin. Our moms are sisters."

"Wonderful. I didn't know you were visiting. Nice to meet you. And Kingston can be shy around strangers but he is extra friendly to your cousin." I leaned in for a conspiratorial whisper, figuring Lola was just a few feet away in her office. "My crow has a huge crush on Lola."

"That's right. I attract all kinds," Lola said as she stepped into the shop front. She was carrying a box with glass trinkets.

I put my hands on my hips. "How on earth did you hear that? Sometimes I think we should combine my sense of smell with your sense of hearing and start some kind of—" They both waited for me to finish, but I couldn't come up with anything clever.

"Superhero club?" Lola provided with a wry smile as she placed the box on the counter.

"Yes, a club for super senses." I turned to her cousin. "Are you in town long?"

Shauna parted her lips to answer but Lola stepped in first. "She's here to run the store and house sit while I'm in France."

I leaned my arm on the counter and turned to face her. "Yes, I've heard rumors of you jetting off to Europe. Normally, it's something one would expect to hear straight from one's best friend but—"

24

"Why are you talking in the third person?" I could tell instantly that Lola wasn't excited or anxious for the trip. Her mouth was turned down at the edges and her shoulders were rounded. "And I won't be gone long. My parents, me and a small cottage does not spell success or a long vacation. I give it three days and I'll be packing up for the airport." Lola started removing the glassware from the box. Most of it was green and muted orange depression glass. The low cost plates and cups that were manufactured and distributed during the Great Depression. "Are you going to miss me?" she asked with a laugh.

"Hmm, that depends. Are you going to bring your best friend back something pretty from France?"

"I could probably find some pretty trinket that my best friend will like."

Lola handed Shauna a green cake plate and pointed to the dust cloth near the cash register. Shauna picked it up and absently wiped the glass as she listened to our amusing chatter.

"In that case, yes, I'll miss you a great deal. But maybe not as much as a certain someone who has been doing more than his share of brooding today."

Lola glanced swiftly toward her cousin and motioned for me to follow her to the office.

Shauna's posture slumped when she realized she wasn't going to get to hear the rest of the conversation.

Lola waved me past her into her tiny office nook. "I don't need Shauna listening in," she said quietly and shut the door. "She relays everything to her mom, my Aunt Ruby, and then Aunt Ruby relays everything to my mom. Only Ruby usually puts her own spin on it. Then the whole thing gets twisted into some sordid tale about me dating the president of a motorcycle club or whatever other fun details get tossed in on the rumor chain."

She leaned against her desk and crossed her arms over the screaming eagle on her Van Halen t-shirt. "Is he really upset?"

"Well, it *was* kind of sudden. Just the other day you mentioned something about rather having a root canal than spending so much time with your parents."

Lola smiled about her analogy. "I guess I did say that. But, you know, my best friend"—She waved her hand toward me—"the oddball who likes to refer to herself in third person, has been such a role model for me. She spent an entire week with her parents and she survived without one meltdown. I thought I'd give it a shot with my own ma and pa." She stared down at the ground then, even though there was nothing of interest on the carpeted floor of her office. Her mouth pursed like a fish and then her chin jutted side to side. All gestures that assured me she had more to say on the subject.

"But . . ." I said as a starting point.

Her thin shoulders poked at the worn cotton t-shirt as she took a deep breath and rested her hands back against the desk. "Not but. *Besides* is a better way to begin. Besides, I think Ryder and I are moving too fast. When I go fast, I tend to lose control. I crash and burn."

"We are talking about relationships and not your terrible driving skills, right?"

"Yes, and I'm not that bad behind the wheel. Ah, who am I kidding? I'm terrible. Yes, I'm talking about my relationship." She put up her hand. "And before you start, Miss Meddlesome Matchmaker, I'm not running away. I'm just putting some space between us. A lot of space actually. And an ocean. So no unwanted advice or prodding."

I shook my head once and pretended to zip my lips, then immediately opened them. "You're right. I was being a meddlesome matchmaker. It's only because I thought you two were absolutely perfect—"

Lola raised her brow at me.

"Oops." I pressed my fingers to my lips but then dropped them quickly. "I guess it's not that easy to drop the matchmaker persona. But I will be the complete opposite of a matchmaker. I'll be a—" I tilted my head to the side. "Does matchmaker have an antonym?"

"Divorce lawyer?" Lola asked and we both burst into laughter.

I stepped forward to hug her. "I really am going to miss you. But I think it's good you're taking a little time for yourself. Well, other than being stuck in a cottage with your parents."

"I plan to do a lot of exploring. I am looking forward to it. I just hope Shauna can handle running the shop. She said some of the old stuff creeps her out. She's always been afraid of everything. Can't tell you how many times we had to cut the trick or treating short because Shauna would see something scary and want to turn back." Lola held up her hands. "I mean, duh. It was Halloween. Scary was kind of the theme. I was thrilled when I was old enough to just go with my friends and leave Shauna behind."

A loud gasp was followed by the sound of glass shattering. Lola's shoulders rose up to her ears. "My mom insisted I let her watch the house and shop. I think it was as a favor to Aunt Ruby, who needed a break from my cousin. But I'm not sure if anything of value will be left by the time I return. That's the third piece she's broken today." Lola headed to the door. "I've got to help her clean up. I don't want Bloomer to get a glass shard in his paw." She stopped before opening the door and lowered her voice to a whisper. "I swear I've caught that dog rolling his eyes twice today. Wait until he learns she's babysitting him for the next week." She opened the door and I followed her out.

Late Bloomer was sitting in front of the counter, watching raptly as Shauna frantically swept up chunks of glass. There was no eye roll but I was sure I caught an amused grin in the folds of his jowl.

Shauna glanced up with round blue eyes. She looked pale with panic about the mishap. "I'm sorry, Lola. The thing just slipped out of my fingers." Her voice wavered as if she might cry.

"Don't worry about it," Lola muttered. She stooped down to pick up the bigger shards.

"I'm so clumsy," Shauna said as she moved the broom back and forth. "Mom calls me butter fingers and she's right. It's like I dip my hands in butter every morning. Only not regular butter. That weird oily stuff they put on movie popcorn."

Lola straightened with a handful of large chunks. "Just make sure your movie popcorn hands get every piece. I don't want Bloomer to step on anything."

"That reminds me," I said as I patted Bloomer on the head. "Briggs and I are going to the Mayfield Four Theater tomorrow night. They're showing Casablanca."

"Sounds serious," Lola quipped. "First Casablanca, then North by Northwest. And before you know it, the two of you are sharing a soda in a Gone with the Wind marathon."

I ruffled Bloomer's soft ears. "Your mom is such a funny woman."

Lola snapped her fingers. "Funny woman. Streisand. No wait. That was Funny Girl."

"I love vintage classic movie night at the Mayfield Four," Shauna chirped. "For Halloween, they always decorate the theater and play one of the creepy black and white monster movies. They're my kind of horror movie because they don't include some awful guy sneaking around with a chainsaw and hockey mask. Those are way too scary." The broom nearly slipped from her hand as she tried to get some pieces out from under the counter. "Sally Applegate, the assistant manager of the theater—" She paused to bend over and pick up a large chunk. "She sets up the special movie nights. She belongs to the same anxiety support group as me."

Lola turned to her. "I didn't know you were in group therapy."

Shauna shrugged. It seemed she didn't mind talking about it. "Yeah, I was getting these panic attacks whenever something worried me, so Mom thought I should go. The therapist, Miss Nader, is a friend of hers. It really helps. I hardly ever have panic attacks anymore."

"Good to know since I'm putting you in charge of everything," Lola muttered with a good dose of sarcasm. She shot me a secret eye roll. I could easily predict what the first topic of conversation would be between Lola and her mom once she landed in France.

I tapped the counter with my fingers. "Well, I've left Kingston in nap mode. I should get back. He's all alone in the shop."

That statement caught Lola's attention. "Kingston's alone? Where is your assistant?"

Shauna's interest was piqued too. "Yeah, when do I get to meet Ryder?"

"Never," Lola said quickly to cut her off and turned back to me. "He didn't tell me he had the day off."

"He didn't but he wasn't in a great mood. So when friends asked him to go swimming at the beach, I told him to go."

It was easy to see by her expression that she was slightly upset about Ryder not mentioning his swim plans.

Lola quickly swept some invisible dust off the counter. "Good for him. I hope he has fun," she said in a tone that didn't match the words. I, of course, kept that observation to myself, but Shauna laughed about it.

"It doesn't sound like you want him to have fun at all," Shauna mused. "It seems like you're kind of mad he went without you."

Lola spun around and scowled at her. "What I'm mad about is the splinters of glass still on the floor. Go inside the office closet. There's a portable vacuum on the shelf. Bring it out here and pick up every tiny piece so Bloomer doesn't hurt himself."

Shauna realized, too late, her mistake. She looked a bit twitchy and nervous as she headed off with her broom. Lola snatched the broom from her hands before she got two steps. "I'll keep sweeping and pick up all the other pieces you missed."

Shauna walked dejectedly to the office.

"Nice meeting you, Shauna," I called.

A smile returned to her face as she looked back. "You too. Have fun at the movies." She disappeared around the corner.

I favored Lola with my own scowl. "Meanie. She just said she's getting over anxiety issues."

Lola waved it off. "Please, the kid was born anxious."

I shook my head. "All right. Let her know if she needs anything I'll be glad to help. When do you leave?"

"Tomorrow morning."

"So soon?" I walked around to her side of the counter. A chunk of glass crunched beneath my sandal. "Oops, think I found a piece only now it's a bunch of pieces." I reached over and hugged her. "Have a safe trip. And remember, I don't want a shirt that says 'my best friend went to France and all I got was this stupid shirt.'"

Lola laughed. "I'm insulted that you'd think I was that boring and unoriginal. I'll find you something."

I patted Bloomer once more and headed to the door. I glanced back at her. "You are going to say good-bye to him, right? Otherwise, I might as well give him the whole week off."

Lola nodded. "Yes, we are going to dinner tonight. Have fun at the movies with Mr. Wonderful."

"I plan to."

CHAPTER 5

*H*ammering woke me from an early evening nap. I sat up groggily from my awkward position on the couch. I leaned forward and stretched my arms up to the get the kinks out. My back was sticky and my hair was glued to the perspiration on my forehead.

Once I got home, I went straight to work opening all the windows in the house. It was an unrewarded attempt to cool the place off. After having a smoothie for breakfast and gelato for lunch, my stomach churned for something solid. I'd decided to throw caution to the wind and make a grilled cheese. I could still smell it throughout the house. I was sure I'd be dreaming about grilled cheese in my sleep.

The hammering started again. I walked to the kitchen window. I couldn't see Dash's roof, but there was a tall ladder leaning against the back of the house. He must have decided to move his construction project outside to avoid the stuffy warmth of the house. It sounded like a good idea to me too.

Kingston stared at me from his cage. It seemed he was mad I'd taken him from his air conditioned perch in the shop. Nevermore had barely touched his food before slinking off to the bedroom for another nap. I tossed a few peanuts into Kingston's bowl. That snapped him out of his glowering mood. It was never too hot for peanuts. Or too cold. Or too early. Or too late.

I grabbed a bottle of green tea from the refrigerator and headed out to the porch to drink it. The hammer cracked the thick, still air. I trotted down the steps to get a view of the noisy action next door. Dash had removed a large swath of shingles from his roof. He was replacing the wood with a new sheet of plywood. His white t-shirt was plastered to his tanned skin. He had wrapped a red bandana around his forehead to keep the sweat out of his eyes. He carefully placed a nail at the edge of the wood and gave it three hard blows.

I walked to his front yard and shielded my eyes to watch him. He still hadn't seen me, but his dog, Captain, greeted me with a lazy tail wag before dropping his big head down on his pillow again.

"I used to help my dad build stuff in his garage," I said loudly.

Dash turned around and wiped his forehead with his arm. His white smile flashed from his tanned face. I'd only recently learned that Dash had been the cause of Briggs' divorce. Briggs had married his high school sweetheart at a young age. It turned out to be a heartbreaking mistake. But the mistake was made worse when his best friend, Dashwood Vanhouten, betrayed him. Of course, there was a good dose of betrayal from Olivia, his wife, too but Briggs wasn't able to forgive Dash. I couldn't blame him, only I was in the awkward position of living next door to Dash. And he'd never given me any reason not to like him as a friend. It was something Briggs was working through. I'd decided to give him as much time as he needed. In the meantime, Dash and I were still friends. Just not close friends.

Dash tromped carefully over to the edge of the roof. He grinned down at me. "I don't picture you as the construction type."

"Considering it usually took me thirty or forty swings of the hammer to put in one crooked nail, you're probably right. Did you have a leak?"

He glanced back at the large patch. "Yeah, I've been meaning to get to it. The house was so hot, I decided to move the work outside."

"I figured that's what happened. It's so hot in my house, I feel like I'm shrinking while I sleep. Like a cotton t-shirt in the hot dryer."

Dash laughed and the movement made him slip forward. My heart nearly popped from my chest, but he easily caught himself.

"Think this is why I avoided patching the roof."

"I'll stop distracting you and let you get back to it. Be careful." I headed back to my porch steps and sipped my tea. From my front yard, I could see down to the water. I couldn't see the marina and pier, but the tall tower of the lighthouse was my favorite focal point. Farther out on the horizon, it looked as if a thin layer of gray clouds was forming. As much as I hated foggy mornings that sent my curly hair into a crazy fit, I would gladly walk around with the Shirley Temple hairdo if it meant a drop in temperature. I pulled out my phone and swiped open the weather app. There was no sign of relief.

I put my phone down and picked up my tea. I sucked in a big, choking gulp when Dash's yell startled me. The clamor of a ladder falling to the ground was followed by a thud and a groan.

My heart pounded so hard I could hear it in my ears. I dropped the tea and ran toward Dash's house. Captain was close on my heels as I pushed through the gate into his backyard. I saw the top of the fallen ladder before I found Dash. He was sitting on the ground, rocking back and forth in pain and holding his arm close to his stomach. The tan on his face had faded to an olive green.

I rushed to him and knelt down. "What can I do? How can I help?" I felt lightheaded from worry.

Dash looked down at the arm he held. "I think I broke my collarbone. My shoulder broke my fall. I'm trying not to move my arm because it hurts. I'm feeling sick from the bone break, but I think I'll be all right to drive myself to the hospital if I just rest a few minutes."

"Nonsense. I'll drive you to Mayfield Medical Center. You sit here and gather your bearings. I'll go get my keys." I raced back through the gate and into the house. Kingston stared at me as if I was nuts as I searched frantically for my keys and purse. My phone rang as I ran down the front steps but I ignored it.

I circled back to where Dash had fallen. He'd gotten himself to his feet, but he looked shaky and pale. He held his arm tightly against him. A wave of nausea rolled through me when, for the first time, I noticed that his right shoulder was lower than the left. The deformity proved his prediction about the broken collarbone.

I hurried to his left side. "Here, put your arm around my shoulder and I'll help you to the car." He was still unsteady enough that when his arm draped around me his weight nearly made my knees collapse.

He sucked in a breath and straightened his legs. "Jeez, sorry about that. I'm still out of it. Thanks for your help, Lacey. I can see now that I probably couldn't drive myself."

We walked awkwardly and slowly out of the backyard. "I'm glad to help. Besides, I owe you. I vaguely recall getting stuck in that stupid old mansion, in the dark, no less, and you came to my rescue. And then there was that time I was trying to get my keys from my silly bird on top of the roof and you caught me. So consider this a debt paid by a friend." Ungainly pair that we were we managed to reach my car.

His face had regained some of its natural color but he was still in a good deal of pain. It took him a minute to lower his large frame into my tiny car. He filled up the front seat and barely had enough room for his long legs.

He carefully pulled the seatbelt across with his left arm while I climbed into the driver's seat and started the motor. My racing heart was finally returning to its normal pace. The surge of adrenaline I'd experienced when I heard Dash fall was starting to subside. Considering it was a fall from a roof, it could have been far worse. A broken collarbone was painful and inconvenient but manageable.

Dash leaned his head back and closed his eyes. "I'm so stupid. And cheap. I should have just called a roofer."

"Probably. You could have been badly hurt, Dash."

"Yeah." He lifted his head and opened his eyes. "As my shoes stuttered down the shingles like a pair of rusty roller skates, my mind went right to survival mode. I grabbed for the ladder but lost my grip and it fell away. Then I was at that point of no return when I knew some part of my body was going to slam cement. I've broken my ankle before and it was not fun, so I sort of twisted around to tuck and roll out of it." He laughed weakly, then winced at the pain the movement caused. "You know, like the stunt people jumping from a moving train. But I didn't get fully into the roll and landed right on my shoulder."

It was my turn to wince. "Sounds painful but it seems quick thinking kept you from being more gravely injured."

"It seems that way." He rested back again with a sigh. "I've got so much work to do down at the marina. This is going to set me back big time."

I felt truly sorry for him.

The emergency entrance was at the back of the hospital. I pulled into one of the many empty parking spots. "Looks like it's not very crowded, which is a good thing. I suppose most people are inside, sitting by their air conditioners and fans."

"Are you saying there was only one person silly enough to climb on his roof tonight?"

"Those are your words. Not mine." I smiled and patted his good shoulder. "Really, I'm just glad it's not worse, Dash."

"Me too." He went to reach for the door and remembered too late that moving his arm was a bad idea. He gritted his teeth at the pain.

"Let me be the chivalrous one and get that door for you." I opened my door. "Just sit tight."

I scurried around to the other side of the car and opened the door. Dash stared up at me with big puppy dog eyes. "I hate being this helpless," he said.

I waved him out with a flourish. "You'll be my strong, helpful neighbor in no time once the doctors patch you up. Do you have your wallet and insurance card?"

He patted his back pocket. "Yep. Maybe I should have landed on my bottom. My wallet is so stuffed with old receipts and useless junk, it might have padded my fall. Although I've had a broken tailbone before and it hurts like heck."

We headed to the big glass doors of the emergency room. "Broken ankle, broken tailbone. Maybe your parents should have covered you in bubble wrap."

He laughed. "Exactly what my dad suggested after my third trip to the emergency room all in the space of one long, accident prone summer. I was sort of fearless when I was young. Fearless and stupid."

The young woman behind the check-in desk went into a mild state of stunned excitement when she saw her next client. Even with a crooked shoulder and a grimace on his face, Dash caused a splash. My phone rang as Dash took a seat at the woman's window.

I leaned over. "I'll just be outside taking this phone call."

Dash glanced up at me. "You can go, Lacey. I'll figure out a way to get home. This could take awhile." His suggestion seemed to perk the ears of the woman checking him in. Something told me he could easily find a ride home from one of several willing hospital workers, but I had no intention of abandoning him.

"My pets are fed and it's much cooler in the hospital than my house. I don't mind waiting." I searched blindly through my purse and found my phone. It was Briggs.

"Hello."

"Hi, did you get my message?"

I thought back to the few harried moments at home. My phone had rung but I was in too much of a state of alarm to answer it. "No, I didn't. I'm at the hospital." I realized instantly that saying those four words over the phone was not the best way to start a conversation. I could hear a short gasp come from his side.

"What's happened? Are you all right? I'll be right there," he shot out his side of the conversation like bullets, and I couldn't get a word in edgewise.

The big doors slid open. I left behind the cool, antiseptic smelling hospital and reentered the sticky, hot night air. The stark difference in temperature was like a gentle slap in the face. "James," I said abruptly. "I'm fine. Dash fell off his roof and got hurt. I drove him to the Mayfield Hospital."

"Couldn't he have just called a friend or an ambulance?"

"James," I snapped harshly. "Shouldn't your next question have been was he hurt badly? You are a police officer, after all. You need to worry about the well being of all your citizens. Even Dash." I stopped my lecture and immediately repeated it in my head, wondering if I sounded far too angry. But in truth, I was angry.

"You told me you drove him so it was easy to deduce that he wasn't hurt badly. I'm a police officer, after all." He threw my admonishing words back at me and they stung. The coolness of his tone assured me my lecture had hit a nerve. (My driving Dash to the hospital had probably already struck a big one too.) It was our first spat since we'd decided to take our relationship past the friendship stage and I didn't like it much.

My voice wavered a little as I spoke into the phone. The fright of the evening had left me more shaken than I realized. What I needed from Briggs was support, not irritation. I decided to continue on letting him know that his dislike for Dash was not going to get in my way. "I should get back inside in case Dash needs me to fill out some paperwork."

"Lacey," he said in a placating tone, but I wasn't having it. I'd done nothing wrong to have him question anything about the evening.

"Really, James, I think it's better if we just end the call for now."

"Yes, you should hurry back in to him in case he needs you." So much sarcasm came with his statement it made my phone feel heavy in my hand.

"Fine, I will," I said sharply and hung up. I blinked the ache from my eyes. This was not a time for tears. All I'd done was something any normal person with a conscience and half a heart would have done. I reached the glass doors and stomped hard on the cement to open them.

Dash was still sitting at the check-in window. Something told me the young woman with the nice smile behind the window was taking just a little longer than usual to check in the patient. It might end up being a very long night. Now I was feeling extra hot under the collar, and it had nothing to do with the heat wave.

I marched back into the hospital and up to the window. Dash glanced casually up at me, then his face snapped toward me again. "Anything wrong? You look upset."

I bit my lip to keep the rant welling up inside of me tucked away. I needed Lola not Dash, but she was out to dinner with Ryder. I'd just have to go home and vent to Nevermore. He tended to be a good listener, even if he was thin on advice.

I felt my forced smile in my cheeks. "Everything is fine. Did you need me to fill out any paperwork?"

Dash grinned back at the young woman behind the window. She had lovely long eyelashes and a small overbite that made her extra cute. "Miss Strathmore was nice enough to fill in the paperwork. All I had to do was scribble a signature with my left hand." Dash turned a concerned expression up toward me again. "Are you sure you're all right?" His face blanched. "Wait, I'll bet I can guess who the call was from. Is he mad that you brought me here?"

I shook my head. I'd made a point of never discussing Briggs with Dash. "It's fine." I heard my own words echo back to me off the window. "Wait. No it's not. I'll be right back." I turned on my heels, pulled out my phone and dialed Briggs.

I considered the possibility that he wouldn't answer but he picked up on the first ring. "I'm sorry, Lacey," he said as I simultaneously barked, "you listen here, James Briggs," into the phone.

I skated right past his brief apology. I needed to get out my thoughts before I lost them. "Dash fell from his roof. Let that scenario percolate for a second, Detective Briggs. He was visibly shaken and frankly, so was I. If you'd prefer the kind of heartless woman who could just walk away from a friend in need, and yes, I said friend, then maybe I'm not the woman you want to be with. What happened between you two is on your plate not mine. It's certainly changed my opinion of Dash, but I wasn't about to let him sit alone in his yard in pain and shock." I stopped and took a shuddering breath. I was on the verge of tears, but I'd managed to hold them back. He was silent on the other side so I continued. "Just what kind of person would I be if I'd left Dash on his own after he'd fallen from the roof?"

"You're right, Lacey. I'm sitting here stewing in my own vat of shame right now. You did the right thing. I know exactly what kind of person you are. That's why I adore you."

His last words made the sob I'd been holding back burst out. I covered my mouth to stifle the next one.

"Are you crying?"

"No," I said through a sob. I wiped my eyes. "I'm still shaken from the whole thing. I didn't know what I'd find when I rushed into his yard."

"How is he doing?" his question seemed genuine and that made my throat tighten a bit more.

I swallowed back the lump. "He'll be fine. But he broke his right shoulder so he's going to be one armed for awhile. I'm sorry I got so snippy with you, but you made me feel guilty for something that I shouldn't have felt guilty about."

"Yes, I did. I put the total blame on my ego and my ignorance. I called earlier to see if you wanted to come over and watch some television. The air conditioner in my house works again. But you're busy tonight, so I'll see you tomorrow."

I glanced back in through the doors. Dash was being taken into a room.

"Just so you know, James, I would much rather be watching television with you in your air conditioned house than sitting in a hospital emergency room."

"That's good to hear. I think. See you tomorrow, Lacey."

"Yep and don't forget our movie date."

"I won't. Good night."

"Good night." I hung up and sighed with relief. The evening had started so simply with a grilled cheese and nap and had somehow ended up an emotional roller coaster ride. But it seemed the ride had ended and I'd survived.

CHAPTER 6

The outside temperature had cooled overnight enough to allow me to cook up an omelet for my convalescing neighbor. I dropped some bread into the toaster to go along with it.

There was always far more waiting than doctoring during an emergency room visit, and the night before had been no different. After waiting an hour for the x-rays to be analyzed, the emergency room doctor called in an orthopedic specialist. That took another hour and the consult, another hour after that. In the end, it was decided to immobilize Dash's arm and let the shoulder heal on its own. Fortunately, it had broken just the right way that the bones could easily fuse back together without the help of a titanium plate. As long as Dash stayed off roofs and ladders for awhile. He was relieved not to have to go through surgery, but he wasn't thrilled about having his arm strapped to his body.

We'd gotten home just before midnight. Dash trudged into his house feeling pretty good on the pain medicine they gave him, and I headed home and dropped right into bed. The alarm went off at seven, but it felt like I'd just fallen asleep. After the third hit on the snooze button, Nevermore took matters into his own paws and started batting at my chin to wake me. Kingston had joined in with a low, grumpy caw from under the sheet on his cage.

I filled a travel cup with fresh coffee and covered the breakfast plate with cellophane for the walk next door. Dash and I had exchanged keys long ago in case of emergency, and feeding my neighbor, who couldn't exactly make breakfast for himself, was a semi-emergency at the very least.

Dash was sitting on the couch with Captain at his feet when I knocked and let myself in. He took a deep whiff. "Breakfast?"

"Cheese omelet, buttered toast and coffee." I held up the cup.

"You win for neighbor of the year, my friend. I was just thinking about pouring myself a bowl of cereal, but it all sounded like too much effort with one hand."

I placed the food on his kitchen table. He was always working on something in the house. I had yet to see it fully furnished or not in some state of disarray. The floor in the kitchen had been stripped down to the subfloor and half of the cabinet doors were off.

"You'll have to excuse the mess," he called as I looked in remaining drawers for a fork. "I'm under construction . . . still. Sometimes it feels like I'll never be finished. And when I do get something done, another problem pops up. I know they sell cars that are called lemons, but I think I bought a lemon of a house."

"Not at all." I handed him the fork. "You're just in a dark mood because you're strapped down like a mummy on one side. The right side and most important side too. Now I'm going to attempt the bike ride to work because I'm feeling like a wimp. Elsie probably ran five miles and baked two hundred treats by now. My accomplishments for the morning are an omelet, toast and a pot of coffee."

"Don't forget earning the neighbor of the year award."

"Oh, right. There is that." I laughed. "It seems like you're feeling a little better. That's good." I headed toward the door.

"Lacey," he said quietly. "I'm sorry if I caused any problems between you and Briggs last night."

I smiled at him. "Everything is smoothed out. Enjoy your day off. I guess *enjoy* might be too strong of a word. Try and get some rest."

He held up his fork. "Thanks for the breakfast."

I walked out and headed across to my garage. The sun had only been fully up for an hour and a half but it was already hard at work baking the town below. Still, I was determined to ride to the shop.

I rolled the bike out and ran inside to get my backpack and keys. I stopped in front of Kingston's cage. He stared back at me. "What do you say? Want to fly to town today?"

He stood up from his perch. But instead of hopping off to walk out the door of his cage, he turned around. His tail feathers spread out for a second, then he relaxed back into a crouched position.

"Guess you made that pretty clear. And rather rudely at that," I added.

It was still early enough in the day that the heat was not yet overwhelming. I climbed perkily onto my bike. (Of course the trip to town was mostly downhill, which made it far less daunting.) The cotton candy pink Crape Myrtle blossoms had begun to shed, carpeting the street with pastel popcorn. The early morning bike ride refreshed me after my long, stressful evening.

As I pedaled past Graystone Church, I noticed the bright red doors were propped open. Welcoming in the cool morning air, no doubt. The old church, like the Pickford Lighthouse, was one of those charming relics from a time long past. The pale yellow storm shutters were open wide, exposing the stained glass window panes running along the side of the church. The lone, slate covered steeple stood proud over the earthy brown shingles covering the exterior of the church. In the bright summer sunlight, it looked quaint and inviting. But I knew, too well, on a gloomy, stormy night with only a hollow moon and the glow through the windows to light the church and its accompanying graveyard, it could look creepy.

The northernmost half of the cemetery was covered in modern, smoothly carved granite headstones. Behind the plot of sleek, polished headstones were the gravestones from Port Danby's past. Some of the markers were crudely carved crosses and arched stones that jutted up in no particular order and not necessarily perpendicular to the earth. Further back were the more stately, skillfully carved headstones, statues and family plots of the wealthier end of society, including the plot of the Hawksworth family.

I took a small detour onto Graystone Church Way just for fun. Briggs had brought up the family murder mystery. I realized I'd been somewhat neglectful of my self-assigned task. Aside from the account ledger, I'd discovered a letter from someone referred to as "Button". The letter recipient was "Teddy". There was no way to misconstrue the content of the letter. It was a poetically written love letter. Button had even included a sprig of dried lavender, which had stayed perfectly preserved in the folded parchment .

I parked my bike and walked over the lumpy grass leading to the older half of the graveyard. The Hawksworth family plot was by far the most majestic. It was surrounded by a black wrought iron fence. Two white columns supported a Greek style portico that framed the massive family headstone. Hawksworth was carved in curly fancy script into the stone. Each of the murdered family members, Bertram, Jill and their three children had their own marker. The mystery that still remained was the unmarked grave right next to Cynthia, the youngest. A gray stone sat perched in front of a stretch of grass but there was no name carved into it. I'd considered the possibility that Bertram had a favorite hunting dog or the family had a beloved cat that they'd buried in the family plot. But then why bother going through the expense of honoring the pet without adding a name to the stone. And it did seem that burying a pet in a human cemetery might have been considered disrespectful or in poor taste. Even from the richest, most influential family in town.

I turned back and headed toward the church. A pair of pigeons had landed on the top step. It seemed they were considering a quick trip inside to look for crumbs. I decided to join them. Only *I* was looking for different crumbs.

The two pigeons were not happy to have me walk through and disrupt their plans. They fluttered off toward the trees. They would have been disappointed anyhow. The small chapel was spotless. There were no crumbs of food in sight.

Bright sun streaked through the colorful window panes casting a rainbow of shapes and colors on the ivory painted walls. The end of the narrow corridor leading into the chapel had the crumbs I was hoping to find. They had nothing to do with baked goods. Someone had neatly arranged a six by four array of framed pictures that showed the church at various stages in time. A small brass plaque attached to each picture frame provided the date of the photo. According to the first photo, one dated June 17, 1899, the church had no steeple or shutters. Old railroad ties were used as steps up to the front stoop. The 1903 picture showed the construction of the steeple and the addition of new front doors. I moved to the next picture. It was dated July 3, 1906, just three months before the Hawksworth murders. The picture was taken at an angle that showed the cemetery. Naturally, there were far fewer headstones and statues at that time. The new section of cemetery was still just a stretch of grass. I pulled my glasses out from my backpack and pushed them on to get a better look at the grainy image.

The wrought iron fence that bordered the Hawksworth family plot was already standing but there were no headstones yet. They were still three months away. It seemed Bertram Hawksworth had purchased the family plot in preparation for the future. But did he know that bleak future was just a few months away? Was it possible that, like the investigators concluded, Bertram Hawksworth had killed his family? Or was he just a man who liked to be prepared for anything? Maybe he wanted to make sure his family had an eventual resting place in Port Danby.

As I pulled my gaze away, my eyes caught something in the picture. I had to press my face closer, near enough that my glasses tapped the frame on the picture. The Hawksworth family plot was empty except for one gravestone, the unmarked stone. It was there. Someone had been buried in the family plot months before the October murder, and whoever that person was, their name was kept secret. It was entirely possible Bertram and Jill had planned to have the stone carved, maybe with some intricate, unique design like the train etched into William's headstone, but their own unforeseen demise stopped those plans.

A woman who had been polishing the pews in the church walked toward the corridor. She was slightly hunched over and her cheeks were pink from work. "Can I help you, dear?" she asked. Her voice trembled as much as her fingers holding the dusting cloth.

"No, I was just perusing these old pictures. It's wonderful seeing the historical timeline of Graystone Church in pictures." I turned away from the photos and took off my glasses. Her blue eyes were cloudy with age. I wondered how many times she'd polished the church pews in her lifetime.

"My Great Aunt Mary started that photo collection back in 1899." She lifted a gnarled finger toward the first frame. "My Uncle Thomas took this picture."

I smiled up at the photo. It was fairly good quality and amazingly clear for such an old image. "He was talented." I turned back to her. "I was wondering about something. Maybe you can help me. I took a walk around the cemetery grounds to look at the old statues and headstones. I noticed that one of the gravestones in the Hawksworth family plot is blank. No name or date mentioned. I saw a grave marker for each of the children. Do you know who is buried there?"

The pillow of gray hair piled on her head wobbled as she shook her head. "Such a tragedy, isn't it? It's terrible to think that a man could murder his own family in cold blood. And three children too." She shook her head again.

"Yes, it is very sad," I noted quickly. "But the unmarked grave, do you know who it is? Or perhaps there are some church records?"

The woman rubbed her chin. "Unmarked grave? I'm not sure." She chuckled weakly. "I rarely walk out there anymore. The grass is so uneven, I can't get across it without my cane. But I think that it's always been there."

"Yes." I pointed up to the picture. "I can see it here. It was there before the family was murdered."

Her gray hair wobbled again. "So terrible. What would drive a man to kill his own children? I just don't know what the world is coming to," she said once again, adding a head shake to punctuate the end of her comments.

It was hard not to smile at her 'what is the world coming to' comment since this particular crime happened more than a century ago.

"Well, thank you for your help. I should get to work. I enjoyed our chat."

She waved her dust cloth as I turned to leave. "Anytime, dear."

CHAPTER 7

*R*yder swept the same spot on the floor for a good five minutes before I decided to clear my throat loudly to let him know it was probably overkill. It shook him out of his sweeping trance.

I poked the last orange rose into a special order birthday bouquet and stepped back to admire my handiwork. "I think we should use these orange roses more. I know most people gravitate toward the traditional red, pink and white, but these orange roses are so vibrant. They make me happy just looking at them." I picked up an extra rose and walked it over to Ryder. "Here. Have a happiness rose. I'm tired of your frown."

He took hold of the rose and twirled the stem in his fingers. "Actually, the orange rose came from an experimental cross breeding of red and yellow species. When you give one, it's suppose to signify love that began as friendship."

I smiled up at him. "Or it could just mean happiness. That's the interpretation I'm sticking with. Do you want to go to lunch early? You look hungry."

"That's not hunger you're seeing," he said mournfully.

"All right, chat time." I took the broom from his hand and waved him toward one of the stools. "Sit and I will give you the miniscule insight I have from being both your friend and Lola's."

Ryder seemed hesitant about the upcoming conversation, but he swung his long leg over the stool and settled on top of it. His glum expression and surrendered posture were not exactly encouraging but I forged ahead.

I sat on the second stool and faced him. "First of all, and I say this not as a friend to either of you but as a woman. There is nothing less attractive than a mopey man. And you, my friend, are making Eeyore, Pooh's depressed, gloomy, pessimistic donkey friend, look exuberant. So stop or I'm going to pin a tail on you. If you want to keep Lola's interest, you have to wear a little less emotion on your sleeve and be just a touch more aloof. She'll be back soon, and I know she'll be thinking about you while she's away."

"You're right about all of this but it's hard. I've never felt this way about anyone before."

I reached over and patted his arm. "Don't forget, you have big plans to travel the world to study plants in other regions. I'm sure Lola is keeping that in the back of her mind. She figures you're going to walk away from her someday. She's keeping her feet on the ground about this whole thing because of your future plans."

Ryder nodded. "I know. I keep asking myself if I'm going to be able to go through with them now."

"You have to. If you change your lifelong dream because of Lola, you'll lose her anyway. She'll never forgive herself if she keeps you from your horticulture adventure. That's still a year or two off, right?" I asked in a moment of selfishness. I dreaded the thought of trying to replace Ryder.

"Two years is the plan. And you're right. I'm going to stick to it." He stood from the stool. "And I'm done with moping and frowning."

I jumped down from my stool too. "Good for you." I swept my hands back and forth. "My work here is done. Not the florist work. The friendly advice stuff." I circled back around to the birthday bouquet I'd been working on.

"Hey, boss," Ryder said as he picked up the broom. "Thanks for noticin' me," he said in an amazingly accurate Eeyore voice.

"Oh my gosh, you can do imitations." I tilted my head side to side. "Of course you can. You can do everything." I pointed at him. "And don't you forget that. Now, since it's such a quiet day—" Right then a loud rumbling sound shook the shop enough to rattle the front window and topple a few empty vases. I instinctively grabbed for the edge of the island counter. Ryder steadied himself too.

"Was that an earthquake?" I asked. My heart thumped loudly just as it had the night before when Dash fell off the ladder.

Ryder hurried to the window and peered out. "If it was, then it seemed to happen only beneath our shop. Everything looks peaceful and normal out there."

"The noise came from Les's side of the sidewalk. I think I'll walk over and make sure he's all right." I stepped outside and walked next door to Lester's coffee shop. I quickly found the source of the earthquake. Les was scooting around picking up his pub style bar stools from the sidewalk. He was muttering angrily to himself as he retrieved all his runaway furniture.

I glanced back toward the outer wall of my shop and took several shocked steps back. Les had set up a massive, industrial sized fan to cool off his sitting area. The diameter of the fan was a good six feet across and the blades were as big as airplane propellers.

Les spotted me standing with my mouth dropped open and my eyes popping from my head. "Lacey," he blurted, "did I cause any damage to your shop?" His face was red and it wasn't just from the heat or the sunny yellow and orange print on his Hawaiian shirt. He raced over to me. "Is everything all right?"

I finally pulled myself from my moment of shock. "Everything is fine, Les, but how are you?" He knew exactly what I was asking and answered accordingly.

"Considering I nearly blew away my furniture and the entire coffee shop with the large fan I borrowed, it seems I might be ready for the funny farm." I followed him to the other fallen furniture and helped him right the stools. He looked thoroughly disappointed that his plan was a disaster.

"I have to say, Les, I think those are the kind of fans they use to create hurricanes on movie sets. Something smaller might be more practical."

The heat was too much for him. He sat on the last stool he set upright. "Little handheld fans, that's what Elsie bought for her customers. She's always one step ahead of me in the brains department." He chuckled. "That's what our dad used to tell us too."

I picked up a stool and sat across from him. "I don't see the handheld fans being a big hit on the other side of the shop either. It's just too hot to sit outside. You should focus more on cool drinks like special iced coffees and frappés. That's where you can easily outshine Elsie. It's hard to make a baked good refreshing, but coffee can be perfect on a hot day if it's done up right."

Les pulled a tissue out of his shirt pocket and blotted his forehead. "You know something, you're right. I should go inside and come up with a brilliant new iced drink. One that will pull people off the hot sidewalk and into the shop. Thanks, Lacey. I needed that pep talk."

I wiped my hands back and forth again. "Pep talks seem to be my specialty today so I'm glad to help. Maybe I should walk up and down the street and pop into each shop to see if anyone else needs a little cheery, sage advice from the local florist." I stood up to leave.

"If you do go out on the Lacey Pinkerton advice tour, be sure to stop in the bakery and keep my sister occupied for an hour. I need to have the guy who rented me this fan come and pick it up before she sees it. She'll never let me live it down. Knowing Elsie, she'll have a picture of the fan carved into my headstone just for fun."

I laughed and stopped in front of the fan for a second. "I think I could use this thing in fall when all the leaves drop in my front yard. It would save me a lot of time raking. Take care, Les, and if you need someone to sample your new coffee frappés, I'm your gal."

CHAPTER 8

I was still on the Lacey Pinkerton super helper tour when I decided to fix Dash a sandwich for dinner. It was too hot in my house to cook anything and a sandwich seemed a little underwhelming for a dinner offer, but it was better than nothing.

I headed across his front yard in my favorite spaghetti strap sundress. It had taken me a good half hour to decide if the theater would be too hot or too cold, as they often are. But after several brutal days of high temperatures, I settled on the idea that if it was too cold that would be a good thing

I knocked and was about to pull out my key when Dash opened the door. He'd removed the sling that kept his arm pasted to his body.

"Uh oh, are you ignoring doctor's orders?" I slipped past him with the sandwich. "I made you a submarine sandwich, but I won't be insulted if you don't eat it tonight. Maybe you've already had dinner."

Dash followed me as I headed to the kitchen with the sandwich. "Actually, a friend is supposed to be bringing over some burgers."

"I see." I'd so easily declared that I wouldn't be insulted and then was instantly insulted. Or maybe it was disappointment. After my heart to heart with Ryder and my pep talk with Les, I was two for two on my helper tour. But it seemed tonight's good deed was a bust. "Well, I'll put the sandwich in the refrigerator for tomorrow's lunch."

"Or a midnight snack." He reached up with his free hand and raked his fingers through his thick head of hair.

I looked pointedly at his right arm. "Aren't you supposed to have that arm immobile?"

He looked down at it. "It is. I'm not using it. Actually, that's a lie. Earlier, I knocked my soda can off the counter. My first instinct was to catch it." He scrunched up his face to let me know that didn't end well.

I scrunched along with him. "You used your right arm?"

"It shot right out. Long story short, I missed the can and spent an hour waiting for the pain to subside. But that restrictive splint was driving me nuts. When I was little, my mom used to make me wear this ugly, tight turtleneck to holiday dinners. No matter how much I stretched that darn turtleneck out my head always got stuck in it. I'd panic and thrash until my head popped free. That splint was bringing back that same claustrophobia induced panic attack."

I raised my brow at him. "Don't you spend half your work day jammed inside engine compartments?"

"Yeah, I know, it's crazy. But when I'm inside the engine compartments, I can move both arms freely." Dash lifted his face and glanced out his front window. "Looks like Briggs just pulled into your driveway."

"He's early. I should get going then. Enjoy burgers with your friend." I headed to the door and snuck a smiling peek back at him. "By any chance, does this friend wear stylish vintage clothes and a new hair color every week?"

His mouth shifted side to side to stop a grin. "It's possible. Did you tell Kate about my shoulder?"

"Nope, wasn't me. But you know how word gets around in this town."

"Do I ever. Anyhow, she called and asked if she could come by with some food. I hesitated at first."

"Why is that?"

52

He tilted his head. "Do you really need to ask? Have fun tonight with Detective Grump."

I rolled my eyes. "And you have a good time with Miss Persistent. Actually, I take that back. Shame on me for saying it. And it is very nice of Kate to bring you dinner." I opened the door. "See you later."

Briggs was just climbing out of his car when I stepped out onto Dash's front porch. I knew darn well that my exit from my neighbor's house was not going to go over well. I steeled myself for his reaction. (Although, the way Briggs looked in his black t-shirt and jeans was not helping my resolve.)

His brown eyes glittered with a touch of something that wasn't outright anger but it wasn't a 'hello how are you' either.

I jumped right into my very acceptable explanation. I flicked my thumb back over my shoulder toward Dash's house. "I was just taking him a sandwich. He isn't supposed to used his right arm and that makes food prep kind of difficult." Naturally, Kate Yardley pulled up right then in her sporty little convertible and her new blonde hair color to throw some water on my explanation. She barely had time to smile our direction in her hurry to get the burgers up to the house.

I turned back to Briggs who had crossed his arms, a gesture that showed off his nice biceps. "Seems Vanhouten is extra hungry from this broken arm."

"Shoulder," I corrected. "It's his shoulder and you know it always takes extra calories to heal from an injury. I'm ready. I'll just check on the pets and get my purse." I continued toward the house but didn't hear Briggs' footsteps following. I stopped and looked back at him. As it turned out, black was the perfect color for brooding. "James?" I asked tentatively.

His mouth was set in a firm line. I could let the whole thing devolve into an argument about Dash, but I'd had about enough of those inane squabbles. "I'll just wait out here," he said quietly.

I climbed the steps to the house feeling less excited about the evening than ten minutes earlier. The flouncy green skirt of my sundress swung around my legs as I rushed around refilling Nevermore's and Kingston's water bowls. I'd put on my favorite dress. I'd even put on a touch of lipstick and the only thing on Briggs' mind was my visit to Dash. It was to say the least, disheartening. But I was determined to get the night back on track. I grabbed my purse and skittered down the steps in my sandals.

Briggs circled around to the passenger side of the car and opened the door when I reached him. He paused and gazed at the dress for a long moment and a faint smile appeared. "You look nice, Lacey."

I was stunned and pleased by the compliment. With any luck, the night had just shifted back to the positive side. "Thank you. My mom always complains that I don't wear dresses enough. I thought Casablanca was just the right movie for it."

"Good choice." He waved me into the car.

He climbed into the driver's seat.

"When are we going to take that motorcycle ride?" I asked. He'd promised several times to take me for a ride on his motorcycle but we'd never firmed up any plans. I'd been looking forward to it.

He backed out of the driveway. "We could go back and get it now, but I think you might regret your fashion choice. And frankly, if I have to choose between my bike and that dress right now, I choose that dress."

My face warmed enough at his comment that I turned toward the window to hide the blush. "You sir, are a scoundrel." I turned back to him. "Is that from Casablanca?"

His longish hair rubbed along the collar of his t-shirt as he shook his head once. "I don't think so. I can't think of any famous movie with that quote, so maybe we can just credit Lacey Pinkerton with that line. And thank you, by the way. It's a first for me, being called a scoundrel. Since I have to spend every day as a law abiding, polite, by-the-book detective, I kind of like the sound of it."

I laughed. "Glad I could boost that side of your ego for a change." It seemed the moment of tension brought about by my untimely exit from Dash's house had vanished. I considered it a win. Maybe we were finally getting past that hill.

"By the way," he reached forward and turned the radio down a notch. "Just by coincidence, Ronald Samuels walked into the police station today to lodge a complaint against Connie Wilkerson."

I blinked at him, confused and waiting for more. "Are these people I should know?" I recognized the names as soon as I asked it. "Right, the movie theater owners. So much has happened these last few days, I'd already erased those names from my mind."

Briggs headed toward the neighboring town of Mayfield. "Really? What happened?"

I shrugged. "I've just been putting out a few fires here and there. Lola left to France this morning. Ryder was feeling glum about it, but I gave him a talking to and he cheered up. Then in an attempt to outdo Elsie and her tiny handheld fans, Les set up a massive industrial fan in his outdoor seating area."

A laugh shot from his mouth. "Massive?"

"Yes, I'm talking blades that were longer than my arm span. Ryder and I were working and all of a sudden the shop shook and the windows rattled. Scared the dickens out of us."

"The dickens," he repeated. "Never had dickens scared out of me but go on. Did the fan work?"

"It worked just fine if he was going for the hurricane effect. Poor guy was picking up his scattered pub stools off the sidewalk."

"Good ole Les. So I guess the Great Table War is still raging." He turned toward the theater. Connie Wilkerson's theater was on the corner of Turner Boulevard and Main Street. A giant neon lit moon and star hung over the marquee. It was easy to tell the new construction, the section that had been restored after the fire, because the original building was covered in used brick. The new section had brick too but the weather and elements hadn't given them that nicely aged brick patina. We continued along Turner Boulevard to the Mayfield Four Theater at the end of the block.

"You never finished your story," I said. "What was the complaint from Ronald Samuels?"

"Samuels came stomping in, fist's balled, grumbling about being wronged by 'that woman'."

I covered my mouth to stifle a laugh. "That woman? He actually used that phrase?"

Briggs nodded. "He did indeed. Apparently someone poured salt into his soda machine. Something he didn't notice until movie goers started spitting soda out all over the theater. It took all day for his crew to clean up the mess and the machine had to be drained and cleaned. 'Big profit loss' he grumbled over and over again. By the way, he is not one of those people you'd go out of your way to invite to a summer barbecue or birthday party. Something tells me he's grumpy, salty soda or not."

"See, that's what I was telling you. Trinity, the girl who works for him had nothing but complaints about the man. So he thought Connie Wilkerson from the Starlight Movie Theater was the culprit? Wouldn't he have seen her standing in his theater with her carton of salt?"

"He thinks she paid someone to sabotage the machine." He pulled into the theater parking lot. It was only mildly crowded. A few people had dressed in forties style clothing for the occasion. There were more than a few fedoras but no one bothered with a trench coat in this heat. "I wrote down the complaint and told him I'd talk to Connie."

"It seems the two Mayfield theaters are locked in a bit of drama." I reached for the door handle. "As long as no one salted the lemon-lime slush machine. I've got my heart set on one."

CHAPTER 9

"Two tickets for Casablanca," Briggs said to the woman behind the counter. Her nametag said Sally Applegate and below in tiny silver print were the words 'assistant manager'. Sally seemed to be the artsy type with big hoop earrings, a gauzy, brightly colored shirt and several handwoven bracelets on her wrist. Trinity had mentioned that Sally was the creative mind behind the vintage movie night only Mr. Samuels rarely acknowledged her hard work. Coincidentally, Lola's cousin, Shauna, knew her from her anxiety group.

Sally smiled smoothly at Briggs and gave him a quick appreciative once over. (Couldn't really blame her. That black t-shirt was really working for him.) I certainly didn't see any anxiety or nerves from the woman behind the ticket window.

"I'm thinking popcorn with my lemon-lime slush. It's always important to balance salty with sweet and sour," I added as we handed off our tickets to a young guy with a mass of wavy blonde hair shoved under his red usher hat. His sunburned nose nearly matched the red of the uniform. It took me a second to reconcile the face with the picture Trinity had shown me in the flower shop. This was her boyfriend, Justin. I'd never been to the Mayfield Four theater but it seemed I already knew half the staff.

"Second theater on the right," Justin muttered quickly as he handed back our stubs.

We stepped into the cavernous lobby of theater. Stairs on each side led up to a balcony area on the second floor. The wall to the left of the long treat counter was lined with three noisy, neon colored video games and a large soda machine, apparently the soda machine that was tainted with salt. The right side of the vast, two story room was decorated with exotic glass lanterns and tall baskets of ferns. A richly carved Moroccan table and chairs had been roped off in the center of the display. My guess was that they were just for ambience and not a place for oily popcorn fingers. Colorful silk scarves were draped around the chairs and tables and someone had rolled in an old piano. There was a handwritten sign sitting on top of the piano that said, 'Do Not Touch'. A life-size cardboard cutout of Humphrey Bogart was propped up next to the piano. A large banner boasting some of the more famous quotes from the movie had been pinned to the wall.

Briggs and I stood for a second to take it all in. "Impressive," Briggs noted.

"Trinity"—I motioned toward the candy counter where Trinity was filling a bucket of popcorn for a customer—"She's the sister of my bridal client. She told me that Sally, the woman in the ticket window, was responsible for all the vintage movie night events. However, Mr. Samuels allegedly takes all the credit for himself."

Briggs looked around. "Ah yes, there is the charming Mr. Samuels over there chewing out the boy taking tickets at the door. Doesn't seem like good form to be barking at your employee in front of customers."

Samuels was talking loud enough that we could catch snippets of the angry lecture between gun shots and torpedo blasts on the video games across the way. It had something to do with Justin not taking the time to scrape gum off of seats.

"I had a boss like that when I was in high school," Briggs said. "Mr. Pepper."

I laughed. "Mr. Pepper does not sound like the name of a mean boss. Mr. Hawkeye or Mr. Scrooge or Mr. Blackthorn, yes, but Mr. Pepper makes me want to pop open a can of soda."

"If you'd met the man, you'd understand. He used to chew a nail while he yelled at me for stacking the oil cans wrong in the gas station window."

"How did you manage to stack oil cans wrong?"

"I didn't. I stacked them one on top of the other like any normal person would. Pepper just needed something to complain about. And he found something every day. I finally decided it wasn't worth the thirty bucks a week to work for the man."

"I don't blame you. I think I'd walk too."

Briggs' eyes lifted to the banner. He gave his Bogie impression another whirl. "Of all the gin joints, in all the towns . . ." He started but couldn't keep a straight face. "Guess we should get in line and order that lemon-lime slush." He lowered his voice. "Before someone sabotages it with salt."

I was slightly disappointed he didn't finish the quote. It was always one of my favorite movie lines, and Briggs was just handsome and cool enough to stand in for Bogart. (At least in my biased view.)

Trinity was looking a little miffed at the two women in front of us in line. They couldn't decide between red licorice and malt balls. Her eyes kept drifting to the door where Justin was taking tickets. Mr. Samuels had apparently finished his tirade about gum removal. I didn't see Samuels but he'd definitely soured the mood of his ticket taker. Justin was snatching tickets from hands with a scowl. Not the best form for the person greeting you at the door but then that could be blamed more on the boss than the employee.

The two women finally decided on a bag of gummy worms. Trinity rang them up but was distracted as she counted back their change. A man skirted the line and approached the counter. He looked to be in his thirties. He was a big man, one that might be described as husky or barrel-chested. Three lines between his brows were creased as if he was worried about something. "Tell my dad I'm waiting for him in his office," the man said quickly to Trinity before leaving the counter.

It took a second for the highly distracted Trinity to recognize me. She smiled sweetly at Briggs. "You're the detective in Port Danby." She winked at me. "Nice work."

"Thanks." I smiled sideways at Briggs and passed the wink on to him.

"What can I get for you two?" she asked.

"I think I'm going to try that lemon-lime slush you were raving about." I looked at Briggs.

"I'll try one too. And a large popcorn."

Trinity scooted off to fill our drinks. I glanced around the busy room and spotted Mr. Samuels tromping down the stairs from the balcony, ushering several kids to walk ahead of him. Their heads were dropped as if they'd been caught doing something they shouldn't. He said something to them at the bottom of the stairs and they scurried out the exit. Justin took time out of his ticket collection to skewer his boss with invisible laser beams as Mr. Samuels marched toward the concession stand.

Trinity caught sight of him while she filled the second cup. "Oh, Mr. Samuels, your son is here. He's in his office."

No expression of joy or pleasure followed. In fact, Samuels looked more put out by the visit than anything. I wondered if there was anything that made the man smile. Possibly counting his money like Scrooge on Christmas Eve.

"Fine," he said abruptly. "And bring me one of the lemon-lime slush drinks." He walked toward a small corridor that was marked 'employees only' and disappeared around the corner.

I leaned toward Briggs. "I would not have pegged that grouchy man as the lemon-lime slush type. He seems more like the bitter coffee or sucking on dry lemon type."

"Or gasoline type," Briggs suggested. "He is not exactly warm and welcoming. It's a wonder he has such a successful business."

"I think that the assistant manager can be credited with the theater's popularity more than the manager."

Trinity returned with our slush drinks and popcorn. I glanced around to make sure no one heard.

"You weren't kidding about your boss," I said discretely. "Is he just the manager? Maybe the owner should know about his behavior."

Trinity sighed. "If only that would work. But Mr. Samuels is manager and owner, so we're stuck with him." She handed Briggs his change. "Enjoy the slush and the movie."

I took a quick sip and raised the cup. "Hmm, you were right. This will hit the spot nicely. Thanks."

CHAPTER 10

*T*he ornate sconces running along the side walls of the theater glowed as we walked several steps down and decided on a row that was halfway between the front and back of the theater. The words "Welcome to Vintage Movie Night" were projected across the gigantic screen. About half the seats were filled. Most of the people waiting were either unwrapping snacks or staring at their phones.

After scooting past a few people, Briggs and I decided on two center seats. As he settled into his seat and reached for a handful of popcorn, a woman called his name from the end of the row.

"James? James Briggs? Is that you?"

I glanced to the end of the row. Briggs leaned forward to see who was calling him. Three women around my age were hugging bottles of water and chewing on red licorice whips. The one who had called his name had sleek blonde hair she had tied back with a pink ribbon. She was wearing a vintage Marilyn Monroe style halter dress. One of her friends was wearing what looked like a vintage World War II women's army uniform, complete with the cap pushed down over her dark hair. A third friend was dressed in pedal pusher length blue jeans and a matching denim shirt with sleeves rolled up like Rosie the Riveter.

They looked enthusiastic and ready for their vintage movie night. I felt a little like a party pooper for not getting more into the spirit with my twenty-first century dress and sandals.

"Teresa?" Briggs asked. "How have you been? Still living in Chesterton?" He was extra jovial in his reply. I sat back out of the way so he could carry on his conversation.

"Just back in town to visit the parents. You remember Mindy and Helen," she said pointing to her friends.

Briggs nodded. "Yes, good to see you. This is Lacey. She owns the flower shop in Port Danby."

I nodded a hello, then turned to stare at the screen that was still just a stationary set of words welcoming us to the movie night. I was, to say the least, frozen in disappointment and quickly trying to pacify myself. Maybe he just didn't feel it necessary to bring up I was his date or his girlfriend. Maybe he figured it was implied because we were obviously out on a movie date together. Maybe he thought my owner-ship of the flower shop was the most pertinent detail to mention in a brief introduction. Yes, those maybes might very well explain the whole thing. Or maybe he just didn't want the women to think he was tied down by a girlfriend.

The rest of their conversation was muted by the analytic thoughts ping ponging through my brain. Briggs finally sat back when the lights dimmed.

I stared straight ahead even though I could feel him looking at the side of my face.

"Friends of yours?" I asked, unnecessarily and with just enough vinegar to surprise even me.

"I went to high school with them." He offered me some popcorn but I shook my head.

"Anything wrong?" he asked. The lights dimmed. A loud commer-cial about theater discounts and snacks at the concession stand blasted through the speakers.

"No, this flower shop owner is quite pleased to be sitting here with the famous James Briggs."

He fell silent. My seat shook as he sat back harder than needed. It seemed he was trying to retrace his steps, or, more accurately, his words from the last few minutes. A quiet sound ushered from his mouth, letting me know he'd stumbled upon the critical sentence. "I like to brag about your business, Lacey. I didn't mean to give short shrift in the introduction. Should I tell them you're my girlfriend?"

I turned to him for the first time. "That would be silly. It's fine."

"I could stand up on the chairs and announce to the whole theater that I'm dating the adorable owner of Pink's Flowers and she has me spinning. In fact I'm so dizzy when I think about her, I sometimes find it hard to believe she's my girlfriend."

He got louder with each word. I finally leaned over and kissed him on the mouth to quiet him. We both sat in silence for a moment gazing into each other's eyes just like we were about to see Bogie and Bergman do on the big screen.

I broke into a giddy smile. "Do I really make you dizzy?"

"Trust me, no one has ever made me more dizzy than you, Lacey Pinkerton."

"Good." I sat back and took a handful of popcorn. "I think."

He was still looking at my profile. He cleared his throat. "By the way, that bit of jealousy or whatever that was a second ago, you might think about it if you see me get grumpy when I see you walking out of Dash's house. Or when I call you and find you've driven my mortal enemy to the hospital."

"I don't know if it was jealousy," I said quickly in my defense. "It was more that I felt slighted." I munched on some popcorn and took a sip of slush that was quickly melting into an artificial tasting lemon-lime syrup. It seemed the crushed ice was the star of the drink. I could still feel Briggs' gaze on my face. I turned to him. "All right, there might have been a tiny seed of jealousy. They seemed so excited to see you in their cute forties fashion. Occasionally, I drop back to high school mode. I'm not proud of that fact but it is what it is. It's not easy dating the extremely sought after Detective James Briggs."

His mouth turned up in a crooked, not terribly amused smile.

I grabbed another handful of popcorn. "Fine. I promise to overlook some of your grumpiness when the subject of Dash comes up. As long as you don't overreact."

"I never overreact," he said wryly. "I'm a detective. It's my job not to overreact." He sat forward and glanced back at the projector room up above the auditorium. The commercials had ended. The screen was blank. The lights had been dimmed low but there was no movie.

He sat back. "It seems like the movie should have started by now." Just as he said it, the assistant manager, Sally, appeared in front of the blank screen. "Ladies and gentlemen, there will be a slight delay due to a problem with the projector. Drink refills are on the house while you are waiting. It shouldn't be more than ten minutes. Our team is working on it."

A low mumble of disappointment made its way around the seats. Several people got up with their soda cups to take her up on the free refill offer. Others turned their phones back on and tiny screen lights lit the room up again.

"Do you want a refill on the slush?" Briggs asked.

"No, I think the novelty has worn off. I think I'll go ask for a cup of water. Do you want anything?" I asked.

"No, I'm fine. Do you want me to go?"

"No, thanks, I might stop by the ladies' room too." I scooted past him, avoiding having to slip by his three friends at the end of the row.

I finished up in the restroom and headed out to get the water. A 'temporarily closed' sign was posted outside the men's room. There was a line in front of the men's room on the opposite side of the lobby. It was nice to see the men having to wait for a change, I thought wryly. It seemed the theater was having more than its share of problems this evening. Maybe there was some sort of sabotage in the works, or maybe it was just one of those nights. I'd had plenty of days in the shop when nothing seemed to work out right.

I was in luck. There was no line at the concession stand. Movies in the three other theaters were in full swing. It seemed only our movie was delayed.

The large, square shaped man, who was apparently the owner's son, was standing behind the concession stand. The frown lines between his brows were still noticeable as he shook an alarming amount of parmesan cheese onto his oily popcorn. He shook and swirled the extra large bucket to coat the kernels with the cheese. I supposed when your dad owned the theater, you could help yourself to the popcorn, candy and drinks. My nose picked up the pungent odor of the parmesan a good fifteen feet before I reached the stand.

Trinity was stooped behind the counter refilling the candy shelves. She popped up and saw me coming across the room. I knew exactly what she was going to ask me and I was ready with my answer.

"Was I right? Wasn't that slush the bomb?"

It was definitely feeling like a bomb in the bottom of my stomach. The taste in my mouth reminded me of the time my cousin dared me to eat a spoonful of dry Kool-aid. But I forced a smile. "You were right. Very lemony and limey. But I've still got a lot of popcorn left. Could I get a cup of ice water?"

Her blue eyes rounded. "But the people in the Casablanca film get a free refill." She leaned forward. "Of course, over at the Starlight, every drink can be refilled as often as you like but—" She shot a peek over at the owner's son. He was still trying to coat every kernel of popcorn with cheese and was far too focused on the parmesan to notice our conversation. "Mr. Stingy would never allow it." She crinkled her nose. "In fact, I have to charge you a quarter for the water."

"I need to go back and get my purse then."

Trinity peeked around, spoke quietly and winked at me as if we were about to pull off the greatest heist of all time. "Give it to me on the way out."

"Are you sure?" I whispered. "I don't want to get you in trouble."

"I'm sure." She grabbed a cup to fill with ice and water.

"Dylan." A deep, grumbling voice echoed through the lobby. It was Mr. Samuels. He was holding his lemon-lime slush in one hand and his phone in the other. His bellow had nearly caused his son to drop his popcorn, which would have been a shame since he'd just spent several minutes getting it to cheesy perfection.

Samuels reached the counter. His son pushed the bucket of popcorn casually behind him as if to hide it.

"I've got to head into the projection room," Mr. Samuels barked. "That nimrod can't get the movie started. I don't have time to finish our talk. I think I've said enough on the subject anyhow." Without waiting for Dylan's response, he disappeared into the employees only corridor. He emerged a few moments later. A tool box had replaced the slush drink in his hand. It seemed the projector being used for Casablanca was as vintage as the movie itself.

Trinity handed me the cup of ice water. "Here you go and enjoy the movie. I'm sure they'll get it started soon."

CHAPTER 11

*T*he theater lights had dimmed more and it took me a second to find Briggs in the center row. I scooted past several people and found my seat.

"You're just in time," he said. "Boredom has caused me to stuff myself with popcorn." He leaned the container my direction.

"No, thanks. Just like the slush is only good when it's cold, the popcorn is better when it's hot."

"Very true." He placed the half-filled bucket on the floor beneath his seat. "I can hear some activity up there in the projector room," he noted.

"The manager was called to help while I was at the concession stand. It seems we are going to be seeing the original version, right from the big metal can. I guess they like to keep vintage movie night authentic." I rested back and stretched my feet out.

The lights dimmed again and the movie started. People clapped to show their appreciation. I leaned my head closer to Briggs. The familiar, pleasant scent of his soap wafted toward me. "We humans get excited about the silliest things," I whispered. Right then he took my hand and I pressed my lips together to contain my excitement, proving my theory right.

"This was a great idea," Briggs said quietly.

"Thanks. I figured it was one movie we could both enjoy."

He laced his fingers through mine and squeezed them. My heart skipped a few beats before I finally relaxed enough to watch the movie.

We were an hour into Casablanca when a flashlight lit up the dark. The audience booed and complained. Another round of audible protests rumbled the theater as the penetrating beam of the flashlight rolled over the seats.

"They must be looking for someone," Briggs said.

Through the harsh glow I could make out the silhouette of the figure holding the flashlight. It was Justin. "Maybe someone slipped in without paying. I wouldn't want to face down Mr. Samuels if I'd snuck into his theater."

The light swept over our heads again like the signal beam on a lighthouse. Then it stopped, backed up and fell right on Briggs. He shaded his eyes and looked back at Justin. The usher was making his way down the steps to our row. Wisely, he turned off the light before a small riot erupted.

"Detective Briggs," he whispered loudly over the other people in the row. Naturally, all faces turned our direction. Even people in front turned back to see what was happening.

"James, were you the guy who snuck in?" I snickered behind my hand. "Don't worry, I'll vouch for you. Or we could just make a run for the emergency exit."

Justin had been booed and hissed at but he had no hesitation scooting past the other movie watchers to reach Briggs. "Sir, we need you in the lobby." Now that he was close enough, I could see he was visibly shaken.

Briggs was off duty but he was always ready to jump into law enforcement mode. He got up from his seat without hesitation. No doubt, Justin's rattled appearance prompted him into action without question.

It was certainly not going to be any fun watching the movie without Briggs, so I got up and followed them out. The first thing I noticed was Trinity standing next to the popcorn maker with her hands over her face as if she were crying or scared. Sally Applegate, the assistant manager, was pale and agitated as she tried to clear the lobby and get people back into the theaters. "Please, everyone, the concession stand is closed right now. We need the lobby cleared. We have a medical emergency, and we need to make room for the paramedics."

Sally was doing an admirable job of taking control of things, but it seemed she was just barely holding herself together. Something serious had happened. I could sense it in the air and on the faces of the few employees who were gathered near the employees only corridor. Anxious glances and whispers were being exchanged by the theater workers. The one person I didn't see in the mix was the owner, Mr. Samuels.

I followed behind Briggs as Justin led him across the vast lobby. "Mr. Samuels is sick," he said. "I went in to ask him about who was closing tonight, and I found him on the floor. It might be a heart attack. But he's not moving. Sally has called the ambulance, but she thought you might be able to help."

Sally spotted us as she ushered several people toward the theaters. "Thank you for your help, Detective Briggs," she called, a gesture that caught the attention of the few people still milling about the lobby. If people hadn't yet figured out something terrible had happened, they certainly knew it now.

"Should I go outside and wait for the ambulance?" Justin asked Sally as she neared.

"I'm on my way to do just that." Sally was out the door and away from the frenzy before anyone could stop her. Justin looked stunned and upset at her decision to abandon the scene.

Briggs hurried toward the corridor. "Let us pass," Briggs said as we reached the distraught group. Briggs pushed through and I stayed right behind.

Mr. Samuels' office was camped with wood paneling, no windows and a large desk in the center of the room. Mr. Samuels was lying on his side with his mouth open and his eyes only halfway shut. I knew instantly I was looking at a dead man and naturally, Briggs knew too. But neither of us let on. He crouched down and placed his fingers on Mr. Samuels' neck.

Some of the employees had inched down the hallway to peer into the office. Some were undecided on whether or not they wanted to see what was happening. Others were eager to peer in and find out why Mr. Samuels was on the floor.

Justin stood in the hallway with an upset Trinity tucked under his protective arm. Briggs stood up and held out his arms. "I need all of you to clear the hallway for the medics." The shell-shocked employees backed slowly out of the narrow corridor. Briggs closed the door slightly and returned to where Samuels was lying.

"Is he?" I asked tentatively.

"Yes, he's dead."

CHAPTER 12

*I*t wasn't an easy call on the part of the assistant manager, but once Sally Applegate was briefed on the gravity of the situation and once she'd recovered from the shock, she decided to stop all of the shows, give out three free passes per person and clear the theater. She mentioned that it was a fairly light crowd for the evening which made the decision easier.

I helped hand out passes. It took some time to clear the auditoriums and move curious onlookers toward the parking lot. Unfortunately, the last handful of people witnessed the arrival of the coroner's van as it pulled up in front of the theater. Eyes popped from heads and mouths dropped open at the ominous sight of the vehicle marked 'county coroner'.

"People are already starting to talk," Sally said. Her hand flew to her mouth to stifle a gasp. "We need to tell his son before he hears it from someone else."

"He was here earlier," I said. "Do you know where he might be right now?"

"Possibly visiting his mother in the hospital. She had heart surgery. It was quite serious, but poor Dylan couldn't get Ronald to even pay her a visit. They've been divorced for a few years."

"Do you have his phone number?"

"Yes, I have it in case of emergencies." Her large earrings twirled as she shook her head. "I can't tell him. I just can't." Her voice wavered close to a sob.

I patted her arm. "Of course not. I just need the number. Detective Briggs will talk to him."

"Thank goodness he was here." Sally sniffled once. Something told me she was more shaken than sad about her boss's demise. Death was always shocking and unexpected. But I could have been entirely wrong. It was possible she felt genuinely bereaved by his loss. I was making a judgment based on my own feelings about the man.

"I'll write down his phone number for Detective Briggs," she said.

The theater was empty except for the employees. Justin, Trinity, Sally, two more ushers and the guy in charge of the projector rooms. Briggs had told the entire crew not to leave and to wait in the lobby until he had a chance to talk to them. There was no indication of foul play, but I knew Briggs well. He suspected something was amiss.

I headed into Mr. Samuels' office. Briggs was doing a visual search of the room.

"What are you thinking?" I asked as I reached the man's desk. It was neat and orderly with several file folders stacked perfectly on top of each other and a matching shiny black metal desk set of a pen holder, stapler and paper tray. The only item that didn't belong with the office supplies and paperwork was the red and white striped drink cup. Mr. Samuels had asked Trinity to pour him a slush while he was rushing around doing manager tasks. His son Dylan had been waiting in his office for him in the midst of his busy night, and Mr. Samuels didn't seem thrilled to have to talk to him. I assumed it was because he had too much to do. It did seem like an inopportune time for a family chat. But then Sally mentioned that the ex-Mrs. Samuels was ill in the hospital, so it was possible the conversation required some urgency.

Briggs rested his fingertips against the desk and stared down at the body. "My first instinct would be heart attack. A middle aged man who, from all accounts, is a Type A personality who spends most of his day agitated. Only he never loosened his tie. It's still bound tight near his throat. That might mean nothing at all. It might have been too sudden, but most of the time, if someone is feeling the pain and spasms of a heart attack, they start by unbuttoning top buttons and loosening up clothes to see if that helps."

"That makes sense. From what I've read, it can feel as if there is a huge weight sitting on your chest. I think I'd loosen up my tie and button just to breathe easier."

I plucked a tissue out of the box. "James, may I pick up this cup? It's mostly empty, just the sticky green remnants of the lemon-lime slush. But I'd like to give it a whirl past Samantha." I tapped my nose, one of the few snouts on the planet with its own nickname.

"Yes, please do. Since his mouth is open and slack, I can see that his tongue is stained green from the slush. He was definitely drinking it. Touch the cup near the bottom where someone would be less likely to hold it. That way you won't disturb any prints if they turn out to be important."

I paused before picking up the cup. "Do you think there might be more here than natural causes?"

Briggs shrugged. It was unusual seeing him at a crime scene dressed in a t-shirt and jeans. "Hard to know. I wonder where the coroner is."

"The van pulled up while I was helping Sally hand out free passes. Which reminds me, she's bringing you his son's phone number so you can call him."

He groaned quietly. "I don't look forward to that."

I placed the tissue in my hand and picked the cup up near the bottom. I brought it to my nose expecting to find the same sugary, artificial lime scent of my slush. But another sweetly chemical smell mingled with the lime. It was faint and not something anyone with a normal nose would notice, but I was sure there was something inside the cup besides the last traces of lemon-lime syrup.

Briggs caught my baffled expression. "Something wrong?"

I took another whiff to make sure I wasn't imagining it. "I'd have to smell another cup of the slush to be sure but there's something off about this one. I noticed that as the ice melted and the beverage warmed, the slush started tasting more and more artificial. Like the cheap fruit punch they serve at kid's birthday parties. But this smells funny, like something has been added to it."

Briggs rubbed his chin as he stared down at Mr. Samuels. "Interesting. Would you mind terribly taking a whiff of his mouth to see if you can find the same scent?"

"Not at all." I walked around to the side of the desk he was standing on. "That's what my sniffer is for, right?"

He glanced back toward the door to make sure no one was near. "For that and for the occasional kiss." He lightly kissed my nose. "Seems our movie night turned out a little differently than planned."

"I don't know about that." I brazenly looked him up and down. "I think I like this Maltese Falcon style Bogart even better than the Casablanca one."

A clamor in the narrow corridor signaled that the coroner had arrived. I stooped down and lowered my nose near Mr. Samuels' mouth. I pulled back instinctively and fanned my face.

"Did you smell something?" Briggs asked.

"Yes, I think he had garlic for lunch. It's strong." I leaned forward once more and twitched my nose side to side, hoping to separate out the various smells. When I worked as a perfumer, I trained myself to isolate each fragrance. It wasn't easy, but with a bit of concentration, I could turn off certain odors to pinpoint the ones I was looking for. It was a skill that made me highly sought after in the perfume industry.

"Detective Briggs, how are you? I'm Doctor Hershonhaus, but you can call me Doc Patty. I'm Nate's assistant." The woman's voice behind me was unfamiliar. Normally, Nate Blankenship showed up when there was a dead body. Apparently, he'd taken on an assistant.

I finished my nasal inspection and managed to catch a faint trace of the same odd smell I found in the cup.

I pushed to my feet. The coroner, Dr. Patty, was less than five feet tall and with glasses so thick it seemed her eyes took up half her face. She shuffled forward on her sensible flat shoes. Her magnified eyes stared down at the body on the floor.

"Certainly wasn't a heart attack," she said confidently. I'd observed

Nate Blankenship examine a body several times, but I'd never seen him jump straight to a conclusion without first surveying the victim. Even when the cause of death was obvious like a gun shot.

"Because his tie is still tight around his neck?" Briggs asked, jumping back to his earlier theory.

Doc Patty's enormously magnified eyes swept down again. "That is occasionally a clue, but his skin pallor is all wrong. Heart attack victims usually have a mottled, almost flushed cast to their skin. Especially if death occurred recently. She popped her face back up. "Do we have any estimate on the time of death yet?"

I spoke up. "I saw him alive and well just an hour ago. I was out at the concession stand as he was called into the projector room to solve a problem."

Doc Patty blinked at me. It was hard not to stare back at her with her thick lenses and gigantic gray-blue eyes. The glasses must have been too heavy for her nose because she kept pushing them up. "Oh yes, you must be the woman with hyperosmia who occasionally helps out with the cases." She looked at Briggs. "Nate mentioned you had an assistant." Her brows scrunched together lifting her heavy glasses high on her nose. "How did you happen to be here to see the victim alive?"

Briggs cleared his throat. "Doctor Hershon—Hersun—" He cleared it again. "Doctor Patty, if you could please examine the victim to find a cause of death, if one can be seen before the autopsy. I need to go make a call to his son." He turned back to me. "Miss Pinkerton, would you mind checking on the employees. I'm sure they are feeling anxious about tonight's tragic event."

"Yes, of course." I followed him down the hallway.

He flashed me an amused grin about the new coroner. "Nate mentioned he hired an assistant. Let's see what she finds." We walked into the lobby. Sally hurried across the room with a yellow sticky note. "Here is the phone number. His name is Dylan. As far as I know that is his only family besides his ex-wife."

"Thank you. Is there some place private I can make the call?"

Sally waved her hands around. "Every theater is vacant. Choose any place you like." Earlier, she was distressed and on the verge of sobs, but she seemed to have cooled her emotions. She spoke calmly as if the entire thing was already far in the past.

Briggs walked off with the phone number. I noticed Trinity sitting alone behind the concession stand sipping a cola. I walked over to see how she was faring.

"How are you doing, Trinity?"

She put her soda down and shrugged. "I don't know. I feel like I should be really sad. I mean he's dead, right?"

"Yes, yes he is."

"That's so weird. One minute he's storming about, throwing out orders, bossing people around and the next he's dead. Doesn't makes sense. Although, my mom told me her great granddad just fell over dead one day. He was getting up to put a log on the fire and he just kept going, face first into the hearth. They said he was gone before he hit the ground." She crinkled her nose. "Probably a good thing cuz falling face first has got to hurt."

"Never thought of that but you're right. And that does occasionally happen with a heart attack or stroke."

She picked up her soda, crunched the ice around with the straw and took a sip. Our brief chat had lightened her mood. It seemed like a good opportunity to find out what was happening right before Mr. Samuels' body was discovered.

"Trinity, when was the last time you saw Mr. Samuels alive?"

She chewed on the tip of her straw in thought, then let it go. "I remember now. He'd gone to the projector room. Then I didn't see him for awhile. I think he was checking time cards or something. He's really nitpicky about us clocking in and out on time." A tiny frown fell on her lips. "I guess I shouldn't talk mean about him. It's just hard to find nice things to say. Except, he did once wear a pair of socks around Halloween that had skeletons on them. It was so not like him. They were cool. I think they glowed in the dark."

"See, there's always something nice to say about everyone. But did you see him at all after that?"

"Yeah, he stopped behind the counter to get a cup of ice water. He was acting kind of strange." She lowered her voice. "I know this sounds weird but he was moving kind of unsteady, you know, swaying back and forth like maybe he'd been drinking. First time I'd ever seen him act like that. He filled his cup and sort of stumbled against the counter. I asked if he was all right, but he didn't answer me." Trinity's eyes grew wet with tears. "This is my fault. I should have told someone. He wasn't feeling well, and I didn't say anything."

I took her hand. "No. You asked. He just didn't answer. Don't blame yourself."

My words seemed to calm her worries. "So . . . you and the handsome Detective Briggs?" she asked in a lightning fast topic switch.

I smiled. "I'm sure Detective Briggs will want to talk to everyone before you go home for the night. It should be soon. Make sure you tell him everything you just told me."

CHAPTER 13

*D*oc Patty was definitely more theatrical than Nate Blankenship. She instructed her two person crew to take various photos of the body while she stood back making every expression from deep, thoughtful concentration to quiet alarm. In the end, she had several conclusions spanning from a brain aneurysm to possible poisoning. I sensed some frustration from Briggs when she announced loudly that he might very well have been murdered. It was something Briggs liked to keep quiet whenever any of the victim's acquaintances were still within earshot.

Since the theater was located in the town of Mayfield, four city police officers were sent to the scene to take statements and collect evidence while Doc Patty and her team prepared Mr. Samuels for transportation to the morgue.

Briggs was writing down a few notes while the activity swirled around him. He was still recovering from having to inform Samuels' son about the death.

"I like this casual detective attire," I noted as I peered over his shoulder at his notes.

"You and me both. I wish the higher ups would relax the detective dress code, but it's still suit and tie. During a heat wave, a suit is nothing short of torture."

"If it makes you feel any better, the first time I saw you in your detective's suit and tie, I thought you looked handsome enough to be a television detective."

A line creased the side of his mouth. "If only I got the same pay as those television detectives." He closed his notebook. "Since Doc Patty has already announced to the world that this is a murder investigation, I thought I might go out back to the alley and the trash bins to see if I can find any evidence. Dylan Samuels should be here in about fifteen minutes. I want to be back inside when he arrives. He sounded extremely upset. I'm sure he'll have a hundred questions. For which, I won't have any answers."

"I'll join you for some sniffing. Whatever was in that drink had a weird sweet smell. Did Trinity tell you about Mr. Samuels acting strangely just before he died?"

I followed him through hallway to the emergency exit.

"She said he was stumbling as if he'd been drinking." He opened the door and held it for me. "There was no evidence of alcohol in his office. Did you smell any on his mouth?"

"No. I think we can rule out that he was drinking."

A large trash bin was pressed up against the outside wall of the theater. "Of course, we'll have to wait for Doc Patty's report," he said the name with a touch of mockery. "But I agree. Unsteadiness and stumbling around could have been the early symptoms of poisoning."

Not to be overwhelmed by smells, I stood back while he lifted the heavy rubber lid. Once some of the odors trapped inside the hot can had been released, I stepped forward.

Briggs peered inside. "Interesting." He gave the lid a toss. It fell back and away from the bin giving us a better view of the contents. I held my breath and cautiously approached the lip of the bin. Since it contained trash from the movie theater and not leftovers from a diner or restaurant, the odor hovering over it was manageable for my sensitive nose.

I peered inside, and my gaze followed Briggs' line of sight. An extraordinary amount of rat poison boxes were piled in one corner. The seemingly empty containers of peanut butter flavored rat bait were sitting on top of the other debris, which included things one would expect to find in a theater's trash bin. Crushed paper products, disposed drink cups, popcorn buckets, napkins and empty candy boxes filled the container halfway to the top. Some of the waste was wrapped in removable trash bags and tied neatly at the top to keep things sealed up.

"Seems like the theater had a rat problem," I noted.

"Yes but that's not the interesting part." Briggs pointed into the bin. "Look how the boxes are all piled in one corner, almost as if someone took the time to stack them neatly. The rest of the debris has just been tossed into the bin without thought. Like one would expect."

"Hmm, you're right. It is sort of odd. And frankly, if my business had been infested by rats, I think I might hide the evidence by shoving the boxes into one of the opaque trash bags."

"Good point." Briggs walked around the side of the can to the corner where the rat poison boxes were stacked. He pulled one free from the stack and checked out the label. "According to the graphics, the poison comes in pellet form. The box is only the outer packaging. The pellets are sealed in a bag to keep them fresh," he read off the box. "So where are the bags?"

"Maybe Samuels has the rat poison stored inside somewhere in the bags. Maybe he decided to get rid of the boxes so no one saw that he had a rat problem." I looked wide-eyed at James. "Maybe he accidently ate some pellets thinking they were—I don't know—candy?" I laughed. "Scratch that idea. I'm sounding silly. Must be the trash odor getting to me."

Briggs walked around with the box. "I know there are a lot of odors around us, and the box is empty but would you mind?" He held it up for me to smell.

I took several long whiffs. "I do smell something similar to peanut butter. Mostly the box just smells like cardboard and a crazy carnival mix of popcorn, soda and candy all glued together with that one-of-a-kind trash can fragrance. Whatever I smell, it's not even close to the scent in the lemon-lime cup."

Briggs put the box back into the bin and glanced inside from the new angle. His eyes swept across the pile of garbage, then his face snapped back toward the front of the bin. "Hold on." He circled back to the front of the trash can. I hopped up on tiptoes and looked inside to see what had caught his interest. A white plastic bottle of coolant was sitting between two stuffed garbage bags.

"Coolant is poisonous, right?" I asked.

"It sure is. It's considered extra dangerous because it has a sweet taste. Most adults would know not to guzzle it, but it's not something you leave around for kids and pets. And it comes in bright colors." He pulled on the plastic glove he'd had the forethought to carry with him for a garbage can tour. He hoisted himself up and leaned over the edge of the can to pluck the coolant bottle free. There was no lid. He shook it to show me it was empty. "Looks like someone used all of it. The question is—did they use it only for automotive purposes or for something more sinister?" He took a whiff and rubbed his nose with the back of his hand. "It smells faintly fruity to me, but I think we need the expert to give it a whiff."

Briggs held the bottle for me to smell. I lowered my nose and breathed in. I did it twice just to make sure.

"Yep." I looked up at Briggs. "That's what I smelled in Mr. Samuels' slush cup."

Briggs looked at the bottle in his hand. "Looks like we have murder by lemon-lime poison."

CHAPTER 14

*B*riggs gave the bottle to the Mayfield officers to mark as evidence. Sally saw us standing out front near the squad cars and came out to fetch Briggs. She was an entirely different person than a few hours ago. She was wringing her hands and playing nonstop with the bracelets on her wrists. I thought back to what Shauna had mentioned about Sally being in her anxiety support group. She was definitely on a thinner thread than earlier.

"Detective Briggs," she said quickly, "Dylan Samuels is here, and he is very distraught. I looked around but couldn't find you." She once again moved the bracelets on her wrist, pushing them back farther only to have them slip forward to her hand again.

"Miss Pinkerton and I were collecting evidence." He seemed to sense he'd said just the wrong thing, but it was too late.

"Evidence?" Sally took a few short breaths and waved her hand in front of her face, causing her bracelets to jangle. "So the coroner was right? It was murder." Her face paled visibly as she said the word. "That's just horrible. Can you please go inside and talk to Dylan. I need to stay out here and catch my breath. I'm feeling slightly sick from all of this."

"Can I get you anything?" I asked. "A paper bag for breathing or a glass of water?"

She rubbed her forehead. "No, I just need fresh air."

Briggs and I started to walk away. He stopped and turned back to her. "One quick question, Ms. Applegate. Was the theater having a problem with rats?"

Her face blanched more. "Did you say rats?"

"Yes. Was there an infestation or something?" Briggs asked.

A weak, nervous laugh fell from her lips. "Gosh, I hope not. I'm scared to death of rats. If there was a problem, Mr. Samuels never mentioned it."

Briggs pulled out his notebook. "Thank you."

We found Dylan Samuels pacing the front of the concession stand, looking upset, which was no surprise given the circumstances. He spotted Detective Briggs and lumbered toward us. His face was red and his eyes puffy, indicating that he'd been crying.

"I haven't told my mother yet," Dylan said weakly as he approached us. "I need to talk to her in person. I had just reached the hospital when you phoned. I hadn't gone up to see her yet. I turned right back around and headed back to the theater." He wiped his palm over his thick, wavy hair before rubbing his hands together. "I don't understand. I was just here talking to him a few hours ago. It doesn't make sense. The coroner doesn't think it was a heart attack." He paced around some, which seemed to help ease the stress. He combed his hair with his fingers again and then stopped abruptly in front of Briggs. "If not a heart attack, then what? My father always ran on high octane gas, if you know what I mean. He was always uptight and he got upset easily." Briggs had fallen into his listening mode. He was highly skilled at just letting people talk. I knew he was cataloguing every word and mannerism and reaction. After all, family members were some of the first suspects in a murder investigation. Although, this particular victim did seem to have a lot of enemies or, at the very least, people who didn't like him.

Briggs pointed to one of the Casablanca prop tables to silently suggest they sit but Dylan shook his head. "I'm better standing at the moment," he insisted. "I'm very agitated. It's been a difficult few days. My mother just came out of open heart surgery."

"How is your mother?" I asked quietly. Dylan didn't seem to notice or mind my presence. My question took his mind off his father for a moment.

"She's doing well. They'll probably move her from intensive care tomorrow. My parents are divorced, but I know she wanted to see my dad before she went into surgery. He's always too busy." He covered his mouth and paused as he closed his eyes. "I'm sorry. I'm still talking about him in present tense." He sobbed once and swallowed deeply. "I have to get strong so I can tell my mom."

"Maybe it would be better if you gave her a few more days to recover before you break the news," Briggs suggested.

"I can't risk her hearing it from someone else. My dad's death was pretty public considering it happened in his theater in the middle of vintage movie night."

"Of course," Briggs said. "You're right."

Dylan's face turned angry. "What happened? I need to know as soon as possible. The coroner mentioned possible poisoning."

Briggs' cheek twitched with irritation. I predicted that he might have a talk with Doc Patty at some point during the night. "We won't know anything for certain until we have the autopsy report. Mr. Samuels, is there anyone you can think of who might have been angry enough at your dad to hurt him?" I was sure he knew the answer to the question, but he wanted to hear it from Dylan. And hear it he did.

Dylan crossed his arms tightly as if trying to contain himself. "That horrid woman, Connie Wilkerson, the owner of the Starlight Theater. She has plenty of reason. My dad's theater gets most of the movie business in town. Connie has always been jealous of it. After that rundown theater of hers caught fire, she started a rumor that my dad paid someone to start it as a form of sabotage. His theater was already doing better than hers. Why on earth would he need to sabotage the Starlight?" He uncrossed his arms, and his thick shoulders relaxed. It seemed the release of rage was helping him cope with the stress of the night. "You need to pull her in for interrogation," he said sharply. "Right away."

"Yes, thank you. I'll be talking to Ms. Wilkerson soon," Briggs said calmly. "Mr. Samuels, you came to the theater tonight to see your father. I saw you when I was at the concession stand ordering popcorn for the movie."

His forehead rolled up. "You were here in the theater when the mur—" He covered his mouth and took a breath. "When my father died?"

"Yes. We came to watch Casablanca," Briggs explained. "What did you come to talk to your dad about?"

He shuffled his large feet beneath him again and shook his head. "I just wanted to let him know the surgery went well and that she wanted to see him soon. He got called off to fix a problem with the projector, so we didn't get a chance to finish our talk." He sobbed once. "That's the last time I saw him alive."

Briggs placed his hand on Dylan's arm. "We won't need anything else from you tonight. The coroner's office will get in contact with you tomorrow. Take care when driving to the hospital to see your mom. She'll need you to be well and strong during this time."

Dylan pulled a tissue out of his pocket and wiped his eyes. "Yes, you're right. Please let me know as soon as you've heard anything."

"I will. Good night, Mr. Samuels, and I truly am sorry."

We watched him walk toward the exit.

"He was extremely distraught," I said.

Briggs was still watching him. I could see the little detective gears spinning in his head, analyzing the last few minutes. Dylan's reaction seemed natural and entirely expected to me, but it seemed my *partner* had different thoughts.

CHAPTER 15

*B*riggs and I filled some cups with ice water to rehydrate. Sally had begun the process of shutting everything down for the night. She turned off the air conditioning first. It took only minutes before the outside heat seeped in to replace the cool air. The coroner had taken Mr. Samuels away, and the weary and bewildered employees looked ready to go home and leave the terrible night behind. I was certain the prospect of being jobless weighed heavy on their thoughts as well.

"I need to let these people go home," Briggs said. "We can head out soon too." His brown eyes looked extra warm under the overhead lights of the concession stand. "Sorry this movie night took such a turn south."

I reached for his hand. "Are you kidding? A murder mystery is always more fun than an old movie. Even one with Bogie." I cleared my throat. "Maybe fun was a tasteless word. After all, a man is dead. Let's just say intriguing. Especially when I'm with my favorite detective."

"And especially for me when I'm with my favorite nose."

I opened my mouth to protest, but he was already one step ahead.

"And the cute, smart assistant that comes with the nose, of course," he added . . . wisely.

I took a drink of ice water. "Nice save, Detective Briggs."

"Thank you, Miss Pinkerton." He drained his cup. "I think we have the source of poison with that empty bottle of coolant, but I'm going to ask the employees to open their lockers for a quick search before I dismiss everyone for the night. I'll have to make it voluntary for now. Sometimes a refusal speaks volumes. I think Miss Applegate is shutting down each theater. I'll go find her and tell her my plan."

Trinity came out of the restroom just then.

"I could get the first one done right now." Briggs nodded Trinity's direction, indicating he wanted me to ask her about the locker since I'd already formed a bond with her.

"Trinity." I walked over to meet her. "Detective Briggs is going to do a quick locker search. Voluntary, of course. Do you mind opening your locker?"

I expected an easy-going shrug. Instead, she bit her lip. Her eyes darted over to Briggs and back to me. "I—I don't have much in there. Just some sneakers and a sweatshirt. The theater lobby gets cold at night. Not tonight of course." She wiped a few tiny beads of sweat from her forehead. "Why is it so hot in here?"

"Sally is shutting down the theater for the night."

"Does that mean we'll be open tomorrow? We're all wondering if we still have jobs." Her eyes turned glassy. "It's too late in the summer to find another job. All the good ones are taken."

"I'm sure a decision will be made soon. In the meantime, you need to go home and rest. It's been a long, difficult night. Do you think Detective Briggs could glance inside your locker?"

She nodded weakly. "Sure. I guess. I mean, like I said, there isn't much inside of it."

We followed Trinity to the employee lounge. A set of ten green lockers stood next to the time clock. Two round plastic tables with plastic chairs sat in the center of the small, windowless room. An ancient looking microwave sat on the counter next to a coffee pot.

Someone had stuck a piece of paper on the front of the microwave that read 'use at your own risk'.

Trinity led us to the second locker from the end. It seemed she'd just realized she was the only person opening a locker. She looked back at us. "Will anyone else have to open their locker?"

Briggs smiled. "Yes, I'll ask everyone. And remember, I'm not the school principal. I'm just looking for something that might help us figure out how Mr. Samuels died."

"All right." She pulled a small key out from her uniform pocket and unlocked the door. She opened it and stepped aside. As Trinity moved out of the way, I noticed her face drop. She stared down at the ground, avoiding eye contact.

Briggs opened the door wider. A photo of Trinity and Justin standing at a party holding hands was taped to the inside of the door. A sweatshirt had been crumpled into a ball and thrown on top of a pair of worn out sneakers. The only things out of place were two containers of salt.

Trinity snuck a peek toward the locker as Briggs reached in and took out the containers. He shook them. They were empty.

"I like to eat salt on my popcorn, but Mr. Samuels doesn't let us use much. He says it's too expensive."

"Salt?" I asked. "Salt is one of the cheapest things at the grocery store."

Trinity's cheeks were a few shades deeper. She fidgeted with the brass buttons on her uniform. "I told you, Mr. Samuels was really cheap."

"So your boss is too miserly to buy salt, and you have a rather unhealthy salt habit," Briggs said wryly. He shook the empty cardboard canisters once more to emphasize his point. "Or just maybe you were behind the salt sabotage on the soda machine."

Trinity covered her face and crumpled into sobs. "I did it. I did it."

I shot a wide-eyed look at Briggs. Was it possible the sweet, fun Trinity had poisoned her own boss? He was unkind and possibly even despicable but murder?

It seemed Briggs understood the confession differently. "So you put salt in the machine?"

Trinity dropped her hands. Her face was splotchy and pink. "Yes, I poured salt into the machine. I was so mad at Mr. Samuels, I couldn't stop myself. Yesterday, a bunch of Justin's friends showed up for a movie. Mr. Samuels yelled at Justin right in front of all of them about some stupid thing like leaving the trash can lid open. Justin was so embarrassed. I decided Mr. Samuels needed to be embarrassed too, so I poured salt in the machine."

Briggs kept the salt containers but closed the locker. "Do you have any acquaintance with Connie Wilkerson?"

Trinity looked baffled. "Who?"

"She owns the Starlight Movie Theater at the other end of the street," Briggs explained.

"Oh right. No, I don't know her other than I know Mr. Samuels didn't like her. He thought she was trying to ruin his business." She covered her mouth. "Oh my gosh, I just figured out why you asked me that." Her face turned red. "She had nothing to do with the salt plan. That was all me. Justin was so mad about being chewed out in front of his friends, we didn't even hang out last night. We were supposed to get ice cream and play video games but he was too upset." She moved closer. "I do think that lady from the Starlight might have done something to Mr. Samuels. From what I've heard, she still thinks Mr. Samuels caused the fire at the Starlight. And who knows? Mr. Samuels was a mean guy." Her hands flew to her mouth again. "I'm sorry. I shouldn't talk badly about the dead. My mom told me that after my Great Aunt Ursula died. She was ninety-eight, so I didn't think it was such a big deal. She was such a sour puss. She never liked us kids. She used to give us each a set of towels for Christmas. Who gives kids towels? I guess she thought we all needed to take more baths."

I held back a smile as Briggs attempted to bring Trinity back to the topic.

"Yes, I had an uncle who gave us coupons for a hair cut at his barber shop," Briggs added. "Now back to Ms. Wilkerson, have you ever seen her here at the Mayfield Four?"

"Hmm, let me think." Trinity tapped her pink fingernail against her chin. She seemed to have gotten past the small guilt trip over sabotaging the soda machine, and she was back to her bubbly self. "Wait, there was that time during winter break when she came here to see him. She rushed right past the ticket window and into the theater and straight into his office. They yelled at each other for a few minutes. Mr. Samuels threatened to call the police on her for coming inside without a ticket. His face was so red, I thought he was going to have a heart—" Again her hands covered her mouth. "Sorry again. Guess it's been a long night."

"Yes it has," I agreed.

Briggs was jotting down a few notes. "Do you know what they fought about?"

"Yes I do," she said, seemingly excited she was having her words written down in a detective's notebook. "The Starlight was serving hot chocolate in the theater for the holidays. There was a big peppermint colored banner hanging below the marquee inviting everyone in for a good movie and a cup of hot chocolate. Mr. Samuels noticed the hot chocolate was popular, so he copied her. He put up a big banner too, only his had snowflakes. She came to yell at him about stealing her idea. Can't blame her. But Mr. Samuels was always arguing with people. The popcorn vendor, the carpet cleaner, the paper towel company, you name it. Even tonight, his son was only here for a few minutes, but I could hear them arguing."

That last detail caught both of our attentions. Briggs looked up from his notebook. "Mr. Samuels was arguing with his son tonight? Could you hear what they were fighting about?"

She shook her head. "I could only hear loud voices behind the wall. I don't know what they were talking about. Since Mr. Samuels was always yelling, I hardly paid attention to it."

Briggs closed his notebook. "Thank you, Miss Falco. You can go home. Do you have a ride?"

"Yes. My mom is on her way."

Briggs and I walked out to find the other employees.

"Interesting," I said. "Dylan Samuels didn't mention any argument with his dad."

Briggs put his notebook into his pocket. "Yes. I find that interesting too."

CHAPTER 16

*J*ustin had wasted no time removing the red double-breasted usher's coat and matching hat once it was confirmed Mr. Samuels was dead. He had balled the coat up and thrown it in his locker. He pulled it out, along with the hat, to show Briggs that the only other things he had inside his locker were the t-shirt, shorts and sneakers he'd worn into work.

"Thanks for showing us the locker," Briggs said. "I know you've already given your statement, but do you remember where you were between the time the projector was fixed and when you came in to ask for my help?"

"Yeah, like I told the officer, I saw Mr. Samuels head up to the projector room. I took my fifteen minute break right after that. When I came back inside, I looked for Sally to see if there was anything else she needed me to do. I couldn't find her, so I went straight to the maintenance closet to get the things I needed to clean theater one. The movie was close to finished. It's my job to clean up trash in between shows."

Briggs looked up. "Since you are part of the custodial team, do you know if the theater was having any problems with rats?"

The question caused him to laugh. "You mean like the kind with tails, or tattle tales, cuz we've got a few of those around here too."

Briggs was amused but he kept his cool. "I mean the kind with tails."

Justin looked at me almost as if to see if Briggs was serious. "I've never seen one in the theater. But I wouldn't put it past Connie Wilkerson from over at the Starlight to buy some at the pet store and plant them in the theater. She hates Samuels." He paused and rubbed his nose. "I mean hated. Kinda weird having to talk about him in past tense all of a sudden. Heck, he was just chewing me out a few hours ago and now he's dead." He seemed to want to walk back the last sentence. "Not that I'd off him or anything like that. He was a terrible guy to work for but I'm more into chillin' and riding waves. I take life one day at a time."

"Yes, I can see that," Briggs said. "Do you know anyone working here who might not be quite as *chill* as you? Someone who disliked Mr. Samuels?"

"Nah, not here. But I think Samuels did set that fire at the Starlight. Maybe Connie wanted to get revenge. Yesterday, someone poured salt into the soda machine. People were spitting cherry cola and orange soda everywhere. It was gross. I think Connie might have paid someone to dump salt in it when no one was looking."

Briggs shifted a glance my direction. Apparently, Trinity had decided to secretly avenge Justin's honor.

The topic of the salty soda machine spurred the same question into my head as the one that Briggs asked. "I understand that Mr. Samuels yelled at you in front of all your friends. I had my dad do that to me once, and I was mad as heck about it. How did that make you feel?"

The new topic made Mr. Chill a little less chill. His otherwise slack posture (to go with the chillin' part) grew rigid. Red flush crept up his neck to mingle with his suntanned skin. "Didn't make me happy. But that doesn't mean I killed the guy." His posture relaxed again. "Can I go now?" He reached into his locker and rummaged through his clothes to get to the sneakers. The t-shirt piled on top rolled out.

I stooped down and picked it up. A scent grabbed my attention. I discretely took a whiff of the shirt and handed it to him.

Briggs put away his notebook. "You can head home. Do you have a ride?"

He scoffed and looked more than a little insulted. "I've got my own car." He slammed shut the locker.

"Of course," Briggs said and backed out of the way. "Drive safely."

Justin sauntered out of the employee lounge.

"We should probably follow him to his car," I suggested.

"He's a big kid." He suddenly sensed I had more to go with my suggestion. Sometimes we were riding along each other's wave lengths. Tonight was one of those nights. "Why?"

"Because the t-shirt he dropped smelled like coolant."

CHAPTER 17

My stunning revelation that Justin's shirt smelled like coolant sent Briggs and I out to the parking lot. Justin was sitting in an old truck trying to turn the engine over but not having a great deal of luck.

He was surprised to see us standing outside his truck and rolled down the window. "Do you still need to talk to me?" His voice was edged with irritation, which might have had more to do with the stubborn truck motor than us.

"Yes, if you could just step out of the truck for a second, I'd like to ask you a couple of questions," Briggs said it calmly, but Justin still looked alarmed by the request.

The door creaked as Justin pushed it open. "I told you, I didn't do anything. I was just doing my job tonight."

Briggs pulled out his notebook and opened to the page he'd started for Justin. "Mr. Lakeford, I just have a few more questions. I'm absolutely not accusing you of anything. You mentioned you went on a break during the time in question. Did you talk to anyone or hang out with anyone on that break?"

Justin raked his thick hair back with his fingers. His wavy locks had that sun and salt bleached look as if he spent a lot of time sitting out in the water on his board. He was just a kid. He certainly didn't seem like the murdering type but then I'd been surprised before.

"Mr. Samuels always made the break schedule so that none of us could hang out together." He added an eye roll. "He said we'd stay too long on our breaks if we were talking and laughing with our buddies. He didn't want us to enjoy one second of working for him," he added with a huff. "I came out here, sat in my car and looked at my phone. We're only allowed to use phones for emergencies when we're in the theater."

While Briggs talked to Justin, I circled around the front of the car. I could smell some of the usual odors that came from a car, especially an older less digitized model, burning oil, the acrid scent of various motor lubricants and something that smelled distinctly like coolant.

Briggs knew exactly what I was doing. He peered my way for a second. I nodded to let him know the car had recently been filled with coolant.

"Mr. Lakeford, have you recently used a coolant product on your car?" Briggs asked.

The question made Justin's brows raise right into his pile of wavy hair. "Y-Yeah," he said with confusion. "I need a new radiator but couldn't afford one because Samuels was so cheap." He wasn't holding back on his unabashed dislike for his late boss. "I keep adding coolant, but this heat wave is making it worse. Is there a crime in trying to keep your car running?" His attitude was starting to grate on Briggs' nerves. His jaw tightened just enough for me to notice.

"Certainly no crime in keeping your car running," Briggs said just sharply enough to let Justin know to cool it. "Where is the bottle of coolant? Do you still have it?"

Justin's defensive posture softened after Briggs' discrete admonition. "I left it here by the car. I bought it on the way to work and filled my radiator when I got here. But I couldn't get the stupid cap off, so I had to break the lid. I was planning to walk back to the trash bin and toss it after work. It's gone now, so someone must have taken it."

Briggs wrote down the statement. Listening in on the conversation, nothing about his coolant story sounded forced or made up.

Briggs closed his notebook. "Thanks. You've been helpful." He looked at the truck. "Do you need some help getting it started?"

Justin's earlier attitude had smoothed out. He looked tired and ready to get home. "Nah, it just takes a few tries to start. Can I go?"

"Yes, drive safely."

CHAPTER 18

riggs sighed audibly as we walked back into the theater. "Considering this was my night off, I'm tired."

I gave his arm an apologetic squeeze. "This was my fault. I came up with the Casablanca plan. I had no idea the night would end up like this."

"That makes two of us."

Sally was the last person left in the theater. Her face was drawn and tired as she wiped down the soda machine.

"Is there anything we can do to help you close up?" I asked.

My voice startled her. She turned around. "I thought you two had gone. I'm almost finished. I left a message for Dylan Samuels. I don't know what to do with tonight's cash. Mr. Samuels was the only person with the code to the safe. Did you get everything you needed with the statements and locker checks?"

Briggs smiled politely. "Yes, but I have one more locker to check if you don't mind."

It took her a second to understand what he was asking. Her lack of clarity was understandable. The trauma of the night and having to shut down the theater on her own was starting to show in gray circles beneath her eyes.

"Oh yes, of course. My locker is mostly empty. I rarely use it. The kids like to bring comfortable shoes and clothes to change into, but I don't wear one of those heavy, uncomfortable red uniforms. I don't bring spare clothes." We followed her to the employee lounge as she spoke.

Her phone beeped just as we reached the lockers. She opened the door, revealing nothing more than one bottle of aspirin and a banana that was a few days past ripe. After some of the stories I'd heard about Mr. Samuels, a bottle of aspirin seemed entirely appropriate.

She glanced at the text on her phone and groaned in disappointment. "Looks as if I'll have to stick around for awhile. Dylan is coming back to the theater to take care of the cash. He doesn't have a key."

That statement caught our attention. "Dylan Samuels doesn't have keys to his father's theater?" Briggs asked. "Seems like it would be a good security measure to have someone he could trust keep a spare key."

"As far as I know, I'm the only one with a spare key. Last winter, before Christmas, I had the flu. I was sick in bed with a fever and terrible aches and pains. Mr. Samuels got delayed at home, so he called me to open up the theater. I live just a few miles away. When I asked him if his son could open up because I was terribly sick and it was freezing outside, he said Dylan didn't have a key." She twisted her mouth into a frown. "He also told me if I didn't open up, I'd be fired."

I couldn't hide my disgust, even though I knew Briggs wouldn't like it. "The man was truly without conscience."

"It seems there were a lot of things not to like about that man," Briggs responded. It wasn't like him to voice his opinion out loud, at least not to people he was interviewing, but Mr. Samuels was a special case. The miserly, mean stories about him just kept piling up. "Ms. Applegate, I know you made a statement to the officers earlier but would you mind filling me on a few details. Where were you during the time between the start of the Casablanca film and the moment Justin told you Mr. Samuels was on the floor of his office?"

The question threw her slightly. She began fidgeting with her bracelets, something I'd seen her do often during the last few hours. "I was tending to an issue in the men's bathroom." The statement produced a touch of pink in her cheeks. "One of the toilets keeps getting clogged."

"Yes, I saw the closed sign on the bathroom when I went to use the ladies' room," I added.

Briggs wrote down a few notes before continuing. "It's a little out of your job description, isn't it? Plumbing in the men's room?"

A nervous, dry laugh shot from her mouth. "Yes, there were a lot of things Mr. Samuels required me to do that were out of my job description. He was too cheap to hire a plumber, so he asked me to deal with it. I unwittingly let it be known that my dad was a plumber and that I'd apprenticed for him after high school. At least until I realized I didn't have the stomach for clogged plumbing or climbing beneath houses. I was working on the—" She cleared her throat. "The restroom issue for a good thirty minutes. Then, as you might expect, I walked outside for a few minutes of fresh air. When I came back inside, Justin was racing toward me as if he'd seen a ghost. That's when he told me Mr. Samuels was on the floor of his office not moving. I checked on him and immediately called the ambulance."

Briggs finished writing the statement.

Sally relaxed some, seemingly relieved to have her part of the story finished. "You know, we all complain about working here, but the reality is going to hit us tomorrow when it seems we are jobless. It's hard to know what will happen to the theater. I don't think Dylan has any interest in this business. He rarely spoke to his dad. He only came around a lot lately because of his mom's health problems. Not sure why," she said sadly. "It's not like his father gave him any support on that matter."

"Trinity told me you are responsible for the vintage movie night," I said. "The decorations were wonderful. It really felt like we'd stepped into Rick's gin joint. Sans the gin, of course. Maybe the Starlight Theater can use your talent. Or maybe if Dylan sells to another theater owner, he'll make sure to put in a good word for you."

Her cheeks blushed again. "To tell the truth, after the flu incident, I pleaded with Connie to take me on as assistant manager. I promised to help her turn the Starlight around. But she's been struggling so much since the fire, she can't afford to hire me." She drew in a deep breath. "Enough of my feeling sorry for myself. A man has died, after all. Even if there won't be a sea of tears at his funeral, it's a tragedy."

"Yes it is," Briggs said. "If you don't mind, we're going to wait out in the lobby for Dylan Samuels. I have just a few more questions for him."

"That's fine." She crossed her arms around herself. "I'm actually glad you're staying. After what happened tonight, this theater feels big, dark and a little sinister."

CHAPTER 19

*D*ylan Samuels walked into the mostly dark theater looking rightly somber. He was a big man with a broad shoulder span and a thick chest and belly that, for some reason, reminded me of a bull. Yet, he didn't look confident like a bull. Even with a large shoulder span, he looked crumpled as if someone had hit him in the gut. It seemed like a normal appearance considering that his dad was recently murdered and his mother was in intensive care in the hospital. I'm not entirely sure I would even be able to stand upright if I'd suffered the same.

Upon seeing him, Briggs seemed hesitant to approach him. He wanted to clarify Dylan's last talk with his dad. Trinity had mentioned that they had argued. That would certainly be something of note in a murder investigation.

I was quickly trying to come up with a reason to get closer to the man, just to check for the coolant scent, but short of walking up to hug him, I couldn't come up with a plausible excuse.

One thing was certain, he was more than surprised to see Briggs and I still standing in the theater.

"Detective Briggs, I didn't expect you to be here. Have you found out anything?"

"I haven't heard anything definite from the coroner yet. We stayed around because Sally was feeling a little uneasy alone in the theater."

"Well, I'm here now, so we don't need to keep you any longer. Please let me know the second you hear something." He seemed anxious for us to leave, or maybe he was just anxious to be done with the night himself.

"How is your mother?" Briggs asked. "I hope the news didn't set her recovery back."

Dylan walked behind the concession counter and helped himself to a bag of chocolate covered peanuts. "If you'll excuse me, the only food I've had tonight was popcorn." He ripped open the bag. "I didn't make it to the hospital. I called halfway there to check on her and they told me she was sleeping. I decided it was too soon to tell her. Then Sally called about the cash, so I turned around and headed back to the theater."

"Mr. Samuels, I know this has been a trying time for you, but I need to ask you something." Briggs hesitated. "An employee noted that they heard you and your father arguing, rather loudly. You didn't mention an argument when I talked to you earlier. Can I ask what you were fighting about?"

His face reddened and contorted. I couldn't tell if it was anger, indignation or sorrow that made his large face squish up almost as if it was made of dough. "Please, it's too painful to think about." He covered his mouth with the side of his fist. It took him a second to continue. "I didn't mention it because it's too painful to know that the last moments I spent with my dad were in a heated argument." He pulled a tissue from his pocket and wiped his eyes.

"I'll get you a cup of water," I said and rushed away. I'd found a reason to get close enough to the man to get a whiff of his clothes or, at the very least, his hand.

Dylan's large frame was more shriveled than when he walked inside. He looked close to passing out. Briggs helped him to one of the chairs in the center of the lobby. He sat with a thud and rested his head back with eyes closed.

I reached them with the cup of water.

"Here you go, Mr. Samuels." I leaned over, getting as close to him as possible without it seeming like an odd invasion of personal space. Rather than place the cup on the table, I waited for him to take hold of it. My plan worked. His fingers rubbed against mine as he took hold of the cup. There was no scent of coolant on his clothes.

I stepped back. Briggs pulled out the chair next to him and sat.

I turned away and discretely smelled my own hand. I smelled traces of parmesan. I'd nearly forgotten about seeing Dylan standing behind the concession stand showering a bucket of popcorn with parmesan cheese. His dad had told him then that he didn't have any more time to talk. That was just before Mr. Samuels rushed up to the projector room.

Dylan drained the cup of water.

Sally came out from the employee lounge. "Oh good, you're here. Detective Briggs and Miss Pinkerton were kind enough to wait with me. I have the money counted and placed in paper bands. I didn't want to use the office"—her voice trailed off, and she looked at me —"It didn't seem appropriate for me to sit at his desk." She caught a tiny sob. It seemed to be a genuine display of emotion and not just one put on for Dylan Samuels.

Briggs nodded. "We are almost through here, Ms. Applegate." It was his polite way of saying he needed for her to leave them alone.

She took the hint. "Of course. I'll just go back into the lounge and wait." She shuffled slowly off. Earlier in the evening, before the murder, she moved with the alacrity of an enthused cheerleader, excited to treat people to a night in Casablanca, but that spirit had drained away completely.

Briggs didn't waste any more time. It was getting close to midnight, and we were both tired. "Mr. Samuels," he started but didn't need to finish his question.

"We fought about my mother," Dylan snapped. The cup of water had apparently revived him. "I just wanted him to visit her. I didn't think it was too much to ask. They were married for twenty-five years, after all. It would have made her feel better to see him. But he couldn't be bothered." His voice went up a few octaves, but he kept a lid on his anger. "That's what we argued about. Don't you think I had a right to be mad? Wouldn't you be mad if it was your mother?" he asked Briggs.

"Yes, yes I would be." Briggs didn't take out his notebook. He patted Dylan on the shoulder. "We're going to see ourselves out. Try and get some rest. I'll let you know as soon as I hear something."

Dylan stood from the chair and nodded. "See that you do."

CHAPTER 20

*I*t seemed there was the slightest break in temperature as I walked from my car to the shop. It was still too early to know for sure, but it seemed the worst was over. Kingston seemed to notice too. He soared on ahead to stretch his wings. He circled right back like a boomerang though when his arch nemesis, a mockingbird who nested nearby, shot out of nowhere and chased angrily after him. Kingston landed on the roof of the shop, looking both frightened and humiliated. The mockingbird landed just a few feet away and stared at Kingston, her long tail lifting victoriously up and down like a lever. Of course there was nothing much I could do. The war between mockingbirds and crows was a longstanding tradition in the bird world. But like a worried mom, I hated to see his confidence shredded by a bully. Even a bully who was a quarter his size.

I stopped and stared up at my crow. "Come inside, King. Remember, you get to spend all day inside air conditioning nibbling on treats, and she's stuck out here in the sticky air searching for worms."

I opened the door and tucked myself aside, knowing full well that Kingston would swoop right past me, anxious to get away from the mockingbird. His wings fluttered against my shoulder as he soared past, landing with a clatter on his perch.

The shop phone rang the second I shut the door. I hurried over and picked it up. "Pink's Flowers."

"Hi, Lacey, this is Jazmin Falco. I've changed my mind about the first peony bouquet. I've decided the buttercups look too much like Easter brunch instead of a wedding. Can I come back by this morning and look at the bouquets again?" While I was relieved not to have to chase down out of season buttercups, something told me this wouldn't be her last change of mind.

"Yes, of course and we don't have to choose from my examples. I can show you a catalog. That will give you a broader range of choices." Even as I suggested it, I knew I was opening up a possibility for a long, teetering decision session. I normally offered a finite number of choices for no other reason except that it saved the client from having to agonize for hours over too many choices.

"That sounds perfect. I'm heading right over, if that's all right."

"Yes, of course." I waved to Ryder as he walked inside the shop. Kingston dropped right down off his perch and trotted quickly behind Ryder's long strides as he headed to the office to put away his lunch. My bird was feeling down about the embarrassing morning and obviously wanted an early treat to wash away the blues. He knew Ryder was an easy target.

"Great, we'll be there soon," Jazmin said and hung up. I wondered who was included in 'we'. Trinity had had a late, stressful night. I doubted she'd be up for another long flower decision session. Maybe the groom was coming this time. That was always a good thing. The grooms tended to get antsy quickly, and that usually prompted a faster decision.

I could actually hear the clicking of Kingston's talons on the floor as he continued trailing behind Ryder on his way to the shop front.

Ryder twisted around and checked behind him. "What does Kingston want?" he asked.

"What do you think?" I replied. "He had a bad morning. That wily, little mockingbird was harassing him. Now he's trying to make himself feel better with food." I paused after my statement. "My gosh, he really is turning human. Go ahead and give him a couple treats before I have to call a bird therapist."

Ryder plucked the treat can from its shelf. Kingston skittered behind him back to his perch. As he dropped the treats into the treat bowl, Ryder stretched up to gaze across the street to Lola's Antiques. He leaned side to side and stared that direction even after feeding Kingston.

"Are you looking for someone?" I asked. Lola was not expected back until next week. Her cousin had been lucky. The heat wave had kept customers to a minimum. The antique shop was so cluttered with items, it was always a little unwelcoming on a hot day.

Ryder pulled his attention from the front window. "Huh? Oh no. Not really. It's just that Shauna stopped me on my way out last night. She looked sort of pale and shaky. She claimed that the antique rocker in the back of the shop had been rocking back and forth on its own. I told her Late Bloomer probably knocked into it, but she seemed convinced an invisible spirit was trolling her inside the shop. I just wondered if she'd calmed herself yet. She looked pretty anxious."

"Uh oh, that's probably not good. Shauna told me she attends a support group for anxiety."

He shook his head. "Why would she have asked Shauna to watch the shop? That's just like Lola not to think about others when she flies off on her continental vacations."

I arched a brow to let him know, in case he didn't already, that he sounded petulant. He caught on fairly fast.

He raked his hair back with his fingers. "How is it that that woman always manages to bring out all my worst qualities," he muttered more to himself than in pursuit of advice.

But I was never great on keeping advice to myself. "*And* your best qualities," I said. "I think they call that a relationship."

"Right again, boss. You should switch your profession."

"Maybe I should." I laughed as I headed to the refrigerator to pull out the peony bouquets.

"Hey, weren't you at the Mayfield Four last night?" Ryder asked as I came around the corner with the flowers. "I heard the owner was killed right in his office."

I froze in my steps. "How did you hear that?"

"It was all over social media this morning. So it's true?"

I placed the bouquets on the island. "It's not certain yet that it was murder, but things are leaning that direction. We were an hour into Casablanca when one of the ushers came in to get James. Wasn't exactly a dream date but life around town is never boring."

"I'll say. Ghosts in rocking chairs and murdered theater owners. What's next?" Just as he said it, the bell on the door clanged loudly and Lola's cousin, Shauna, burst inside the shop. Her eyes were round with fear, and she was panting to catch her breath.

Ryder and I both rushed to her side. "I don't have a paper bag," I told her in as calm a tone as I could muster under the circumstances.

She shook her head, cupped her hands over her mouth and took a few deep, steadying breaths. We waited patiently for her to gather her wits. It seemed in one aspect, Ryder had been right. Shauna might not have been the best choice for running the antique shop.

When it seemed her breathing had slowed, Ryder took her arm and led her slowly to the stool. That was when I caught it. It was just the tiniest hint of admiration on Shauna's part, but I was sure I saw it. Even in the final stages of a panic attack, Shauna took a moment to favor Ryder with an eye twinkle.

She settled herself on the stool and smiled broadly at him. "Thank you," she said with an extra dose of sugar. "I didn't know what else to do, so I came here. I'm sure it's nothing, but I was sitting in the shop browsing through a couple magazines." She pulled her gaze from Ryder for a second to look at me. "There aren't many customers in this heat," she offered quickly, seemingly thinking she had to explain to me why she was just looking at magazines.

"Yes, we are slow too," I noted.

"Anyhow, I was looking at a magazine. Then I heard this strange howling sound." She closed her reddish-gold lashes and crooned a long ghostly sound. "Just like that. I swear it was coming from the storage room." She blinked her blue eyes at Ryder. "I hate to bother you, but do you think you could come across the street with me and check out the storage room?"

Ryder looked at me for permission.

"Of course," I said. "Ryder will take a look around. I'm sure there is a perfectly logical explanation for the sound you heard."

Shauna moved her head back and forth slowly. "I don't know about that. There wasn't anything logical about the sound I heard. It was just like this." Once again, she favored us with her unexplained howl impression.

Shauna was right in the middle of it when Jazmin walked inside the shop. Trinity shuffled in behind her on a pair of pink flip-flops. She looked energetic and bright eyed. Apparently, a shocking night of murder hadn't set her back too much.

Shauna saw there were customers and snapped her mouth shut. She didn't look too thrilled to see that two pretty young women had just entered the shop. She quickly led Ryder out the door and across the street to Lola's store.

"Good morning," I said. "I've pulled out the peony bouquets, including the one with buttercups, just in case you decide they are what you want after all. Although, I sort of agree with the Easter brunch look." I circled around to the open shelf side of the work island and pulled out my wedding bouquet notebook. It was filled with laminated photos of bridal bouquets. "Are you still set on peonies?" I circled back and set the notebook down in front of her.

"Yes. I promised my grandmother. She used them in her bouquets and my mom did too." She placed her large bag on the floor. Her tiny dog popped its head up and looked around before disappearing back into the purse.

I laughed. "Will your dog be in the ceremony? I've always pictured my wedding with Kingston." I motioned toward the perch. "I thought he could swoop in with the gold rings in his talons. I think he'd be quite the showstopper."

Trinity laughed.

Jazmin smiled. She didn't seem terribly entertained by my idea. "I think Tootsie would be terrified of all the people. But we are taking her on the honeymoon."

Trinity rolled her eyes. "She never goes anywhere without her precious, annoying little Tootsie." She made sure to put a strong accent on the double O in Tootsie.

"Just like I never seem to go anywhere without my annoying little sister." Jazmin sat on the stool and pulled the notebook closer. "And now that she doesn't have a job, she'll be bugging me even more."

Trinity placed her hands hard on her slim hips. "You don't know that. I still have a job. Someone has to keep the theater going. I think Sally will just be put in charge. That's even better than when Mr. Samuels was—" Her words trailed off as she seemed to conclude it wasn't nice to talk about a dead man.

"I'll give you some time to look," I said. "I've got a few bouquets to arrange. Just let me know if you have any questions."

Jazmin started to pore over the dozen or so pictures. Trinity was more interested in my bouquet arrangements than in her sister's wedding. She leaned against the work table at the back sink as I cut the stems on some pink roses.

"Where did that cute assistant guy go with that girl who was howling? And why was she howling?"

"Ryder was just going to help her with something. She's running the antique shop while Lola is out of town." I didn't feel like going into the whole story.

"She seemed kind of strange," she said snippily and then did an about face on topics. "Did you tell anyone about the salt? I'll lose my job if anyone finds out."

What I wanted to say was you should have thought of that before you poured salt into the machine. But I was part of the investigation, and it wasn't my place. "No one else knows." Since we were on the topic, I decided some unofficial prying wouldn't hurt. "Have you spoken to anyone? To your coworkers? Does anyone have a theory about who might have been wanting to harm Mr. Samuels?"

"I've only talked to Justin." She picked up one of the wilted roses I'd set aside and twirled it around in front of her nose for a whiff. "He says Detective Briggs thinks he killed Mr. Samuels."

I glanced up from my task. "Where did he get that idea?"

She shrugged casually, only I could tell the topic upset her. "He was asking Justin about the coolant he put in his car. Justin said that might have been the poison. He said the stuff looks and smells like green punch, so maybe someone snuck it inside the lemon-lime slush Mr. Samuels was drinking." She stared down. There was the slightest lip quiver happening beneath her freckled nose. "I gave him the drink, but I didn't put any poison in it," she said emphatically and loudly enough to catch her sister's attention.

Jazmin looked across the shop at us. "Is she bothering you, Lacey? Just send her back over here."

Trinity scoffed in the direction of her sister. "What am I? Your trained puppy? Not that your pup is anywhere near trained," she muttered as she turned back toward me.

I pushed a rose into the vase. "She's not bothering me," I called and then lowered my voice. "You don't need to worry about that. Detective Briggs will find the real killer." My statement didn't alarm her, which was a good thing. I hated to even consider her as a person of interest. She just didn't fit the mold of murderer. "That's why, if you hear anything from any of your coworkers, even Justin, you need to let me or Detective Briggs know right away."

"Justin would never do something like that. Even if Mr. Samuels ruined his life's dream of working in the surfboard shop."

"Oh," I said casually as I wiped down my counter. "How did he do that?"

She snuffled as if just having to tell the story made her angry. "Justin has been wanting to work in Mayfield Surf Shop ever since he was a little kid. Problem was, no one ever left their position there because it's a cool place to work."

"I'm sure."

"Well, a miracle finally happened, and someone left the shop. They needed a new salesman. Justin would've been perfect for that. He knows a ton about surfboards. He applied for the job. The only reference he had was Mr. Samuels at the theater. And that mean old man told the surf shop owner not to hire Justin. He told him he was unreliable and lazy." Her voice wavered for a second. She quickly rubbed her nose to stop a sniffle. "Justin was really upset, but he would never kill anyone."

I stopped my task. "No, of course not. That wasn't very nice of Mr. Samuels. Don't worry about the investigation. Like I said, Detective Briggs will find out who did it."

Trinity glanced back over her shoulder at her sister. Jazmin was too focused on the bouquet pictures to notice or care about our conversation. Trinity turned back to me. "I think Connie Wilkerson has been trolling the Mayfield Four with bad online reviews. She might be paying people to write terrible one star reviews. There were a whole bunch lately. It was making Mr. Samuels red in the face every time one showed up. He assumed they were legitimate and took it out on all of us. That was why he was yelling at Justin about not cleaning the theaters better between movies. A lot of the reviews complained that the auditoriums were really dirty and that there were rats running around the place."

The last part caught my undivided attention. "Rats? Was there a rat problem?" It was still a puzzle why there was an almost methodically stacked pile of empty rat poison boxes sitting in the trash bin.

"Not that I knew of. No one liked Mr. Samuels but Connie liked him least of all." She seemed to be trying to lay the blame on Connie. I was certain Briggs had her on the list to interview, especially since there had been a rather public ongoing feud between the two theater owners.

"I've got it narrowed down to six bouquets," Jazmin stated proudly from her stool.

Trinity rolled her eyes and looked back at her sister. "Oh my gosh, Jaz. They're just a bunch of flowers. They'll be dead before you open the last wedding gift. Just pick something."

Trinity turned back to me with a satisfied huff. "Justin and I have already decided we're not going through the hassle of a wedding."

I finished cleaning my work counter. "Is that right?"

"Yep. I won't even need one of those expensive dresses. We're going to put on our bathing suits and paddle out past the breakers on our surfboards and get married out on the water. And the only people invited will be people willing to paddle out on boards too."

"So the only flowers will be seaweed." I smiled. "That sounds like a unique wedding indeed."

The bell on the door rang. Trinity's face lit up when she saw that Ryder had returned. He looked calm, so I could easily conclude that there were no ghostly encounters.

"Did you take care of the problem?" I asked.

He was holding back a grin. "Apparently, Shauna had tripped over Bloomer's rawhide chew bone so often she got mad and put it on a shelf in the storage room to get it out of her way."

I laughed. "Bloomer was howling for his rawhide?"

"Seems that way." He shook his head and muttered as he walked past to the office. "Something tells me that won't be my only ghost busting mission this week."

CHAPTER 21

*A*fter a long morning with Jazmin, who finally decided on one of my first bouquet examples with pink peonies and yellow roses, I was more than pleased to meet a certain handsome detective at Franki's Diner for lunch.

Briggs had texted that he'd gotten us a booth in the back, away from the clatter of the kitchen and the busy foot traffic along the counter. Franki spotted me as I walked into the diner. She whirred past me with a large tray of food. "I figured that's why he waited for the booth in the back." She winked. "Lots of privacy for a romantic lunch."

I shook my head. "Not sure how romantic a bowl of chili can be, but I'm sure we'll give it our best." I headed to the back corner of the diner.

Briggs had gone casual, or as casual as his job allowed. He had wisely left his coat and tie behind at the station. There was something extra pleasant about the way his strong forearms looked with the sleeves of his shirt rolled up.

He put down the menu he was holding when he saw me. I slipped into the booth across from him. He patted the menu. "I don't know why I bother to look. I always order either the burger or the bowl of chili. I'm thinking chili is too hot for this weather."

"I agree. I'm going for the chicken salad sandwich. Nice and refreshing because Franki puts chunks of grapes in it."

"Hmm, that does sound good. Maybe I'll step out of my comfort zone today and try the chicken salad."

I stacked the menus on top of each other. "A few months together and I've turned you into a wild risk taker."

Franki swept over and quickly took our order. She was particularly harried today. The tables and the counter were filled with lunch customers. She pushed a stray hair off her forehead. "This heat wave is great for business. No one wants to turn on a stove at home. But I'm exhausted. I'll be right back with your teas."

I leaned back and relaxed for the first time all morning. "I know Franki insisted this was to be a romantic lunch, but I'm about to change all that by bringing up the investigation. Any word from the coroner?"

"Nothing definitive. Still waiting for the lab results. But Doc Patty," he said the name with the usual hint of mockery, "is still leaning toward poisoning. She managed to get a health history from Samuels' doctor. He was on a lot of different medications for cholesterol, blood pressure and a few other ailments. Doc Patty mentioned that would make him much more vulnerable to poisoning."

"*And* for a possible heart attack," I suggested. "Maybe this wasn't murder after all. Maybe this was just a grumpy man with frail health who worked himself into a lather about something and his heart gave out."

Franki delivered the iced tea. I picked mine right up for a cooling sip.

Briggs reached for a sugar packet. "No, that's been ruled out. There's a certain enzyme that spikes in the blood after a heart attack. Initial blood tests came back negative."

"Troponin," I stated confidently. He looked properly impressed. "Two years of medical school," I reminded him. I was well on my way to becoming a doctor when my super sensitive nose had other plans.

The smells and odors of the anatomy lab were just too much for me. "Then I guess the heart attack theory is put to rest for good."

Briggs stared at his tea in thought as he stirred in the sugar. He had that faraway look in his brown eyes that he got whenever he was trying to puzzle something out.

I sat forward. "Detective Briggs, I can see the gears spinning in your head."

I jarred him out of his thoughts. He smiled and took a drink of tea. "I was just thinking about the conversation I had with Dylan Samuels last night. When I called to tell him that his father had been found dead on his office floor."

"Yes? How did he react?"

"His reaction was what I expected. Shock, despair. He immediately asked how he died. He had to have known with all the medications his dad took that he was a textbook case for a heart attack. He didn't ask if it was his heart. Even we jumped to that conclusion at first and we didn't know his health history." He shook his head. "I'm just grasping at straws." He swirled the straw in his drink and smiled. "Literally and figuratively, it seems."

"I think your speculation is valid. It seemed he lied about his last conversation with his dad. It was more agitated than he first reported. By the way, Trinity, the employee from the theater who poured salt in the machine, came into the shop this morning. I think I mentioned to you that her sister is getting married, and I'm working on her flowers. She told me a couple of things that may or may not be significant. First, she mentioned that Justin, the theater usher, had been trying to land his dream job at the Mayfield Surf Shop. Apparently, it's not easy to get a position there."

Briggs nodded. "Makes sense. Probably a cool place to work if you're a surfer."

"Exactly. Well, a position opened up and Justin applied. But he had to put Mr. Samuels down as his reference."

Briggs nodded. "Let me guess. Samuels gave him a terrible review."

"Yes. It blew Justin's chances. And speaking of reviews, Trinity also mentioned that she thought Connie Wilkerson had been paying people to leave bad reviews online for the Mayfield Four. Including reviews that claim the place is crawling with rats."

Briggs' brow lifted. "Rats? Maybe there was something to all those rat poison boxes in the trash."

"Maybe."

Our chicken salad sandwiches arrived. "Anything else I can get you two?" Franki asked. She looked at us both with a 'how cute is this' smile.

"Nope, I think we're good," I said. "Thanks, Franki."

"You bet."

Briggs watched her walk away. "Why do I get the feeling that our dating has added a whole new topic of conversation to the town's gossip chain?"

I picked up my sandwich. "Because it has. That's only because it's new. Another fresh topic will come around to replace it soon enough." I took a bite and Briggs did the same.

He nodded as he chewed and swallowed. "Good choice."

"What's your next step?" I asked

"I'm going to head over to Connie's house for a chat. If you can get away, I'm going this afternoon. If you'd like to—"

"Yes I would," I said quickly.

He laughed. "You don't even know what I was going to say. Maybe I was going to say if you'd like to mow my lawn that would be great."

"I know you need *the* nose to snoop about the place. And since Samantha and I come as a team, it was easy to predict what you were going to say. And I've got my own lawn to mow, thanks."

"I guess then the *three* of us will head over to Mayfield after lunch. We have no witnesses that place Connie at the scene, but she does seem to have a motive. In fact, with Mr. Samuels being disliked by so many people, it seems there is no shortage of motives for this murder. Now, if we could just find the person who disliked Samuels the most."

CHAPTER 22

*B*usiness was slow and Ryder had no qualms about running the shop while I took a quick trip to Mayfield. He'd set himself the task of cleaning up all the ribbon spools and reorganizing them for easier use.

Briggs checked the map on his phone. "It's just a half mile ahead." The street we traveled along was quiet with nicely kept houses. A bright blue Toyota zipped past us. We both happened to glance at the driver as she drove past. Briggs looked quickly over at me. "Was that Sally Applegate?"

"I was just about to ask you the same thing. Now that I think about it, I did see a bright blue Toyota just like that in the theater parking lot. It's a striking color. Easy to remember. It must have been her. Do you think she was coming from Connie's house?"

"Unless she happens to live on the same street, that would be my guess."

"Maybe she's trying to find a new job and she's hoping Connie can finally afford to take her on," I suggested.

"That doesn't sound too farfetched." Briggs turned right at a small dead-end street called Clover Road. He parked under a massive poplar tree to keep the car cool. There was no car parked on the driveway in front of Connie's house, a cute pale green bungalow with white trim and a jutting front porch.

"Do you think she's home?" I asked.

"Guess we'll find out." We walked up the driveway.

There was no way for my nose to ignore the warm, penetrating smell of a car engine hovering over the empty driveway. "She might not be home, but I'm certain there was a car sitting in this driveway just moments ago."

We climbed the porch steps. A hand painted welcome sign that was covered with stars greeted us on the front door. Briggs knocked. It opened quickly, almost as if Connie was expecting someone. Or maybe she thought her previous guest had forgotten something.

"Detective Briggs," she said with a good degree of surprise.

"Miss Wilkerson," Briggs said with a nod. "This is my assistant, Miss Pinkerton. May we come in? I'd like to ask you a few questions."

Connie Wilkerson was forty something. Her white summery dress was covered in yellow polka dots. Her short reddish-brown hair was pushed back with a matching polka dot headband. I could smell onions, tomatoes and basil drifting out from the kitchen as we stepped into the house. An overhead fan was spinning at top speed, pushing mostly hot air around.

She stopped in the center of the front room. The walls were decorated with framed classic movie posters, including one from Casablanca. "What can I do for you, Detective Briggs?"

Briggs didn't pull out his notebook right away. I'd seen him delay it whenever he didn't want to put someone on defense before he even got started. "Miss Wilkerson, I'm sure by now you've heard the news about Ronald Samuels."

"Yes, I have and I can't say I'm sad or upset. I know that sounds callous, but that's how I feel. I never lie."

Briggs cleared his throat. "Yes, I understand. I know there had been some tension between the two of you."

Her nostrils flared in indignation at his mild statement. "Some tension? The man set my theater on fire. I nearly lost everything because of him." It seemed to dawn on her that the show of anger wasn't the best way to present herself to the man investigating Samuels' murder. She relaxed and dropped her chin. "Of course, I would never resort to anything so heinous as murder." She shot a curious look my direction. I smiled politely in return. What I needed was to find a way to get into the garage to sniff for coolant. Even that was probably going to prove worthless because if coolant had been the culprit, then the murderer had access to it at the theater.

My sniffer did help me devise a way to bring up Sally Applegate. "Did you and Sally make pasta for lunch? It smells delicious. I'm a big fan of basil."

My simple, innocuous question threw her off guard. She stumbled over a few syllables before deciding on an answer. "Sal—Sally who? I'm cooking some spaghetti sauce for dinner."

Briggs stepped right up to bat. "So Sally Applegate didn't leave here a few minutes ago?"

"Sally Applegate?" She placed her hand on her chest for effect. "Why would she be here? As I said, I've been cooking spaghetti sauce."

Briggs casually pulled out his notebook. Connie shifted on her sandals. The movement and the jet engine speed fan above caused the flouncy skirt of her dress to flutter up. Her cheeks darkened as she pushed it quickly down.

"Cute dress," I noted. "You're daring cooking spaghetti sauce in a white dress."

Briggs snuck a sideways peek at me. He knew too well that I was pointing that fact out to him, a man, someone who might not notice that a white and yellow polka dot dress was hardly practical for cooking with tomatoes.

"I was wearing an apron," she said crisply. "Can we hurry this along, Detective Briggs? I need to get ready for work."

"Just a few more questions. I'll make it fast. I'm sure your theater will be extra crowded tonight since the Mayfield Four is closed."

Her brows rose with an innocent blink. "Oh wow, I hadn't even considered that possibility."

Her statement about never lying seemed to be what one might refer to as a lie. Especially because I was convinced Sally's car had been in the driveway just seconds before our arrival. No other cars had passed us, so unless a neighbor had driven over parked in the driveway and driven right back home, it had to be Sally.

"Miss Wilkerson." Briggs flipped open his notebook. "Can you tell me where you were last night between the hours of seven and nine?"

"Yes, of course," she said and then paused. "I arrived at the Starlight at noon to help with the matinees."

"So you were there all afternoon and night, until closing?" he asked.

"No, actually, I stayed until almost six to do some paperwork and make sure the evening shows went off without a hitch. Then I came back home for a few hours to eat dinner and rest before heading back at ten to help clean and close up."

He wrote down some notes. "What time was that dinner break at home?"

"I think I got home around six and I was here until half past nine. I remember because I was just getting into my car when the phone rang. My ticket manager called to let me know about Mr. Samuels' death."

"I see. Did you have company or were you alone?"

She laughed dryly. "Alone. I'm hardly in the mood to entertain during my few hours of rest."

Briggs looked up from his notebook. "Is there anyone who can confirm you were here? A neighbor who saw your car in the driveway?"

Her face turned smooth and pale. "Certainly I'm not being considered a suspect. I was here those hours. I made myself a tuna sandwich and sat with my book right there on the couch. Right below the Gone with the Wind poster. I can ask neighbors if they saw me pull into the driveway, but I always park in the garage."

Briggs lowered his pen. "Is it possible to see the garage?" He'd read my mind.

It seemed as if she was going to deny his request at first. Her shoulders had grown more rigid, and her chin jutted forward in defense. "Yes, I have nothing to hide, so by all means. Right this way." She led us to a door in the kitchen that led out to an attached garage.

A white Chevy sedan was parked in the center of the garage. A washer and dryer took up one top corner. One wall was lined with boxes that were labeled for seasonal decorations like Halloween and Christmas. Shelves on the opposite side contained floor cleaner solution, a box of tools and gardening supplies. At the end of the bottom shelf there were at least ten bags of brown pellets. Something told me they were peanut butter flavored rat bait.

Briggs walked over and touched the center of the hood on Connie's car. "You're certain that Sally Applegate wasn't here earlier?" The question stunned Connie.

"Yes, I think I would know if I had a visitor."

"There was the smell of a car motor lingering on your driveway when we walked up," he said plainly.

She fidgeted enough to assure both of us that she'd been caught in a lie. "I went out for a moment. To buy some basil," she added to give weight to her story.

"Except your car is cold," Briggs said.

Her shoulders relaxed with a long groan of surrender. "Fine. Sally was here. We celebrated Mr. Samuels' demise with a pasta lunch. Nobody is sad that man is dead. I can tell you that with confidence."

Briggs glanced around the room casually, but I knew he was calculating and planning his next words. He turned back to her. "Why did you lie about Sally being here?"

"Isn't your being here enough to explain it? I didn't want you to start coming up with some crazy farfetched theory that Sally and I had conspired together to kill Samuels. I didn't want to raise any suspicions."

"Lying to an officer is never a good way to avoid raising suspicions. And no matter what your feelings about the man, a celebratory lunch just hours after his death is a little much. Don't you think?" Briggs asked.

She smoothed her hand primly down the skirt of her dress. "If that's all, I need to get ready for work."

I walked an extra wide berth around the car to sniff the bags of pellets on the shelf. It was an artificial smell that mimicked peanut butter. "Do these work?" My question bounced around the tension in the garage and landed squarely Connie.

She blinked in confusion at me.

"The peanut butter flavored rat bait? Does it work?" I repeated.

Briggs' eyes flashed toward the bags as I spoke.

I picked up a bag and examined it. "Does it take care of the rat problem? I've noticed some of them are chewing the boxes in my garage."

"Uh, I—I'm not sure." She stuttered over her answer. "I mean I haven't tried it yet."

"I see." I smiled mildly at Briggs. "Are we through here, Detective Briggs? It seems we're keeping Miss Wilkerson from her busy night at the theater."

"Yes. Thank you for your time."

Connie hit a button to lift the garage door to show us a faster way out.

CHAPTER 23

Since I'd taken an extra break from the shop to visit Connie Wilkerson with Briggs, I gave Ryder the rest of the afternoon off. Business was so slow I contemplated closing up early. I couldn't blame the entire slump on the heat wave. It was my first year as a florist. I was slowly seeing trends and peaks and valleys in business. Most of it was connected to the time of year. Holidays were booming, along with early spring when most of the wedding orders came in. Jazmin was my only bridal customer at the moment, but I expected more orders near Christmas. Winter weddings were growing in popularity. But the end of summer was a time when people were using their extra cash for back to school items and last minute vacations. Flowers were probably an unnecessary expense. Wisely, I'd learned to save during peak seasons and scrimp during the valleys.

I'd finished up purchase orders, reorganized my office and found myself with time to think about the murder investigation. Briggs had driven back to Port Danby deep in thought. We'd both agreed that Connie's behavior and the lie about Sally, along with her outright disdain for Samuels, put her in the person of interest category. In fact, the piles of unused rat poison and her general lack of a good alibi had moved her higher on that list. The question that remained was how could Connie have poisoned the slush without anyone seeing her? Certainly, given her reputation as Samuels' vocal enemy, theater workers would have noticed Connie Wilkerson walking through the Mayfield Four. It seemed far more plausible that the murderer had been inside the theater all along.

Kingston's nemesis, the pushy mockingbird, had flown off earlier in the day. My crow had found enough courage to take a tour around the neighborhood. He'd been gone a good hour, so I walked outside to look for him.

The blast of hot air I expected was followed by a gentle coastal breeze. It seemed the worst was over. We were headed back to being a coastal town with beachy weather rather than a town that had somehow been dropped onto the surface of planet Mercury.

I shaded my eyes and scanned the sky and the trees, but there was no sign of Kingston.

"Lacey," a voice called from across the street. Shauna glanced both directions quickly before hurrying over to my side. She looked frantically into the shop window. "Is Ryder around? I think there's something or someone in the attic of the shop. I can hear footsteps, like someone is moving something around." She didn't wait for my response and rushed past me to the front door.

"Ryder is off for the afternoon."

She froze with one foot inside the shop, then turned around and joined me on the sidewalk. "What will I do? I can't possibly go back inside that store. What if it's a ghost or an ax murderer?"

"Or a ghost who is also an ax murderer," I chided.

Her lips puckered in displeasure. "This isn't funny. Can you call Ryder for me?"

"No, it's not funny. I'm sorry. I'll walk over to the antique shop with you and see if I can find out what's going on."

Her disappointment in not having Ryder come to her rescue was palpable. It seemed a good fright was much more fun when there was a handsome knight to come to your rescue, instead of a curly haired, sarcastic flower shop owner.

I locked my shop door and took one last sky survey for my bird before walking nervous Shauna back to the antique store. It was easy to see why she needed an anxiety support group. That thought pushed an idea into my head. After I solved the ax murderer problem, I hoped to grill her a bit on her group mate, Sally. I hadn't considered Sally a person of interest until the strange incident at Connie's.

Shauna stopped a foot back from the door with a frightful gaze as if something might jump out at us from inside. I was sure going to have a few good stories to tell Lola when she returned. I wondered if she realized that her humble little antique shop was a favorite hot spot for menacing spirits.

"I'll go in first," I suggested, but there seemed to be no question about it. Late Bloomer lifted his head from his pillow as we walked back inside. The ghost didn't seem to have Lola's dog too agitated.

Shauna stood plastered to the door. Her eyes darting back and forth, again waiting for something to jump out at her. I patted Bloomer on the head. I might have been imagining it, but I could have almost sworn the dog shot me a secret eye roll.

"Where did you hear the sound?"

Shauna finally peeled herself off the door, her emergency escape hatch, apparently, and tiptoed toward me. Her shoulders were up around her ears as she peered cautiously up at the ceiling. She was just halfway when a quick succession of taps was followed by a rolling sound. Before I could peel my gaze from the noisy ceiling, Shauna was outside the door, hugging herself and pacing the sidewalk.

I listened again. After a few seconds of silence, the tapping sound continued. Once again a strange rolling sound followed. Naturally, with the day I'd had, my mind went right to rats. I knew Lola was vigilant about pests in her shop. A rat could cause catastrophic damage to antiques.

Shauna was at the door now, staring in with eyes as wide as saucers, waiting for her volunteer ghost buster to get to work. Lola had a ladder in the storage room. The small attic door was in the same room. I didn't relish the idea of having to climb up into the dark, cluttered space above the store, but if I didn't determine the source of the noise, there was no way Shauna would ever step foot inside the antique store again.

I headed along the short hallway to the storage room. As I reached for the door, a tapping sound skittered across the ceiling. It sounded vaguely familiar. I waited for it again. Titter tatter, titter tatter. My laugh was stifled in the narrow passage. It was a sound I'd heard far too often.

I headed outside. Shauna stepped away from the door as I opened it. She was white as the sidewalk below her fidgety feet. "Did you see anything?" she asked.

"Not yet." I walked out to the middle of Harbor Lane and got up on tiptoes to get a view of the roof. The menacing ghostly culprit appeared, only he was far from ghostly and only slightly menacing. Kingston saw me standing on the sidewalk below and dropped the shelled walnut he was holding in his beak. The nut rolled quickly down the roof. My crow titter tattered after it.

Shauna looked baffled. "Is that Kingston?"

"Yes, and I'm afraid he's the one making the noise on the roof. It seems he found a walnut and carried it up to Lola's roof to eat. Only the pitch of the roof seems to be making that task difficult."

Shauna released a long breath. "Thank goodness. I was sure something terrible was lurking up in the attic. Are you sure it was Kingston making the sounds?"

"Yes, I recognized his footsteps pretty quickly." I whistled for Kingston to come down. He picked up the walnut and flew across the street to the roof of the flower shop.

"I'll walk back in with you to make sure the problem is gone, but I'm sure the tapping noise just flew over to my side of Harbor Lane. Shauna was still tense about walking inside the shop. I decided to get her mind off the earlier scare.

"Have you heard from Lola?" I asked. "Is she having a good time?"

Shauna's steps lightened as she followed me across to the counter. "She seems to be having a good time, but it's always hard to tell with Lo-lo. She can be a little sarcastic."

"Who? Lola?" I said with a chuckle. "I'm sure she's having fun. I mean it's France."

"Well, thanks for figuring out the sound. So Ryder isn't coming back for the rest of the day?" she asked casually as if it was just an afterthought. (Which it clearly wasn't.)

"I don't expect to see him again until morning. He watched the shop for me while I went on an errand. I was going to ask you—you mentioned that Sally Applegate, the assistant manager at the theater, was in your anxiety support group."

She gasped slightly. "My mom said the theater manager died right in the middle of a movie. Just dropped dead in front of the audience."

Lola had mentioned her Aunt Ruby liked to put her own spin on things. It seemed she was right. "No, that isn't exactly how it happened. He was in his office. No audience." I pulled her back to the original topic. "Do you know Sally well?"

"Not really. She's about ten years older than me, so it wasn't like we hung out or anything." Shauna walked around to the other side of the counter and picked up the bottle of glass cleaner and the rag she had sitting near the register. "Mostly what I know about her is what she's talked about at group."

"I see. Well, I guess that kind of information has to be kept in the group." I looked expectantly at her, hoping she'd still drop a few tidbits. I was in luck.

"We're not really supposed to talk about stuff outside of group, but I'm thinking of quitting so I guess that rule doesn't apply anymore."

"You're not going to group anymore?"

"Nah, I don't really need it." It seemed she'd entirely wiped away the last half hour from her memory. "But I can tell you, Sally is a good candidate for the group. She has so much stress in her life. Poor lady."

I inched closer to the counter and tried to contain my enthusiasm for hearing more. "Stress?" I asked lightly. "What kind of stress?"

She sprayed the cleaning fluid on the glass top of the counter. I rubbed my nose to stop it from twitching into a massive sneeze.

"The usual kind of stuff," she continued as she wiped the glass. "She was struggling to pay her bills. Her mom is sick with some kind of nerve thing. I guess the doctors don't know what it is but she's always in bed. Sally is taking care of her and trying to make sure her mom doesn't lose the house. Then there is the stress of working for that awful boss of hers." She looked up wide-eyed from her task. "I guess that stress has been removed now."

"Yes but a new one has sprung up," I noted. "Sally might not have a job if the theater closes down."

"I hadn't thought of that. But they'll open it again. The Mayfield Four is way nicer than the Starlight."

"Do you think so?"

"Everyone thinks so," she said confidently.

I patted Late Bloomer's head again. He didn't stir from his nap. "I better go open up for Kingston to get to his perch. He's probably worked himself into a lather trying to break open the nut. Sorry he gave you a fright," I said on my way out.

"He didn't give me a fright."

Yep, she'd definitely forgotten the entire last half hour.

CHAPTER 24

My chat with Shauna sparked my interest in the online reviews for the Mayfield Four Theater. Trinity was sure Connie had paid people to leave bad reviews.

I opened up the shop and Kingston swooped past me. The walnut was still wedged in his beak. He flew to his perch, holding tight to his prize. The second I picked up his treat can, with goodies that took much less effort to eat, he dropped the walnut. It fell onto the tray beneath his perch. While he was busy eating his treats, I grabbed the nut, carried it to the work island and used the handle end of a screwdriver to crack it open. I dug out the nut meats and carried them back to the perch.

"Here," I said. "And let's just be glad your mockingbird friend wasn't around to witness that sad display of bird-ness."

I headed into the office and sat down at the computer. Mayfield Four had over a hundred reviews with an average of three stars. It seemed ratings were either five or one, with very little in between, which, frankly, made both sides a little suspect. For me to give a five star rating to a regular old neighborhood theater, I'd expect the seat to recline like my dad's easy chair and gourmet snacks to be served by the movie stars themselves. Some of the rave reviews seemed to indicate that my wish list had just about been met, sans food delivery by movie stars. Comfortable seating, attentive staff and great sound system were among the things complimented. But there were plenty of negative reviews too. One person's entire review complained about there being far too many unpopped kernels in their bucket of popcorn.

I scrolled down to some of the more recent reviews, in particular, the one stars. Some stated plainly that the theater was disgustingly dirty. One reviewer went so far as to post a picture. I clicked on the review, and it opened up wider. Interestingly enough, it was a photo of a stack of rat poison boxes sitting in the trash bin. The reviewer who called themselves Mary J. wrote— "enter this theater at your own risk. They have a rat infestation. Just look at this trash bin behind the theater. I think I'll spend my movie money at the Starlight up the street instead. At least that theater isn't crawling with rodents".

It was just a touch too obvious to include a comparison of a competing theater. It seemed Trinity was right about Connie possibly paying people to write bad reviews of the Mayfield Four. Only, after finding the evidence sitting right in view in Connie's garage, I'd say the staged photo of the rat poison and one star review that came with it was posted by Connie herself.

CHAPTER 25

I finished my review search and was shutting down the computer for the evening when Elsie's sing song voice was followed by a delicious aroma. A mix of butter and brown sugar, according to my infallible nose.

"Yoo hoo, Pink," she called. "I've got cookies."

My chair rolled across the floor as I leapt out of it at the word *cookies.*

Elsie was standing at the island with a plate of goodies and one of her mini handheld fans. "I come bearing gifts."

"You know I love all of your gifts." She handed me the plate and the fan. "Why are you handing me this? Don't your customers need it? I saw a few of them holding them in front of their faces while they nibbled baked goods."

"Turns out they aren't a very efficient way to keep my customers cool. I had to keep replacing the batteries. I'm giving up on them. Batteries are way too expensive. It'd be cheaper to hire people to stand with giant ostrich feather fans and wave them at the customers."

I decided not to bring up Lester's gigantic fan. I didn't need to *fan* the flames of sibling rivalry between my two neighbors. I put the plate on the counter. The cookies were filled with everything from bits of chocolate and nuts to chopped cranberries.

I picked one up and bit it. It was a mix of flavors all wrapped in a buttery, brown sugar cookie. "Hmm, very good. What are they called?"

"I call them Clutter Cookies. I make them whenever I decide to clean out the clutter in my bakery pantry. It's a nice way to get rid of half used bags of chocolate and nuts and fruits. The cookie is just a basic chocolate chip dough recipe."

I swallowed another bite. "There is nothing basic about anything you bake, Elsie." I picked up a second cookie and turned it back and forth to admire it. "Clutter Cookies. A new favorite."

Elsie climbed up on a stool. "So what's with the murder at the theater? I assume a certain charismatic detective is on the case."

"Gosh, that's right. I haven't talked to you since our movie date."

Elsie spun on the stool to watch me as I grabbed the watering pot to give the plants in the front window a drink. "Were you two at the theater when Ronald Samuels died?"

"Yep, right in the middle of Casablanca. They pulled James out of the movie. Poor guy. Even when he has the night off, he's still on duty. At least in everyone else's eyes." I leaned into the window area and poured the water.

"I went to city college with Ronald Samuels," Elsie said. "That was forty years ago, but I can tell you he was as unlikeable then as he was now. Always grumpy."

I straightened from the window and walked back to the island with the watering pot. "Interesting. I had no idea you knew him."

"Not well. He wasn't exactly the kind of person you wanted to befriend. Still, it's sad that he died," she added with a touch of sincerity. "I hear he dropped right in front of one of his audiences. Poison?"

"He died alone in his office. Boy, rumors sure do get big and swirly in this town. Looks like poison. Normally that detail wouldn't be out yet but the new coroner, Doc Patty, as she prefers to be called, sort of announced her findings to all the employees. It always makes James' job that much harder when crucial details are leaked out."

"Yes, that makes sense. From what I've heard, Connie Wilkerson of the Starlight Theater has been in a feud with the man. Especially after he set fire to her place."

"That was never proven, and I seriously doubt Samuels would have taken the risk. His theater does far better business."

"I suppose that's true. Connie has tried hard to make a go of it with the Starlight, but she just never seemed to gain traction. She comes into my bakery every Thursday for a peach muffin, and I always have to hear her long list of problems."

"Does she?"

"Nine in the morning. Like clockwork. Unless she's too busy now with overflow business from the Mayfield Four."

"I might just drop casually by tomorrow while she's buying her muffin. There's a few things I want to ask her."

CHAPTER 26

*K*ingston decided to take advantage of the early evening cool down. He took off over the town and headed toward the Pickford Lighthouse. The tall trees that bordered the west side of town were always a hangout for other crows. I sometimes fretted like a worried mother that he didn't have enough friends, or at least friends that weren't human. He never mingled with the other crows much. He just led way too different of a life, but occasionally, he liked to perch nearby the crows. Kind of like the outcast sitting near the popular kids, wanting to be one of the gang. That thought often saddened me and made me wonder if I was doing the wrong thing keeping him domestic. I was sure he'd have a terrible time trying to adapt to the wild. He was just too set in his ways. And, selfish as it seemed, I was too used to having him around.

Briggs' car was out front of the police station. A visit with my favorite detective would be a great way to fill the time while I waited for Kingston to get the call of the wild out of his blood for the night.

Hilda was just cleaning up her desk at the front counter as I walked inside. "Hello, Lacey," she chirped. "Perfect timing. He just got back." She buzzed me in and swept past me with her purse. "Have a good night."

"You too, Hilda." I knocked on the office door and poked my head in as he called good night to Hilda. "It's me. Are you busy?"

His white teeth sparkled. "Never too busy for you."

I sashayed in. "I can remember a time when Miss Pinkerton's unexpected visit was considered a nuisance."

"No, never a nuisance."

I stood over his desk and stared at him.

"O.K. maybe a tiny bit of a nuisance. But that was before I discovered that the highly curious Miss Pinkerton and her turbo charged sense of smell were brilliant at solving crimes."

I sat down. "Brilliant, huh? I like that word. Really captures my essence." I leaned forward and rested my forearms along the edge of his desk. He had his notebook out and was transcribing some of it onto the computer.

"I found out a few things of interest," he said.

"Me too."

He leaned back. "You first."

His wonderful brown eyes stole my breath for a brief second. "Uh yes, all right." It took me a moment to remember what I was going to tell him. "First of all, and this is just sort of a side note about the victim's character. More affirmation that Mr. Samuels was unpleasant and not well liked. Elsie told me she went to city college at the same time as him, and even back then, in his twenties, he was a grumpy, disagreeable sort. I know that doesn't push the case forward, but I thought I'd mention it. Also, I decided to check out the reviews for the Mayfield Four Theater. Remember when I told you, Trinity seemed to think Connie was using online reviews to sabotage Samuels?"

"Yes, right." Briggs peeled a note off the bottom of his monitor. "Had a note to do just that. What did you find?"

"People either loved the Mayfield Four or they hated it. There were few in between reviews. Which leads me to believe that while Connie was paying people to write bad reviews, Samuels was paying people to write good ones. Although, I could be totally wrong about both assumptions. However, there was one reviewer, a person who called themselves Mary J., who took the time to post a picture to give weight to her assertion that the Mayfield Four was infested with rats."

Briggs' chair squeaked as he sat forward with interest. "Was it a picture of rats?"

"Not quite. Remember that nicely stacked set of poison boxes in the trash bin?"

His forehead relaxed. "So Connie Wilkerson bought the poison to stage a picture that went with her infestation claim." He tilted his head side to side. "Elaborate but I guess if you're going after your enemy, you have to be crafty. Of course, posting a staged photo of rat poison doesn't mean the next step is murder. But it does show just how far she was willing to go to hurt Samuels."

"Not only that," I said, "but I keep inadvertently making the connection between the rat poison and the method used to kill Samuels. What if Connie bought the poison and hoped to also use it to kill Samuels. It has a peanut butter flavor. Maybe she was conspiring with Sally to somehow get it into his food."

"Possible but probably farfetched. Those pellets might trick a rat into thinking its eating peanut butter, but I doubt it tastes anything like the real thing."

I shrugged. "Just a theory."

"And a good one. I'll keep it in mind."

"What did you find out today in your detective adventures?"

His chuckle was always pleasant to hear. "My adventures took me to the hospital."

I nearly popped off my chair. "What? Why?"

"I guess I phrased that badly. I went to visit the ex Mrs. Samuels. I called ahead and the doctor told me I could see her for ten minutes to ask a few questions as long as I didn't upset her."

"How was she doing? Still recovering from the shock?" I asked.

"She didn't seem to be shocked or sad. She was weak, of course, from surgery and hooked up to a lot of machines, but it seemed she wasn't the slightest bit upset that her ex-husband was dead."

"I guess that falls in line with most people's reactions." I shifted back in the chair. "But it doesn't fall in line with what Dylan Samuels told you regarding their argument."

Briggs pointed and winked. "Bingo. She practically laughed when I asked her if she was upset that her ex-husband never came to visit her in the hospital. Dylan insisted she was hoping to see him. But she told me that would have only sent her right into cardiac arrest. She says she can't stand the sight of him. She blamed her heart disease on the stress of living under his constant verbal abuse for twenty-five years."

"I wonder why she stuck it out so long," I said.

"Who knows? Maybe it was because of Dylan. Which brings me to one last detail. Since Virginia, that's her name, wasn't feeling too distraught over the death, I brought up Mr. Samuels' will. It didn't seem too impertinent, given that she didn't seem the slightest bit emotional about the murder. And that gave me another clue as to why she could have cared less about his death. As could be expected, she was no longer one of his beneficiaries, but apparently, neither was Dylan."

My eyes rounded. "His only son was not a beneficiary?"

"Nope. According to Virginia, Samuels changed his will a year ago and left everything, including the theater, to an unknown beneficiary. The lawyer has the document, so she and Dylan are left in the dark about who will inherit his money and theater. I put a call into the lawyer to find out if and when the name can be made public."

"I guess that Dylan Samuels doesn't have a money motive then."

"My thoughts exactly." He reached his arm out across the desk, and I happily placed my hand in his. "I thought we could have dinner tonight."

"I like that idea, only I defrosted a dish of lasagna my mom left in the freezer for me on her visit. I have to eat it or it will get mushy. Why don't you come over. Technically, my mom's cooking, and she's way better at it than me."

"Sounds good. I'll be another hour or so." He got back to his notebook.

"And I have to round up my bird, so that works out perfectly."

The aroma of my mom's cheesy, tomato filled lasagna circled the kitchen, making me hungry and homesick all at the same time. That crafty woman knew just what she was doing when she prepared and froze some of her best homemade dishes for me to heat long after she and Dad had gone home. If I'd had a spare moment, I would have called to let her know I was on to her culinary scheme. But as it was, I was scurrying around getting dressed and ready for my dinner date.

After I left the police station, I walked back toward the flower shop to pick up my car. I drove to the town square to look for Kingston. He was sitting with a group of crows that had pulled a bag with French fries out of a trash can. Again, like the mom of a kid who didn't always fit in, I hung back and let him be a crow for a few more minutes without the embarrassment of having mommy tell him it was time to come in for the night. I started to feel just a touch hurt that he was ignoring me, but the second the last fry was gone, he flew toward the car with hardly a glance back at his new friends. Apparently, it had been more about the French fries than the buddies.

I opened every window in the house to get a fresh breeze flowing through the rooms. More moderate coastal temperatures were returning, and I welcomed the salty, cool air. I dashed into the bathroom once more to check my lipstick when a knock sounded on the front door.

It had only been an hour since I saw Briggs but a smattering of butterflies took a quick tour around my stomach. I hurried to the door and opened it.

Dash was standing on the front porch with a pickle jar in his left hand and his right hand pasted to his side. "Yes, I understand the irony of this scene, but I need help getting the jar open. I'm trying to make a sandwich, and in order for it to be a success, it requires a pickle."

I laughed. "Of course it does." I lifted my arm and curled it to reveal a terribly unimpressive bicep. "You came to the right person," I said in a deep voice. With no small degree of confidence, I took hold of the jar and gave it a good twist. I added in a manly grunt, which fell hilariously flat when I realized I hadn't budged the thing. "Or maybe you didn't come to the right person. But you're in luck. I have faced down a stubborn jar on more than one occasion and I have another trick up my sleeve." I motioned for him to follow me into the house to keep the moths fluttering around the porch light from flying inside.

I carried the jar into the kitchen and pulled out the can opener to pry the lid and release the vacuum.

Dash took a deep breath. "Smells good." He glanced around at my spotless kitchen. "You are a very tidy cook."

"No, actually, I'm the opposite of tidy. This was a prebaked lasagna my mom made. My only part in it was putting it in the oven to heat."

Dash noticed the two place settings on my table. "I guess you're expecting Briggs." He took hold of the jar. "I will take my pickles and get out of your way. Thank you, by the way. This injury has hurt my masculine pride far more than it's hurt my broken shoulder. Hopefully, the pickle jar is the low point and things will look up after this."

"I think it takes a man comfortable in his own skin to admit when he needs help with a pickle jar."

"Maybe I'm being too hard on myself," he said with a chuckle.

I reached for the door and opened it for him. Pickle jar in hand, he stopped suddenly as if someone had glued his feet to the floor.

"Briggs," he said quietly.

I peered around the edge of the door. Briggs looked at me before facing Dash.

"Vanhouten," he said. If not for the fact that it seemed to come from between clenched teeth, it almost sounded polite.

Coward that I was, I stayed mostly behind the door, using it as a shield of sorts.

Dash held up the jar. "Turns out pickle jars are hard to open with one hand."

"Yes, I heard about your accident. Hope you're feeling better," Briggs said.

I sucked in an audible breath and quickly covered my mouth to stifle it.

"Thanks. Not sure what I would have done if Lacey hadn't been kind enough to drive me to the hospital." They continued their amicable conversation over my front door threshold. I held my breath hoping, against all odds, it didn't crumble into an argument.

"Yes, it's a good thing." There was a hint of sarcasm in Briggs' words, but I was still giddy at the overall tone of their talk. I wanted nothing more than for Briggs and Dash to be civil with each other. I never expected their old friendship to bloom again. Far too much damage had been done by Dash's selfish behavior, but it would be wonderful not to have to worry about bringing up Dash in conversation.

"I'm friends with Tim Rogers at the coast guard. He mentioned you flew one of the search planes when a pleasure boat went missing," Briggs said. "He said you located the boat even in dense fog. Nice job."

A small squeak came from my throat before I could stop it.

"Lacey, are you going to hide behind the door all night making little sounds?" Briggs called from his side of the threshold.

Dash stepped aside to make room for me to emerge from behind the door. I knew my smile was ear to ear but I didn't mind. "I was having too much fun listening to the conversation. I didn't want to spoil it." I looked up at Dash. "You never told me about the boat rescue. That's wonderful, Dash."

Dash smiled weakly. "It was no big deal. Anyhow, I'll let you two eat dinner. Thanks again for opening the pickles."

Dash nodded at Briggs as he slipped past.

Briggs stepped inside and I shut the door. I spun around on my heels and kissed him.

"Nice appetizer before dinner," he said. "What did I do to deserve such a nice welcome kiss?" The twinkle in his eyes assured me he knew exactly how he'd earned the kiss.

I hopped on my toes and kissed him once more. "Thank you, James."

CHAPTER 28

I got to work early to finish a few things before my unofficial stake out at Elsie's bakery. It was perfectly plausible that the neighboring shop owner might be sitting at one of Elsie's outdoor tables eating an apricot scone. Plus it gave me an excuse to eat an apricot scone. Elsie's were a splendidly flaky adventure with just the right balance of sweet and tart.

"Heading next door for an apricot scone," I called to Ryder as he washed his hands in the work area. "Do you want anything from Elsie's?"

"No, thanks. My mom made a big breakfast this morning."

"I won't be long."

It was early but a few people were sitting at Elsie's tables, sipping Les's coffee and eating pastries. I didn't see Connie Wilkerson but it was only just nine. And then there was the possibility that she was too busy for a peach muffin now that the Starlight was the only movie venue in Mayfield.

I stepped into the bakery and was instantly lightheaded from the hurricane of delicious aromas swirling around the shop. I had to concentrate not to get overwhelmed by the incredible mix of smells. Customers with regular noses, or noses of this world as my dad liked to say, were treated to the usual charming mix of butter, cinnamon, sugar frosting and fruity scents, but I had to work hard to not *drink* it all in at once.

Elsie finished up with the customers at the counter and waited for them to walk out before greeting me. "Did you come here for an apricot scone fix or for detective work?"

"Both," I said cheerily.

Elsie walked to the end of the counter with the scones and pulled out a golden scone that was dotted with chewy chunks of apricot. "This will probably be the last batch for the summer. Fresh apricots are getting harder to find."

"That's sad to hear but I'm sure you'll find something tasty to replace them." I glanced back toward the sidewalk tables. "No sign of your peach muffin customer yet?"

Elsie glanced up at the clock on the wall. "Huh, not yet. She's late. Maybe she's too busy." She placed the scone on a paper plate and handed it to me. "You sure look extra pink cheeked and happy this morning. Anything I should know about?" She looked pointedly at my left hand.

"If you're looking for an engagement ring, *Mom*, I mean Elsie, we've only been officially dating for five weeks. Might be a little soon for a ring."

"So why the skippy walk and pink apple cheeks this morning?" she asked.

I broke off a corner of the scone. "James and I had a nice dinner last night. My mom's lasagna. My freezer is filled with several husband winning casseroles. She pretended she was doing it because she thought I wasn't eating enough home cooked meals, but she had an ulterior motive. She's still old-fashioned enough to think the best way to a man's heart is through his stomach. Unless I'm doing the cooking." I took a bite of scone.

Elsie laughed. "How is your mom?"

"Great. She and my dad are going on a cruise next week."

The door opened behind me. Elsie smiled. "Morning, Connie."

A crumb of scone stuck in my throat. I covered my mouth and

cleared it as Connie approached the counter. She looked my direction and forced a smile. She didn't seem thrilled to see me.

"Morning," I said brightly and held up my scone. "Nothing like one of Elsie's treats to get the day started."

Elsie didn't bother to ask Connie her order and, instead, headed over to the glass case and pulled out a plump peach muffin topped with cinnamon streusel. Connie's somewhat cold expression left me searching for a polite way to change topics to the murder investigation. I didn't want to upset one of Elsie's customers right inside the bakery, so I held my tongue.

Connie paid for her muffin. Elsie had given it to her on a plate. With any luck, she'd eat it outside at the tables. The heat had mellowed enough to allow for it. She walked out.

Elsie whispered behind me. "I think your interrogation suspect just escaped. She usually sits at the corner table."

"I didn't want to do anything that left a bitter taste in her mouth while she was standing inside your bakery." I turned back to her. "I'll talk to you later. I might still have a chance to get in a question, but I have to be stealthy and clever. I went with Briggs to her house, and she wasn't terribly pleased to talk to him about the murder."

I picked up the rest of my scone.

"Have you heard from Lola?" she asked before I walked out.

"No, but next time she leaves she might have to rethink hiring her cousin, Shauna. The poor girl is a nervous wreck. She seems to think the store is haunted. She might very well be over at the flower shop right now convincing Ryder to come check out a floor creak or unexplained moan."

"Maybe she just likes to find excuses to have Ryder come to her rescue," Elsie suggested.

"Yes, you and I think alike, my friend. See you later."

I made a point of walking past the corner table where Connie had sat to eat her muffin. She was looking at her phone, which ruined my chances for another conversation. But luck was on my side.

"Is Detective Briggs in his office this morning?" she asked during my slow motion journey between the tables.

I took it as an invite to move closer to the table. "Yes, he should be." I lingered after my answer, hoping there would be more. Luck again. Maybe the apricot scone was my rabbit's foot.

"I've found someone to verify that I was at home during the hours when Samuels was killed. I was so flustered when he questioned me, I completely forgot that the neighbor boy came by just before eight with raffle tickets for his football team. I'm going to let the detective know so he can check me off his list of suspects." She blinked up at me from behind blue framed sunglasses. "I assume I was on the list." She was waiting for affirmation, but it wasn't mine to give.

"You'll have to ask Detective Briggs about that." Since she had opened the discussion, I decided it wouldn't hurt to bring up the reviews. "I was reading through some of the online reviews for the Mayfield Four. According to one review, Mr. Samuels was having a problem with rat infestation. The person took the time to post a picture of some boxes of rat poison in the bin outside the theater." She fidgeted on her seat and picked absently at the muffin as I spoke.

"Well, if that's what the review said and if there was a picture to prove it, then I guess it must be true," she said flippantly.

"It's just that you had all those bags of rat poison in your garage, the same brand as in the picture."

She dropped the piece of muffin back onto the plate. "Fine. I posted the review. And I might have even paid a few other people to post bad reviews too. Everyone does it. The man set my theater on fire."

"Allegedly," I stated quietly.

"He did it. No one else believes me, but I know it was Samuels. Anyway, posting fake reviews doesn't make me a killer. And now that my alibi is solid, Detective Briggs will have to snoop somewhere else for his suspect."

She was getting red in the face. It was a good time for me to end the conversation.

"Absolutely. I'll let you finish your muffin then so you can get down to the station. Have a good day."

CHAPTER 29

*B*riggs pulled up in front of the shop and my heart did a skippity do. The relationship was still new, but I hoped that the tiny heart dance at the sight of him would never leave. My mom once told me she still got misty eyed when my dad dressed up for a special occasion. It was one of the cutest darn things the woman had ever said, and I kept every word of it in my memory.

I'd forgotten that I'd already locked up for the night. I hurried over to open the door. "What a nice surprise, James. I was just about to head home."

"Were you?" He lifted his sunglasses up to his head. "I won't keep you then."

"Nonsense." I waved him inside. "Come in off the sidewalk."

He stepped inside the shop. "I wanted to let you know the lab tests showed that Samuels had ethylene glycol in his bloodstream. That's the toxic substance in coolant. So we have our murder weapon. If I could just find out who put the coolant in the slush cup. The evidence is scant. While there seems to be numerous motives, there are also plenty of alibis."

He followed me into the office to get my purse. "I take it Connie Wilkerson visited you then?"

"Yes, how did you know?" He leaned against the door jamb while I shut down my computer.

"I just happened to run into her eating her usual Thursday morning peach muffin at Elsie's."

"Just happened, eh?" His mouth tilted on one side. "Coincidences follow you around like kids follow the ice cream truck."

I reached the doorway where he was standing. "It does seem that way, doesn't it?"

"I'll have to check out her story with the neighbor if any more evidence points to her. I'm heading back to the theater right now to talk to Dylan. He's trying to make sure everything is secure in the building until the lawyer contacts the new owners. Sally gave him her key. She didn't want the responsibility."

"Oh? I wouldn't mind going along for that. Unless you don't need your assistant tonight." I batted my lashes at him dramatically.

"I can't tell if you're trying to be coy or flirtatious or if you have something in your eye."

I smacked his arm. "Can I tag along or what?"

"Sure. That's why I stopped by."

We headed through the shop. "Where's Kingston?"

"He wanted to stay home today. We won't be too long, will we? I need to feed the pets."

"Nope. I need to feed Bear too. If he hasn't already helped himself to the coffee table."

I turned off the lights and we walked out to the car and climbed inside.

I pulled the seatbelt around me. "I was thinking maybe it's time our families meet."

Briggs' face snapped my direction. "You mean the parents?"

"No, gosh no," I said as if he'd suggested we pack up and move to the middle of the Sahara Desert. "I meant the furry family members."

Briggs checked the side view mirrors and pulled out onto Harbor Lane. "That could still include my dad. He has hair everywhere."

My laugh was cut short by a sudden thought. "Gosh, I hope *that* doesn't run in the family."

"I take after my mother's side."

"Thank goodness. Anyhow, maybe you should bring Bear over tonight. Kingston has already met him. But the big test is with Nevermore. I'm hoping Bear is still young and silly enough to not seem like a threat to Never. He doesn't mind Dash's dog, Captain," I added and quickly decided I should have kept that nugget to myself.

"I see," he said. "I'm glad because that had me worried."

"Oh stop, James. I was just using it as an example. Nevermore doesn't meet many dogs. What do you say? Should we give it a try?"

"What if they don't get along?" he asked.

It wasn't a question I expected, and I had no good answer. "It'll be fine. Nevermore is a very reasonable cat. Usually."

"If you say so, I guess I could bring Bear around later tonight."

"Perfect." I relaxed back against the seat. "What triggered this meeting with Dylan?"

"I called him to tell him about the autopsy report. He gave me an earful about going to see his mom in the hospital. He said I had no right to talk to her without asking his permission. I told him I had her doctor's permission. That seemed to satisfy him, but I think he's feeling edgy about the whole thing. I'm sure he realized his mom wouldn't corroborate his reason for the argument with his dad. He insisted it was because his mom desperately wanted to see Ronald Samuels before she went into heart surgery, but that seems far from the truth. I need to find out the real reason for the argument and find out why he lied."

"Sounds like he's back on your persons of interest list."

"He never left it." He glanced back and changed lanes. "By the way, the slush cup Samuels drank from contained the coolant. Unfortunately, condensation on the paper cup prevented any good fingerprints. The coolant container we found inside the bin had some smeared prints near the top and on the handle. One set of the same prints on both. I'm certain they'll be Justin's prints since he admitted it was his bottle of coolant. Not stellar evidence so far. I'm hoping a few more interviews will get someone to crack."

"Or maybe there is still a key piece of evidence just waiting to be uncovered," I said brightly. "You never know what might turn up."

"I like your optimism, Miss Pinkerton. I just wish some of it would rub off on me."

CHAPTER 30

*T*he rose colored dusk sky hung low over the town of Mayfield as Briggs turned the car down Turner Boulevard. A long line of moviegoers stood outside Starlight Theater. It was easy to predict an explosion of business at Connie's theater with the Mayfield Four being indefinitely closed.

"Samuels' death sure gave Connie Wilkerson a nice boost in ticket sales," I said as we passed.

"Yes. I'd say she benefited from his death almost as if she'd been one of his benefactors. In a convoluted, disconnected way of course." The vast, empty Mayfield Four parking lot had attracted a group of kids on skateboards. They had taken the time and effort to carry a makeshift ramp to the empty lot to use for tricks.

Briggs sighed. "They know they're not supposed to be skateboarding here."

"Oh, let them stay. It's a big slab of empty asphalt. They're being resourceful. Besides, it can't be for too long. I'm sure whoever inherited the theater will open it back up soon. After all, I bet you would have done the same thing at their age."

Briggs peered sideways at me. "I preferred BMX bikes to skateboards. And since you're making me feel like an old fist shaking curmudgeon for even bringing it up, I'll ignore them."

He pulled the car up to the theater. Dylan Samuels spotted us through the tinted glass of the ticket booth. He waved and circled around to let us into the theater. "Come on in. I was just locking up all the cash drawers." He hooked the set of keys on his belt loop. "They're empty, of course, but I wanted to make sure everything was secured before I lock it up for good. My dad put his heart and soul into this place. I'd hate to see it get ruined by vandals. There's no telling when the new owners will reopen it."

"Did you find out who the new owners are?" Briggs asked. In a murder case, it was always good to find out who benefited financially from the death. It seemed we already knew of one person who would benefit. Connie Wilkerson had been struggling to compete with the Mayfield Four, but with its owner's demise, her business was going to be booming. But someone else would soon inherit Ronald Samuels' theater. Knowing who would give Briggs an entirely new path of inquiry.

"I'm in the dark about all of it." Dylan's tone darkened. "That was the way my dad did things. He kept everything to himself. My mom and I were always the last to know about anything." He straightened, stretching his barrel chest and shoulders to full width. He was a large man, but it seemed that size had never helped him feel big enough to stand up to his dad. "I suppose most men of that generation are like him. Keeping business matters to themselves and never opening up about anything."

Briggs nodded. "I suppose you're right. I do have a question for you, Mr. Samuels. When I spoke to your mother, she mentioned that she didn't want to see you dad before her operation. Or any other time, for that matter. She made that fairly clear in our brief conversation."

Dylan's jaw twitched, and he blinked more than usual. "They didn't get along. I suppose she thought it would only aggravate her to see him."

Briggs casually pulled out his notebook. I always admired how calm and cool he stayed when he was about to start a small spark. "Of course." He flipped through a few pages. "But when I asked you about the argument overheard by some of the theater employees, you said it was because your mother would feel better if Mr. Samuels visited her before surgery. You were upset that he couldn't be bothered to see her."

Dylan's tank-sized torso shrank down, and he covered his face. "I wish you wouldn't bring up those horrible last moments." He rubbed his eyes and lowered his hand. "Do you understand how hard it is to know that our last conversation was an argument?" He was obviously trying to avoid answering. He pulled a tissue from his pocket and blew his nose.

"I'm sure it's very difficult," Briggs said and then stood waiting in resolute questioning silence. He didn't have to say a word to assure Dylan that he was still expecting a response.

Dylan got the message. He pushed the tissue, which I suspected was fairly unnecessary in the first place, back into his pocket. "I suppose it doesn't matter either way. I asked to borrow some money. I'm between jobs, and with Mom in the hospital, bills have been piling up. I thought he could help out." His face sagged with disappointment. "I was wrong. Now I have to live with those final moments knowing we never patched things up." His voice trailed off and he shook his head.

"I am sorry, Mr. Samuels," Briggs said. A light knock pulled our attention toward the glass entry doors. Justin was standing outside.

Dylan grunted. "That kid," he muttered. "He's here to pick up his last paycheck. My dad was planning to let him go this week anyhow. He was sure Justin was stealing from him. Said he found a wad of twenty dollar bills in Justin's locker. When he confronted Justin about it, he told him he'd sold a skateboard to a friend but according to my dad, he was acting pretty cagey about it. Dad never trusted anyone, but he was probably right on this account. I never liked that kid."

Briggs and I exchanged glances as he walked to the door to let Justin in. "Guess I should talk to Justin again," Briggs said quietly from the side of his mouth. "I wonder why Samuels is only just mentioning the stealing issue."

I followed Briggs as he headed to Ronald Samuels' office. The room had remained untouched since the night of the murder. Aside from the key piece of evidence, the poisoned drink, the room had given few clues.

Briggs went to the file cabinet and pulled it open. I circled around to Mr. Samuels' desk and pulled open the first drawer. It was neatly organized with blue pens in one tray and black in another. Paper clips were layered in a neat pile next to a roll of tape. A flash of yellow caught my eye as I moved to close the drawer. A sticky note was pressed on the inside front of the drawer.

Briggs noticed me pulling it out. "Please tell me you found a note that names the murderer," he said wryly.

"Afraid not." I held it up. "It's a note Samuels wrote to himself. Fire Justin. That's all it says."

Briggs walked over and looked at it. "Seems like that is something you could remember without a sticky note. I think I'll talk to Justin before he leaves."

We left the office and found Justin looking angry and red faced as he stood toe to toe with Dylan Samuels. Dylan was holding what looked like the paycheck behind his back.

Justin spotted us walking across the lobby. He pointed at Dylan. "Detective Briggs, he won't give me my paycheck. I earned every dollar of that check. He has no right to keep it."

Dylan had apparently decided to take theater matters into his own hands. He put on a collected tone, trying to show he was the adult and that he had the upper hand of the situation. "I've simply told Mr. Lakeford that he needs to first return all the money he stole from the theater."

Justin's suntanned face turned an orange-red. "And I've told you, I never stole one dime from this place. Now give me my paycheck." Dylan was much bigger in stature than Justin, but the boy looked way more agile. His arms were sinewy but curved with muscles from surfing. I had no doubt he could throw a mean punch if he wanted. And from the look on his face, he very much wanted to do just that. Briggs' presence was probably the only thing keeping both men from throwing the first fist.

Briggs seemed to come to the same conclusion. Without an ounce of hesitation, he placed himself squarely between the two men. "Mr. Samuels, do you have any direct evidence that Justin stole from the theater?"

"No, he doesn't," Justin started angrily, but Briggs put up a hand to stop his rant.

Dylan fidgeted on his wide shoes for a moment, then shook his head. "I only know what my father told me."

"Then I need you to give me Justin's check." Briggs put out his hand. Dylan was about to smack it down on his palm but then thought better of it.

Briggs turned around and handed the check to Justin.

Justin muttered thanks and hurried toward the door.

"Hold on, Justin," Briggs called. "I need to talk to you."

Justin's shoulders sank. He spun around with one of those classic 'what now' expressions you perfect as a teen to flash at pesky parents. Slightly rude considering Briggs just snagged him his paycheck.

Briggs turned back to Dylan. "I'll let you know if there are any further developments on the case."

"Yes, that would be nice," he said bitterly. The sting of the last few minutes had turned him sour. "It seems that you aren't getting anywhere on the case."

Briggs gave him a grin that bordered on smug. "I'll find the killer. Sometimes they are hiding in plain sight." His final comment made Dylan's face darken. His eyes looked more bulgy than usual too.

I sidled up next to Briggs and walked with him toward Justin and the exit. Once outside, Briggs managed to corner Justin long enough to ask him a few questions. Justin seemed put out by the whole thing. I feared he'd be less cooperative to have two of us facing him. I stood off to the side, pretending to be interested in the movie posters hanging in the glass cases along the wall, but I kept an ear tuned to the conversation.

"Two things, Justin. I need you to find time to get to the Mayfield Police Station and leave a set of fingerprints." I peeked from the corner of my eye and saw Justin was predictably stunned by the request.

"I didn't steal any money, and I didn't poison that old grump." His voice teetered on the edge of crying.

"No, I'm not accusing you of either. I just need to confirm that the prints on the coolant bottle belonged to you."

"Of course they do. I told you, I bought it for my car. How would I be able to put coolant in my radiator without touching the bottle?"

"I know. We're looking for evidence that someone else touched the coolant. That would help us find the killer. But while I have you here, Dylan Samuels mentioned that his dad was going to fire you. He found a wad of money in your locker and thought you'd stolen it from the theater."

"Yeah, how do you like that? Samuels was nosing through everyone's lockers when the break room was empty. Must be some kind of law against that."

"Technically, they were Mr. Samuels' lockers. He was just letting his employees use them. Surely, you knew he had a key to the lockers, giving him free access at any time? Sort of like the high school principals."

"Yeah, that's pretty sketchy too. Anyhow, someone else gave me that money. I didn't take it from the theater, and Samuels knew it. There was never any discrepancies between receipts and the money in the registers. He was just looking for an excuse to fire me."

"Someone else handed you a wad of twenty dollar bills?" Briggs asked.

"Yeah." Justin shrugged. "I did someone a favor and they paid me. That's all."

"Any chance I can get you to tell me the details of that favor without me having to call you in for questioning?" I was certain Briggs didn't have enough to go on to call the kid in for questioning, but the mere suggestion of it certainly sparked fear.

"Fine. I wrote a review. A bad review about the Mayfield. I mean what do I care if the place gets a bad review? Samuels deserved it. He ruined my chances to work in the surf shop. I was happy to write it."

Briggs peered briefly back toward me. "Did Connie Wilkerson pay you to write the bad review?"

"Yeah. I told her I'd do it for a hundred bucks." A half hearted laugh fell from his mouth. "Didn't think she'd take me up on it but hey, whatever. Can I go now? I'm trying to find a new job."

"Yes, and don't forget about the fingerprints. They're expecting you."

"Great. That guy is still a melted wad of gum on my shoe and he's dead." Justin turned and strutted back to his car.

Briggs joined me at the Casablanca poster. "This is where it all began." I tapped the glass over Bogie's face.

"And we never even got to finish our popcorn." He took my hand. It was rare for him to hold it when he was on official business, but I wasn't going to complain. Far from it.

The oven-like atmosphere of the last few days was gone and a fresh cool breeze tickled the early evening air. Briggs was churning the last two conversations around in his detective's brain.

I swung my arm, taking his with it for a brief hand-clasp pendulum. "What have you concluded after talking to Justin and Dylan? Anything significant?"

He mulled over my question. "Not anything significant but I am leaning toward one person. And I'm not even sure why except my gut just keeps telling me to look that direction."

"Let me guess," I said. "Dylan Samuels?"

He looked over at me. "How did you know?"

I smiled. "I just know you too well, I guess. Plus, you left him with a rather cryptic, accusatory comment. The one about the killer hiding in plain sight. At least, if I'd been on the receiving end of it, I might have worried I was under suspicion."

Briggs opened the passenger door for me. "Good. That's exactly the effect I was going for. That way it won't be such a big shock to him when I walk up to his door with handcuffs."

CHAPTER 31

I made sure to feed Nevermore an extra helping of cat kibble. I figured if his belly was full, he'd be drowsy and happy. Nevermore wasn't prone to freak outs, but Bear was more rambunctious than most dogs. I was in the midst of my own freak out, certain that I'd pushed this meeting of the pets too quickly, when the phone rang. I sighed in relief as I rushed to it. I was sure it was Briggs letting me know he'd changed his mind. It was Lola.

"Hey, or should I say bonjour? How is it going? Must be really late there. Or early, I guess. I'll stop talking now so you can get a word in." I sealed my lips shut.

"Well, I haven't sent my parents adrift on a rudderless sailboat yet and they are still talking to me so I guess things are fine. It is beautiful here. I miss Franki's chili. Everything here is so light and frilly."

"I'll try not to be hurt by the confession that the thing you miss is a bowl of chili and not your best friend. Have you talked to your cousin? She is—she is—hmm." I paused.

"Yeah, she is," Lola said. We didn't need to fill in the blank to know we were both thinking of the same nonexistent adjective. "Is she fully into her plot to try and steal Ryder away from me?"

Her question kicked my next sentence from my head where I was planning to mention that Shauna seemed to be finding numerous excuses to see Ryder. "So you expected it?"

"Yep. Growing up, Shauna was only ever interested in boys I dated. She managed to make quite the fool out of herself many times. She's five years younger. My mom and Aunt Ruby were inseparable back then, so Shauna was always at our house. One time I was sitting out on the front porch with my first boyfriend, Tate, an older man of seventeen, and Shauna came sashaying out of the house wearing one of my skirts. She had also helped herself to my makeup. I think she used all of it at once. Let's just say the circus would have hired her on the spot as a clown."

I laughed. "Her plan is more elaborate this time, and it includes poltergeists and unexplained noises, all of which require Ryder to come to the rescue."

"Actually, she is kind of a scaredy-cat, so that's not so elaborate. Anyhow, I called to see what was up with you. How is the handsome detective?"

Headlights lit up the front window. "The handsome detective," I gasped.

"Uh oh, sounds like trouble in paradise," Lola said.

"No, no trouble. It's just that I talked James into bringing Bear over to meet Nevermore. But now I'm rethinking it. Only they just pulled up so it's too late."

"Wow, you're at the pet meeting stage already? Sounds like things are heating up fast," she quipped.

"France and time with the parents hasn't dulled your sarcastic wit."

"Are you kidding? They bottle and sell sarcastic wit over here. I'll let you go. Send me pictures of Nevermore gripping the ceiling like a spider. I'll be back soon."

"All right and thanks of the confidence boost. Now I'm really regretting this. Bye. Safe flight back."

Nevermore had settled into his usual spot up on the top of the couch. His eyes were closed, and he was far off in cat dreamland. It only took Bear's first paw step on the porch to make him bolt upright.

Briggs knocked lightly, but the other sounds coming from the front porch were just a little too frightening. Nevermore shot off the back of the couch and raced down the hallway to the bedroom. I was relieved. The first cat and dog introduction could still be delayed until Bear grew more mature.

I opened the door. Bear loped right inside, ignoring Briggs' command to stay. His big, wet nose went straight to the floor, and before either of us could stop him, he galloped down the hallway, following the intriguing new scent. A carnival act followed that, under different circumstances, might have been hilarious, or at the very least worth a hundred thousand likes on Instagram. Briggs and I clashed shoulders as we both tried to squeeze through my narrow hall doorway together. We jammed together for a second, but my mother instincts kicked into super strength mode. I pushed free and shot like a torpedo down the hall to my room. I reached the doorway just as Nevermore flew out of the room (flew was not an exaggeration either. All four paws were off the ground). His fur stood up on end, and his eyes bulged as he headed for the nearest exit, the front door, which we'd left open during the chaos. The last thing I saw was his tail, looking spiky and round like a bottle brush as he vanished down the front steps.

Before either of us knew what was happening, Bear galumphed past us out the front door. We nearly repeated our cartoonish, stuck in the doorway trick but Briggs, now realizing that my cat mom adrenaline was at full throttle, waved me through first. Nevermore tore across the front lawn. His heavy dinner didn't slow him down as he quickly climbed into the branches of the spruce tree across the street. Bear reached the tree seconds before us. He was standing on his back paws, with front paws braced against the rough gray trunk, smiling happily up at the cat.

"Bear," Briggs said sternly. The dog turned his face our direction but kept his stance against the tree. Briggs pointed to the ground next to him. "Bear, heel," he said sharply. Bear's ears drooped. The big, wet smile faded as he walked, head low and paws heavy, back to Briggs.

"*Now* he listens. I'm sorry, Lacey. I was afraid this might be a bad idea. I'll put him inside the car and see if I can get Nevermore out of the tree."

"No, James, that's all right. I'll come out here with a piece of fried chicken after Never calms down. It might take thirty or forty minutes for the trauma to wear off." I turned to him. I knew my expression would give away my worry, but I just couldn't put on a fake one.

Briggs commanded Bear to stay. He obeyed. The dog seemed to understand that the fun chase through the house after the small fluffy beast had not won him a treat or an atta-boy.

"I know what you're thinking, Lacey. I can see a microscopic twitch in your nose, which means you're working hard to hold back tears."

"No, you're imaging the twitch." I looked down because I was a terrible liar, and he knew it.

He took my hand. "It'll just take time. And Bear needs to mature before he can handle something as exciting as a cat. Maybe we should start with a stuffed animal cat and work him up to the real thing. He's still in that big goober stage. Once he grows up, he'll know how to handle himself like gentleman." He looked back at Bear. The dog was sitting as still as a stone statue, except his eyes kept darting sideways toward the tree. "And he's learning to listen more. That should help."

I took a deep breath and silently chided myself for immediately thinking all was lost. "You're right, James. Next time we need to strategize better. I'm sure, eventually, they'll be the best of friends." I knew there wasn't an ounce of optimism in my tone, but I couldn't tamp down the disappointment. What if I'd finally found the man of my dreams but I had to give him up because our pets didn't get along?

Briggs held my hand tightly as we crossed the street back to my house. "I suppose I should just head home for the night, otherwise Nevermore will never come down," he suggested.

"That would probably be for the best."

He opened the back door on his car. Bear took one last gander at the tree before climbing inside. Briggs turned to me and gave me a quick kiss. He held my shoulders and looked pointedly into my eyes. "Don't over think this, Miss Pinkerton."

"I won't. I promise," I insisted with a voice that sounded anything but insistent.

He kissed my forehead. "That was the weakest sounding promise I've ever heard. I'll see you tomorrow." He opened the car door. "Call me if you need help getting the cat down from the tree."

"Oh, I don't know. I'm always looking for a reason to call one of those broad shouldered Mayfield firemen."

He squinted one eye at me. "Funny woman but I'm glad to see you smiling." He climbed into his car, started it and rolled down the window. "And everyone knows those firemen are just a bunch of hot heads."

I blew him a kiss as he rolled out of the driveway. I decided to push the evening's disaster out of my mind for now. That was going to be easier once I coaxed my neurotic cat out of the tree with fried chicken.

CHAPTER 32

*A*pparently, we were back to peonies and buttercups. I was now going to have to scramble and make a dozen calls to find a grower who could provide me with yellow and pink buttercups, or ranunculus, as they were more formally known. I wanted Jazmin to be absolutely certain before I started the search. I pulled out the example I'd created a few days ago. With all that had happened, it felt like months had passed.

After standing beneath the spruce tree holding up a cold drumstick and talking sweetly to my cat for a good half hour, he finally climbed out of the branches and followed me back inside, tail and nose in the air as if nothing had happened. He nibbled on the chicken, performed several of his masterful yoga stretches, licked his paws and toddled off to bed for the night. Briggs called to make sure the cat survived his ordeal. We ended up talking until midnight. (Which nicely counteracted the earlier disaster.)

Ryder walked in a half hour late. "Sorry, boss. I got stopped on my way here by a certain antique store clerk."

"What was it now? Furniture moving on its own?"

He laughed. "How did you know? Apparently the old Victorian pram Lola has in storage, the one she uses in her annual Christmas window display, was moving back and forth on its own. It was perfectly still and lifeless as a baby carriage should be when I walked into the storage room. I suggested that Late Bloomer might have knocked into it, setting it in motion."

"Was she satisfied with that explanation?" As we spoke, Jazmin walked in with Trinity trailing behind her.

Ryder pulled his cap off his head and fluffed up his hair with his fingers. "I honestly have no idea if she was or not, but I'm getting tired of being the local ghost buster. It would be a whole different thing if there were some actual ghosts. I mean that would be cool. But prams moving on their own and dogs moaning for lost treats? Not exactly the stuff made for television." He nodded politely to Jazmin and Trinity before heading back to the office to put his stuff away.

I waved my hand toward the bouquet. "Of course, it will look far fresher on your wedding day."

Jazmin bit her lip. Something told me a mind change would soon follow it. She walked to the bouquet and turned it around several times to look at it from every angle. She climbed up on the stool and pulled out her phone.

"Oh boy, here we go again," Trinity muttered.

"Shush," Jazmin told her. "You came here to tell Lacey something, go ahead while I take a few more pictures."

I looked expectantly at her. "What is it, Trinity?"

Trinity reached up and fiddled with a hoop earring as she looked toward Kingston's perch. "Where is your crow?"

"He likes to fly around the neighborhood in the morning and pretend he's a bird. "

She laughed. "How cute is that?" She was still staring at the empty perch, making it more than obvious that she was having second thoughts about whatever it was she wanted to tell me.

"Is there something else?" I asked.

She released a half-sigh, half-groan. "I hate being a snitch and the whole thing is silly and I'm sure it has nothing to do with the case. It's just that I noticed something kind of weird and now they are asking Justin for his fingerprints." Her rambling was stopped by a hiccough that seemed to be the result of a suppressed sob. Two more shoulder wracking hiccoughs followed.

Her older sister heard the noise. She lectured her without taking her focus off her task. "Take a few deep breaths and out with it Trinity before you work yourself into one of those annoying hiccough fits."

Trinity didn't put up her usual snarky defense and instead followed her sister's suggestion. I waited while she took a deep breath, held it and released it like a steam kettle. She went through the process two more times, then did what I liked to term the impending hiccough pause where you wait to see if they've gone away. Trinity appeared to be in the clear.

"I've got a bottle of water in the office refrigerator," I suggested.

Trinity's bangs swayed back and forth as she shook her head. "No, I'm good. I sometimes get hiccoughs when I'm nervous."

"You have nothing to be nervous about. If you don't want to tell me directly, maybe you can write it down." I wasn't about to let this go. It seemed to have something to do with the murder case. At this point, any piece of information would help move it along.

Trinity mulled over the idea of writing it but shrugged it off. "No, I'll just tell you. I'm sure it's nothing important anyhow. It's just something I'd forgotten. That was such a scary, weird night, the night Mr. Samuels died," she added in case I was thinking of a different scary, weird night. "I pushed it out of my head. But then I was thinking it was kind of strange."

Jazmin growled in frustration." Oh my gosh, Trini, just say it. Lacey has more important things to do than listen to you babble on and on with no point or purpose."

Trinity took a second to stick her tongue out at her sister before returning to our conversation. "I'm sure you remember that the projector was having problems that night."

"Like it was three days ago," I quipped. Jazmin giggled at my sarcasm, but it went over Trinity's head.

"When Mr. Samuels got called up to the projector room to help, he told his son he didn't have time to talk anymore. That was after I heard them yelling at each other through the concession wall. Dylan was doing what he usually did when he came to the theater, raiding the concession stand for snacks."

"Yes, I remember him coating his popcorn with parmesan cheese when I came out for the cup of water."

"That's right. You were standing there too. Mr. Samuels went up to work on the projector, and Dylan Samuels took his popcorn and walked out the door. His face was pretty red. I almost thought he was choking on a popcorn kernel or something. Right after, the counter got super busy because the movie was delayed and people came out for their free refills. But then the weirdest thing happened. We ran out of popcorn buckets, so I headed to the storage room at the end of the hallway. It's just past the employee's lounge and Mr. Samuels' office. I was staring down at the ground and nearly plowed right into Dylan Samuels coming out of the storage room. His face wasn't red anymore. It was sort of white, like a piece of paper. He didn't say anything as he scooted past me and out into the lobby. I didn't see him after that so I just assumed he left. It was weird because I'd already seen him walk out the exit but then, boom, he was there again. And of all places, inside the storage room."

"Could you tell what he was doing in there? Was anything out of place?"

Trinity shrugged. "Looked like the usual storage room packed with boxes and supplies. Not really sure why he would be in there. I thought it was weird at the time but then Mr. Samuels was dead and the whole thing kind of flew out of my head."

Jazmin mumbled something under her breath as she browsed through the bouquet photos on her phone. I wasn't thrilled about having to chase down out of season buttercups but I was glad Jazmin had changed her mind yet again. Otherwise, Trinity might not have told me about Dylan Samuels' unexplained reappearance the night of the murder. Briggs seemed to be leaning toward Dylan as the main person of interest. Up until now he had only scant evidence and little direct motive. But I was sure the nugget Trinity just reluctantly dropped was going to be worth its weight in gold.

"Thanks for letting me know, Trinity. I'll be sure to pass on the information to Detective Briggs."

"And tell him Justin didn't kill anyone. I just know he didn't do it." Her bottom lip quivered some.

"Don't worry about Justin."

Jazmin hopped off of the stool. "I've made my decision and its final. I want to go back to the bouquet with just peonies."

Trinity looked over at me and rolled her eyes. I nearly did the same but refrained. I was a professional, after all.

CHAPTER 33

*J*azmin and Trinity hadn't taken more than one step out of the shop, and I was on my phone calling Briggs.

I nearly chewed off a fingernail waiting for him to answer.

"Hello, Miss Pinkerton," he said in that smooth, cool tone that made my cheeks warm.

"What took you so long to answer? I've got news, big news, giant news. In fact, expensive dinner out as a reward news."

His smooth, cool laugh had the same effect on my cheeks. "What is it? A signed confession, I hope, because I'm beating my head against a wall here."

"Nothing quite as succinct as a signed confession, but Trinity came into the shop with her sister this morning."

"Another bouquet change?"

"Yes, well sort of. She went back to the original, but that's beside the point. Trinity told me something she'd forgotten in the chaos of the night. The store is quiet, and Ryder doesn't mind watching the shop. Can we drive to the theater and I'll fill you in?"

"We could do that. Dylan mentioned that he had to turn the key into the lawyer today. I'll call him and see if he still has it."

"That's right. Dylan has the key at the moment," I said, thinking aloud. "That's all right. He has no idea why we're going back to the theater."

I heard a pair of keys clink. "I take it that the information Trinity forgot has something to do with Dylan Samuels."

"It sure does and it's a doozy. So hurry up. Not that dallying will take the dooziness factor out of it, but I'm anxious to tell you what I learned."

"I'm on my way," he said.

"Ryder, I'm going to take off with James for a bit. Can you hold down the fort?"

Ryder looked up from the rose arrangement he was making and glanced around the empty shop. "I think I can handle it."

I chuckled. "Just enjoy this slow period. The holidays are around the corner." I stepped outside. My bird swept down from the roof and landed at my feet. "I thought you'd run off to marry a carrier pigeon or something." I opened the door. "Look who has decided to grace us with his presence. Make sure he gets some snacks. I'm sure he's extra hungry after his adventure."

"King, ole buddy," Ryder said as I closed the door.

Briggs pulled up to the curb. He was on the phone as I climbed inside. "Yes, that would be great. If it's not too much trouble. We're heading there right now. Thanks." He hung up. "Dylan had already turned in the key. I talked to Ronald Samuels' lawyer. He gave the key to the new owner. They are meeting us at the theater to open up. I'm sure whoever inherited the theater is anxious to get this murder case solved, so the rumors and bad press can stop."

"Did the lawyer say who the new owner was?" I asked.

"Nope. I told him I needed to get inside. I didn't tell him why." Briggs looked over at me. "Because I don't actually know why."

I turned slightly in my seat to face him. "Trinity was agitated and worried to tell me because she knew she had left out something pretty important. Although, I doubt she realized it at first. But she's so worried about Justin being a suspect, it seemed to jog her memory of that night."

He stared out the front window, but it wasn't the mostly empty road he was focused on. His unshaven jaw moved side to side in thought.

"Why do I have the distinct feeling I'm about to get my bubble burst and lose out on an nice dinner to boot?"

"No, sorry. It's just that if her motive for suddenly remembering something crucial came out of her fear that her boyfriend would be arrested for murder, we might have to take it with a grain of salt."

I twisted back to face front and slumped against the seat. "Well poop. I guess you just showed me why I'm not sitting in the driver's seat wearing my detective's suit and tie. That didn't even occur to me."

"Or I could be entirely wrong and she just forgot. After all, I'm sure it was the first time she had been witness to a murder. What did she have to say?"

"All right, I'll tell you, but the wind has been taken right out of my sails."

He reached over and squeezed my hand. "What if I still promise to take you to a nice dinner?"

I sat up straight. "Yep, the wind is back. Trinity told me that she watched Dylan walk out of the theater, red in his face and angry, after his dad told him their conversation was done. Then Ronald Samuels went up to the projector room and Dylan left. After a busy rush on soda refills at the counter, Trinity left the concession stand to get more popcorn buckets from the storage room." I paused. "Did the team search that room?"

"The storage room? Yes. It's at the end of the hallway past Samuels' office. It was mostly stacks of unopened supply boxes. They didn't find anything of note. Why do you bring it up?"

"Trinity claims that as she headed into the storage room, Dylan was walking out. She added that he looked white as paper too."

"But she saw him leave the theater?"

"Yes. That's why she thought it was weird. He left but something made him come back."

Briggs nodded. "If her story is accurate, then that is a pretty explosive detail. Can't believe she left that out when we interviewed her."

"Maybe she just didn't think it was important," I said.

"At least not until Justin was asked to give fingerprints. Which he did, by the way. His prints were on the coolant. Only his." We drove along Turner Boulevard. The Starlight was offering two popcorns for the price of one and a free bag of gummy worms with every ticket.

"Looks like Connie's business is doing well enough to toss in some freebies," I noted. "Wait until she hears that the new owner has been given the keys."

Briggs pulled into the empty Mayfield Four parking lot. The skateboard ramp and the skaters were gone. I glanced over at Briggs.

"Don't look at me. I'm sure the local police told them to move their skate park elsewhere. But it wasn't this grumpy old fun destroyer."

I sat back with a satisfied smile. There was one more car in the parking lot, a bright blue Toyota.

"I know that car," Briggs said. "I wonder—It can't be. Maybe it's true."

"Care to cut me in on your odd conversation?" I asked.

Briggs parked the car and pointed through the windshield. "Looks like the new owner is here already. Look who it is."

I squinted through the sunlight reflecting off the glass to the shadowy entrance of the theater. Sally Applegate was unlocking the theater door.

"Sally? Do you think Samuels left everything to his assistant manager?"

"Seems that way." Briggs turned off the car and unfastened his seatbelt.

"Does that give her a motive?" I asked. "Or maybe they were seeing each other," I suggested.

"Neither. When I talked to the lawyer, he said he'd only just informed the new owner. He mentioned the person was extremely shocked and thrilled. I don't think Sally knew."

I unfastened my seatbelt. "Well, well. Maybe Mr. Samuels wasn't such a terrible guy after all. Sally is taking care of a sick mom and struggling to make ends meet." We climbed out of the car. "So Dylan is still at the top of the list?" I asked.

"He never left it," Briggs said. "Now let's see if we can find something to prove he did it."

CHAPTER 34

*S*ally Applegate let us into the theater and then drifted around in her flowy batik dress gazing at the lobby like a kid lost in a candy shop. "I can't believe this is happening. It's too much to absorb." Her words might have been meant for us, but it was hard to tell because they floated up and away as she twirled slowly around.

"Congratulations, Sally," I said. "I think you'll make this place better than ever."

She stopped her semi-dance and smiled at both of us. "I still can't believe he left this to me."

Briggs cleared his throat lightly. A signal that he was getting down to business, which for him meant solving the murder. "The lawyer mentioned that you had no idea Mr. Samuels left the theater to you."

"I never would have guessed in a million years. Frankly, he was just never that nice to me. I was convinced he didn't even like me but kept me on because no one else wanted to work for him. But the lawyer told me Mr. Samuels said it should go to me because I would take good care of the theater." Her voice broke. She pressed her fingertips to her lips. "Excuse me. It's just that this is so overwhelming."

"I'm sure it will take some time to get used to," Briggs said. "I'm certain it will be much better for business if we find the person who poisoned Mr. Samuels. If we could just take a look around one more time."

"Of course. I'm sorry. I forgot why you came. Please feel free. Like you said, the quicker you arrest the murderer, the better."

"Thank you." Briggs and I headed toward the hallway with the office and storage room. There was a brown metal door at the end of the hallway that said emergency exit. Briggs opened it and peered outside into the alley. "That's what I thought. This leads right to the trash bin."

He opened the storage room door and switched on the light. It was just as I expected, a small closet like room with metal shelves packed high with unopened cartons of popcorn kernels, candy treats and paper goods. The one wide open box was filled with latex gloves.

"You take the right side and I'll take the left, and we'll meet in the middle," Briggs said with a wink.

"Right. The right. What are we looking for exactly?" I asked.

"Not too sure. Something that looks out of place. Something that would explain Dylan's unexpected visit to the storage room."

Most of the boxes were taped shut, waiting to be opened, which in a way was a blessing. It would have taken all day to search through every box. "I assume that if the box is still sealed shut, we don't need to look inside."

"Right. Unless it looks like it's been unsealed and sealed back up." He reached into a shelf. "Like this box of straws." He tore free the masking tape someone had pulled over the box to seal it after the packing tape had been broken. "Just straws." He taped the box shut.

I found one opened carton that contained Milk Duds. "Yum, my childhood favorite." I plucked out a box and shook it. Nice and hard too. Making it the perfect candy for removing unwanted fillings or loose teeth." I stuck the box back into the carton but couldn't get it to go all the way down so that it was flush with the rest of the boxes. I pulled it out to turn it the other way. That was when a whiff of some- thing other than Milk Duds tickled my nose. I pulled the box closer to the edge and put my face near to catch the scent again.

"Briggs, I've got something. Unless Milk Duds have changed their formula—" I pulled the entire box free of the shelf and set it on the ground. Briggs joined me as I crouched down to get a look inside the box under the light.

My face popped up. "Latex gloves?"

He reached into his pocket and pulled out a pair of tweezers. "Sure looks that way." He plucked out the latex gloves that were jammed into the space between the candy boxes. As he drew them free, a faint scent drifted toward me.

"Coolant," I said. "Even though they are turned inside out, I can smell coolant. And something else, but I'm not sure what."

Briggs couldn't hold back a smile. "What would I do without Samantha? And the cute Miss Pinkerton attached to her, of course."

"Of course. I'll make sure to order a lush dessert with my expensive dinner to reward Samantha."

Briggs held the gloves in the tweezers. "You can order any dessert you want."

Briggs searched in his pocket with his free hand and pulled out an evidence bag. I leaned to the side and looked at his pocket. "What else do you have in those endless pockets, Inspector Gadget?"

"I think that's about it. With any luck and a lot of science, we'll be able to lift some prints off the inside of the gloves." He handed me the bag to open. I held it out for him. As he dropped the gloves inside, the second odor came to me.

"Parmesan cheese. How could I not tell that was parmesan. There are few aromas like it."

Briggs looked puzzled. "Why are you talking about parmesan cheese?"

"Because I can smell it on the inside of the gloves." I snapped my fingers. "And Dylan Samuels was eating popcorn with parmesan just before his father was killed. I saw him pouring it on his popcorn. Loads of it."

Right then, agitated voices rolled down the hallway to the storage room.

"I can't believe this," a man yelled. "How could he do this?" I'd never heard him yell before, but it was easy to recognize that the agitated man was Dylan Samuels.

"Sally," I gasped.

Briggs nearly dropped the bag in his rush to get out to the lobby. Dylan Samuels was pacing with a face as red as a tomato. His nostrils were flared like an angry bull's. Sally stood behind the concession counter, apparently trying to put space between her and the angry man in the center of the lobby.

I walked over to stand with Sally. Dylan spotted Briggs. He lifted an arm and pointed angrily at him. "And you, you incompetent fool. I might just sue your police department for incompetence. When will you find my dad's killer?"

Briggs stepped into the lobby. "Actually, I've found him."

The red rage in Dylan's face drained. "You have? Where is he?"

"Dylan Samuels, I'm arresting you for the murder of Ronald Samuels."

Dylan stood there listening to his rights being read and looking almost sad enough to make me feel sorry for him.

"He was a monster. He verbally abused my mother and me for years and then cut us out of his will. I didn't plan it. The judge will see that. It was a moment of extreme anger. I saw the coolant so I ran inside and got his drink." He dropped down to his knees. "I almost didn't put the drink back in his office. But he wouldn't even lend me money to pay bills. I'm his only son." He crumpled further, his thick shoulders folding in on him as his head dropped forward. "I was his only son," he muttered again.

The sorry sight brought tears to Sally's eyes. I put my arm around her shoulder.

CHAPTER 35

*R*yder burst into the shop so exuberantly the goat bell fell off. He was holding an extra large book with a frayed and tattered cover in one arm as he bent down to retrieve the fallen bell.

He attempted to tie it back onto its ribbon with one hand but gave up and carried it with him to the work island. "Look what Lola brought me from France. It's dated 1885. It's filled with fantastic lithographs of flowering plants."

I gently lifted the cover. The binding along the edge of the book was worn from time and use, and I feared the book would fall apart if I wasn't careful. "Wow, the pictures are stunning, Ryder. It's gorgeous."

Ryder was beaming from ear to ear. Lola had left suddenly and it had hurt him plenty, but it seemed she'd made up for her abrupt departure with one magnificent, thoughtful gift.

"I'm anxious to say hello too," I said. "Is she already across the street?"

"Yes, she just opened up. Shauna packed up last night and went home. I let Lola know that there are a lot of ghosts and ghouls hanging around her antique shop and that I was now officially a ghost hunter if she needed help."

"I think we'll have to get you a pair of coveralls with a ghost buster badge. I'm going to head over there and say hello." I walked out into the bright day. The heat wave had been over for a week. There was even the tiniest touch of fall in the air which excited me.

I walked inside. Lola was moving glassware around in the shelf to make room for a few new items.

"So are you fluent in French?" I asked.

She spun around. "Pink!" We hugged.

"So good to see you," I said. "When we have time I want to see pictures and hear stories. How are your parents?"

"They're fine. I realized as I grow older, I can tolerate hanging out with them much more."

"I'm finding the same thing," I said. "I was homesick after my parents left Port Danby last month. I guess we're both really growing up."

"I don't know about that." She pointed down to her signature style. Today's outfit included a faded Grateful Dead t-shirt, shorts and cowboy boots. "My mom tried to buy me some new clothes in Paris, but I wasn't interested. Speaking of Paris, I spent hours in an old bookstore."

"Ryder is floating around the shop with little wings on his shoes. It was the perfect gift for him."

"I've got something for you too." She disappeared into the back for a second and returned with a book shaped package wrapped in a Paris newspaper and twine.

"I do love gifts that come wrapped in French newspapers. Of course this is my first, but I already know I love them." I slipped off the twine and carefully pulled away the paper. The book was old and bound in embossed, bronze tinted leather. "Edgar Allen Poe, *The Raven and Other Poems*. I love it. It's perfect." We hugged again.

"It's not first edition but it's quite old. Someone named Margaret gave it to her brother James for Christmas in 1920. There's a hand-written note on the inside cover."

"James?" I asked. "Even more perfect."

"Glad you like it. So what have I missed? Anything interesting happen while I was gone?"

"Oh, you know, the usual. Murder, peonies, poison, that kind of stuff. We'll go have a bowl of chili at Franki's later, and I'll tell you all about it."

CLUTTER COOKIES

View online at: www.londonlovett.com/recipe-box/

Clutter
COOKIES

Ingredients:

1 cup light brown sugar
3/4 cup granulated sugar
1 cup (2 sticks) butter, softened
2 eggs
2 tsp vanilla
2 1/4 cup all-purpose flour
3/4 teaspoon baking soda
1/2 teaspoon kosher salt

6oz semi-sweet chocolate, roughly chopped
4oz white choclate, roughly chopped
1/3 cup dried cranberries, chopped
1/3 cup toffee bits
1/3 cup chopped pecans
1/3 cup chopped walnuts
1/2 cup oats

Directions:

1. Preheat oven to 325°

2. In a stand mixer or by hand whip softened butter, brown sugar and granulated sugar until light and fluffy.

3. Beat the 2 eggs into the mixture and add vanilla.

4. Add salt, baking soda and flour. Mix just enough to combine.

5. Fold in the chocolate, cranberries, nuts, toffee bits and oats.

6. Using a 1/4 cup measuring cup scoop the dough onto a greased or parchment lined baking sheet. (Note: 1/4 cup makes the giant sized cookies seen in the pictures. You could also make smaller cookies.)

7. Bake for 15-17 minutes until the edges begin to brown and tops are dry. (Note: If you're making smaller cookies you'll need to adjust this time.)

8. Remove from oven, transfer to a cooling rack and ENJOY!

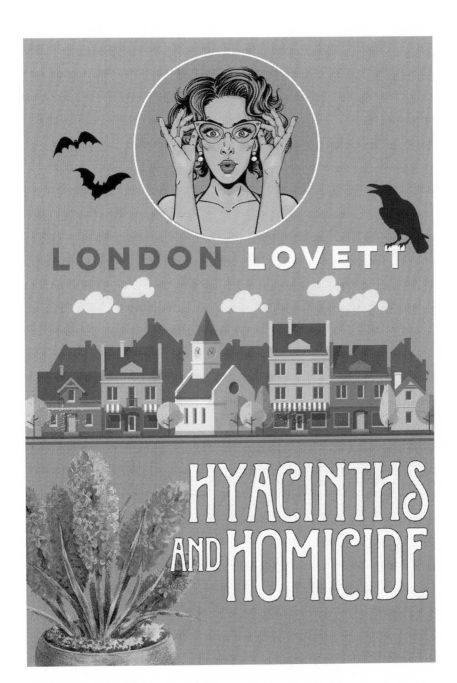

LONDON LOVETT

HYACINTHS AND HOMICIDE

CHAPTER 1

$\mathcal{T}$he store bell clanged behind me as I carefully placed the last potted hyacinth on the counter. The lush blue stalks had cost a pretty penny due to the fact it was late fall and the fragrant flowers were a good six months early for their natural bloom.

Ryder's coat rustled as he pulled it off to hang on the hook. "It's definitely big toe weather."

I pulled my admiring gaze from the flowers and cast him a quizzical brow. "Did you just say it was big toe weather?"

"Yep." He walked over to the work island and took a moment to breathe in the heady scent of the hyacinths before continuing. "My grandpa always knew when it was going to rain. He'd hang onto his gray suspenders with his thumbs—" He nodded. "Yes, he did that, cliché as it sounds and his belly was round too." Ryder stepped back, pushed out his stomach and hooked his thumbs around invisible suspenders. "He'd stand just like this and bellow, 'my toe's achin' so it's gonna rain, sure as I'm standing here.'"

"My dad always says his bones hurt when the weather is changing, but I don't know if I've ever heard someone predict weather with his toe. Was he usually right?"

"Spot on every time but that's not the crazy thing about it."

Kingston gurgled from his window perch to catch Ryder's attention. Ryder walked over and grabbed the crow's treat can and pulled out a peanut butter dog bone. "The *crazy* part about the story was that Grandpa didn't have any big toes." Ryder handed Kingston the treat and walked back to the counter. "When my grandpa was fourteen, he and a group of friends had gone off on a hike in the snow behind his dad's farm. They got lost for three nights. His work boots had so many holes, he ended up with frostbite. They had to cut off his two big toes."

"That's terrible. Poor guy. But then how did he predict the weather with them?"

"He claimed he could still feel the toes. You know how people can still feel their limbs after they've lost them? Same thing with toes, I guess. And he claimed that they'd be throbbing in his shoes when the weather was turning bad."

"He sounds wonderful. Is he still around?" I moved the hyacinths back farther on the counter so I could design the centerpieces for the high school reunion.

Ryder's shoulders dropped some. "No, we lost him to a bad heart four summers ago, but he had one of those personalities that just permeated our lives. Still does. That's why we always say it's bad toe weather when it's about to rain."

"I'm sorry to hear that. He sounds adorable and grandpa-ish."

"Yellow roses, right?" Ryder asked as he headed toward the refrigeration unit where we kept roses and cut flowers fresh for bouquets.

"Yes, thanks, and I'll get the vases."

Ryder and I met back at the work counter to create the arrangements. He took another whiff of the spike of bluish-purple flowers. "You know, I don't think these hot house blooms smell nearly as strong as the ones that bloom naturally in spring."

I leaned forward and ran my fingers gently along the petal laden stems. Each bloom resembled a tiny purple starfish packed snugly into clusters of waxy florets. Glossy green leaves framed the bottom of the stalk, providing the perfect contrast for the bluish-purple flowers. "You might be right about the fragrance. When I worked for the perfume industry, I spent a lot of hours with my sniffer poked into stalks of hyacinths. They're a popular fragrance for cosmetics. And as I recall, they always made me sneeze. These have a rich, heady scent but no sneezes. Of course, now that I said it, my nose is tickling." I rubbed it a few times to stop the tingle. "All I know is these forced bloom hyacinths cost four times as much as the blooming bulbs do in spring. But Debra Geppler, the woman in charge of the reunion, insisted that the centerpieces for the luncheon contain Blue Jacket Hyacinths and Bright Canary Yellow Roses. Supposedly the two flowers are a perfect match for the school's colors, royal blue and yellow."

Ryder started trimming thorns and ends off the roses. "What's the name of the high school? Is it local?"

"It's the ten year reunion for the Rockmore Royals. Rockmore High is about fifty miles inland but they decided to hold the reunion at the Chesterton Regency Hotel."

"That's a nice hotel. We had our prom there."

"I'll bet you looked adorable in a tux." I smiled as I pressed a foam base into each vase. I'd chosen tall, clear glass vases, the only ones tall enough to hold the stalks and roses.

"Not really," Ryder said. "I was stiff and uncomfortable. I would have much preferred to show up in jeans and a flannel shirt, but my mom and the girl I was dating had different plans. Pure torture, those tuxedos. I'm getting married in shorts and a t-shirt. And something tells me, Lola would go right along with that plan. She'd probably pull out one of her special rock band t-shirts for the occasion."

Of course, I'd stopped hearing anything after he tossed Lola and getting married into the same sentence. I stared up unblinkingly at him over the vase. It took him a second to discover he had my undivided attention.

"Hypothetically, of course," he said quickly. "Boy, you and my mom have the same way of interpreting conversations. Every subject goes right to weddings."

"You're right. And I'm sorry for jumping to conclusions." I pushed several hyacinth stalks into the foam and added the yellow roses. I stepped back and tilted my head to admire it. "These colors are striking together. No wonder she requested them."

"It's sort of strange though considering their reunion is just a few days before Halloween. Seems like autumn colors would have worked better for the occasion."

"Actually, these are for the meet and greet lunch. From what I understand, there'll be a Halloween costume party in the evening."

"Sounds like a good time." Ryder dropped six more yellow roses in a water vase and stopped to admire my arrangement. "Very nice. Guess you can't go wrong with hyacinths. Did you know the name of the flower came from a Greek mythological figure called Hyakinthos?"

I picked up my pruning shears to trim some leaves. "I did not but something tells me, my assistant, the walking encyclopedia, is going to tell me the story." Ryder was one of those people who once he learned something, he never forgot. I'd found I could ask him just about anything, and he could pull up some source or detail or historical fact. After a rough patch, my best friend, Lola, was once again smitten with my shop assistant. She seemed to have come to her senses when it came to her relationship with Ryder, but I was sure she still didn't know how lucky she was. Ryder's feelings had always been solid when it came to adoring Lola.

Ryder grabbed a towel to wipe the trimmings off the counter. "Apparently, the god, Apollo, was teaching a young Hyakinthos how to throw a discus and Zephyr, the god of wind was jealous of their friendship. He blew the discus back and it hit Hyakinthos in the head and killed him. A flower grew from his blood. Or something like that. Not sure if I have it exactly right but you get the gist."

"Those Greek gods and their constant jealousy and envy. They sure had insecurities, considering they were gods."

The bell rang and Lola floated into the store with her nose held especially high in the air. She was wearing a red and white striped beanie that reminded me of Where's Waldo and a gray vintage Cat Stevens t-shirt. "I smell flowers and cookies. Guess that makes sense in this location." Lola sauntered up to Ryder, hopped up on her toes and gave him a quick kiss. "Can I just say that I have the sweetest smelling boyfriend in the world. I swear his clothes smell like roses and brown sugar. Seriously, they should make an aftershave that smells like flowers and cookies. It's a surefire way to gain affection."

Ryder laughed. "Now that every ounce of my masculinity has been drained, I think I'll get to work on a new window display. Something orange and red like the trees, what do you think, boss?"

"Love it. I'll get these centerpieces finished and put them in refrigeration. I'm delivering them to the hotel tomorrow morning."

Lola put her hands on her hips. "What about the cookie cloud coming from next door?" she asked me.

"What about it?"

"What do you think? Elsie is probably desperate for our taste testing opinions. We can't leave her hanging."

"You do have a point. Wouldn't be neighborly of us not to offer our expertise." I pushed another rose into the vase. "Let me finish these and I'll meet you over at the bakery in a half hour."

Lola took heavy steps toward the door. "I suppose I can wait, but I'm not happy about it." She twisted back and blew Ryder a kiss. "Good-bye sweet smelling boyfriend. Half hour, Pink, don't be late," she admonished as she walked out of the store.

CHAPTER 2

*E*lsie was in the middle of helping a customer when Lola and I marched in with our official taste testing postures and attitudes. Those same confident postures deflated with disappointment when her customer, a slim, young woman with large, expressive eyes was buying up every cookie tray.

Elsie was pouring on her ingratiating charisma, something she saved for her very best customers, and with the amount of cookies being purchased, this woman definitely earned that title.

Elsie stacked the pink boxes on the counter. "Can I help you out to the car with these?" she asked.

The woman smiled politely at us. "I don't want to take you away from your other customers."

Elsie waved her hand. "No, they aren't customers. They're just neighbors."

"Feeling a little insulted," I muttered quietly to Lola.

Lola leaned her head closer to me. Her focus was still on the cookies. "Do you think she left the broken ones on the tray?"

"She better have," I mumbled from the side of my mouth. "She owes us after that *just neighbors* comment. I won't accept anything less than three broken pieces, and I'm not talking crumbs either."

We forced smiles as Elsie walked by us with a stack of pink boxes. She seemed to know she'd just insulted her best friends and avoided making eye contact on her way out.

Lola and I perused the incredible goodies behind the glass case while we waited for Elsie to return. (We found it easy enough to swallow our pride when it came to Elsie's cookies.)

Lola pointed to a tray of pumpkin muffins, each topped with a swirl of cream cheese frosting. "I've had four of these muffins in a week. I wonder how many calories they are?"

I put my hand on Lola's shoulder. "Stop wondering. There's no happy ending to the story. One bite probably requires ten thousand steps just to break even."

Elsie stepped back into her bakery.

I swung around and pressed a hand to my chest in Scarlett O'hara fashion. "Well, I never," I added in a Southern twang. "Just neighbors, indeed."

"Sorry. Guess I got carried away when a highly sought after caterer came to me for cookies. I saved you both a few a samples. Hopefully, that will erase those frowns."

Lola nodded. "Yep, that should do the trick."

Elsie circled to the back side of the counter. "Chocolate chip, oatmeal raisin or peanut butter shortbread?" she asked.

"Yes," Lola said with the same emphatic head nod.

"All three it is." Elsie turned and walked to the back counter and piled cookies onto a paper plate.

"So that woman was a caterer?" I asked.

Elsie turned back with the plate of cookies. Lola and I each grabbed one. "Yes, her name is Katrina Jessup, and she owns Elegant Edibles. She is catering a high school reunion over at the Chesterton Regency Hotel. She needed cookies for a coffee social." Elsie primly smoothed the front of her apron. "And she'd heard that Elsie's Sugar and Spice Bakery was the best in the area."

I held up the last bite of chocolate chip cookie. "Can't argue with that." I pushed the bit into my mouth.

Lola reached for an oatmeal raisin. "Aren't you making floral centerpieces for that same high school reunion, Pink?"

"Yes. In fact I was working on them when you walked in earlier."

Elsie set to work wiping down her counters. Her prideful grin had washed away, and she looked deep in thought.

"What's up, Elsie? Something troubling you?" I asked.

She glanced up from her task. "Huh? Oh no, nothing troubling me. It's just that I'm going to have a visitor for the next six months."

"A visitor? Anyone we know?"

"I may have mentioned her a few times. Hank's niece—well, my niece too, of course. Britney is the middle child of Hank's sister, Carla. I haven't seen her since she was a little girl of eight. She's twenty-five now, so we'll be like strangers." She moved closer to lower her voice even though we were alone. "She was a shy, awkward kid. I'm not sure what I'll do with her. Hank's brother-in-law, Britney's dad, was in the army and stationed in Europe most of her childhood."

"So she's lived in a lot of exotic places," I said. "I doubt she'll be shy after that kind of upbringing."

Elsie's chin swished back and forth in thought. "I don't know. She was extremely shy. She'd hide behind her mom whenever an adult spoke to her. I once ended up alone in the same room with her. I cheerily asked her what her favorite hobby was. She ran from the room crying for her mother."

"Wow, that's taking shyness to a whole new level." Lola took a break from cookie consumption long enough to toss in her opinion.

Elsie stacked the empty cookie trays. "Tell me about it."

"Why is she coming to stay with you?" I asked.

"That's where the bigger worry comes in," Elsie said. "Her parents are trying to help her get her career started. Guess what she studied in Europe?"

"International relations?" Lola asked.

I handed Lola another cookie to keep her busy. "I'm going to assume that since they are sending Britney to you, Elsie, that Hank's niece wants to be a baker."

"A pastry chef to be more exact," Elsie said.

"Maybe your search for the perfect assistant is finally over," I offered, although I knew better. Elsie had been through at least ten assistants since I'd moved to Port Danby. None of them ever met the high standards Elsie expected. Most quit after the first two weeks.

Elsie's dry laugh assured me she wasn't expecting any success with her new assistant. Only this one came with a family commitment behind it. It would be much harder for her to get rid of a bad assistant if that person was her husband's niece.

"I'm preparing for the worst—a shy, clumsy, awkward young woman who will probably hide when a customer walks in. I'll have to put on a brave, friendly face though. I don't want to disappoint Hank."

The door swung open, ushering in a moist ocean breeze. Ryder's big toe weather prediction was proving correct. A drizzly rain had begun to coat the asphalt, sidewalk and my neighbor Dash, who'd walked in with the breeze. He wiped the water drops off his forehead.

"Am I interrupting a meeting of Port Danby's sensational business women?" he asked.

"No, Lola and I just came over to sample cookies. It's a nice diversion from the work day," I said.

Elsie walked down to the end of her pastry shelves without even waiting for Dash to make his request. "The usual?" she asked, sounding just like a salty bartender behind a saloon counter.

Dash smiled with a shrug. "I've grown a little obsessed with Elsie's pumpkin muffins." He patted his hard, flat stomach. "I'm going to have to get the next size of jeans soon."

"Pleeze," Lola puffed behind me.

Elsie pulled a muffin out from the shelf. "Do you want it in a bag?"

"No need," Dash said. "I'll eat it on my way back to the marina." It was off season for Dash's boat repair business, but he'd been kept busy by some of the local fisherman. Many of them had boats that, according to Dash, should have been at the bottom of the sea by now. But new boats were expensive, and most of the local fisherman preferred to keep their own vessels ticking and sputtering and burping smoke.

Dash picked up his muffin and bowed. "Ladies, I'll leave you to your cookie sampling."

"By the way, Dash," Elsie called before he let the door shut behind him. "This is the last week for those pumpkin muffins."

Lola choked and sputtered on a cookie crumb that had gone down the wrong way. "Why is that?" she managed to cough out.

Dash walked back inside with a bereft expression as if someone had just told him devastating news. "Are you out of pumpkins? Rhonda Martin down on Dawson Grove was just at the marina complaining to me that so many stores had pumpkins this year, no one bought any from her patch. She says she'll be making pumpkin stew until her husband can't stand to look at another squash. I'd be happy to cart some back here for you."

A light laugh burst from my lips. "You really are obsessed with them," I quipped.

"Guilty as charged," he said.

"Well, you can bring all the pumpkins you want, Dash," Elsie said. "I'm still done making those muffins. I need to start thinking about Christmas treats."

"Christmas?" Lola asked. "I haven't even given out my Halloween candy yet and you're talking about Christmas. That reminds me, I've got to order a new string of lights for the shop." She grabbed another cookie. "Thanks for the samples. See all of you later."

"Yes, thank you for the energy boost." I grabbed a cookie for Ryder. "See you both later." I turned back to Dash. "And if you need a friend to talk you down off the ledge when you're going cold turkey off those muffins, I'm right next door."

CHAPTER 3

$\mathcal{T}$he rain had cleaned the streets of autumn debris and left behind a crisp, clear dusk. Any remnants of the gray clouds had drifted out to the horizon to harass passing boats and vessels. Ryder and Lola had gone out to an early dinner, leaving me alone in the shop with my crow and my thoughts.

Kingston paced along the edge of my desk, poking at my paperwork and tapping out a clamor on my metal stapler with his talons. He gripped the pen on my desk, carried it to the edge and dropped it on the floor. His black beady eyes stared at me with a mischievous glint.

"You are always so helpful. At least you're a diversion from this dull paperwork." I closed out my account spreadsheet and took a hop over to Facebook. Social media was the crowned jewel of procrastination. It was so easy to slip into the world of friends' vacation pictures, relatives' political rants and photos of children and pets. I'd avoided posting pet pictures after one post with a cute shot of Kingston and Nevermore sitting on the couch together. I thought it was adorable and it got many likes. But it also invited every opinionated person to ask why I was keeping a wild bird hostage in my home, and with a cat, no less. I was devastated but mostly it made me question my decision to keep Kingston as a pet. Of course, the people chewing me out had no idea that Kingston wasn't the least bit wild. He preferred a waffle breakfast and sitting on the couch to fighting off mockingbirds and stealing eggs from nests. But it would have been useless to try and explain it to people who had already solidified their opinions of me. I deleted the post soon after and spent weeks anguishing over the question of whether or not I was wrong to keep Kingston. I easily reminded myself that after I'd saved Kingston, I made a valiant effort to release him back into the wild. He returned every time and made it clear that he preferred his quiet, docile existence with me. I wasn't going to let anyone else throw shade on my decisions. And just as that thought tumbled through my head, a post came up from Anita Cabrillo, my close friend and study partner from medical school. It seemed she had landed a huge job at a prestigious hospital. I typed the obligatory congratulations and clicked out of Facebook. I'd been so excited to start medical school, and it felt like a natural fit. But my overactive nose had other plans. I couldn't stand the smells in the anatomy lab, and my sensitivity to substances like formaldehyde made it impossible for me to continue. I made the heartbreaking decision to quit medical school, a decision that was even more disappointing to my parents than me.

I rested back against my chair with a sullen sigh. Kingston had retrieved the pen but dropped it as he jumped back on the desk. The frenzied caw of several crows outside the shop snared his attention. He trotted quickly out of the office to the front of the shop to see what all the excitement was about. I wandered half-heartedly after him, lamenting how, yet again, he'd be missing out on a natural crow activity as he stared longingly out the window. He flew up to his perch and gave his sleek black feathers a good shake before settling in for the show.

I peered past him through the window. The shadows were stretching long on the sidewalk as the last bits of sunlight lit the sky. In a tall cypress standing behind the shops, a great horned owl had settled in to wait for his night of hunting. It seemed the local crows were not happy about the intrusion. They cawed loudly darting in and out of the branches in an attempt to send the unwanted visitor on his way. In a true show of pecking order, the owl barely flinched at their angry protestations. Kingston's sharp gaze was glued to the window. He cooed and clucked a few throaty sounds, his way of joining in with his kind.

I walked heavy hearted back to the office to finish my work. It was hard to watch Kingston stare out the window. In my mind, he was envious of the other crows. Although, I could have been totally wrong. I hoped I was wrong.

I plunked down hard in my chair. Between worrying about Kingston's mental health and the latest news that Anita, who always scored below me on tests, had landed a big job in medicine while I pored over flower and vase orders, my mood had gone south.

My phone buzzed, and I was glad for the pity party interruption. The text was from Briggs. Just seeing his name on the screen helped lighten my spirits.

"Why does this job have to come with so much paperwork?" he texted.

I stared at my own pile of receipts and purchase orders. Paperwork was definitely not the highlight of being a business owner.

I texted back. "I assume that's a rhetorical question, unless you really want me to list the various reasons your job would require paperwork."

"Yes, rhetorical. I need a break. I'm on my way to your shop with some of Franki's split pea soup."

"Yay, you're my hero. You just saved me from the abyss of self-doubt."

"Then it's a good thing I ordered extra corn bread. See you in five."

I pushed the phone away. "See, Anita Cabrillo. I'll bet you don't have a handsome detective who brings you pea soup and cornbread."

The prospect of dinner with Briggs pushed me to finish up a few more purchase orders. He knocked on the locked door, and I practically skipped out to let him inside. Briggs had pulled a winter coat on over his dress shirt. He'd left his tie in his office. A black fedora was pulled low over his head, shading his face but not his brilliant white smile as he lifted a brown paper bag in each hand. "Dinner for two and an extra piece of cornbread for the gentleman with the long beak and impressive feathers."

I ushered him inside and immediately hopped up on my toes to give him a quick kiss. "You saved both Kingston and me from glum moods." Kingston heard his name being thrown around amidst a cloud of delicious fragrance and quickly skated back and forth along his perch.

Briggs carried the bags of food to the center island. "Why were you both feeling glum?" He pulled Franki's famous cornbread out of the bag and plucked off a chunk of the golden yellow bread.

"It's really me, more than Kingston," I confessed. "He was watching some crows across the street as they harassed an owl. Worry wart Mom that I am, I convinced myself that he was missing out on all the excitement."

Briggs dropped the chunk of cornbread on Kingston's feeding tray. The crow immediately set to work devouring every crumb. Briggs walked back toward me. "I'll bet if you gave those wild crows the choice between sitting out in the wet trees fretting that an owl had invaded their territory and sitting in a warm, dry flower shop nibbling hot cornbread, they'd pick Kingston's life every time."

"And that is why you are my boyfriend. You turn my frown to a grin with a cup of hot soup and an outlandish hypothesis about crows."

Briggs climbed onto the stool. "Not that outlandish. Just no way to prove my hypothesis. And is that the only reason I'm your boyfriend?" He pulled the spoons out of the bag.

"Well, you do look good in a suit and tie. And you ride a motorcycle when you're not playing detective. I can probably come up with a lot more, but Franki's soup smells delicious and I'm hungry." I plunged my spoon into the soup. Franki laced her split pea soup with chunks of ham and potatoes.

"Did you say you're making centerpieces for the Rockmore High reunion?" he asked. His question reminded me that while Anita was busy saving patients, I was arranging flowers in vases. It seemed it was going to take more than soup with Briggs to pull me out of my mood.

"Yes, my important task for the day is sitting in my refrigeration unit."

Briggs stopped the spoon halfway to his mouth. "Why was that statement peppered with so much sarcasm?"

"Was it?" I dipped cornbread into my soup and pushed it into my mouth.

"What's up, Lacey? And don't tell me it's still about Kingston's social problems."

I took a deep breath. "It's silly. My best friend in medical school just got a lofty position at a prestigious hospital and I'm arranging flowers."

"You make the world more beautiful with those flowers." He reached over and ran his fingertips down my cheek. His touch left behind a tingling warmth on my skin. "And just by being you," he added. "Besides, how many murders do you think your friend has solved?"

I smiled. "I guess I have been doing some pretty- good detective work."

"Best partner I've ever worked with." He gazed at me with his wonderful brown eyes. "Don't sell yourself short, Lacey. You moved to a new town and started a successful business all on your own." He reached over and took hold of my hand. "I, for one, am extremely glad that you chose Port Danby to restart your future."

I lifted his hand to my lips and kissed his knuckles. "I am too, James. Thank you for the pep talk. I needed it and you are just the right cheerleader for the job."

He cleared his throat. "I prefer to be out on the field than on the pep squad. In fact, the Rockmore Royals were big rivals of Chesterton High. We beat them every game but one."

"Must have been an *off* night for Chesterton's star player." I winked.

"Must have been." He returned to his soup.

"I'm feeling better, so thanks. I think I just need a new . . ."

He looked up. "Don't say it. As soon as you say you need a new murder mystery someone winds up dead."

"That makes me sound positively diabolical." I picked up a chunk of bread.

"Yes, it does. But you're also adorable so it all sort of balances out."

I nodded. "I can live with that."

CHAPTER 4

I'd barely opened the shop for the day when Lola burst through the door like a hurricane force wind. "Shy and awkward, my foot," she grumbled. "I met Elsie's niece this morning. I got to the antique store early to do some dusting and saw they were busy at work baking and creating. She's confident and beautiful and nice and beautiful and from all accounts talented and beautiful."

"Since you mentioned the fact that she's beautiful three times, I'm going to assume that's what has you in this volatile mood."

Lola pressed her straw boater down over her red hair. It curled out at the sides. "Ryder is going to take one look at her and ask 'what on earth am I doing with the flighty redhead and her wacky rock 'n' roll t-shirts.'"

My gaze dropped to her Bruce Springsteen t-shirt. "First of all, I can think of many adjectives to describe Bruce Springsteen, but wacky is not one of them. I love that shirt, by the way, but then it's hard to go wrong with Bruce. And secondly, Ryder adores you, so stop with the worry."

Elsie walked in right then. I couldn't quite read the expression on her face. It seemed to be a mix of surprise and concern. She swept right past Lola to me. "She's a better baker than me. She's over there right now finishing up the most delectable tray of pistachio macarons, and she made them so easily it was as if she was just buttering toast. Not only that, she's fast and efficient and organized." Elsie's shoulders drooped. "I've met my match, but I don't have a chance because she's almost forty years younger than me."

I took a deep breath. "Here I go again." I nodded at Lola before turning back to Elsie. "First of all, you might be *around* sixty, but you can outrun and outwork most twenty-year-olds, so age is irrelevant. Secondly, you're the best baker in town, and just like we all grew up loving our mom's food, people in this town have grown up loving your baked goods. Dash was practically in withdrawals when you told him you weren't making pumpkin muffins anymore. And thirdly—" I started but was interrupted by Lola's dismayed chirp.

"I only got first of all and secondly," Lola complained.

"That's because Elsie walked in." I turned back to Elsie and paused. "You didn't by any chance bring a macaron sample? I love pistachio."

"No but you can walk next door and get one. Then you can see for yourself that my days as premier town baker are numbered."

"That's right. I didn't get to number three. For the last year, you've been searching for an assistant who can live up to your high standards, but no one is ever good enough. Now you've found that person. You'll have the help you've been wanting. I think you'll be glad she came. Trust me, having a great assistant can make your life much easier."

An unsuspecting Ryder walked in. His face lit up instantly when he saw Lola.

"There," I said to Lola. "That was number three right there."

Lola smiled coyly and headed over to talk to Ryder. She knew too well that he was nuts about her. She just needed to believe she was worthy of his adoration.

"Ryder, I'm going next door for a minute to meet Elsie's niece." I walked to the door with Elsie.

"Sure thing."

Elsie and I walked outside and through her elaborate sidewalk sitting area, which she had decorated with Halloween themed tablecloths and skull shaped lights. Her niece was in the kitchen when we walked inside. She hurried out at the sound of the door. Britney Norris had a tall, statuesque physique. Her shiny, coffee brown hair was pulled back from her face. Dark brown eyes sparkled out from flawless golden skin and her smile came right out of a toothpaste commercial. No wonder Lola was in such a frenzied state.

"You must be Lacey, the florist." Britney strode confidently forward with hand outstretched. "I'm Britney but please call me Brit. My aunt has told me so much about you. She says you have a special nose that can pick out the faintest scent."

"Yes, it's called hyperosmia. It's as much of a curse as it is a blessing. And by blessing, I mean when I'm standing inside your aunt's bakery. Everything she makes is delicious."

I snuck a sideways peek at Elsie. She was holding back a grin.

"You are so right," Britney said. "I've been taste testing everything. I have so much to learn from her."

Elsie seemed to be standing taller than when she'd walked into my shop a few minutes earlier. "Oh, you two, you're making me blush. But Lacey isn't here to sample my treats. I was bragging to her about your perfect macarons."

"Hardly perfect," Britney said humbly. "I'll get you a few." Britney moved with the fluid grace of a runway model as she walked to the kitchen.

I leaned closer to Elsie. "Shy and awkward?"

"I'm as stunned as I could be," she whispered. "She's an entirely different person."

Britney returned with a paper plate piled high with pale green macarons. "Some have a caramel layer and a few have white chocolate ganache."

"Both sound heavenly." I lifted the plate. "And they are beautiful." The crisp bite instantly melted into sugary delight on my tongue. "Elsie's right. They are delicious."

The door opened and Lester walked in holding a large cup of coffee. He barely gave me a cursory nod as he proudly presented Britney with the coffee. "I added an extra squirt of hazelnut syrup."

"Thank you, Uncle Lester. I'm afraid I'm going to be so spoiled here, I won't ever want to leave."

That proclamation made Elsie tense. This was going to be a major adjustment for her but I was sure it was going to be a good thing in the end. Elsie worked so hard and having someone on board who was talented and, by all accounts, highly capable, would give my friend the break she needed.

The door opened again and Dash walked inside. Apparently, he was going to make sure to enjoy the last days of Elsie's pumpkin muffins. His eyes traveled directly to the tall, brown eyed girl with the white apron and shiny smile.

"Dash," Elsie spoke up, "this is my niece, Britney. Dash is a local. He fixes boats down in the marina."

If it was possible, Britney's smile widened even more. "Please, call me Brit." She stuck out her hand. I was certain I caught a lingering gaze of mutual admiration between the two. I peeked over at Elsie. Her tight expression told me she noticed it too.

Elsie held up the muffin, but it took a moment for Dash to pull his attention away from Britney. He handed Elsie his cash and nodded good-bye to all of us. It wasn't like Dash to be shy, but he sure backed out of the bakery looking like a timid teenage version of the real guy. Elsie and I exchanged conspiratorial winks.

"I've got to get back to the shop. Thank you for the delicious macarons, Brit. It was wonderful to meet you."

"Yes, you too. Enjoy."

CHAPTER 5

*D*ebra Geppler, the woman in charge of the Rockmore reunion was so efficient, the second I texted her that I was in the hotel parking lot, she came rushing out with a utility cart to help me carry the centerpieces inside. She spotted me easily with my vase of blue hyacinths, and I recognized her easily by the large bold print on her nametag. She was dressed in royal blue slacks and a bright yellow blouse to match the flowers.

"Hi, I'm Lacey, and I can see by the bright blue lettering on your tag that you are Debra." I held a centerpiece up for her to get a good view of it.

Debra rested her hand on her chest. "It's far more spectacular than I imagined. The colors are perfect."

"I'm so glad you like it. And thank you for thinking of the cart. I was planning to carry them in two at a time but this will save me the extra trips."

Debra and I placed the vases on the cart and rolled it carefully along the asphalt to the hotel entrance. I'd driven by the Chesterton Regency Hotel several times, but I'd never stepped inside. The facade was a mix of brown brick and white and black trim, giving it a sort of Tudor-like appearance. Hanging baskets of moss, overflowing with red and pink petunias hung along each side of the massive portico leading to the glass doors.

"I've never been inside this hotel. It is much grander up close," I said as we worked in tandem to make sure the vases stayed upright.

"Yes, I've always loved this hotel," Debra said. "My parents and I always stayed here when we came down to the coast for vacation. I knew it would be the perfect venue for the reunion."

"I'll bet it's a lot of work to be in charge of a high school reunion," I said.

"Yes, I suppose I was asked because I was social director for our graduating class. I love doing this kind of stuff."

I grabbed a vase of flowers that nearly toppled over the side as we pushed the cart over the mosaic of tile at the entrance.

"Are you a party planner?" I asked, thinking maybe I'd just made a nice business connection.

Debra laughed. She had round pink cheeks that bunched up when she smiled. "No, I've got two toddlers at home. I work from home doing data entry for several medical offices. But party planning is a dream of mine. Someday."

"Well, if you need a good florist, you've got my number."

"I do and looking at the quality of your work right now and the fact that you showed up exactly on time, I'll be sure to call you if I ever get that dream started. I'm still waiting for an actual party planner to deliver the pumpkins I ordered for the costume party. They were supposed to be here this morning at eight. I've put in three calls but there's been no reply."

"That's a shame. If you need pumpkins just let me know. I can find you some."

The lobby of the hotel was grand in scale and decorated somewhat glitzy with massive chandeliers hanging down from a paneled ceiling. The glossy marble floors were partially covered by richly hued rugs and upholstered furniture. It was outdated but in a good way. In fact, it transported visitors back to a time of old Hollywood glamour.

A man wearing one of Debra's bright nametags was pacing near the entrance as we walked inside. The name on his badge was Clive. He gave a cursory nod toward Debra but was too absorbed in what seemed to be a tense phone conversation to do more than that. His shirt sleeves were rolled up exposing an eagle tattoo on his forearm. It looked oddly out of place as if that tattoo was an afterthought and possibly even a regret. As he turned away from us, I heard him ask, or more from the tone of his voice, plea, for a little more time. Debra didn't seem to notice Clive's tension or the subject of his conversation.

She did tilt her head in Clive's direction. "You know how every high school class has their big shots, their stars," she said with no small amount of derision. "We had a trio of them. Clive was probably the most likable of the group, and that's not saying much. His two friends, Riley and Dane, are already here. They are just as arrogant as ever. The two of them made it rich with some real estate venture. Don't see how it's fair considering that they were nothing but big bullies at school."

We passed through the lobby toward the convention and meeting rooms at the other end of the hotel. Blue and yellow signs had been posted along the way welcoming Rockmore Royals to their tenth reunion.

"That never seems fair does it? What about Clive?" I asked. "Was he in on the get rich scheme?"

Debra stopped to hug a few women who appeared to have gotten spray tans and fancy hairstyles for the reunion. They did a quick exchange of 'you haven't changed a bit' with each other, then Debra and I continued on down the hall.

"As far as I know," Debra picked up our conversation, "Clive was left out of the deal. He was always kind of the third wheel with that group. Not that he didn't do his share of being an unlikable big shot, but Dane and Riley both came from money. Clive had just managed to latch onto them and stay friends."

We reached the large event room where hotel workers were setting up tables and chairs for the lunch. Blue and yellow balloons hung in clusters from the ceilings. Blown up pictures from the class yearbook were pinned to the walls along with colorful banners welcoming the group.

"Darn," Debra grunted. "I thought the tables would have been ready by now. We can put the centerpieces over on this long table." We rolled the cart to the table along the wall, while the hotel workers finished setting up furniture.

"The caterer won't be bringing out the hot food trays for another hour. I was so lucky. Elegant Edibles is always booked solid, but the owner, Katrina Jessup, reached out to me when she saw my Facebook post about the reunion."

I was about to mention seeing the caterer, Katrina Jessup of Elegant Edibles, at Elsie's bakery but thought better of it. I didn't know if Debra knew about the caterer handing out another baker's cookies, and I certainly didn't want to step into it.

We placed the vases on the table. Debra leaned back to admire them. "They'll be the highlight of the lunch." Her phone rang. "It's the party planner with my pumpkins. I need to take this. If you can wait a moment, then I'll get your check."

"No problem. I'm just going to peruse the pictures." I walked along the wall of the room. Blown up to poster size, the pictures were fairly grainy, but the kids in the photos were wearing the same hairstyles and fashions that my friends and I wore. I'd skipped my tenth reunion and seeing the pictures gave me a twinge of regret about missing it.

Deep voices echoed through the mostly empty room as I stared up at the various sports teams.

"Debra sure has put on some pounds," a man said behind me. I turned around and came face to face with three men. Clive was one of them. After the rude comment about Debra's weight, I deduced that the two men standing with him, smirking up at the pictures, were his notorious friends. Their nametags, Riley and Dane, confirmed my suspicions.

Riley had a wide forehead and baby fine blonde hair fringed over deep set eyes. He laughed about something Dane said, but his expression was hard and mean. His voice and laugh were big and booming, but he was only average in size. And, ironically enough, he was carrying a few extra pounds in the middle. His deep set eyes focused on me. He seemed to be trying to guess my name.

Dane was covered head to toe in expensive clothing and shoes. He was wearing a gold Rolex on his wrist to show off his success. I supposed that was what people did at reunions.

Riley pointed rudely at me. "Cindy, right? You used to work in the library. You are way hotter now."

"I didn't go to school with you."

Riley made an overly dramatic frown. "Are you sure?"

"Trust me, I'd remember." My tone could not have been misinterpreted, but he managed it.

Riley nodded arrogantly. "Yeah, I get that from chicks all the time."

Debra entered the room again. She glanced frantically around for me.

"Excuse me," I said quickly and rushed past them.

Debra spotted me and raced toward me with a look of desperation. "Something terrible has happened," she said.

"What is it?"

"The pumpkins aren't coming." She announced it as if she was telling me a giant asteroid was hurtling toward earth. "You mentioned you could find some pumpkins for our costume party."

The morning before, in his attempt to extend Elsie's pumpkin muffins, Dash had noted that Rhonda Martin on Dawson Grove still had a patch full of squash. That nugget of information was going to come in handy today. "Yes, I know of a farm that still has some. I'll bring the pumpkins back this afternoon."

Debra grabbed my hands. "I'll be forever grateful," she said in a tone that made it sound as if I'd just saved her from that same hurtling asteroid. "Do you want to just write up a new invoice and add the pumpkins to it?"

"That works. I'll see you in a few hours with arms full of pumpkin."

CHAPTER 6

*A*s I hurried back to my car, a text came through from Tilly Stratton, the librarian in Chesterton. "I've found something I think you'll be interested in. Tilly."

I texted right back. "I just happen to be in Chesterton. Can I stop by right now?"

"Absolutely. See you soon."

I climbed in and headed straight to the library. Debra's pumpkins would have to wait. I'd been slowly peeling away the layers of a century old murder mystery and I didn't want to lose the opportunity to find more details. Hawksworth Manor, the dilapidated, yet stately, mansion looming over my neighborhood from Maple Hill had been the site of a grisly family murder. In 1906, when the tragedy had taken place, the local police had quickly written it off as a murder-suicide. They'd concluded that Bertram Hawksworth, a wealthy businessman, had grown despondent, possibly over the failure of his bid to build a large shipyard in Port Danby, and, in his anguish, had shot his wife and three children before turning the gun on himself. But pictures from the murder scene didn't make sense. Bertram was holding the murder weapon in his right hand, but I'd found pictures of him proving that Bertram had been left-handed. The officer at the time had discovered the same inconsistency but was quickly transferred, not only off the case, but out of the Port Danby precinct. I found it all too suspicious and had taken it upon myself to find out what really happened. Clues were sparse and mostly disconnected so far, but I was determined to press on. Since Chesterton Library housed a plethora of local newspapers and records from the turn of the last century, it had become my go-to place for research. Tilly Stratton, the industrious and helpful head librarian, knew I was interested in everything Hawksworth and tended to keep an eye out for things that might be significant in solving the case.

The Chesterton Library was a charming blend of rustic and quaint with its barn red exterior, white trim and dark blue door. The inside was just as inviting. Tilly Stratton took care to keep the bookshelves organized and flush with every book a reader could want. A tall shelf at the front of the main reading room boasted, with a bright orange sign, that it held all the latest bestsellers.

Tilly was just coming around from the stacks with two school girls as I entered the room. She waved at me to follow her to the circulation desk. Tilly had changed up her usual bowl haircut by clipping a few strands back with a plastic bow. Her smiled revealed her large front teeth as she greeted me. "I haven't seen you in so long, I thought maybe you were no longer interested in the Hawksworth murders."

"I'm still interested. It's just that life keeps getting in the way. In fact, I don't have much time today either. I'm off to buy a bunch of pumpkins for a high school reunion."

"Wonderful, you're going to your reunion," she said with a cheery whisper.

"No, I'm just helping with the floral arrangements. And squash arrangements too, apparently."

Tilly adjusted her glasses and searched around on the bottom shelf of the circulation desk. "Well, you know how I ask that people leave the newspapers out on the research table so I can put them back in proper order?" she asked as she continued her search.

"Yes."

"Ah ha." She pulled a newspaper out. It was yellowed and crisp from time but in nearly perfect condition. "Some high school students were writing a paper on the history of Port Danby." She shook her head. "Those silly girls must have pulled out every paper on the shelf. They were doing so much giggling, I doubt they got any work done. Anyhow, I was putting the papers back and I found this one. It's one of the first editions of the Chesterton Gazette." She turned the paper toward me. It was dated May, 1890. She pointed to the headline at the bottom of the front page. "Bertram Hawksworth takes a bride." *See Society Section page four* was written in small print beneath the announcement.

"You found the wedding announcement," I said too loudly and pressed fingers to my lips to shush myself.

Tilly nodded enthusiastically enough to make her glasses slip down her nose. She pushed them up and leaned forward. "There's some commentary from the society reporter that I thought you might find interesting."

A woman approached the desk looking for Tilly's assistance.

I carried the paper to a nearby table and sat down. The paper felt brittle in my fingers as I carefully opened it to page four. Right at the top was a fuzzy gray and white picture of the happy couple on their wedding day. Only happy wasn't exactly the right adjective for their facial expressions. I'd only seen Jill Bertram in the grim photo taken at the crime scene. It seemed she'd been a pretty woman with large eyes and a tiny bow shaped mouth. It was pursed rather tightly for the picture. Her late Victorian gown had large puffy shoulders and layers of lace. A tiny crown on her head held a long, gauzy veil that trailed down behind her shoulders. Bertram Hawksworth stood stiffly next to her, and from the expression on his face, it seemed he would rather have been anywhere but standing for a wedding photo. According to the caption, the couple got married in Mayfield Chapel and were postponing the honeymoon due to Bertram's business conflicts. Farther down on the page was a snippet written by a woman named Nellie Singleton. She started the short article by claiming to be the town's 'expert on high society'. It seemed to be a gossip column of sorts, which made me smile. It seemed even in the stodgy Victorian era, people liked a good dose of scandal and rumor. Of course, without television or radio, most forms of entertainment fell on the written word, so it made sense. Back then, wealthy elites were like our modern day celebrities.

Nellie Singleton seemed confident about her credentials, so I read on.

"The rumors have been confirmed. Bertram Hawksworth, Port Danby's most eligible bachelor has taken a bride. The lovely Jill Elizabeth Stoddard will soon be society's new darling. But my dears, don't blame yourself too much for not being the chosen Hawksworth bride. The rest of us never had a chance. This reporter has it on good authority that the marriage had been arranged a decade earlier by the two families. Jill brings to the union a hefty dowry from her father, George Stoddard of Stoddard Shipping and Exports. We hope the two will be very happy together and wish them many years of joy."

I smiled at the playful tone of the article. It was unexpected and surprising, especially knowing a woman had written it. Back then, women writers hid behind male pseudonyms just to be taken seriously. I'd only read one piece by Nellie Singleton, and I was an instant fan.

My phone buzzed, attracting the attention of a few people sitting nearby studying and working on laptops. I shrank down and flashed them all an apologetic grin. I reached into my coat pocket and glanced at the text. It was from Lola.

"I'm taking a lunch break. Where are you?"

I quickly replied. "I'm just leaving Chesterton Library. I'll treat you to lunch if you come with me on a pumpkin picking expedition on Dawson Grove."

"That autocorrect is hilarious. I assume you didn't mean to say pumpkin picking expedition."

"That's exactly what I meant. Are you in or not?"

"Sure. I haven't been pumpkin picking in years."

"Great. I'll meet you at Rhonda Martin's farm in twenty minutes." I stuck the phone in my pocket but pulled it back out when Lola returned a text.

"What about the free lunch?"

"Squash plucking first. Then lunch. See you in twenty." I gingerly folded the paper back up to its original form and carried it back to the desk. Tilly was busy looking something up on a computer for two girls. I waved and mouthed the words 'thank you', then headed out to the car.

It wasn't an earth shattering clue for the Hawksworth case, but it certainly pointed out that the Hawksworth marriage might not have been all kisses and roses. Just maybe the romantic letter from "Button" I'd found in Bertram Hawksworth's trunk was not written by Mrs. Hawksworth. Maybe Bertram Hawksworth had a mistress. It was all just speculation for now, but it definitely added a touch more scandal to the mystery.

CHAPTER 7

$\mathcal{L}$ola and I stood at the edge of the Martin property, a quaint farmstead that, like most of the farms in the area, was land that had been handed down to the next generation to keep it in the family. Rhonda and Burt Martin were just about reaching that age where running a farm, even a small, family one, was becoming a burden. That was made more evident by the fact that they both stayed securely in their porch rocking chairs as Lola and I picked the pumpkins.

Lola took a selfie standing in the middle of the patch. "Nothing says fall like a haphazard cluster of future jack-o'-lanterns." She lowered the phone. "You're kind of late on yours though. Halloween is in three days. I carved my pumpkin last night, and I must say it's a masterpiece." She spent another minute searching for her jack-o'-lantern before proudly holding up her phone. She'd carved an intricate picture of a scarecrow into the side of the pumpkin.

"Impressive. Perhaps you've missed your calling. Instead of antiques, you should become a master pumpkin carver." I bent over to pick my first pumpkin. The vines and leaves were dried and brittle making it easy to break the squash free from the plant. While some of the pumpkins had softened and caved in from the weather, most were still bright, solid and happy to be chosen.

"And you should be a comedian." Lola tucked her phone into her windbreaker jacket. The chilled air coming off the coast was mixing with a breeze coming from inland. It was just turbulent and cold enough to require a good coat or windbreaker. "I've been hinting to my parents that our business is booming online and that I probably don't need to spend so much time at the shop," Lola said as she traipsed through the vines. "My time would be better spent packaging and mailing the items purchased online. Ooh, here's a symmetrical beauty." Lola picked up a pumpkin and yanked it free. "Ahh," she shrieked and dropped it to the ground where it made a proper splat. Lola wiped her hand on her jeans. "It was only a beauty on the top. Mush on the bottom."

We continued our search for twenty presentable, medium pumpkins. There were still plenty in the patch. I carried two nice ones to the side and hiked back through the sinewy vines to find more. "I think it's great that the antique business is doing well online. I can see where that makes sense. Reach the entire world with your antiques instead of just locals and weekend vacationers. Do you think your parents might consider letting you limit the shop hours so you can devote more time to the online business?"

Lola braced a good-sized pumpkin on her shoulder and carried it to our collection. "The only problem is that the online business works great for small items but not so much for furniture and fragile items." She swung around. "I nearly forgot to tell you. Remember those strange pictures of that old house on the east coast?"

"The ones with the ghostly figure staring out from the front porch? How could I forget? Still wonder if it was some kind of photography trick."

"We'll never know for sure. I sold them. And get this, Sunni Taylor, the woman who bought them, is the current owner of the house. She was anxious to get them, even paid extra for overnight shipping."

"Makes sense if it's her house." I grabbed two more pumpkins and carried them to the side of the patch. Wheels squeaked behind me.

"Thought you might want to pile them in this wheelbarrow." Burt Martin had kindly left his comfy rocker to roll his wheelbarrow out to the patch. He was wearing an old flannel coat and a knitted cap on his head. "Just don't fill it too much. The front wheel is shaky."

"Thank you so much. I guess I should have asked the price before we started picking them. Is two dollars a pumpkin enough? I'm taking twenty."

Burt laughed. "I should be paying you to pick them. It'll save me the work. Seems everyone's patch went crazy this year. Now there's a surplus and Rhonda refuses to make pumpkin pie before Thanksgiving." He glanced back and waved to his wife.

"Take as many as you like," Rhonda called from the porch.

"Her arthritis is acting up in this cold weather," Burt said. "Otherwise, she'd be down here tossing those squash into that wheelbarrow faster than you can roll them to your car. They're starting to attract all kinds of critters too. Last night, the dogs were barking like crazy. I turned on the porch light. Three fat and sassy raccoons were nibbling away in the middle of the patch, just like fat, old men with their bellies bloated from pumpkin. I yelled and waved my arms to shoo them away, but they just stared at me and kept eating."

I laughed. "Raccoons are persistent. Thanks for the wheelbarrow. That'll save us a few trips to the car."

"Sure thing." Burt made his way back to the porch.

Lola and I continued our quest for the prettiest pumpkins. "Why do they need so many pumpkins for a high school reunion?" Lola asked as she stooped down to examine her next prize.

"Since the reunion is so close to Halloween, they decided to have a costume party. The woman in charge, Debra, is very particular about everything. Every high school has one—the energetic, hard-working, peppy person who makes sure all the school events are memorable."

"Yes, I know exactly who you're talking about. Brenda Thistle, head of the pep squad, class treasurer and all around cheer inducer. It's funny how no matter the generation or location, every high school is made up of the same general types of people."

Her statement reminded me of the three guys I met while delivering the flowers. "Including the big men on campus who were too arrogant to socialize with the little people, namely, the people not invited to their lunch table. Rockmore High has three and I met all of them. They are still reliving their glory days as the class big shots, even ten years later."

"For my class, it was Katie Harris. She was so mean. The only reason she carried so much clout was because her father was rich and helped pay for the new football stands."

"I guess bullies come in every shape and size." I picked two more pumpkins and walked them over to the wheelbarrow. I stared down at the collection. "We're going to have to fill every nook and cranny of my car with pumpkin." I glanced over at Lola. "How do you feel about being strapped to the roof like a Christmas tree?"

"As long as I still get a free lunch. And by the way, all this pumpkin picking has given me an expensive appetite. I'm going to require a lot of sustenance after this adventure."

"I'm right there with ya." As usual, we'd covered many subjects, but one topic had not come up until Lola tossed it out for discussion.

"You haven't told me what you think of Elsie's niece," Lola said as she trudged past with full arms.

"She bakes delicious macarons. Having two bakers next door will be both delightful and scary. I'm going to have to keep a check on myself."

Lola returned with empty arms. "I wasn't asking about her baking talents."

"I know you weren't. What can I say—she's lovely. Tall, beautiful, confident. I think she'll be good for Elsie. She needs a good assistant. You have to stop always worrying about your relationship, Lola. It's impossible to enjoy it when you're always afraid it's going to end. And it's not—" I said quickly. "Anyhow, I witnessed a small interaction today that was more than interesting."

I had her full attention. "Between Ryder and Britney?"

I huffed loudly. "Truly, you are a loon. The interaction, which was more or less just an overlong gaze, was between Dash and Britney."

Joy and relief instantly washed across Lola's face. "Oh, they'd be perfect for each other."

"All right, tamp down the enthusiasm, friend. It was only a long gaze. There was no proposal yet."

The notion that something might grow between Dash and Britney put a little spring into Lola's step. "Let's get these pumpkins piled into your car. I'm starved," she said cheerfully.

CHAPTER 8

$\mathcal{I}$ tried unsuccessfully to leave Rhonda and Burt forty dollars for the pumpkins. They refused to take it. Lola and I had a fast lunch of premade turkey sandwiches and sweet potato chips outside the Corner Market, before heading back to our shops.

I was covered in dust and debris from the pumpkin patch. Ryder insisted he could keep shop the rest of the day while I went home and showered before delivering my heavy load to the hotel.

My car chugged as if it was dragging a twenty foot trailer up Myrtle Place. I turned into the driveway. Kingston paced the back of the seat, anxious to get to his cage and his snacks.

Dash's truck was sitting in front of his house as I pulled into my driveway. He was hard at work painting the railing on his front porch. Dash had only just recuperated from a nasty fall off the roof. I was glad to see him standing on firm ground instead of loose roof shingles. Kingston flew up to the roof to wait for me to go inside. In an unusual display of energy, Dash's dog, Captain, came plodding across the yard to greet me. The dog's moment of unexpected energy caught Dash's attention. He turned to see where Captain was heading. His smile was blinding white under the shade of the porch.

He put his brush into the paint can and followed Captain's path to my side. "Hey, neighbor, you're home early."

I held my hands out and stared down at my dirt crusted shoes. "I've been hanging out with Linus in the patch waiting for the Great Pumpkin, so I decided to take a shower."

He stopped and took note of my shoes. "I see that. Any luck with the Great Pumpkin?"

"No but I do have a car filled with fat orange squashes." I waved back at my poor little car still panting from the drive up the hill.

"That would explain why the chassis is nearly touching the driveway." Dash was in a better mood than I'd seen him in a long time. I wondered briefly if it had anything to do with the town's new visitor. Turned out, I didn't have to wonder long.

"I saw you in the bakery today," he said unnecessarily. He looked down and kicked at a few blades of grass. It was another rare moment of shyness for Dash. "Guess you met her niece, Britney." Apparently he wasn't finished stating the obvious. Or *being* obvious, for that matter.

I paused to pat Captain on the head. "Considering I was gobbling up her macarons, I had no choice but to say hello." Usually Dash and I were in sync when it came to humor, but I sensed that he was in no mood for my silly sarcasm. He had something more important on his mind. Oddly enough, I felt the tiniest twinge of jealousy about his keen interest in Elsie's niece. I pushed the ridiculous twinge away. "Elsie told me that her niece had been a shy, awkward little girl. I think she worried she was going to have to deal with the same nervous girl. I'm still trying to work out if Elsie is relieved or dismayed about the fact that Britney has left behind that bashful, little girl and bloomed into a confident, beautiful woman. Her baking talents are nothing to be sneezed at either. I think that has Elsie on edge more than anything. You know she doesn't like to be out-baked."

Dash smiled. "Little chance of that. I'm still trying to figure out how I'll survive without those pumpkin muffins."

"Which reminds me—thanks for the heads up about the Martins' pumpkins. That nugget of information came in handy. I just cleaned out half their patch. They looked pleased to see the back sides of them." I tapped my chin. "Do pumpkins have back sides?"

"I guess that depends on how you carve them." He had lightened up in this new thread of conversation. It felt strange talking to Dash about a woman, and I was just as glad to change topics. If only he felt the same.

"So, do you think I have a chance?" he asked. His question was incomplete, but I knew exactly what he was asking.

"Dash," I said matter of factly. "As hard as you are to look at, you know with those outlandish broad shoulders and smoldering green eyes, I'm sure Britney will be able to look past all that unpleasantness and see the true man beneath." It seemed I was still pushing my luck with my sarcastic wit. My mom often told me I didn't know when to wrap it up and tuck it away. Apparently she was right . . . again.

"I can see this is a serious question, so I'm going to straighten up and be a good friend, instead of a babbling nincompoop. Yes, Dash. I was there when the two of you met, and my hair nearly stood on end from the static charges shooting through the air."

His smile returned. I'd never seen him so unsure of himself. "Then, I wasn't just imagining it."

"Not unless I somehow crawled into your imagination. I'd give her some time to get settled in though. She only just got to town, and she and Elsie are in the middle of trying to figure out their relationship. She probably doesn't need anything new thrown into the mix. Although, she does seem like a woman who knows exactly what she wants and how to get it."

"She does. I guess that's why I'm feeling unsure of myself," Dash said.

"Well don't. Be yourself. Bring back the sure of himself Dashwood Vanhouten. That's all you need."

A soft thud against my front window carried our attention to the house. Nevermore was twisting and turning though the curtains, balancing on the windowsill, making sure I knew that he was waiting for me to come inside.

Dash raked his fingers through his thick hair. I was about to add that performing that gesture occasionally wouldn't hurt either, but I decided to keep that advice to myself.

"That's what I've always liked about you, Lacey. You're so easy to talk to. How is it going with Briggs?"

Dash and I rarely spoke about my relationship with Briggs. Their rough history of friendship, betrayal and competition made it a subject better left untouched.

I smiled up at him. "Things are going great. I enjoy being with James."

He nodded. "I'm glad to hear it. Well, I've got to get back to painting. Got off work early today so I decided to tackle the job I've been putting off forever." He rolled the shoulder that had just healed. "All the parts are back in working order, so I don't have any more excuses."

Nevermore thumped his paw against the window. "That's good to hear. I better get inside before Never busts through the window pane."

"Thanks for the pep talk," Dash called as he headed back across his lawn.

"Anytime."

CHAPTER 9

*T*he cart Debra used to help me carry in the floral bouquets was not going to work for twenty pumpkins. Ronald Sexton, the hotel manager, was gracious enough to lend us several luggage carts. Debra and I piled as many pumpkins as we dared on each and began a slow, careful journey into the hotel. One bump or sudden movement might have sent our cargo rolling away like cue balls.

"These are perfect." Debra pushed the cart with both hands as she gazed admiringly at the pumpkins. "They are just the right size for the straw bales I have stacked in the corner of the room. I thought it would give the party a real country Halloween kind of feel."

"Absolutely. Pumpkins are so simple and understated, so unassuming yet where would autumn be without these rotund vegetables? Or are they fruit?" I asked.

She shook her head. "I couldn't tell you."

"I know just the person to ask. I'll text him when we get these beauties to their straw bales because now I need to know. I'm thinking seeds inside mean fruit, like watermelons and cantaloupes."

We drew quite the flood of curious gazes as we pushed our unusual luggage through the lobby. A few people with Debra's easy to spot blue nametags lingered around the lunch room, even though the hotel crew was clearing away tables and chairs.

"We raffled off the hyacinth vases," Debra said as we chugged past the room where the luncheon was held and onto the next room. "I kept one for myself," she admitted sheepishly. "They are so beautiful. I wish there was some way to preserve them."

"If only nature's beauty wasn't always so fleeting. I'm glad you liked the arrangements, and I'm especially glad you took one for yourself. You deserve it with all the work you're doing for this reunion."

Several of the reunion guests were helping to hang black and orange balloons around the vast event room. As Debra had mentioned, one corner of the room was stacked with straw bales. An impressive scarecrow wearing a class t-shirt and black top hat loomed over the bales. Three fake crows sat on the top bale mocking the scarecrow with their black wings. "I could have brought you a real crow for a prop if I'd known ahead of time," I mused as I texted Ryder "pumpkins—fruit or vegetable?"

Debra's brows were bunched in confusion. "Did you say a real crow?"

"Yes, I have a pet crow named Kingston. I'm joking, of course. He would be helping himself to every goodie in the buffet line."

"That's an unusual pet." Debra stopped her cart in the corner.

"Kingston is an usual crow. How do you want these displayed?" I picked up the first pumpkin.

"Along the top edge but not in a line, sort of haphazard like they might be in a patch. A photographer is going to take pictures of people in this corner of the room."

"What a fun backdrop for the costume photos." I placed the first pumpkin right between two of the fake crows. Ryder texted back. "Fruit because it comes from a seed bearing plant."

I texted back "thanks" and held up my phone. "Pumpkins are a fruit, in case you were still wondering, which with all you have to do today, you probably weren't." I pushed the phone into my pocket.

Debra shook her head. "Guess not all fruit is sweet."

"Debra, as usual you've outdone yourself," a voice said from behind. The man's nametag read Grady. He was average height with shiny black hair and kind brown eyes. "I can't wait to put on my costume."

Debra beamed at his enthusiasm. It seemed he was a different sort of classmate than the first three men I met while carrying in the flowers. "Thank you, Grady. Lacey, the florist who brought the Hyacinths, saved the day by harvesting some pumpkins for the picture backdrop."

Grady bowed politely. "Then, I suppose the Royals are forever in your debt, Milady."

I curtsied in response.

"Grady Ramone was our class valedictorian," Debra boasted. "He also has a black belt in karate and he recently was promoted to head engineer at NASA."

Grady tossed his shoulders in a humble shrug.

"Yeah, once a nerd, always a nerd." A deep laugh followed the rude remark. I wasn't surprised to look back over my shoulder and see Riley, one of the class big shots.

"And once a bully, always a bully," Grady chided back, taking the words right out of my thought bubble.

Even though the men were similar in size, Riley strode over with his chest forward in a futile attempt to intimidate Grady. A long, tense moment followed. Debra sucked in a breath and held it, while I quickly imagined a scenario with me stepping between the men. A fleeting vision of me getting a black eye from a flying fist helped flatten the notion. Fortunately, a rush of relief followed when Riley chuckled and shucked Grady, none too gently, on the shoulder.

"I'm just horsing around with you, Ramone," Riley said. "Where's your sense of humor?"

Before Riley lumbered away to catch up to his friend, Dane, Grady got in one good stinger. "I save my sense of humor for people who are actually funny."

Debra hid a giggle behind her hand. Apparently, she didn't want to show sides, even when it was easy to see which side was right.

Grady's jaw was still tight from the moment of tension, but Debra deftly changed his focus. "So, Grady, can we get a hint about your costume? I still remember when you showed up at Veronica's costume party as a scary clown." Debra turned to me. "Some of us hid in the bathroom for the first ten minutes after his arrival, but Grady, who was always the gentleman, soon had us laughing and perfectly at ease." She shivered once. "Although, confession time—" she continued. "I was too afraid to walk home that night. And I lived literally two houses away. I spent the night at Veronica's house, and she was happy to have me."

Grady smoothed his hair down in the back. "I remember that costume. My sister did the makeup. Now she's working on movie sets."

Debra looked my direction. "Which tells you just how scary he looked. What can we expect tonight? Willing to share any details? Your secret is safe with us."

It was obvious from the expression on his face that Grady was anxious to give some hints. He pulled out his phone. "I'll show you the hat, which will pretty much give it away. My sister had a costume designer friend make it for me." He swiped through his pictures and held the phone up for us to see the picture of the red, purple and green jester's hat.

"Wow, that's amazing," I said. "That is no store-bought costume hat. It looks like it's made of velvet and satin."

Grady put the phone in his pocket. "Good eye. And the same designer made the rest of the costume to go with it. I was thinking about some gory makeup for a scary jester, but I think this time I'll avoid giving the women nightmares and just go as a jovial jester. They're meant to be amusing, after all." Grady leaned down and picked up a pumpkin. "I finished with the balloons, Deb, so I can help you with the pumpkins."

A loud whistle split the air as we continued setting up the display.

"Whooee, aren't you something." The three of us stopped and turned back toward the front of the room. I instantly recognized Katrina, the caterer, from Elsie's shop. She was carrying in a tray of Elsie's cookies, and at the same time, coolly ignoring Dane's taunts.

Dane's gold Rolex glittered on his wrist as he made a show out of surveying Katrina from head to toe. She tried to walk swiftly past him to the exit, but Dane stepped in front of her. He tried to engage the woman. The stiff set of her shoulders and back showed just how angry she was at his obnoxious behavior. She managed to sidle around him and brusquely leave the room without further incident.

"It's like they never grew up," Debra said quietly.

I glanced at Grady. His jaw was tight with rage again, and he seemed to be unfurling his fingers from fists. "One of these days those guys are going to be paid back for their cruelty. They're long overdue for a big heaping pile of karma."

CHAPTER 10

$\mathcal{T}$he pumpkins looked ripe and fall-ish sitting on bales of straw. Debra was still running around, trying to get things ready, so I volunteered to roll the luggage carts back to the lobby. They were cumbersome enough that it would take me two trips, but I was in no particular hurry.

Ryder had texted that he'd be staying late to finish up his window display while he waited for Lola to finish work across the street. They had planned a sunset picnic on the beach, which sounded divine and romantic. I was just considering calling Briggs to suggest a dinner out when he called me.

"Hey, Lacey, are you still in Chesterton?"

"As a matter of fact I am. I just finished setting up a display of pumpkins."

"Great. I'm finishing up some work at the office, then I'm heading that way. I've got to feed Bear and take him on a walk. I thought you could stop over. There's a great little Italian place around the corner from my house. Unless you need to get back."

"Actually, I was just having a green with envy moment about Lola and Ryder's sunset picnic, so a cozy Italian dinner sounds perfect and wipes that green color right away."

Debra's harried voice sounded in the hallway between the lobby and the event rooms. She was asking for help with the table linens, but everyone seemed to be anxious to get back to their rooms to get dressed for the party. "I'll stick around here for another hour and help with setting up the reunion. Text me when you're home and I'll head over."

"See you soon."

I hung up and hurried off to catch up to Debra. She darted into the event room. I found her setting up a small table with pictures and memory cards for two students who had died since graduation. Debra straightened the picture of a young girl who was wearing a big smile that was filled with braces. The name on the plate beneath the frame was Jessica Trumbo.

"Debra, I have time to help you with the table linens."

She looked up from the table. "That's so kind of you, Lacey. I don't want to take up more of your time."

"Please, I'd like to help. I mean, look at all this." I waved my arm around the room, laden with balloons, hanging bats and ghosts and crepe paper spider webs. I turned back to the table. "You even remembered a memorial table for classmates who died."

Debra's round cheeks blushed pink. "Thank you. I have put a lot of time into all this. Everyone went upstairs to get into their costumes, but I still have to set the tables. I would love your help." She gazed sadly at the picture of Jessica. "She was such a nice person," she said. "Always willing to help out too. And so talented. She was on her way to becoming a concert pianist. She could play the classics beautifully. Unfortunately, her extra long nose and the big ears that she always tried to hide from view under hats, made her the terrible trio's favorite victim. Dane used to call her Dumbo, a cruel twist on her last name. And Riley and Clive always encouraged it. They really were an awful group of friends. And I thought they might have grown out of it, but I guess for some people being mean is just part of their character."

"It seems that's the case. So tragic that she never got to live out her dreams as a musician. How did she die?"

Debra led me away from the table toward a stack of black and orange linen tablecloths. "I never heard many details, but from what I read, from the snippets posted on Facebook, she was visiting her grandparents. They had a farm in the Midwest. She lost control of her car and it flipped several times."

"That's terrible. She was way too young to die."

Debra picked up the second framed picture of a young man who seemed to have been forcing a smile for his senior portrait. "Norton Allred died on a trip to Africa just last year. He was one of those intellectual types who was always taking life too seriously. But he was quite successful in finance. From what I heard, he contracted some illness and died a few days later."

"Was he also a target for Riley and his buddies?"

"Who? Norton? No, I'm sure they never allowed him to eat at their table, but I don't think they harassed him. Clive, Riley and Dane saved most of their ruthless teasing for two people, Grady and Jessica. I'm sure you saw how Grady's mood changed when Riley came near. They didn't like Grady because he won all the academic awards and the teachers loved him. He was voted most likely to succeed, and he's lived up to that title. I suppose those three are still proudly wearing their bully titles too." Debra took one last look at Jessica's picture and pushed up a faint smile. "I suppose we should set the tables, if you're sure you have the time."

"Absolutely."

Debra handed me a tablecloth and pointed across the room. "You can start at that end, and we'll meet in the middle."

"Sounds like a solid plan."

CHAPTER 11

$\mathcal{T}$he delicious fragrance of garlic bread and lasagna circled the room as the caterer and her team carried in hot trays of food. The aroma gave me a moment of giddiness about my date with Briggs. It seemed Katrina had easily dismissed Dane's rude advances when she brought in the cookie trays. She looked cool and collected as she instructed her crew on where to place the food items on the buffet.

Debra and I were working at the guest tables tossing out plastic spider rings and glowing plastic fingertips on each table as party favors.

"After putting together flowers for many big occasions like weddings and anniversary parties, I'm always impressed by the caterers. It seems like such hard work."

"Katrina Jessup is one of the best. She is extremely talented. I got to taste test some of the food we're having tonight. Katrina calls it a trip through Italy. It's delicious. I think everyone will be pleased."

The first of the guests started trickling into the room. Two versions of Dracula, one with a punk hairdo of red tipped spikes and another, the more traditional, with a cap that was supposed to resemble slick black hair with the obligatory widow's peak. A princess, a Darth Vader and a nicely created Edward Scissorhands walked in next. Debra looked anxiously toward the door as people strolled in. The song "Monster Mash" began streaming from the speakers overhead.

"Debra, I'll finish putting these goodies on the tables. Go up and get changed. Just because you're putting on the party doesn't mean you shouldn't enjoy it too."

"Are you sure? You've already done so much."

"I'm enjoying this."

She handed me her bag of party favors. "Be sure to help yourself to a plate of food before you leave."

"Actually, my boyfriend is taking me to, coincidentally enough, an Italian restaurant tonight, but thank you anyhow. Now hurry up and get dressed."

Debra checked with the caterer that everything was going smoothly and readjusted a few of the decorations before heading out to get changed.

I quickly distributed the rest of the party favors. It seemed people weren't waiting to be invited to the buffet table. Plates were already being filled and the clamor of music and voices grew louder. I checked my phone, but there was still no text from Briggs. I was glad I'd showered after harvesting pumpkins, otherwise I would have been going out on a dinner date coated in dust. I only wished I'd pulled on something a little more spectacular than jeans and a gray sweater.

"Oh man, I thought I'd be the only Dracula," Clive barked through the noise in the room. He was holding his plastic fangs. He'd entered with someone wearing a gruesome zombie mask. It was easy to recognize Riley under the mask because he was still wearing his bright orange high top sneakers. Clive's two partner vampires seemed to shrink under his complaint as he approached them. "At least I didn't go punk like you, Roland. That is you under that white pasty stuff, isn't it?"

Roland muttered yes and then made his way to the buffet table, apparently not up for a long conversation with Clive. Dracula with the plastic hair didn't wait around either. His cape fluttered out behind him as he dashed behind vampire number one.

"At least I didn't wear the stupid cheap plastic hair with the costume." Clive laughed loudly at the guy's back. Clive hadn't spent too much time on makeup other than some white foundation and a drip of red painted near his mouth. His thick, brown hair was slicked back with copious amounts of hair product to give his mop the shiny, smooth look of Dracula. He and Riley roared with laughter when their third partner, Dane, strolled in dressed like Prince Charming complete with sash, red cape and black boots. Although, I'd never seen Prince Charming wear a Rolex watch. I had to grin at the irony of someone like Dane pretending to be a prince. His thick, burly build made him look even less right for the part. And as unlikeable as the three were, instantly people were flocking around to hang out with them.

"Just like high school. People never learn," a voice said from behind. I spun around to find a colorful jester with brightly colored tights, tunic and hat standing behind me with a plate of food. "Are you staying for dinner?" Grady asked. He picked up a garlic bread stick. "It's delicious."

"Yes, my mouth has been watering since the food was carried in, but I'm leaving the party to the Royals. I was just helping Debra out so she could get dressed."

"Good ole, Debra. She worked hard to make this a success. It almost would be if those three losers hadn't shown up."

I glanced back at the three. They were loud and arrogant and full of themselves, just the kind of people I avoided in high school. I smiled back at Grady. "Debra was telling me how awesome you were in school, always winning the academic awards. Someone like you should never have to think twice about bullies like that."

He sighed and it made the tips of his multi-pointed hat vibrate. "Told myself that again and again, but sometimes it's hard to forgive and forget."

"I know." I bowed my head to him. "Well, I'll leave you, royal jester. Enjoy the costume ball."

He dipped the bread stick into his spaghetti sauce. "I intend to make the night unforgettable. Good night, my fair lady."

CHAPTER 12

*a*fter a five minute exuberant greeting from Bear, Briggs picked up his keys. "We should get going, Mama Ricci's gets busy at this time and there are only ten tables."

"Ten?"

"It's a little mom and pop place, which is why the food is so good. Nothing commercial. Just authentic home cooking."

I smiled weakly. I hated to let on that after being surrounded by the aroma of Italian food for the last hour and a half, I was no longer in the mood for anything with garlic or oregano. No doubt, a person with a normal nose would still be craving pizza and spaghetti, but for me it was sensory overload, like aversion therapy. As much as I looked forward to a cozy, romantic dinner with Briggs, I couldn't stand the thought of being once again immersed in the heady fragrance of Italy. "Sounds yummy," I said with little enthusiasm.

Briggs never missed a detail. "Are you not hungry?"

"I'm starved." I moved my nose side to side. It seemed to kick up some of the aromas from Katrina's Elegant Edibles. "It's just that I spent the last hour helping set up the costume party for the Rockmore reunion."

"You do like to go above and beyond for you customers," he quipped.

"Well, I mostly volunteered because I was waiting for dinner with my favorite detective boyfriend."

Briggs' lazy smile creased the side of his mouth. "Glad to hear I'm at least the favorite on your list of detective boyfriends."

I walked closer to him and absently straightened the collar on his flannel shirt, a blue and gray one that went nicely with his skin tone. "The caterer was serving Italian food at the buffet, rich smelling sauces and garlic breads and oregano," I said the last with distaste as just the thought of it was making me queasy.

"You don't like oregano?" His brown eyes were shiny with confusion.

"Yes, when I haven't been immersed in it for an hour," I said somewhat curtly, frustrated that I had to spell it out for him. It wasn't as if he could forget about my supersonic nose. I'd helped him solve more than one murder case with it.

He tapped the side of his head. "Of course. You've been smelling it with that powerful button nose of yours, and you can't stand the thought of spaghetti and garlic bread. By the way, Mama Ricci's is the best. The garlic butter drips off the—" He stopped when he saw the tight, firm set of my mouth. "Sorry, I guess I've been sort of daydreaming about that garlic bread since we made the date."

"See, now I feel bad. You were craving Mama Ricci's."

He pulled me in for a kiss. I could smell the lingering fragrance of soap on his skin. "The only thing I was craving was spending time with you. Any kind of food will do."

I peered up at him after the kiss. "Since you're flexible about the food, how about a little flexibility on transportation?"

Briggs' brow arched. "You are talking in puzzle pieces again."

"I'll be more direct then. When I walked up your driveway, I was admiring a very shiny and fun looking motorcycle. I could almost swear it whispered 'take me out for a ride' as I walked past."

Briggs lowered his arms. "Ah ha, so now my motorcycle is talking to you, eh?"

I held out my arms to point out my casual outfit. "Earlier, I was lamenting that I was dressed in jeans and a sweater for our dinner date. Now, it seems, my fashion choice was fate." I could see I was losing him fast and had to jump into pleading mode. "Please, James. You promised we could take a ride, and I've been waiting very patiently for the chance. I mean, what's the use of having a cool, easy rider style boyfriend when he always drives me around in his sedan, his work sedan at that."

Briggs blinked at me for a moment. "Quite the salesperson."

I shrieked and threw my arms around him for a hug. "I'm so excited, and you don't have to go slow for me. Zoom right along at whatever pace you like. In fact, the faster the better."

"I think we'll stick to the speed limit, if you don't mind, Speed Racer. Come into the garage so we can fit you with the right helmet. One that fits over all those curls."

I followed him at a skip to the garage. "What part of my sales pitch worked best? Just so I can make note of it for next time."

"The cool, easy rider style boyfriend pretty much clinched it." Briggs had an array of different motorcycle helmets sitting on a shelf in the garage. They ranged from full face helmet, like the kind racers used, to a simple bowl shaped Harley Davidson helmet. He reached for a shiny blue one that had a tinted visor. "A friend gave me this one. It's too small for my head."

We had an amazingly flirty few moments standing face to face as he adjusted the chin strap to hold the helmet securely on my head. He spent a few extra seconds gently pushing my curls back off my face and beneath the helmet. Then he leaned back and before I could protest, he took a picture of me wearing the helmet.

"What are you doing? I must look like a big bobble head with this helmet."

He looked at his phone. "Yes, but a cute bobble head."

He grabbed the Harley helmet. "There's a burger stand off the highway about five miles west. Does that sound like an exciting enough journey for your first ride?"

"Hmm, that depends, are there fun swerves or dips in the road?"

He laughed and took hold of my hand. "No, but I can always add in a few swerves just for fun."

"That works."

Five minutes later, Briggs and I were turning the corner onto the main road that would take us to the highway and eventually our dinner destination. It wasn't the cozy booth in a quaint, charming restaurant that we'd planned. It was way more fun than that. The nighttime sky was lit up by a nearly full moon, and the night air had absorbed a chill. My face felt numb from the cold as I peeked up over Briggs' shoulder. I cuddled closer both for warmth and because I quickly discovered that hanging tightly onto the driver was the best part of the entire ride. Despite his earlier hesitation, Briggs didn't seem to mind it either.

The glowing moon lit the rustic landscape along the highway, blurring it into a smear of shrubs and small farms as we rode toward the burger stand. The dips in the road felt a little like a roller coaster ride, and I couldn't keep myself from laughing.

Briggs turned his face and spoke loudly. "Everything all right back there?"

"Couldn't be better," I called back. I curled my arms tighter around him and stared over his shoulder at the road as it slipped past under the motorcycle. Right at the time when I could no longer feel my face, Briggs slowed the bike down and turned off onto a dirt road. The burger stand was set a good five hundred yards back from the highway. There was a cluster of pale green metal tables sitting to one side of the lot where several people were dining on burgers and fries.

Briggs parked and put his feet down. I braced my hands on his broad shoulders and climbed off. He helped me unfasten my helmet and gently lifted it off.

I reached up and fluffed up my curls. "Helmet hair, one of the risks of riding a motorcycle."

He shook his head. "Yes, that's the one insurance companies worry about as well." He took off his own helmet and rested both of them on the seat. His brown eyes glittered with amusement as he looked at me.

I pointed to my face. "You're laughing at my permanent smile," I spoke through my grin. "It's a combination of my face being frozen along with the general thrill I'm still feeling from the ride."

"Maybe this'll help warm it up." He leaned forward and kissed me.

"That's a start." He took my hand and led me to the stand. It looked as if it had been a produce stand at one point but now a roof and grill vent had been added to the back. Acrid gray smoke twirled up from the vent, filling the air with the smell of charred meat and onions.

"I recommend the bacon cheeseburger," Briggs said.

"Then, that's what I'll have. And fries, of course."

"Of course."

I staked out a table that was out of the stream of smoke oozing from the stand. A few of the other diners glanced my direction. I sat up straighter, feeling pretty darn cool after riding up on a motorcycle. Then I caught a glimpse of my half flattened, half wild curls in a window on the side of the stand and came to the disappointing conclusion that rather than ogling the biker babe, they were most likely intrigued by my clownish hair. I shrank down. Using that same window reflection as a mirror, I made a quick attempt at resurrecting my pre-helmet hair, which, by itself, was nothing to brag about. But I'd given up straightening my natural curls during my first month living in a coastal town.

Briggs walked back with a cardboard box of food and drinks. "I hope it's all right that I ordered the fries with nacho cheese sauce. I had a salad for lunch and I'm feeling the need to balance the nutrition with something off the charts in bad food choices."

I reached for a fry and pulled it out of the cheesy pile. "Nacho cheese is just like a fluffy new pillow. Pure comfort and I never say no to either of them."

He laughed as he threw his leg over the bench and sat down across from me.

I took the burger and my drink. "Thank you for dinner. And for the motorcycle ride."

"My pleasure." He unwrapped his burger. "So, how was the reunion going?"

"Seemed to be running smoothly. They were having a big costume party tonight. As I was leaving, a lot of vampires, zombies and members of royalty were streaming in for the party. And all the usual high school characters were there too. Pre-costume characters, that is. Unfortunately, for the Rockmore Royals, their three main bullies did not mature in the last ten years. They were easy to spot and easy to dislike. And I never even went to school with them."

Briggs washed down his bite with soda and swallowed. "We had our share of bullies too. Not sure what drives people to be so mean, but I suppose it's usually because they have miserable lives at home."

"Well, at least two of the Rockmore bullies had nothing to be bitter about. They've been successful in real estate, yet they were still obnoxious." I took another fry. "The ambience is lacking," I said as I glanced around at the mostly dirt and weed lot. "But the food is scrumptious."

He winked at me. "And so is the company."

My cheeks warmed at his comment. I busied myself with the burger while the color in my face faded. We ate in silence for a few minutes, enjoying the yummy food and each other's company, but there had been one thing weighing on my mind lately. A problem that we hadn't really tackled yet. We'd tried once, only it turned out in disaster. I cleared my throat.

"So, James, I suppose we should talk about the elephant in the room."

He paused on his way to a burger bite and stared at me. "Since we aren't in a room and I don't see any sign of an elephant, I assume we're about to discuss something big and looming . . . and *obvious*?" He said the last word as a question.

I put down my soda. "After Nevermore and Bear's first meeting calamity, I've been worried. What happens if they never get along?"

He visibly relaxed when I revealed the elephant. Yes, it was a small, maybe even tiny elephant, but it was still a concern.

"Lacey, Nevermore was just afraid because Bear is still a big, slobbering goofball. Eventually, he'll mature, and we can get them slowly used to each other. Last time was a disaster because we didn't plan ahead. Bear just loped inside your house like he owned the place. I can't blame the cat for taking off."

I nodded but it was still a point of concern. "I'm sure you're right. Maybe if we just take it easy and let them see snippets of each other a few times first. And like you said, eventually Bear will grow out of puppyhood."

"I sure hope he does. My couch is only a facade now, like those fake movie sets on the production lots. The entire back side has been chewed hollow. I figure I'll wait to buy a new one until he grows out of the chewing stage. Someday," he added.

I pushed the worry about our pets to the back of my mind for the time being.

We finished our burgers and talked about bits of everything. We never grew tired of each other's company. I could have sat at the smoky burger stand all night just staring into his brown eyes and listening to funny stories about his rookie years, but the temperature was dropping and we still had to ride back on the motorcycle.

We were in the midst of making sure my helmet was on correctly when his phone rang in his coat pocket. He reached for it. "It's Chinmoor." He answered the call.

One minute into the call, Briggs' expression grew serious. "Right. Let them know I'm on my way." He hung up and looked apologetically at me. "It seems our dinner date is over."

"What's going on?"

Briggs picked up his helmet and pulled it on. "Seems as if the Rockmore ten year reunion just took a deadly turn."

CHAPTER 13

*T*he parking lot of the stately Chesterton Regency Hotel was packed with a sea of flashing red lights. Every type of emergency vehicle had arrived at the scene. A uniformed police officer, a man with thick red hair and an equally thick moustache, walked toward us when he recognized Detective Briggs climbing off the motorcycle.

"Officer Clark," Briggs said as a greeting.

"Detective Briggs, this way," Clark said without stopping to give details.

Officer Clark led us along a pathway that followed the outline of the building. We passed several side entrances and the rear parking lot where a group of curious and shocked looking spectators had gathered.

Officer Clark paused to give some information. "It appears the victim fell from the fourth story balcony." He pointed up to the fourth floor where curtains fluttered around an open sliding glass door. Other guests were standing out on their balconies looking on in horror at the scene below.

Emergency personnel stood in a semi circle around something on the sidewalk. They were calm and quiet, as if there was nothing they could do to help. We reached the circle of uniforms. A large white sheet had been drawn over a body. The only things showing were the victim's shoes. Orange high tops.

"Riley," I gasped.

Briggs looked over at me. "Do you recognize the shoes?"

"Yes. He was here for the reunion."

Briggs walked to the opposite end of the body. He stooped down and lifted the sheet. Riley's head was sitting in a puddle of blood. Briggs lowered the sheet and stood up.

Officer Clark joined him. "The hotel manager is on his way. It was his night off. Megan Sharpe, the woman standing with Officer Coolidge, witnessed the fall." A very shaken looking woman was standing a good distance away from the scene being comforted by a woman police officer.

"Thanks." Briggs walked over. He discretely motioned for me to follow. It was always hard to contain my excitement when he allowed me in on an investigation. I had earned his trust with my sleuthing skills. Of course, it helped that I always carried around a turbo charged nose. Samantha, the name Briggs had given my nose for always twitching like the nose of the television witch, had helped solve a number of murders in the past year. I was always glad to lend my sniffer to a good cause.

The woman who had witnessed the tragic fall looked properly shaken. Her lips were nearly white from shock. Briggs noticed her distress too. "Officer Coolidge, I'm just going to ask a few questions, then I need you to get her inside to rest." His calm tone and gentle suggestion immediately helped soothe his witness. He pulled a tiny notebook and pen from his coat pocket. It made me smile. Apparently the man never left home without his trusty tools of the trade.

"Miss Sharpe?" he asked.

"Yes, Megan Sharpe," the woman said shakily.

"I understand you witnessed the fall," he continued.

Megan covered her mouth to catch her breath. "Yes, yes. It was awful. I came outside to look at the moon." She looked up toward the sky. "It's a hobby of mine, moon watching."

"Do you know what time that was?" Briggs asked.

"It was about a half hour ago. Just after 8:30, I think. I was just coming around the corner of the building." She pointed back to the corner where the pathway took a right turn. "I heard a yell and the body flashed in front of me." She covered her face. "It was horrible." She muttered through her hands.

The phrase 'heard a yell' was significant. It made the possibility that Riley was pushed off the balcony much more likely.

"I'm sorry, Miss Sharpe, it's hard to hear you behind your hands," Briggs said.

She lowered them. Most of the color had returned to her face and lips. "He hit the pavement so hard. It was a terrible sound. I'll never forget it." She took a shuddering breath.

As she recounted the fleeting seconds when she'd witnessed Riley fall to his death, the victim's classmates, still clad in costumes, slowly filtered out to the pathway. Hands covered mouths in disbelief and shock as word streamed through the crowd that the body under the sheet was Riley. Even the caterer and some of her helpers stood with the others in their green and white aprons looking utterly horrified.

It was hard to see clearly through the clutter of costumes and huddled people, but I didn't see Clive or Dane anywhere in the crowd. It seemed more than a little strange that Riley's best friends and business partner were absent.

Debra pushed through the crowd, and even though an officer told her to stay back, she forged ahead wearing a blue gingham checked dress, ponytails and red sequined shoes like Dorothy of Oz. In contrast with the cheery costume, her face was pale gray under the moonlight as she spoke quickly to the officer. He tried to coax her back, but she was persistent.

I headed over to her. "Lacey," she said urgently. "I didn't expect to see you here. I can't believe this has happened." I nodded at the officer to allow her to come to me. I hugged her for a moment. She was shaking from head to toe.

"I was out with my boyfriend. He's a detective." I never liked to brag, but I loved the sound of having a boyfriend who was a detective. And, in this case, it explained the reason why the local florist was standing in the midst of a possible murder scene.

Debra pulled out a tissue and blew her nose. There didn't seem to be tears with it, so I could only assume it was just a sinus thing. It was terrible to think about right then but I didn't hear or see any sobbing or tears in the group of onlookers. Riley had died but the expressions were more of the usual stunned looks people wore when faced with the grim certainty of death. Everyone always had mortality in the back of their minds, but seeing it firsthand, especially when that person was alive and well just moments before, made it all too real.

Briggs was still taking the statement of the eyewitness. I decided to do a little interview of my own.

I walked Debra off to the side, away from her classmates and away from the other spectators. "Debra, did you see Riley leave the party?"

She took her time to think about it. "I didn't actually see him walk out, but at one point, I heard the three of them—"

"You mean Clive, Dane and Riley?"

"Yes." She rolled her eyes slightly. "I overheard them complaining that the party was cheesy and that they were bored and wanted to go to a nearby bar." It was obvious their comments had hurt her. Leave it to them to make sure she overheard.

I put my hand on her arm. "It was not cheesy. You did a wonderful job."

"Thank you but after all the hard work, the night has ended in a calamity."

"Not your fault, Debra. So, all three were planning to leave the party?"

Her ponytails swung as she nodded. She shuffled in her bright red shoes. "If only these were really Dorothy's shoes. I'd click my heels together to transport myself back home. I had such big hopes for this weekend. Now I just want it to end."

"I don't blame you." In between trying to comfort her, I was sprinkling in more questions. She didn't seem to notice. I was certain she assumed the tragedy was an accident. "Did you see the three men leave?"

"I didn't see when but soon after I heard them talking, I realized they were gone. They were so loud and boisterous, it was easy to notice their absence."

A low murmur went through the crowd as Nate Blankenship, the coroner walked up in his bright colored jacket with lettering on the back announcing that he was, indeed, a coroner. Briggs' gaze caught mine for a moment, then he turned his attention to the scene.

The sight of Nate's team caused Debra to gasp.

"My gosh, this is such a nightmare," Debra said. "Can't believe this has happened."

"It's a terrible tragedy," I agreed quietly, then continued. "Debra, I never took notice whether or not you were serving alcohol at the party. Were the guests drinking? In particular, was Riley drinking?"

"We did have some beer and wine but no hard liquor. There just wasn't enough money in the budget for it. Everyone had a coupon to limit the beers and wine too. But that didn't stop people from bringing in their own flasks or buying drinks in the hotel bar. And I do remember seeing Riley and his friends with glasses from the bar." She pressed her hand to her chest. "Is that how he fell? Was he drunk?"

"I have no idea, but I'm sure the coroner will perform a blood test for that. Do you know where Clive and Dane are now?"

Debra turned back to the group and stretched her neck to look over heads. "I don't see them."

"What are their full names?" I asked. "I'm sure Detective Briggs will want to talk to them."

"Clive Jergens and Dane Caputo. I think they were staying on the other side of the hotel."

"Thanks. I won't keep you, Debra. And I'm truly sorry about how badly the night ended."

Just as she started heading back to the group, the officers at the scene were directed by Briggs to clear the area completely. Onlookers were instructed to go back inside the hotel or to their cars. I still didn't see Dane or Clive in the group.

I reached Briggs' side. "That was Debra Geppler, the woman in charge of the reunion. She said the victim and his two friends had complained the party was too boring. They made plans to go to a local bar. I have their names."

Briggs smiled weakly. "Best partner a detective could ask for. Let's go find his friends."

CHAPTER 14

The other officers were containing the scene outside while Briggs and I headed up to Dane's room. We had a few minutes alone in the elevator on our way up to the fifth floor where Dane Caputo was staying. We hadn't had much time to talk before that.

I leaned back against the brass railing at the back of the elevator. "Are you thinking murder?"

"The witness heard the man yell before his body plummeted from the balcony. It's a good indication of foul play. I have the team in his room right now with instructions not to touch anything until we get there."

I couldn't hold back a smile. "We. I love that word."

Briggs was just about to take a quick second to kiss me but, to my dismay, the elevator stopped and the doors opened. It was a vast hotel with two distinct wings. This side was calm and quiet. Light music played through the hallway, which was lined on each side by dove gray doors set in peach colored walls. The crystal lights hanging overhead provided a warm glow and long shadows through the otherwise deserted hallway.

"It's hard to believe there's a horrific scene out on the sidewalk of the second wing." My voice echoed in the hallway. "Everything here seems as it should be for a pricey hotel."

"It's definitely quiet." Briggs looked down at the key card in his hand and nodded for us to turn the corner. We reached Room 511. Briggs knocked hard. "Mr. Caputo, this is Detective Briggs of the Port Danby Police." We waited. There was no movement behind the door. Briggs tried again, knocking harder and longer. No answer.

He motioned for me to step away from the door as he put the card into the lock. It clicked open. Since we'd come from dinner, Briggs had no weapon on him. He remembered that little detail too late as he reached instinctively for his gun, the gun that wasn't there. His gesture to reach for his weapon made a flutter of nerves rush through me. I hadn't even considered that he might be facing danger as he walked into the room.

Briggs stopped in the doorway and called into the open room. "Mr. Caputo? Dane Caputo? Port Danby Police."

Since I'd scooted back, I couldn't see inside the room. I crossed my arms to stop the rush of fear as I listened for some kind of response or action. Seconds later, I heard Briggs speaking into his phone. "This is Briggs. Looks like we'll need the coroner up in Room 511 when he's finished below. Send someone for evidence collection."

The blood drained to my feet. Another body? How could that be? I approached the door cautiously. "James, can I come in?"

"Yes, sorry, Lacey. Come on in. The room is clear. At least of any possible danger," he said as I turned the corner.

Dane Caputo was slumped on the floor at the foot of the bed. His Prince Charming costume was tossed haphazardly on the bed. He had changed into pants and a sweater. The lamp on the desk was turned on, but the heavy, decorative shade dimmed the light.

I moved closer to get a better look. "Is that a phone charger cord around his neck?"

"Looks like it." Briggs glanced back at the dresser. "Not from his phone though. It's plugged into the wall right now." Briggs pointed out a phone connected to a charger on the nightstand.

I walked over to a cart from room service sitting on the far side of the bed. "Cocktails and chocolate chip cookies," I noted as I looked over the tray. "Interesting combination. Debra said they weren't serving any hard drinks. I guess he decided to call room service instead."

"I'll have to make a visit down to hospitality. With any luck they keep good records on the time food is delivered to each room." Briggs walked to the door again and checked both sides. "No signs of forced entry. Not even sure if that's possible on these electronic key doors but it seems whoever killed him was invited in."

"Or maybe they were already here, waiting for him," I added.

Briggs nodded. "Entirely possible. If that's the case, then they had a key."

"Like room service?" I asked.

"Yes. That's why we'll need to talk to them soon." Briggs walked back and crouched down next to the body. "Looks like cause of death is fairly obvious." He took a closer look at Dane's face and throat, then lifted up his right hand. His thick fingertips were red and bruised. "He tried his best to pry the cord off his neck but without luck." He looked closer at Dane's wrist. "It seems he was wearing a watch at some point."

I clapped once. "Yes, you're right. I noticed his watch because it was one of those pricey Rolex watches." I glanced over at the costume crumpled on the bed. "He was wearing it when he came down to the party. I remember because it was sort of humorous to see Prince Charming with a Rolex. Do you think the motive could have been theft?" I asked.

"Possibly, if the watch is missing. We'll know after we search the room and his belongings." He lowered Dane's arm into the same location. "Lacey, would you mind? Before everyone else gets here."

I knew exactly what he was asking. I tapped my nose and gave it a little side to side swish. "At your service, Detective."

Briggs backed out of the way, and I knelt down next to Dane's body. Before I could take one whiff, loud voices and footsteps filled the hallway. A middle aged man barreled into the room. His tie was askew and his shirt collars were sticking out at various angles as if he'd gotten dressed hastily. His face took on a greenish cast when his troubled gaze landed on Dane's limp body.

"Good lord," the man muttered and stumbled into the bathroom to get sick.

Briggs and I exchanged brow lifts. "He looks a few years past his tenth reunion," Briggs said wryly. "I'm going to assume that's the hotel manager." Briggs walked to the bathroom and tapped on the adjacent wall. "Mr. Sexton?" he asked gently.

"Yes, I'll be right with you," Mr. Sexton mumbled back. Seconds later, he emerged from the bathroom holding a wet washcloth. He made a point of not looking in the direction of the body. "You'll have to excuse my reaction. I've never seen a—" He paused and looked at Briggs. "Is he dead for certain?"

"I'm afraid so, Mr. Sexton. And I'm sure you're aware of the incident on the opposite side of the hotel."

Sexton looked as if he might be sick again. "Can I get you a glass of water?" I asked.

"No, thank you." Sexton wiped his forehead with the cloth. "I don't understand what's going on? Are my other guests in danger?" The waver in his voice made his whole body shake.

"We haven't connected the two incidents yet, but there are some precautions—" Briggs was interrupted when Officer Clark's head popped into the room with a knock. "Detective Briggs, I have someone who needs to see you right away."

"How will we ever recover?" Mr. Sexton groaned to himself.

I stood up and waited next to Briggs. Clive came around the corner, his face ashy gray and his chest heaving with breaths. His hair was wet and cleaned of the hair gel.

"I think someone was trying to kill me," Clive said on a gulp of air.

Mr. Sexton released an unearthly sound and raced for the bathroom again.

Clive's wide, frightened eyes coasted to the body on the floor. Instantly, he grabbed for support on the wall. Officer Clark took his arm, as well, to keep him from passing out. Clive took a few deep, steadying breaths and moved tentatively forward on shaky legs. "It's

Dane, my good friend Dane. They told me Riley had died, but it was Dane."

Briggs and I exchanged glances.

"I can't believe it." Clive reached blindly for the bed next to him and sat down hard. Briggs cleared his throat. "Mr.?" He asked, pausing for him to fill in the name.

"Jergens, Clive Jergens." Clive peered up from a snow white face. But it wasn't makeup from his costume. He had seemingly showered and washed everything off, hair gel included. The three had planned to go out to a bar and obviously headed up to their rooms to change out of their costumes first.

"I'm sorry but your friend Riley Morrison is also dead. He fell from his fourth story balcony on the other side of the hotel." Clive covered his face, and his shoulders shook with silent sobs. I suddenly felt guilty for thinking so badly of him. His empathy and sorrow were palpable. Something I wouldn't have expected. While I was busy psychoanalyzing a high school bully, Briggs showed me that he was still the true investigator. I'd completely forgotten about Clive's alarming declaration when he walked into the room.

"Mr. Jergens, when you walked in here, you said someone tried to kill you."

"Yes. I think so. They snuck up on me in the hallway outside my room. I'm sure he was planning to strangle me just like poor Dane. But he ran off. Lost his nerve, I guess."

"He?" Briggs asked. "Did you get a look at the person?"

"Not directly. But I know who it was and I have proof."

CHAPTER 15

*A*fter Mr. Sexton marginally composed himself, Briggs advised him to shut down the parties, the restaurant and bar and *calmly* ask visitors to get to their rooms for the night. Briggs let him know he needed to talk to the hospitality and room service staff before they left their shift. It was not an easy thing trying to gather evidence and piece things together in a vast hotel that was, by Mr. Sexton's estimation, two thirds full for the night.

Nate Blankenship was just finishing up with the first body and was heading up to Dane's room. Briggs instructed Officer Clark to not pick up or move anything until he returned.

Sexton had confirmed that the room next door to Dane's was vacant. There was a connecting door between the two rooms. Briggs opened it and ushered Clive through to hear his story. Before Briggs followed him through, I pulled him aside and whispered what I knew about the two victims and Clive.

"From snippets I heard while helping set up the reunion, Riley, Dane and Clive were best friends. They were also bullies, getting a great deal of joy out of making fun of and teasing their classmates."

Briggs leaned his head closer. "In other words, people didn't think too highly of them."

"Only those poor souls who are inexplicably drawn to bullies. And you know every bully has their group of fans."

Briggs' mouth turned up on the side. "You should become a psychologist." He reached forward and brushed his fingers against my hand, sending a warm tingle up my arm, before walking into the next room where Clive was waiting.

I hung out near the open door, watching as Nate prepared to examine Dane's body. Clive was a naturally loud speaker. If I tilted my head enough, I could catch most of the conversation.

"I'll start by saying that Riley, Dane and I were close friends in high school. We were, well, let's just say we were rambunctious. We occasionally teased the other kids. You know, just for fun."

I rolled my eyes on my side of the door.

"Fun for who?" Briggs asked.

I smiled at Briggs' perfect response. (As if I needed any more reason to adore him.)

Clive was too rattled to notice the sarcasm. "I know we could get mean occasionally and a few people were always targets. But there was still no reason for Grady Ramone to commit murder."

I stifled a gasp and inched closer to the room. I had no doubt Briggs felt me hovering in the doorway, but Clive didn't seem to notice. He was too busy tossing out accusations. Grady seemed like a genuinely decent guy. He'd already suffered enough at the hands of Clive and his pals. Now it seemed he was going to be cast as a murderer as well.

"I've got proof it was Grady," Clive said. I couldn't stop myself from moving close enough to see into the room. Clive was digging out his phone and standing at an angle that faced away from the door. Briggs' brown gaze flickered my direction before returning his attention to Clive.

"You have evidence connecting this person, Grady Ramone, to Dane's death and Riley's fall from the balcony?" Briggs asked as Clive pulled up something on his phone.

"Not to their deaths but to my near attack. And it's easy enough to connect the dots. Grady must have killed them after his failed attempt to kill me." He held up his phone. "Take a look at this picture. I was in the hallway at my room door and a very distinctive shadow appeared on the wall next to the door. The person was standing right behind me. I snapped a quick picture and swung around to greet the person but they were gone."

Briggs took hold of the phone. I badly wanted to be in the room, looking at the picture. Knowing how unsatisfied curiosity could make me bananas, Briggs kindly described what he was looking at. "It seems to be the outline of a jester's hat," Briggs said louder than necessary for my benefit.

I was once again stunned. Grady was definitely wearing a jester's hat. It was an impressively made costume from top to bottom. Could it be that the class valedictorian and successful engineer had been so badly scarred mentally by the bullying he'd endured that he came to the reunion for revenge?

"Grady was the only person wearing a jester's costume," Clive continued. "At first, I'd taken the picture because I thought the shadow of the hat was kind of funny. When Grady had run off, I assumed it was because he didn't want to talk to me. We weren't exactly friends, you know? Dane could be particularly ruthless, especially when it came to Grady and Jessica Trumbo."

Briggs looked up from the phone. "Jessica Trumbo?" he asked.

Clive shrugged half-heartedly. "Yeah, I feel extra bad about her. She had a long nose and these big ears." He reached up and put his hands next to his own ears and waved them like elephant ears. "Sometimes we called her Dumbo. Mostly because of her name," he said in a weak point of defense. "Anyhow, Jessica died in a car accident a few years back."

"Do you know what time you took this picture?" Briggs asked.

"It was just after the guys and I split up to go to our rooms. We left the reunion around eight. It was a real dud. We decided to change out of our costumes and meet downstairs at nine to go to a bar."

"After the man in the jester's hat disappeared, what did you do next?" Briggs asked.

"I brushed the whole thing off as a failed prank and went inside my room. I answered a few emails and then headed in to shower off makeup and hair gel. I was Dracula," he added. "I don't know how women do it. Took me forever to get all that stuff off."

A scoffing sound popped out before I could stop it. The dimwit was under the illusion that all women caked themselves in theatrical makeup just to look presentable.

"I don't think women generally walk around in vampire makeup and hair gel," Briggs said. (Earning yet another gold star on a long list of gold stars.)

"What happened after your long shower?" Briggs asked.

"When I got out, I heard all the chaos and the emergency sirens and figured something was up." He shook his head and his face dropped. "Never could I have imagined that it was my two friends." He took a moment to collect himself before continuing. "That's when I decided that Grady must have been sneaking up to hurt me."

"But you didn't see a weapon or anything else to lead you to that conclusion. Just his shadow behind you?"

Clive's laugh had a touch of anger. "Isn't that enough? After all, he ran when I turned around."

Briggs rubbed his chin in thought. "But you didn't see him running down the hallway?"

Clive was ready with his answer. "Room 420, my room, is on a corner. He must have dashed around it before I saw him. Like I said, I figured it was just a prank. Ramone was always kind of the nerdy guy in class. He was into things like comic books and practical jokes. Just never would have counted him as a killer."

"Alleged killer," Briggs reminded him. "So far all we have is your picture. Please refrain from starting any rumors and let us do our investigation."

"What should I do in the meantime?" he asked sharply. "After all, it's my neck on the line. My two best friends are dead. It's easy to conclude there is some kind of theme here."

Briggs was still holding the phone. "Do you mind if I send this picture to my phone?"

"Not at all. Especially if it'll help nail Grady—if he's guilty, of course," he said with a touch of sarcasm. It seemed Clive had already wrapped the whole thing up and put a guilty tag on Grady Ramone.

"I'll have Officer Clark escort you back to your room. Just make sure to lock the door. I'll be in touch with you shortly." Briggs quickly typed his number into Clive's phone to send the picture. "And now you'll have my direct number. Just call if anything seems off or suspicious. I'll be in the hotel for the next few hours."

"I hope you're not leaving before you catch the guy. Otherwise, I'm out of here. I'm not sticking around to get knocked off too." It seemed he'd recuperated from the shock and sadness of his friends' deaths quickly. He was in full defense mode.

Briggs paused. "Is there anyone else here, aside from Grady, who might have had a vendetta against the three of you?"

Clive shook his head. "Like I said, we were kind of tough on a few people, but Grady and Jessica were always our main targets."

Briggs nodded. "Any regrets now about bullying your classmates?" I was stunned and pleased by his question.

Clive stuttered over a few syllables. "Uh-uh, I—I don't think we were bullies. Like I said, we were rambunctious. That's all."

"Mr. Jergens, I have a large puppy who lopes around the house pushing over lamps and chewing on furniture. That's rambunctious. Calling a young girl Dumbo to remind her that she has large ears, an attribute I'm sure she was well aware of—that's bullying."

Clive's mouth was sealed shut in a straight line as they walked out. I shuffled out of the way and made it seem as if I'd been watching the coroner all along.

Briggs turned to Clive again. "Since the victims were good friends, I assume you know who we should contact for next of kin."

Clive nodded. He was still recovering from Briggs' words. "Uh, I suppose their parents. Dane was single and Riley was divorced. Twice," he added.

"If you can give the names and phone numbers of the parents to Officer Clark when you get back to the room, we'll take care of notifying them. Unless that's something you want to take care of?"

Clive's face smoothed to pale marble at the suggestion. "No, no absolutely not. I haven't spoken to any of them for several years."

"Officer Clark, can you escort Mr. Jergens back to his room and see that he gets safely inside? In fact, do a quick search of the room before he enters. And get the next of kin information."

"Right away, sir." Clark escorted Clive out the door. Before Briggs could get caught up in a conversation with Nate, I grabbed his hand and tugged him my way.

"First, let me represent bullied kids everywhere by saying thank you. That was brilliant."

Briggs pulled his mouth to the side in disbelief. "You were bullied?"

"I'm a little insulted you don't remember," I said, placing hands on hips and then looking cross eyed down at my nose to remind him.

"Ah, that's right. You couldn't eat because you could smell too many things around you. You were so skinny, the other kids thought you were sickly."

"Yes, exactly, and I can tell you that after hearing the phrase stick figure Lacey a few times, I was filled with anger. But if I met Terrence Connnor, the boy who loved to tease me, at a ten year reunion, I don't think murder would cross my mind. Especially if I was extremely successful like Grady Ramone. He was valedictorian and he's head engineer at NASA. Who wouldn't love to show up to their reunion and rub that shiny chunk of achievement in people's faces?"

Briggs nodded. "That does seem like a much gentler and more effective plan of revenge." He pulled out his phone. "But then there's this photo." He tapped open the picture and held it up for me to see.

The picture was at an odd angle and caught mostly the shadow on the wall. The overhead lights showed a silhouette on the wall that was clearly the outline of Grady's jester hat. It was cropped so that you could only see the hat in the shadow.

"There's no denying that it's a jester's hat, and I know that Grady was dressed as a jester." I tapped my chin in thought.

"What's ping ponging through that constantly calculating head of yours?" Briggs asked.

I dropped my hand. "If you were about to sneak up and kill someone, would you wear a large, highly visible hat? Seems like it might get in the way."

Briggs winked. "Good point."

"I'm just getting started but I'd say this man died in the last hour to two hours," Nate piped up from across the room.

"That's what I figured." Briggs turned back to me. "Looks like Nate is going to be here for awhile. Do you want to stay? I'll be here late. I could get one of the officers to drive you home if you're tired."

I tilted my head. "A double murder complete with jester hats and bodies falling off balconies. What do you think?"

"Right. Let's go over to Riley's room and look around."

CHAPTER 16

$\mathcal{T}$wo uniformed officers were standing watch in the room, waiting for Detective Briggs' orders. "Detective Briggs," the older officer with leathery skin, as if he'd spent a lot of time in the sun, came forward. "On your orders, we've looked around but haven't touched anything. There's a small metal table on the balcony that's been turned on its side, showing a possible sign of trouble. As for neighboring rooms, the one to the right is vacant, and a couple is staying in the one on the left. They were out to dinner when the victim fell, so they didn't hear anything. Nothing else seems out of place, unless you count the zombie mask sitting on the bathroom sink." He leaned his head toward his partner. "Gave us both a good startle," he chuckled.

"Thank you, Officer Tremaine. I'll take it from here. If you would, could you find one of the hotel guests for me? His name is Grady Ramone. He was here for the Rockmore Reunion. Let him know I want to talk to him."

"Absolutely." The two officers walked out.

The glass door to the balcony was half open. Briggs and I walked out into the moonlit night. A fresh breeze wafted through the tall alder trees dotting the hotel grounds. "This was supposed to be a nice romantic evening," Briggs said quietly.

"I just sat behind my *easy rider* boyfriend on the back of a motorcycle, and even though I was smiling ear to ear for the entire ride, I didn't get one bug caught between my teeth. I'd say that qualifies as romantic."

"That's what I like about you. No wild expectations and you're easily pleased."

I took his hand. "Besides, any time I spend with you is romantic as far as I'm concerned."

"Said the woman standing on a balcony overlooking a large smear of blood on the sidewalk below," he quipped.

"True. The murders sort of take the shine off, but at least you're including me in the investigation. There was a time when I had to sneak around to find out clues."

He smiled at me as he pushed a curl off my face. "If that was your idea of sneaking around, then I don't recommend cat burglar as a profession. And why wouldn't I include you in the investigation? I've never worked with someone as dialed in as you are. Then, of course, there's Samantha. Can't forget how often she's popped in to save the day."

"Only I didn't get a chance to sniff Riley's body," I reminded him.

Briggs nodded. "I decided to spare you that one. Falls from high places always produce gruesome injuries. The back of his skull was basically obliterated by the pavement. I'll make sure you can examine his clothes once they are in evidence. If it's even necessary." Briggs surveyed the balcony. "Unless Riley was stumbling drunk, the overturned table is a pretty good indication that, like his friend Dane, he put up a fight. Nate is going to take tissue samples from under his fingernails to see if he managed to scrape some skin off his attacker."

I stood at the balcony railing. It was made up of the popular white coated composite lumber that people used for fences and gates. The top railing was wider than the balusters running perpendicular to the deck. The entire railing came to my waist. "This is a fairly short guard rail. If Riley was your height or even a few inches shorter, it seems like it would be fairly easy to fall over the top. There would be more weight on top than on bottom with the railing at this height."

"Still, it would take someone with a good amount of strength. You've seen Grady Ramone. Is he a big guy?"

"I'd say he's pretty average. Not small. Not big." I shrugged. "Guess that's not very helpful." I snapped my fingers. "Wait. Here's something. Debra mentioned that Grady had a black belt in karate."

"That would certainly make him a formidable opponent in a fight." He added that fact to his notebook. "I'll have to ask him about that. I'll be talking to him soon enough." Aside from the overturned table there was nothing else of note on the balcony. The hotel was well kept and the balcony was free of dust, leaving little chance of finding footprints.

Briggs walked around the room, looking in drawers and at Riley's belongings. I headed into the bathroom. Since Riley had been wearing the mask earlier in the evening, it was the one item I could think of that might contain some clues for my nose to pick up.

I hopped back as I turned on the bathroom light. I'd been expecting it, yet the mask, with its hollow eyes, gaunt face and decaying skin was frightening. Riley had it sitting upright, leaning against the mirror as if it were a disembodied head. I poked my head out of the bathroom. Briggs was searching through Riley's phone.

"James, is it all right if I pick up the Halloween mask to give it a smell? I can put it right back in the same place."

He pulled his attention from the phone screen. "Yes, that's fine."

I walked out. "Did you find something on his phone?"

"No, it's just he received a text from Dane at 8:04." Briggs read the text aloud. "Hey, got the munchies after that joint. I'm going to order some cookies and drinks if you want to head over here before we meet Clive downstairs. Riley shot back the thumbs up emoji. That's the last text he sent."

"Guess that explains the odd combination of cookies and liquor."

"Wonder why he didn't invite Clive," Briggs said.

"Debra told me that Dane and Riley were business partners. It's easy to assume that they were closer to each other than to their third counterpart. Plus, they might have figured Clive was going to take a long time to get out of his costume. You know, because of *all that makeup* like we women wear."

Briggs laughed. "The man did display an incredible amount of ignorance in one short interview."

"I'm just going to give Samantha a whirl around that disgusting zombie mask." I walked back into the bathroom. The rubbery dead skin of the mask stretched and bent as I picked it up. A thudding sound hit the tile vanity as I lifted the mask. The unexpected noise startled me into briefly imagining the mask had groaned in complaint. As I lifted the latex face up, I discovered Riley had propped it on top of a shampoo bottle, possibly to help keep its shape. I didn't know much about Halloween masks, but one that was so realistic and detailed had to cost a pretty penny. Of course, not as many shiny pennies as a Rolex watch. I wondered if there was anything of value missing from Riley's room. If the murderer had been after Dane's watch, why would he have needed to kill Riley too?

As anticipated, my olfactory cells were overwhelmed with the smell of rubber and latex. The shredded neck around the bottom of the mask had the faint smell of aftershave, the same fragrance I smelled when I walked into the bathroom. It made sense that the fragrance was stuck to the neck portion of the mask if Riley had splashed it on after shaving. I held the mask upside down and lowered my face toward the opening. Two deep breaths resulted in the same latex odor, and the earthy fragrance that I smelled on the shampoo bottle. There was nothing else of note and no smells that were out of place. I lowered the mask back onto the shampoo bottle. It stared up at me with deep, hollow eyes. Its distorted, blood covered mouth gaped open, as if it was about to bite a brain. I shivered once at the sight of it and found myself rushing back out to Briggs.

Briggs caught my sudden rush. "Did you find something?"

"No, unfortunately. That mask is so creepy, I scared myself."

Briggs had a good chuckle about my confession. "Nate texted that he's about to move the body. I told him to hold off so you can give it a once over. So far, there's not much to lead to any suspects."

"Other than the jester hat picture and Grady's possible motive," I noted.

"Yes. Officer Clark did locate Grady Ramone. We'll go see him after we revisit the second murder site. Are you tired yet?"

I shook my head. "Nope. Just getting my nose warmed up."

CHAPTER 17

he murder weapon, in this case the thin cord to a phone charger, was just being dropped into an evidence bag as we walked into Dane's room.

"Wait," I said too abruptly to Officer Tremaine as he held the cord between tweezers. "I just need to smell that cord."

Officer Tremaine looked at Briggs for a rational explanation.

"Please hold onto that cord with the tweezers so Miss Pinkerton can smell it." Briggs' response left enough holes to cause the officer's thick brows to bunch into fuzzy caterpillars.

I ignored the quizzical expression and moved my nose along the length of the wire. I was unsure that I'd be able to smell anything on the narrow casing over the cord but was surprised how many scents I picked up. There was aftershave identical to the kind Riley had been wearing. It made sense that the two men might wear the same brand. It was a good, expensive fragrance too. The slightest hint of the metallic smell of blood wafted up from the center of the cord. It made sense if the cord had tightened and dug into Dane's neck. It was also possible his fingertips bled as he tried to pry the cord from his neck. There was one more scent, an oily scent that I couldn't match to anything in my vast mental encyclopedia of odors.

Officer Tremaine was apparently entertained by my sniffing session. His suppressed smile twittered in his face, wanting badly to break free.

I nodded politely at him. "Thank you so much. You can continue."

"Tremaine, when you're done with that, I need you to search this room and the victim's belongings for a Rolex watch." Briggs looked questioningly at me for more detail.

"It's gold with a silver dial," I added.

Briggs and I walked over to Nate. "No question that he died from strangulation," Nate said. "The red fingertips show he was working hard to break free of the cord. I don't see any other sign of struggle, but I'll know more when I get him on the table." Nate looked at the room service cart with the bottle of whiskey and cookies. "The odor of alcohol is faint, but perhaps you'd like the master nose to take a tour before I put him on the gurney." Nate had seen me at enough crime scenes to know all about my hyperosmia.

I walked to where Dane was stretched out on the carpet. Nate had moved his body so that he was flat on his back. I caught a whiff of his aftershave, the same scent I smelled on the cord and on Riley's mask. I lowered my nose inches above his face and then trailed it along his chest. It was always a little surreal being so intimately close to someone who was no longer living and breathing. It felt slightly wrong, rude, as if I was invading his personal space. Then there was always that terrifying, creeping feeling that the body presumed dead might suddenly move. That unsettling fear came from watching one too many horror movies and from the fact that, aside from the unnatural pallor of his complexion, the body was still a solid, muscular man who looked capable of movement.

Laundry detergent, soap, aftershave fragrances were mingling in my saturated olfactory cells. Just like with Riley's mask, nothing smelled out of place. I swept my nose back up and caught a whiff of something different. "Garlic," I muttered to myself. Sometimes, it was as if I was having a quiet conversation with my nose, as if we were two separate entities. "And lemon," I continued. "Garlic *and* lemon."

"What's that?" Briggs asked.

I sat back on my knees and peered up at him. "I smell garlic and lemon. They're not two separate aromas but rather they are layered on top of each other."

Nate clucked his tongue. "That has to be most talented nose this side of the Rockies."

Briggs grinned with pride as he gazed down at me. "The whole woman, nose and all, is pretty darn talented."

My cheeks warmed as I leaned down to smell along the sweater sleeves and Dane's hands. "A bit more of the garlic, lemon mixture." I reached his hand where the imprint of his missing watch was slowly fading. I smelled a stronger whiff of the same garlic, lemon mixture on his hands. There was also the light scent of marijuana on his fingers, a plant that had a distinctively skunk-like smell. It was not surprising considering Dane's last text to Riley mentioned a joint and munchies.

I reached my hand up, and Briggs popped me to my feet. "The only thing that seems out of place is the garlic, lemon smell. It's on his sweater and his hands."

"Do you know what kind of food they were eating at the party?" Briggs asked. "Wait," he continued before letting me answer. "It was Italian. That's why we changed our dinner plans."

"Yes. I saw pizza and lasagna and garlic bread. Not sure where the lemon comes in. But that doesn't explain why I'm smelling it on his sweater. Dane came down to the party dressed as Prince Charming." I walked over to the bed. The costume had been checked for evidence but not bagged up yet. I picked up the blue coat and red cape and ran my nose around the fabric. There was a mix of smells, including garlic, tomato sauce and even beer. I put the costume back on the bed. "That's strange. I can smell the garlic again, but this time there's no lemon. It makes sense that his prince costume would smell like Italian food, but it doesn't explain why the aroma is on his sweater."

Nate patted his chest with both hands. "What if he tapped his chest frantically as the cord went around his neck? It could have come off his hands. Maybe he wasn't big on napkin use."

"That's very possible," I said. "Well, I'm finished with the nasal inspection."

"Briggs, how do you want me to take this body out of the hotel? Maybe the manager has the best route where we won't be seen by many people."

"Right," Briggs said as he walked to the hotel phone. "I'll give him a call and see what he suggests."

While Briggs made the call, I perused the room. The room service cart had been untouched, except it seemed both high ball glasses had been removed for evidence. The plate of cookies sat sadly in the middle of a white linen napkin. I stooped down next to it just to take a whiff around the items on the cart. My nose stopped short on the handle of the cart. "There you are again," I muttered. The lemon and garlic were slapped together in one fragrant aroma. A perfectly plausible explanation was that Dane grabbed the handle and transferred the lemon and garlic to the cart when he moved it to the corner of the room.

I walked across the carpet. Dane's reunion nametag was sitting on an itinerary for the weekend. Debra had the entire two day event planned out and printed neatly on stationary that was lined with the Rockmore Royals colors and school motto. After today's meet and greet luncheon, with the hyacinth centerpieces, the classmates were to enjoy a ghoulish night of festivities at the costume ball. She even had a costume contest planned for later in the evening. Poor Debra had worked so hard on this. The culminating event was to take place tomorrow morning with a Sunday brunch put on by Katrina's Elegant Edibles.

I moved the itinerary and picked up a card that was framed by bright orange jack-o'-lanterns. Listed in the center, in a creepy font, were the foods on the party menu. Various pizzas, lasagna, spaghetti and meatballs, green salad and garlic bread. Desert was fudgy brownie sundaes. I was no chef but I couldn't understand where the lemon came in on the dinner menu.

Briggs finished his phone call. "The manager is coming up here to lead you to the service elevator and out the back entrance. That way you can avoid standing in a guest elevator with a dead body. He also preferred to not have the gurney rolled through the lobby," he said dryly. "He's asked the guests to stay in their rooms, but he can hardly enforce that. It's been a long time since I've been to a double homicide . . . thankfully. It's hard to keep track of it all," he said with a sigh. The long night was starting to get to him. He looked weary.

"I think we're looking at the first victim—" Nate started. "I think the balcony victim died after this man was strangled. After examining both of them, I'd say they died at almost the same time, but I think this victim has been dead longer. Rigor mortis was just starting to set in on this man. Of course, I got to him last, so it's hard to know for sure. But I'm solid in my conclusion that they died just a short time apart from each other."

"Yes," Briggs agreed. "All the events, including the alleged near-attack on Clive, all seemed to occur between eight and nine. And that's about the only thing I know for certain. There's an entire hotel of guests and workers who could be possible suspects, but I think we'll start with the man who wore a jester hat to the Halloween party." Briggs turned to me. "I'm sure you aren't anxious to watch the removal of the body. I've heard from Officer Clark. He's with Grady Ramone, waiting for questioning. Are you still with me? You look a little tired."

"I was just about to say the same thing to you. Maybe we can get some coffee down in hospitality after you finish talking to Grady," I suggested.

"Yep. Or maybe Grady will confess to everything and that will bring a swift end to an otherwise long night."

I took his arm as we walked out into the hall. "I always love an optimist."

CHAPTER 18

*N*ot wanting to alarm Grady or let on that he'd been implicated in a double murder,, Briggs arranged to meet him downstairs in the lobby's coffee bar. It was also a convenient way for each of us to get a reviving cup of coffee. Since Grady and I had met and had a friendly conversation, he didn't seem averse to having me sit at the table with them once Briggs introduced me as his girl-friend. Since the party ended abruptly several hours earlier, Grady had changed out of costume and into a pair of pants and a t-shirt. He'd pulled on a navy blue cap with the NASA logo.

I hugged my cup of coffee in both hands and took a sip. My sigh caught both men's attention. "Sorry, it just tasted so good." I smiled coyly.

Briggs motioned toward the hat. "Lacey tells me you work for NASA. I always dreamed of working for NASA. I'm afraid my math skills had different ideas for my future."

Grady reached up and tapped the logo. "Yes, it was always a dream of mine too. Although, I'm one of those guys who sits behind the computer and not inside the space capsule. But I get about as close to it as a civilian can. And on a good day, I get to eat lunch with astronauts."

Briggs lifted his coffee. "Very cool." Briggs was a pro at getting people to relax when he questioned them, only I was certain Grady would figure out quickly that this wasn't just a friendly chat about his awesome job.

Grady fingered his cup but didn't lift it for a drink. "The officer said you needed to see me concerning the—" He paused and lost some of the color in his face. "Are they really both dead? Riley and Dane?"

"I'm afraid so," Briggs said.

"That's terrible." Grady's expression saddened some. "I knew them, of course. But I'm not sure how I can help you."

"Mr. Ramone, can you tell me what you wore to the costume party?"

The first question threw Grady for a loop, and an involuntary laugh shot from his mouth. "That's why you needed to see me? To find out my costume choice?" The set of his jaw grew more tense as it seemed to dawn on him that the question was serious. He sat forward. "I wore a custom made jester's costume. Lacey saw it earlier in the evening." He added to show that he was certain Briggs already knew what he wore.

He reached for his phone, rather suddenly, and with the late night and double murder, the movement caused Briggs to straighten to attention. Grady noticed his defensive reaction and his expression grew grim. "Trust me, Detective Briggs, we scientists rarely walk around with a weapon in our belts," he said snidely. He pulled out his phone. "Here's a picture of me in the costume."

Briggs seemed slightly ashamed of his reaction but said nothing of it. He looked at the picture. "It's a nice costume."

Grady sat back on the chair and put down the phone. "Yeah, so nice that someone stole the hat. It seems some people never outgrow high school."

"When was the hat stolen?" Briggs asked.

"Not exactly sure. I guess around seven thirty. I'd finished my dinner and headed to the restroom. I took the hat off and put it on the marble counter in the lounge area around the corner from the bath-room stalls. Thought it might get in the way." His slightly embarrassed gaze flicked my direction. I picked up my coffee and pretended to only be half-listening.

"And that's when it went missing?" Briggs asked.

"Yes, I used the restroom, washed up and headed out. My head was spinning with the night's activities. I absentmindedly walked through the lounge and out of the restroom. It wasn't until I got back to the party and someone asked where my hat was that I remembered I'd left it in the restroom. I hurried back but it was gone. I think someone took it while I was using the restroom. That's why it was so easy for me to walk out without it. It's a large, colorful hat. It would have been hard to miss, even with my head filled with conversations and class-mates. But since it wasn't there, I streamed right past without giving it another thought." He smiled weakly. "It's not as if I usually pick up my jester's hat on the way out of the restroom."

Briggs nodded with a grin. "I suppose NASA would frown on you showing up to work dressed as a jester."

We all had a short laugh, then Grady looked at Briggs. "Detective, I still don't understand why I'm being questioned about my evening, or my hat, for that matter."

I sensed that Briggs was not ready to mention Clive's picture yet. But he had another plausible angle to work from. "Mr. Ramone, it's come to my attention that you were—" he hesitated looking for the right way to phrase it. Grady stepped in to fill the void. (He was, after all, class valedictorian.)

"Tormented, bullied and harassed by the two victims?" Grady asked plainly.

"Yes." Briggs answered even more plainly. Bullying wasn't really something you could soften up with flowery language.

"Clive, Riley and Dane took every opportunity to make me miser-able. They tried to make me feel small and an outcast, but in truth, they were the outcasts. Sure people pretended to like and admire them, but that was only out of fear. With those three, it was a 'you're either with us or against us' type of mentality. I was the top student in the class. I knew I sure as heck didn't need to be *with* them, so I always made it clear I was against them. And they made me suffer for it."

Grady looked at both of us. "I know this is wrong to say so close to their deaths, but maybe those two got what they had coming."

Briggs didn't comment. He let Grady continue without interruption.

"Since the party was obviously over, a bunch of us were helping Debra collect up some of the decorations. We were absorbing the news that Riley had fallen to his death from the hotel balcony when we got word that Dane was dead too. People were stunned, but I can tell you without hesitation that not one tear was shed for either of them. That's the legacy they left behind. A group of classmates who couldn't work up even one tear at their loss. Of course, I haven't seen Clive all night. I would think this has hit him pretty hard."

That was Briggs' cue, it seemed. He sat forward and pulled out his phone. "Actually, that's something I wanted to ask you about," he said as he thumbed through to the picture.

Grady's curious gaze landed on the phone. It seemed he couldn't imagine what a detective might have on his phone that would have to do with him.

"First, exactly when was the last time you saw Clive Jergens?" Briggs asked.

Grady rubbed the side of his jaw. "Wasn't really paying attention. To be frank, I was trying to avoid contact with any of them. I guess I saw him in the food line. That was just after seven. All three of them were piling their plates with food and laughing so loud no one could hear their own conversations."

Briggs pulled out his notebook and wrote a few things down. I'd witnessed many times how when the notebook came out the defenses went up. Grady was no different.

He shifted on his chair. "I don't understand. Am I on some kind of suspect list just because I hated the guys?"

"Hate can be a motive for murder," Briggs said. "But I'm just collecting statements and evidence right now. There is no suspect list yet."

Briggs' explanation didn't seem to lessen his worry. Grady fiddled with brim of his cap adjusting it lower over his face. "I can't even kill a spider without feeling remorse for a week," he said lightly, but there was a nervous edge in his tone.

"I walk a wide berth around a trail of ants," I confessed. Grady smiled weakly at my attempt to lighten the tension that seemed to be building around the table.

"Did you see Clive or his friends after you left the buffet line?" Briggs asked. He was clutching his phone, apparently looking for the right time to spring the incriminating picture on him.

"No. We hung out with different people in high school. It was no different tonight at the reunion. They went their way and I went mine. Never saw any of them after that."

Briggs cleared his throat and repositioned himself to face Grady more. "Clive Jergens claims to have taken this picture outside his room just after eight."

It took Grady a few moments to figure out he was looking at a shadow of his jester hat. He handed the phone back to Briggs. "I don't understand. So the silhouette of my hat showed up on a wall. Why is that significant?"

"Clive said he saw the shadow and thought it was funny. He took the picture and then turned around, assuming you were going to play a prank on him. But whoever was wearing the hat raced away out of sight. Clive went in to shower and when he got out, he discovered that not one but two of his friends were dead. He concluded that you might have been there to do him harm as well."

Grady's expression was a mix of confusion and disbelief. "That's ridiculous. Besides, I told you, the hat was stolen when I used the restroom. I haven't seen it since. I figured because I had a Hollywood costume designer sew the hat, someone decided it was valuable and took it. Guess I shouldn't have been bragging about who made it."

"Then you weren't at Clive's room around eight o'clock, waiting to either play a joke on him or do him harm?" Briggs asked.

"Absolutely not. I have everything I want in life. Why would I throw all that away just for revenge on a couple of rubber headed high school bullies?"

"One more thing," Briggs asked. "Did you come straight back here after the restroom, after you saw your hat was missing? And do you have names of people who saw you at the party at eight?

Grady paused to think about the question. "I headed back to the party to look for my hat. I thought someone might have found it and was waiting to return it. No one had seen it." He reached up and adjusted his cap again. "The costume hat made my hair look flat and funny, so I went back up to my room for this. I stayed there for a half hour or so just to relax. I get overwhelmed in big parties with lots of people."

"So you had no contact with anyone, someone who could corroborate your whereabouts between eight and eight thirty."

"I guess that's about when I was in my room. So no. I told you I was resting, taking a break from socializing and people." He sat forward. "Look, I hope you catch who did this, but you're wasting your time with me. Obviously, whoever stole my hat was up to no good. I'm not going to mourn Dane and Riley's loss, but I certainly would never commit murder." He pushed his chair out.

"I hope you don't mind but I'll be sending Officer Clark with you to your room just to do a quick search for the jester's hat."

Grady did seem to mind. His mouth straightened into a thin line. "No problem. I hope he finds it for me. It cost me a lot of money."

"Thank you for your time, Mr. Ramone," Briggs said.

CHAPTER 19

*T*hus far, my nose hadn't given us any good leads. Briggs and I headed down to the hospitality kitchen that supplied room service to the hotel guests. Since an unenforceable curfew was placed on the guests, Mr. Sexton, the hotel manager, wisely offered room service for fifty percent off. Because of the discount and people reluctant to leave their rooms, the hospitality workers were too busy to stop and answer questions.

The woman in charge of room service for the night, Ms. Acton, took a few minutes out of her chaotic shift to check the name of the server who delivered the cookies and drinks to Dane's room. Briggs and I worked hard to stay clear of the foot traffic and carts being wheeled in and out of the hospitality kitchen, but it wasn't easy.

We pressed against a wall as yet another cart covered with silver plate domes and baskets of bread rolled past.

"I guess people decided to take advantage of cheap room service," I noted. "I'll bet most of them had dinner long before they were asked to go to their rooms. They just wanted to order something because the bargain was too good to pass up." I looked over at Briggs. "Like when I buy oodles of paper towels because they are half off and then I quickly discover that I have no place to store them. That still doesn't stop me from repeating the bulk buy. Mostly because the bargain is too good to pass up."

A young man with his white coat unbuttoned and the flaps flying behind him like the coat of mad scientist ripped past us with an empty cart. Briggs had to scoot his feet back out of the way or risk getting his toes run over.

"I guess we've begun the really romantic part of our evening out," Briggs said.

"No, that came while we were examining a dead body for evidence." A cart rolled past with three slices of cheesecake. "Yum, that looked good. I'm trying to figure out what I'd order if I was told everything on the menu was half off. I suppose cheesecake would probably be on the list." I laughed as a funny story came to me. "I just remembered when my two friends and I took a weekend trip to a hotel on the beach. My friend, Donna, got the place for free. Her parents had to cancel their trip, so they let us go instead. We were such silly girls. We didn't realize that room service was extra, and the hotel had cleverly, and underhandedly, not listed any prices. So we ordered a brunch fit for three queens. Eggs Benedict, croissants, strawberries and fresh squeezed orange juice." I pressed my arm against my stomach. "I'm hungry just thinking about it. We were such newbies to the adult world of hotel living, we thought a dollar was an appropriate tip for the server. He was not happy. Boy, did we turn green when were checking out, thinking everything was covered, only to be handed a bill for eighty-five dollars. Thought we were going to have to wash dishes or something just to get out of there. Fortunately, Donna's mother gave the clerk her card number. But we had to pay her back. Most expensive eggs I've ever eaten."

"Detective Briggs," a woman's voice called over the clatter of carts and trays and glasses. Ms. Acton, the woman in charge of the servers, came through the maze of carts to where we were standing. She had a piece of paper clutched in her hand. "The server who delivered the cookies and drinks to Room 511 is Nina." Ms. Acton stretched up her neck to look over the heads in the kitchen area. "I don't see her, so she's not back from her last delivery. She is easy to spot." Ms. Acton pulled her top lip down in disapproval. "She showed up to work today with blue streaks in her hair. I told her they had to come out before her next shift, but tonight, those blue streaks should help you spot her." The doors pushed open, and Ms. Acton's eyes rounded. "There she is. She just came back."

Briggs and I turned around. Nina was a tall girl with a short, spiky haircut. Just as Ms. Acton had mentioned, there were blue streaks running through her otherwise blonde hair.

"Nina, Nina," Ms. Acton had to practically yell over the din in the room. Nina spotted her boss and headed over. She had large green eyes that landed directly on Briggs. A pretty smile followed.

"Nina, Detective Briggs would like to talk to you about a delivery you made tonight."

Nina pushed her rolled white coat sleeves up exposing a trail of star tattoos on her wrist. "Which delivery?" she asked and bit her lip with concern as if she was suddenly facing the school principal.

"The cookies and liquor to Room 511." Briggs found he was having to yell. He looked at Ms. Acton. "Is there somewhere quieter we can talk? I'll have my assistant Miss Pinkerton with me, so we won't be alone."

Ms. Acton motioned the three of us to follow her to her office. "It's small, but if I close the door, you should at least be able to hear each other." She waved us inside.

"Thank you," Briggs said and shut the door to lock out the noise.

Nina was pushing nervously at her sleeve again. It seemed odd for her to be worried about just doing her job. Maybe it was knowing she was talking to a detective that made her antsy.

"Nina, right?" Briggs asked. I knew he always liked to use last names but wasn't given one. He hadn't even called me Lacey until we knew each other for several months.

"Yes," she said quietly as if she wasn't sure. "This is because that guy died in that room, isn't it?"

"Yes," Briggs said. I always knew when he was having to work to keep a straight face.

"I didn't have anything to do with it. I didn't even see the guy."

Briggs' face popped up. "But you delivered food to his room. Who answered the door?"

Nina fidgeted with her sleeves again and glanced around as if she was hoping someone would pull her away from the questions. "Uh, I'm not sure who opened the door."

"Can you describe the person?" Briggs asked. "Start with something simple, man or woman?" He was getting tired and maybe a touch cranky. I was feeling the same amount of weary frustration, and I wasn't doing the interview.

"It was a man, I guess," she shrugged and looked out the office window for a rescuer, but her coworkers were far too busy to notice or bother.

Briggs' posture tightened, indicating he was getting fed up. It was rare for him to become irritated with a witness, but it was late and it was entirely possible the strong cup of coffee did more harm than good. Or it might just have been the utter lack of cooperation from Nina.

He tried a different angle by retracing her steps. "So, room service got the call from Mr. Caputo, the guest in Room 511 at eight, and you were sent up to his room with cookies and drinks a few minutes later."

She didn't nod or respond.

"Is that correct or am I getting something wrong?"

Nina sensed the agitation in his voice, which prodded her to open up a little more. "That's what happened only—" She stopped there.

"Only?" Briggs urged her to continue.

Nina fidgeted with her sleeves again. Her hesitation caused Briggs to fidget as well. "Please explain," he said sharply.

"If I tell you, you can't mention anything to Ms. Acton, my boss. I'm already on her hit list, and she'll fire me for sure."

"I'll keep this between us," Briggs promised.

"While I was waiting for my next delivery, a woman, the caterer from the reunion, I think, had come in to ask Ms. Acton something. I think they'd run out of dishes in the caterer's kitchen or something like that. They talked for a few minutes. As the woman walked out, Ms. Acton shouted out my next delivery was for Caputo in Room 511. Mickey, the guy who makes sure the order is ready to go, rolled the cart out. I took it and headed out for delivery just like usual. I got to the service elevator. The caterer was waiting for it to open. We stepped into the elevator. That's when she approached me about delivering the cart up to the room herself."

Briggs and I exchanged perplexed glances. He turned back to Nina. "The caterer asked to deliver the cart to Room 511?" he asked slowly to make sure he was understanding.

A faint blush rose up along her neck. "She paid me ten dollars to let her do it. I took the money. That's why you can't tell my boss. She'd fire me if she knew."

"Did the caterer say why she wanted to pay you to do your job?" Briggs asked.

"Nope, just that she wanted to deliver that cart to Room 511. I offered to let her deliver some of my other room service orders too, but she didn't think that was funny. She was kind of uptight now that I think about it. I know she wasn't doing it to ease my burden, if you know what I mean." Now that the big confession was off her chest, Nina was free with her comments. "I guess she just wanted to meet the guy or something."

"What happened after you took the offer?" Briggs asked. He was reaching for his notebook.

"I handed off the cart. She got off the service elevator at the fifth floor. I tucked the money in with my tips and headed back here for the next order. That's the last I saw of her, the caterer, that is. Caterers who are hired for special events use a different kitchen. It's at the opposite end of this floor, past the meeting rooms. Has its own entrance and everything."

Briggs jotted a few notes down. "Thanks for your help, and I won't say anything about the ten dollars."

Nina flitted off, looking much more relaxed than a few minutes earlier.

"Looks like we need to talk to the caterer," Briggs said as we walked back out of the boisterous kitchen. "I wonder how the caterer is connected to all this."

CHAPTER 20

e headed across the hotel to the caterer's kitchen. The lobby was quiet and deserted. The guy behind the reception desk was stifling a yawn as we walked past. The scene at the front of the hotel was the direct opposite of the scene we'd just left in hospitality.

We were halfway to our next destination when I connected a few dots in my mind. "I just remembered an incident. Not sure if it's relevant or not."

We stopped in a quiet recess of the hallway.

"The name of the caterer is Katrina Jessup. She owns a business called Elegant Edibles. I learned that yesterday morning when Lola and I shamelessly showed up in Elsie's bakery to beg for cookie samples. I can tell you, sometimes the buttery, brown sugar bliss coming through my north wall is intoxicating but I digress. Katrina was there buying cookies for a snack at the reunion. Elsie was beaming with pride because apparently Katrina's business is very respected." I shook off that line of topic. "Oh my, I'm tired and I ramble when I'm tired."

Briggs' crooked smile turned up. "You're the only person I know who makes rambling adorable. But it's late, less ramble. How does this connect Katrina to Dane Caputo?"

"I was here helping with the pumpkins when Katrina carried the cookies in. Dane and Riley were in the room, not helping like the others but just standing around being in everyone's way. And Dane certainly got into Katrina's way, making a rude display of ogling her. He tried to block her from leaving, but she walked brusquely around him, ignoring his taunts."

"Did Dane touch her at all?" Briggs asked.

I thought about the incident for a moment. "No, he never went that far, thank goodness. She marched out angrily but then who wouldn't after that kind of uninvited attention."

"Did Riley join in with Dane on the harassment?"

"Not technically but there was a certain level of comradeship, a silent cheering on of sorts. Something tells me those two were ruder and more bold when they were together than alone. In fact, I had a similar but not quite as brazen incident with the two of them when I was delivering my flowers."

Briggs straightened his posture and his expression hardened. Moments earlier, the weariness of the long night showed in his face. Now, it looked as if he'd been shot with a dose of adrenaline. "What do you mean, Lacey? You never mentioned anything before. Did they touch you? Did they—"

I pressed my hand against his chest to stop him from firing off any more questions. "James, it was nothing. I didn't say anything or even remember my brush with them until just now when I recounted the story about the caterer."

My attempt to mollify his sudden mood change wasn't working as well as I expected. I continued. "They merely mistook me for someone else they went to school with and said some off handed remark about my appearance. It was, apparently, their way of being charming. And what does it matter now? They are both dead."

That stark reminder seemed to erase some of the tension. "You're right. It's late and the thought of someone being rude to you—"

"Wouldn't be the first time, James. But thank you. Now should we get to the caterer's kitchen before they close up for the night?" His reaction had me slightly overwhelmed. It was wonderful to feel safe and protected.

We walked in silence toward the caterer's kitchen, each of us perhaps absorbing the last few minutes. A light slipped through the bottom of the door leading to the caterer's kitchen and the distinct clang of pots and pans being put away let us know the team was just about cleaned up for the night.

The lingering aroma of the evening's buffet, garlic and onions struck me as we entered but Briggs didn't seem to notice, signaling that the smell was faint. At least for a normal nose.

As we passed the area that was dotted with two small utility sinks, the fragrance of lemon cut through the garlic and onion. My gaze landed on a bowl of lemon halves sitting near the sink.

Two women and a man were in the food preparation area filling storage bowls with cut vegetables and sliced strawberries. A boy who looked to be around eighteen could be seen through the window cut out leading to the dishwashing area. He was drying pots and stacking lids.

As I followed Briggs along the massive industrial stoves, we both immediately noticed our shoes were sticking to the cement floor. I lifted my feet exaggeratedly. "I must be extra tired because gravity seems to be working against me."

"The cleanup crew must have missed a spot," Briggs quipped.

I took another sticky step. Shoeprints and dirt were glued to the sticky substance. My nose was telling me maple syrup. "A really big spot."

The woman wearing the chef's coat noticed us staring down at the ground. "Watch your step there," she called as she approached us. "One of the assistants spilled a gallon of maple syrup earlier in the day and we've been dealing with it ever since." The woman wiped her hands on her apron. "I'm Anne, executive chef for Elegant Edibles, how can I help you? I don't generally like people walking through the kitchen, but as you can see, we're almost finished for the night."

Briggs pulled out his wallet and badge as she spoke.

She caught a glimpse of it, and before he could say a word she continued. "I assume this has something to do with the deaths. I have no idea how we can help. We're just the caterers."

"Actually, I'm interested in talking to the owner, Katrina Jessup."

That statement caused her eyes to pop. "Katrina? She's not here. It has to do with this sticky floor in fact. She left earlier to find an all night market. We need to replace the maple syrup before tomorrow's good-bye brunch."

"They're still going on with the brunch then?" I asked, unable to hide my surprise. Since there was no introduction, the chef seemed to assume I was also a detective. (And who was I to deny it?)

Chef Anne shrugged. "Food has been bought and paid for. And Debra, the woman in charge of the reunion, thought even though there was a tragedy, people would still be hungry before their trips home. Although she did caution us not to be surprised if there were a lot of leftovers. She expects many people to take off first thing in the morning to get away from the doomed reunion. Those were her words, not mine. Poor thing worked so hard to make it a successful weekend."

"When do you expect the owner back?" Briggs asked.

She pushed up the sleeve of her coat and looked at her watch. "Oh my, it's almost midnight. Where does the time go? She should be back soon. I can't tell you for certain."

Briggs pulled a card from his pocket. "Here's my number. Could you have her call me when she returns? And do you have her business card as well?"

Chef Anne swiveled her chin side to side. "Seems strange you need to talk to her so urgently. Anything wrong? In general, the guests seemed pleased with the food, even with the turn of events."

"I'm sure the food was fine. I just need to talk to Miss Jessup, so if you could let her know. I'll be in the building for a bit longer, so I'm available. If you could get me one of her cards?" Briggs was getting short and I couldn't blame him. The last thing he needed was a nosy coworker with prying questions.

Chef Anne eyed us both suspiciously for a second. "Sure, I'll get you a business card. But the rest of us are leaving in the next ten minutes. It's possible we won't see Katrina tonight."

"Surely you could text her the message," Briggs said curtly.

"Yes. Of course. I'll go do that just as soon as I get the business card."

While we waited, one of the other cooks sidled past us with a polite nod.

"Excuse me," I said to her.

She turned back to me and pushed her oversized hat back on her forehead.

"This is a silly question but were there any foods on the menu tonight that included both garlic and lemon?"

As expected, my question threw her. "Uh, tonight? No, not that I can think of. Plenty of garlic, of course but nothing with lemon. We have plenty of recipes with lemon. But we didn't use any tonight."

"The food was delicious, by the way," I said, reminding myself the occasional white lie was necessary. "I was just wondering because I thought I smelled lemon in the sauce. I thought maybe I was missing out on a key element in my own spaghetti sauce. I noticed the bowl of cut lemons over there."

The woman glanced back at the bowl of lemons near the sink. "Oh, we call those our garlic soaps. Whenever we're cutting a lot of garlic, the aroma stays on our hands. Fresh lemon is the best way to cut through it. Otherwise, everything we touch picks up the garlic smell."

"Brilliant. I'll have to try that in my own kitchen," I said cheerily.

Chef Anne returned with a business card. "I sent a text message to Katrina, but I haven't heard back from her yet. I'll leave a note and your card on her laptop just to be sure. My crew is tired and we'll be leaving soon."

"Of course." Briggs held up Katrina's lavender colored business card. "Thanks so much."

My shoes were still lightly gripping the cement floor of the kitchen as we walked out. It seemed the stickiness would be with us for awhile.

We stepped out of the kitchen and into the hallway. Briggs turned to me with his half grin. "I'm going to assume you weren't really interested in recipes or techniques for cleaning away garlic odor."

"Nope. I use spaghetti sauce from a jar. Much to my mother's dismay. Remember when I was sniffing around for evidence on Dane?"

He snapped his fingers. "That's right you mentioned something about garlic and lemon mixed together."

"Right. I figured if it was a food item, something in the buffet that contained the two ingredients, then it was a possible reason for the smells to show up on his sweater. Some people aren't great with napkins. Both lemon and garlic are strong. The aroma might have transferred to his sweater when he changed out of his costume. But nothing at the party contained the two ingredients. I definitely smelled them in combination as if they were layered together. Which means it had to be—"

"Someone from the kitchen," he finished enthusiastically. "It seems not only did Katrina deliver the cart to Dane's room, she must have had some sort of physical struggle with him."

"At the very least, she touched his sweater," I added. "Although maybe I misread her reaction when I thought she dismissed his comments earlier in the day."

"What are you suggesting?" Briggs asked. "That she went to his room to let him know she *was* interested?"

"Very interested, if her hands were all over his sweater."

"Or she went to tell him off and things got physical," Briggs said. "But did that lead to murder? Still doesn't make much sense. Not to mention it doesn't explain Riley's death at all. Or Clive's alleged near miss."

I sighed loudly. "That brainstorm session just made me exhausted."

"I can call an officer to take you home," Briggs said.

"And miss my ride home on the back of your motorcycle? Nice try, buddy." I moved my feet and still felt the maple syrup. It gave me an idea. "James, we should return to the two rooms."

"I was thinking the same thing," he said. "Maple syrup?"

"There would probably only be traces of it, and I'm sure it'll be hard to smell in the carpeting. At the very least, it would have left a sticky residue."

Briggs dropped his arm around my shoulder. "Do you ever stop being perfectly clever?"

"Sometimes," I smiled up at him. "When I really make an effort."

CHAPTER 21

*B*riggs and I headed toward the elevators. As we passed the room where the costume party had been held, I happened to glance in through a slightly open door. Debra was taking down some decorations.

I nudged Briggs and pointed her out. We made a detour into the room. The tables had all been cleared, but Halloween decorations still dotted the walls. Debra was on a chair pulling a large cardboard witch off the wall behind the empty buffet table.

"Debra, do you need some help?" I asked.

Debra turned around on the chair with the cardboard cutout dropping over her. I raced over to grab it from her, before she lost her balance.

"Thank you. I purchased most of these decorations with my own money so I figured I'd save them before the hotel workers tore them down. I live on a street that gets hundreds of trick or treaters. Thought I'd hang them up on my porch."

Briggs had wandered over to a table where some pictures were fanned out. "Miss Geppler," Briggs called from across the room.

"Debra, please," she said as she hopped down from the chair. "The photographer printed some of those out for us on his portable printer.

294

Of course, they were all taken before—" She stopped there, not needing to go further.

Briggs held up one. "These group shots—do you know when they were taken? I see there are quite a few of them."

Debra and I joined Briggs. "Yes, I divided everyone according to different clubs." She patted a yearbook that was sitting next to the display of pictures. "I thought it would be fun, for example, to see the girls' softball team standing together. Only instead of royal blue uniforms, they are in costume." She picked up a photo of seven women standing arm in arm. "Not everyone from the team was here of course but it was still fun to see them together. The photographer was patient enough for me to call together the various groups. I made sure that everyone was in at least one group picture." She picked up a photo with a nurse, a witch, a lumberjack and an alien. "We called it the *no club* group picture." She moved the pictures around on the table. "They turned out nicely but then no one is really interested in seeing them now. I thought I'd just lay them out for people to peruse. I didn't want to bother anyone about them." She made a sort of ho hum sound. I patted her on the shoulder.

Briggs continued his interest in the photos. "The photographer took one picture with the three friends, Clive, Dane and Riley." He showed us the image. The three were standing in front of the straw and pumpkin display. Riley was holding his gory mask. They looked as if they were howling up at an invisible moon.

"I noticed that one. It's sad to think just a few hours ago they were playing around and now they're dead," Debra said.

"Do you know when this was taken?" Briggs asked. "In fact, do you know what time any of them were taken?"

"I'm certain the photographer can tell you exact times, but I do remember the three friends howling." She stopped herself short of an eye roll. "Even ten years later those three craved attention, any attention. Even negative attention. They made such an annoying clamor with their howls, my friend Jessie and I couldn't hear ourselves talk. Jessie was telling me how much she enjoyed the meal. That was at about seven. I remember glancing at the clock because I knew it was almost time to start the group photos."

Briggs sifted through the pictures casually. "So the group photos happened around . . ." He left the blank for her to fill in.

"I called the first group over at 7:45. That was the chess club. When it was time to call the varsity football team up, it was after eight. She picked up the football picture. There were only eight men standing in front of the straw bales. "Clive, Dane and Riley had already left the party, so it was a small group."

"Miss Gep—" he started. "Debra," he continued, "I wonder if I could ask you a favor."

"Certainly."

"If possible, could you go through the group pictures and find out who else was in attendance at the reunion but missing from their group photo? Aside from the three you already mentioned."

"Absolutely, that won't be a problem. I made a list of names for each group photo. I just have to check names with the pictures. There were a few people who had either gone off to the bar or back to their rooms so they missed out. I can't remember who exactly. The night has been such a blur." She shook her head. "A terrible, horrible blur."

I patted her shoulder again. "I'm sure you'll be glad when this weekend is over."

"Definitely." She gathered up the pictures. "I'll get right to work on the names. Will you be here long?"

"Probably another hour." Briggs looked apologetically my direction but I didn't mind sticking around at all. "Should we stop by your room?"

"No, I'll be here at least that long. I want to collect all of my decorations. After I go through the pictures, of course."

"Thanks for your help," Briggs said.

We walked out of the room. "What do you hope to see on that list of names?" I asked.

"We can assume the killer knew both victims which means the person was probably attending the reunion. That list will provide me with the possible suspects. Anyone who wasn't around during the group photos will need to explain where they were in the eight o'clock hour. We already know Grady was in his room for part of that time. With any luck, another name or two will pop up. At the very least, it'll give me the names of people I need to talk to first thing in the morning."

"Including Katrina, the caterer?" I asked.

"Especially Katrina, the caterer."

CHAPTER 22

"I promise this is the last thing we'll do before heading home," Briggs said as we stepped off the elevator onto the fifth floor. "It's just that this kind of murder scene, in a big place where there are lots of people, is hard to contain. Then, there's the annoying fact that most of the people associated with the reunion and therefore the two victims will be scattering off in a hundred different directions."

We turned down the hallway to Dane's room. It seemed the mad rush on cheap room service had finally slowed. Guests had settled in for the night. "I was thinking, James, since both men were in business together, and successful according to Debra, have you considered that this might have something to do with their business. Maybe a disgruntled worker or customer? Debra mentioned they were in real estate together."

"Yes, I've got that on my list for tomorrow. If nothing significant points to anyone at the reunion, then I've got to look elsewhere. Their business would be the obvious place to start since it connects them."

The hotel's front desk had given Briggs a master key card for easy access to the two rooms. He unlocked the door and we went inside. The room service cart had been cleared away. The room was neat and orderly. It was hard to believe just hours ago it was the scene of a murder.

"I suppose there is no other way to do this except for me to get down and sniff the carpet for the maple syrup." I was about to drop to my knees when Briggs held up his hand.

"Hold on, we might be able to narrow down the area." He walked to the edge of the bed and crouched down to rub his fingers over the carpet. I stood over him to see what he was looking at.

"This hotel is basically spotless," he said. "But do you see these smudges of dirt on the carpet?" He rubbed his fingers together. "They are sticky," he said, enthusiastically. If we could place a person from the caterer's kitchen at the murder scene it would be a big break for the case. We knew only from Nina's account that Katrina paid her to take the cart to Dane's room. But we had no actual proof she had followed through.

I dropped down next to Briggs, held my hair back and lowered my nose to the carpet. "Phew, they use a lot of chemicals to clean this carpet."

"Too many?" Briggs asked. "Maybe you won't be able to find the scent of maple syrup in between the chemicals."

I sat up and wiggled my nose. "Never underestimate Samantha. Unless they are also using a carpet product that smells like Sunday morning breakfast, the sticky substance is definitely maple syrup."

"That makes it very likely that someone from the catering kitchen walked through this room. And since we know that the owner of Elegant Edibles paid Nina to take the room service cart into Dane's room, we can assume this maple syrup was dragged in by Katrina. Even though I always try to avoid assumptions."

"Don't forget the lemon and garlic aroma on Dane's sweater. It seems that would not only put her in the room but in physical contact with the victim," I added.

"Maybe this long night is going to bear fruit after all. I'll have to borrow some scissors to cut a few fibers out of the rug before we go home. Now, we need to connect Katrina or someone from the kitchen to Riley's death. We don't have access to his clothes yet, but I wonder if we can find traces of maple syrup in his room."

"Let's head over there and give it a look." We walked out of the room and Briggs shut the door behind us.

"The coffee didn't help much, but I'm feeling revived now that we are on to something," I said as we headed to the elevator. "Thank goodness someone was clumsy and unlucky enough to spill a gallon of maple syrup in the kitchen." We stepped inside the elevator.

Briggs took advantage of our short ride alone in the elevator for a kiss. His brown eyes gazed into mine. "And thank goodness I was *lucky* enough to find Lacey Pinkerton."

"Excuse me but I think I found you." I reached up and rubbed my fingers along the rough black stubble on his jaw. It had grown thicker since the evening began.

"No, I found you. In the middle of a pumpkin patch with a dead woman, as I recall."

"You're right. I was at the crime scene first."

"Either way, it was my lucky day." He kissed me again. He growled in disappointment when the elevator beeped and the doors opened. "Why did elevators have to become so fast and high tech?" With the hotel split into two distinct wings, it was a shorter journey to go to the ground floor and walk across to the elevators on the opposite side.

"It occurs to me that it would have taken the killer a good ten minutes to get from Dane's room to Riley's," Briggs said. "It makes me wonder if the maple syrup would have still been stuck on the person's shoes after such a long trip. Some of it is carpet and some tile floor."

I made a point of pressing my foot against the tile floor. A hint of stickiness remained on my shoe. "I can still feel it on my shoes, but it's very light. But then we were standing in it after the floor had been cleaned, presumably several times. There might have been more stickiness earlier on in the evening."

Briggs' earlier jaunty pace, a result of our success in Dane's room, suddenly slowed. "I must be tired to be considering this as a plausible way to nail a suspect."

I took his arm as we waited for the elevator to take us up to Riley's room. "If you were just any old detective instead of the handsome, brilliant Detective Briggs with his talented assistant then I might say, yes this is as far-fetched as the man in the moon. But don't give up just yet."

"How do you stay so energized this late in the evening?" he asked.

"Easy. I'm with you. And I have no doubt that as soon as I get home, I will drop into a coma the second my head hits the pillow."

We walked along the corridor to the room where Riley had been pushed off his balcony. Briggs opened the door and we stepped inside. No one had touched the room yet. Riley's belongings were still sitting in the closet and the bathroom. The metal table was still turned over on the balcony. Briggs turned on all the lights in the room, and we carefully examined the carpet for dirty spots like we'd found in Dane's room.

"I don't see anything, do you?" I asked.

"Maybe my theory was right. It was far enough that the person's shoes were free of sticky syrup by the time they reached this room." Briggs walked back to the door.

"Are you leaving already?" I asked.

"Nope. Just going to do a little reenactment. There's no sign of forced entry, so let's assume Riley opened the door for the person." Briggs walked in and headed straight through to the balcony. He surveyed the carpet as he walked. "It seems any person heading to the balcony would walk straight down the middle to the glass door. I mean why would you zig zag? Shortest distance between two points and all that geometry stuff."

"Makes sense."

He stooped down and rubbed his fingers over the carpet. "Nothing sticky. No dirt. I think our theory has hit a dead end."

"But there's still a chance they were here. They just had clean shoes," I noted.

"True." Briggs shifted his chin in thought. "But what motive would Katrina Jessup have to kill the two men? Killing one person is big enough but taking out two in the same night, that takes planning, guts and a very large chunk of hatred. I can't believe that the incident you witnessed when Dane was harassing her was enough to send her on a murder spree."

"I have to say, I've run into her a few times and nothing about her says homicidal maniac. She's an attractive, confident, well-put together business woman." Something else occurred to me as I spoke. "Another thing. Katrina's not a large or particularly strong looking woman. I saw Riley when he was alive. He was an average sized man, but still a large body for an average sized woman to throw over the balcony."

"Yes, that's a good point." He looked out toward the balcony. "Although, the barrier is short enough that it might be easier than you think to topple someone over it. But like you said—how would an average sized woman manage to overpower Riley in a struggle? Unless, of course, she's a karate expert or something."

I pointed at him when another light bulb went off over my head. "Like Grady. In all of our maple syrup excitement, we forgot that key detail about Grady."

"You're right. I'd nearly forgotten what you told me about his black belt. I'll have to ask him about that when I talk to him tomorrow."

Briggs noticed something on the dresser and walked over to it. He picked up the phone charger cord. "They took Riley's phone for evidence. This looks like the same kind used to kill Dane, a very common type, according to Officer Clark." He placed the cord back down. "I guess we know Riley didn't kill Dane first before getting knocked off himself."

"I hadn't ever considered that," I said. "Two killers. Like a domino type killing or something? Maybe that explains why we can't find anything to place Katrina in this room."

"It's always possible but more likely we're just missing something. And we don't know for sure the maple syrup visitor wasn't here. As we've discovered, it's a long trip from that side of the hotel, long enough to wear off even the stickiest mess on the bottom of a shoe."

We headed to the door. "With the exception of a wad of melted gum," I noted. "I once stepped on a wad, in my new sandals, no less. I could have walked around the earth three times and that blue glob would still have been stuck to the otherwise pristine sole of my sandal."

Just as Briggs reached for the door, a noise on the other side told us someone was trying to get inside the room. Whoever it was seemed to be using a key card. The green light beeped to show the door was unlocked.

Briggs motioned for me to get back out of the way. My heart bumped into my ribs as I waited for him to open the door. He grabbed the latch. Footsteps pounded down the hallway as Briggs wrenched the door open. "Stay here," he said and raced out the door.

A sickening thud was followed by a grunt of pain. I was never good at following an order in dangerous situations. I raced out the door and followed the sound of the groan. Briggs was stooped down rubbing the back of his head.

"James." I crouched down next to him. "Who should I call? Can I get you something?"

He lifted his face. It was a few shades paler. He winced in pain. "Not sure what they hit me with. Might just have been a hard fist." He turned his neck side to side. "Right to the back of my head." I helped him to his feet. He swayed for a second but the color was already coming back to his face.

He looked down the hallway. "They must have come out of that utility closet as I ran past. Come on." I followed him to the emergency stairwell. Again, he told me to stand back as he swung the door open. He stepped inside and looked around. "They could be anywhere and on any floor by now." He rubbed the back of his head again.

I walked around him to inspect where he'd been hit. I touched the spot he was rubbing. He flinched. "We need to get you some ice. That's going to be a big lump."

"Probably, a few aspirin wouldn't hurt either," he muttered.

"Let's get down to the kitchen area and see if we can get some ice."

We walked toward the elevator. "Why do you think someone would want to get into Riley's room?" I asked.

"Not sure but then I'm about done trying to do any coherent thinking tonight. Still seeing a few stars."

"Maybe I should take you to the emergency room," I suggested.

"No, it'll clear in a few minutes. Not the first time I've been clobbered in the head. And I'm sure it won't be the last. But I can come to one solid conclusion in my foggy head," he said.

"What's that?"

"Whoever the killer is, they are still in this hotel."

CHAPTER 23

$\mathcal{B}$riggs looked somewhat recovered by the time we reached the bottom floor. We had a short argument in the elevator when he insisted we didn't need to bother with ice. I won the debate easily when he reached back to discover the tender lump on his head.

But he insisted we stop by the room where Debra had been taking down decorations to see if she had finished the list. The attack in the hallway convinced him that the person was staying, or, at the very least, working in the hotel. Katrina's small venture as part of the hotel hospitality staff still had no reasonable explanation. Then there was the lemon and garlic aroma on Dane's sweater and the maple syrup on his rug. Briggs didn't say it out loud, but I knew Katrina was high on his person of interest list, even if we couldn't find evidence that she'd been to Riley's room.

Debra was taking down a garland of paper pumpkins when we stepped into the room. She turned at the sound of our footsteps echoing through the space. She quickly wound up the pumpkin garland. "I have the list for you. I could only find six people who were not in their group photo, including the three men." She hurried over to the table where the yearbook and pictures were piled.

Debra instantly noticed that something wasn't right. "Detective

305

Briggs, if you don't mind me saying so, you don't look well. Maybe you should call it a night."

"Yes, that's probably good advice." Briggs absently reached up to smooth his longish hair down and quickly remembered there was a tender bump on the back of his head. He dropped his arm as Debra handed over a yellow piece of paper with six names written in perfect penmanship.

I peeked over Briggs' shoulder to read the list. The two victims and Clive Jergens were the first three names on the list.

"The first three were easy to remember because I know they left my *dreary* party to go barhopping. Maybe they should have stuck it out," she added wryly. "Then there's Grady Ramone. I think there was a situation with his jester's hat. Terry Brickman got sick from eating too much and left the party early. He should have been in the football picture. Then there was Emma Sanders. I'm not sure where she was, but she should have been in the girls' volleyball and the math club pictures."

"Were Terry and Emma ever bullied by Riley and Dane?" Briggs asked.

Debra fiddled with the pumpkin garland to make sure it was folded nicely. "Terry? Never. He was our star quarterback. He's not in football anymore. He's in car sales. Emma Sanders was a little like me in high school, too busy to make any close friends. She spread herself too thin, just like me. But I don't think Riley and Dane ever paid attention to her. Just like me, I wasn't on their radar, fortunately."

Debra placed the garland in a box she had stored under the table. She lifted up a large punch ladle. "Oops, I nearly forgot about this. It was left behind when the caterers cleaned up. I'll take it to the kitchen after I'm done here."

"I think the catering team has left already," I said.

"Yes, I'm sure they have, but Katrina, the owner walked past the room just a few minutes ago on her way to the kitchen. She popped her head in to make sure the brunch was still on for tomorrow." Debra shrugged. "Figured people will need to have a meal for the trip home and the food was already paid for."

"That makes sense," Briggs said. "Since you were kind enough to provide me with this list, Lacey and I will return the ladle to the caterer's kitchen."

"That would save me some time." She handed it to Briggs. "Thank you."

Briggs held up the list. "And thank you for this."

My eyes traveled to the table where the ten-year-old yearbook sat amongst the pictures. "Debra, would you mind terribly if we borrowed this yearbook? We could return it tomorrow, or I could mail it back to you."

"Certainly, if you think it will help." Debra seemed unconvinced by the prospect.

"It will help us match faces and names." I picked it up. "I'll get it back to you as soon as possible."

Debra waved off that plan. "I don't need it back. My own yearbook is packed up somewhere in my parents' attic with twenty years of holiday decorations and spiders and cobwebs. Needless to say, I was in no mood to dig it out. I bought this one at a yard sale in my neighborhood for ten cents. The original owners had left it behind with a large pile of old books."

I held it to my chest and patted it. "Great. Thanks so much for your help."

"You're welcome." Debra smiled at Briggs. "And get this man home. He looks terrible."

CHAPTER 24

I was in full agreement with Debra that Briggs needed to get home. He winced as he reached up to rub the kinks from his neck. He held the punch ladle in his free hand. "Last stop, I promise," he said as we headed back to the caterer's kitchen. "Obviously, I can't let a chance pass to talk with the caterer. Katrina Jessup has several big questions to answer." His footsteps were heavy as we walked. "I have to say, I'm at a loss on these two murders. There's something big missing. It feels like I'm looking into a hole and seeing nothing. The only connection between them is the two men knew each other well, worked together even and they both died within a few minutes of each other. And that's where the similarities end. They even died in very different ways."

"You're forgetting another big connection, James. They both bullied a number of people in high school and many people disliked them. I'll bet some even hated them. Like Grady Ramone."

"Yes, I haven't forgotten about Grady Ramone and his jester's hat. I'm hoping once I sleep on this and the ache clears from my head, I'll have a clearer picture."

"We didn't get that ice or the aspirin," I said. "And I still think you should see a doctor."

"No, I'm fine. I'll call the Chesterton station to get someone over here to pick us both up though. I'm afraid we'll have to put your midnight motorcycle ride through town on hold."

"All right but I'm holding you to it."

We stopped just short of the caterer's kitchen. Light seeped beneath the door. It had been a long, arduous day for the owner of Elegant Edibles. Especially if she had found time to murder two men in between all the party food preparation.

Briggs took out the miniature notebook he'd produced when we arrived at the scene outside of the hotel.

I couldn't stop the smile. "There is nothing more sexy than a man who doesn't leave home without his pen and paper."

He tossed the tiny notebook on his palm. "It's true, I'm a nerd. But at least it's good to know I'm a sexy nerd."

I tugged at the sides of his coat as I hopped up and kissed him lightly on the mouth. "You are indeed."

"Besides, I like to be prepared. You just never know when someone will be tossed off a balcony or strangled with a phone charger." Briggs tapped the kitchen door with the ladle before reaching for the handle. It opened from the other side.

A surprised Katrina Jessup greeted us. Her eyes were a pretty hazel color and shaped like large almonds. She had her laptop bag on her shoulder and a steaming cup of tea in her hand. "Hello, I was just on my way out." Her brows bunched in confusion. She paused when she looked at me, as if trying to recollect where she'd seen me before, then she turned to Briggs. "Are you—"

Briggs pulled out his badge. "Detective James Briggs. I wonder if I could ask you a few questions before you leave."

Katrina reached up and gripped the strap on her laptop bag. "Yes, of course. I got your card. I was going to call you in the morning. It's late and I've had a long work day," she said quickly, seemingly trying to postpone the questions. But I knew that Briggs wasn't going to let her slip out for the night without asking a few of the whopper questions he had for her.

She reluctantly led us back into the kitchen area where she placed her bag on the counter. I noticed a slight tremble in her hands as she took the ladle from Briggs. She put it on the counter next to her laptop and crossed her arms defensively. Not a good start to her interview. Briggs was an expert at picking up body language cues. I was just an amateur, but I certainly could see she was agitated about having to talk to Briggs, and it wasn't just over her delayed departure.

Her bottom lip vibrated a bit, which brought attention to two white scars on her chin. I'd never noticed them before but then I'd never been so close to her.

Katrina's gaze flicked my direction again. Her eyes dropped to the yearbook in my arm. "I thought you were the florist?" she asked.

"This is Miss Pinkerton, my assistant. I've asked her along as a matter of protocol," he explained.

"Protocol?" she asked abruptly. "Am I being interrogated?"

"Not at all. But if there is anything you'd feel more comfortable talking about with an attorney present, then we can make this a more formal interview. It's late and I'm just hoping to firm up some details regarding the two incidents in the hotel tonight."

"You mean the murders?" she asked. She lowered her arms, but there was still a tremble in her hands. "Terrible tragedy. It had promised to be such a wonderful weekend for the reunion. I'm making brunch tomorrow for everyone before they leave. I was here late making sure everything was ready for the morning. We need to start first thing." She was speaking fast as if she thought she could just fill the time with unimportant details.

"Yes, I've heard there is to be a good-bye brunch. Can I ask if you knew either of the two victims personally?"

It was a simple, straight question, but she seemed to be analyzing it for a proper answer. "Well, only that they were two of the classmates attending the reunion. I'm sure I passed them at some point during the day, since I was helping serve the food."

Briggs nodded as if that was a reasonable answer. "Miss Jessup—" he started.

"Mrs. Jessup," she corrected.

"Mrs. Jessup, several people witnessed an incident where one of the victims was making unwanted advances toward you as you delivered food to the room."

"I can't recall that," she said. "It was such a busy day. He might have said something suggestive to me, but I was far too occupied to notice."

"I'm confused," Briggs said. "Did it happen or not?"

Katrina got flustered and crossed her arms again. For the first time, I noticed the impressive diamond on her wedding ring. She also had a short scar on the back of her hand. "I suppose that Mr. Caputo said something to me and tried to stop my progress to the door."

Her statement perked my ears, and Briggs hadn't missed it either.

"I didn't mention which victim was bothering you," Briggs said. "The witness mentioned it was Mr. Caputo."

Katrina sighed loudly. "All right, yes, he did. But frankly, it's not the first time that I've had a man make unwanted advances toward me and none of those men ended up dead."

Briggs' face popped up. "I wasn't suggesting that you killed him. I just wanted to know if the incident happened." Even tired and with a splitting headache, Briggs was cool and smooth.

"Yes it did. Is that all? I'm exhausted and I need to be back here very early."

"Yes, I understand. Just a couple more questions. Did you pay one of the hotel servers money so you could roll Mr. Caputo's room service cart into his room?"

The pink in her cheeks drained away. Her eyes flitted back and forth between us, before dropping away completely. She stared down at the floor.

"Mrs. Jessup, if you prefer to wait and come to the station with a lawyer, then we can arrange that."

She lifted her face. "It's a minor crime. It was only a few dollars."

Briggs discretely rubbed the back of his neck. It was still stiff from being hit in the head. But could this woman have thrown a fist hard enough to knock him down? She also physically didn't match the description of someone who could have thrown Riley off the balcony. But then, sometimes strength was hard to see.

"Mrs. Jessup," Briggs said tightly. "You and I both know that I'm not asking this to arrest you for bribing a hotel worker with a ten dollar bill. Again, if you'd like to further this conversation at the station—"

Katrina unfolded her arms and huffed in exasperation. "All right, yes. I was angry that he tried to come on to me right in front of so many people. I happened to be inside the hospitality office when there was a room service call from Mr. Caputo in Room 511. I decided to confront him and give him a piece of my mind. But he was alive when I left the room."

"Why don't you recount the entire event the best you can," Briggs prodded.

It seemed that now that it was out, Katrina didn't mind talking. She dropped her defensive stance. "I knocked and he opened the door. He was surprised to see the caterer pushing the cart in and even laughed and said something about the hotel being short on staff. He motioned for me to roll in the cart while he went to his wallet on the dresser."

Briggs waited for her to continue. It seemed she was picking and choosing the details to retell.

"When he tried to tip me, I waved the money away and told him I didn't appreciate what he'd done when I was carrying in the cookies. I let him know it was rude and inappropriate."

"How did he react to that?" Briggs asked as he jotted a few notes.

"I think he was stunned silent. I guess he wasn't used to be confronted about his obnoxious behavior. Then I turned on my heels and walked out of the room."

Briggs cast a cursory glance my direction. "So you never touched him or got into any kind of physical struggle with the man?"

His question sent her back to an arms crossed stance. "No, I said what I had to say and walked out. That's the last I saw of him."

"Mr. Caputo died shortly after eight, around the time when you were in his room. Did you see anyone else in the hallway when you got to the room or after you left it?"

She reached up and rubbed her temple. "Like I said, it's been a long day, but no, I don't think I saw anyone in the hallway or near his room."

"Just two more questions," Briggs said. "Were you at all worried about walking into a stranger's hotel room to confront him about his behavior?"

It was a good question that I hadn't seen coming. Neither had Katrina, apparently.

"Well, he wasn't a stranger," she said hesitantly.

"He wasn't? So you knew Mr. Caputo?"

"No, of course not," she said sharply. "I just meant he wasn't a stranger because he was a guest at the reunion. I saw him at the lunch and the costume party. He wasn't just some off the street random stranger."

Briggs nodded in agreement, but I sensed that he considered it a weak answer. Without thinking, he reached up to rub the back of his head, then quickly thought better of it. I was certain the lump was still tender and swollen.

"Last question and then we'll let you go," he continued. "Did you personally cut any garlic today or was that task left to your chef and food preparers?"

She laughed dryly and rightly so. It would have been impossible to see his question coming, unless you knew he was standing next to the most skilled nose on the west coast.

Katrina looked a little insulted by the question. Her chin lifted. "I'm the owner but I always lend a hand in the kitchen, especially when there's a lot of work to do. Today was no exception. And yes, I cut around twenty cloves of garlic today." She reached for her bag. "And now if you'll excuse me, I'm very tired. I'm going home."

Briggs stepped politely aside and she brushed past us. We followed her out and watched her walk with sharp footsteps toward the exit.

"What are you thinking, Detective Briggs?" I asked.

"I'm thinking I need aspirin and bed. With any luck, all of this will make sense in the morning."

CHAPTER 25

*K*ingston's loud, cranky caw woke me from a dead sleep. As I popped up, Nevermore ejected off of me. I'd been sleeping so soundly, I hadn't noticed my thirteen pound tabby had curled up on my chest.

I glanced at my alarm clock. It was only nine but to my crow that was way too late to be stuck under his cage cover and it was far too long to be waiting for his breakfast. The heavy cloud in my head made me long for my weekends as a teenager, where I'd occasionally burrow under my sheets undisturbed until noon. Although the amount of time I could sleep in usually depended on my Mom's mood.

A late morning sun was poking around the edges of my bedroom curtains. Kingston cawed again. "I'm coming, *Milord*," I groaned into the hallway.

I pushed into my slippers and grabbed my robe. I'd fallen into bed so exhausted, I'd forgotten to adjust the thermostat. The chilly morning air had permeated the house, waking me further from my sleepy state. I tied the robe tightly to keep out the cold and squinted at the thermostat as I turned the temperature higher.

Kingston flapped his wings angrily as I pulled the heavy cover from his cage. He skewered me with his beady black gaze.

"Puh leaze," I said with an eye roll. "It's nine. You act like you've been stuck in that cage for three months." I unlocked his door but he didn't budge. Instead, he walked over to his snack tray and poked at it with his long beak.

"You poor crow, I'm surprised you have the strength to stand upright on that perch." I reached under his cage for the can of dog treats and rolled a few onto the tray. "I'll cook you a couple of hard boiled eggs to make up for the suffering you've endured." I turned to head to the kitchen and stumbled over my cat. A slipper popped off of my foot. "You know, Never, if I fall over you and break my neck, there won't be anyone to feed you. Then it's just you and the angry big bird fighting it out to see who the true predator really is." A knock on the front door stopped my rant, one that I was sure I'd feel guilty about once the tiredness left my head.

If there was one sight you wanted to see after a long night and not enough sleep on a drowsy Sunday morning, it was Elsie with a plate full of something delicious. She was wearing her running shoes and sweat pants as she walked brusquely past me with her plate.

"I ran eight miles then baked a batch of walnut and date scones." She headed straight to the kitchen. "No coffee? Why isn't there any coffee in the pot? You always have a pot on for Sunday morning."

"You sound just like Kingston." I tilted my head side to side. "Well not exactly like him. Your syllables are far more diverse and altogether less deafening." As if he knew I was talking about him in a disparaging way, Kingston released another caw. Crow calls were loud when they were out in infinite space, but inside a small house they were enough to make the plaster walls crack.

"I've got to put some eggs on for King. If you wouldn't mind putting on the coffee. I just got up."

Elsie placed her plate of scones on the counter and put her hands on her hips to give me a mom style once over. "I think the robe, pajamas and single slipper gave it away. You don't usually sleep so late."

"It was a long night," I started but was abruptly halted by Elsie's own narrative.

"I haven't slept a wink in two nights," she said as she rambunctiously dipped the measuring cup into the coffee can. Her hand emerged with a mega scoop of coffee. She dumped it into the basket. "I just ran from here to the harbor and back again on three hours sleep. But I was still so anxious, I decided to try out a new scone recipe."

I opened a can of food for Nevermore. The cat danced around me until his dish was full. "I'm sorry to hear that, Elsie. The part about you not sleeping and feeling anxious. Obviously, the scone recipe part is music to my ears." I plopped four eggs into a pot of water, deciding I'd make extra for later. Four eggs would help make up for me leaving Kingston in a dark cage all morning. "What has you so worked up? Or should I easily guess?" I'd been so busy, I'd nearly forgotten that Elsie's niece Britney had recently moved to town.

"Of course, it's Britney," Elsie said.

I grabbed some plates for the scones. "Did she do something wrong? Is she hard to get along with?" I'd only briefly met Britney but she seemed extraordinary in every way.

"No, she's talented in the kitchen and hard working. She is sweet and likeable, although some of my sarcastic humor goes right past her."

I put a scone on each plate and returned to the cupboard for coffee cups. "Then what's the problem?"

"Two things. And I'm sure you'll think I'm nutty as my fudge walnut brownies but here I go. First, there's the obvious. She's a far better baker and people will soon realize that they've been eating inferior baked goods all these years."

I blinked at her over my scone. "You're actually serious?" I said as a question. "You're right. You've lost your fudge walnut brownie mind, Elsie." I took a bite of the scone and my mouth was instantly filled with the flaky buttery magic that only Elsie could create. I closed my eyes to put on an extra show of appreciation as I finished the bite.

"Elsie, I don't care if she can create éclairs that dance and perform tricks, no one bakes like you. No one. And do you know why?"

Elsie picked at her scone and didn't look too cheered by my pep talk yet. "Why?"

"Because Britney is missing one major ingredient that only you have. Passion. The Elsie passion that can only come from the woman sitting in front of me."

"I don't know if that's enough anymore. She knows all these new tricks of the trade—"

"Stop right there, Elsie. Do you think state of the art techniques are what make a baked good memorable? Nope. It's knowing that the person who created the treat put her heart and soul into it. My mom's recipe for chocolate chip cookies used shortening."

Elsie's eyes opened in horror as if I'd told her my mom liked to kick puppies.

"Yes, that's right. Our dirty family secret is out in the open now. My mom added a big dollop of disgusting, greasy shortening to her cookie dough. But you know what? I loved those cookies. They were baked with love, so they were the best darn cookies in the world to me. Until I tasted yours, of course. But we can keep that between you and me." I reached across and squeezed her hand. "Elsie, everyone within a hundred mile radius of your shop craves your sweets. Dash is probably pacing his house right now because he's not going to have any of your pumpkin muffins until next fall."

Elsie sat up straighter. "And that brings me to my second reason for tossing and turning all night. Dash," she said with no added details. But I could easily interpret her facial expression.

"Are they dating?" I asked. "Did Dash ask Britney out?"

"Not that I know of yet, but obviously you noticed there was something there too?"

I was instantly torn. Normally, I got excited about the prospect of playing matchmaker, but this one was too complicated and fraught with friendship problems. I didn't want to betray Dash's friendship by mentioning the conversation I'd had with him on exactly this subject.

"Let's just say the attraction was pretty clear, at least on Dash's side," I added.

"Trust me, the feeling is mutual. Dash came into the shop yesterday on the premise that he was hoping I still had some pumpkin muffins. I could see right thought his act."

"In his defense, he craved those muffins long before he met your niece." Kingston fluttered down from his cage and trotted over to beg for a piece of scone. My mom guilt caused me to drop a chunk onto the floor for him. Something told me he was going to use his Sunday morning imprisonment as a way to get everything he wanted today.

"Dash is a nice enough guy," Elsie said. I had never told Elsie about Briggs' divorce and Dash's betrayal, mostly because it wasn't my story to tell. But it happened long ago, and it seemed Dash had felt both remorse and shame about it all.

"Then what has you worried?" I asked.

Elsie gave me a 'do you really have to ask' head tilt. "Come on, Pink. Just look at poor, pitiful Kate Yardley. She dated him for a few months and she still pines for the man."

"I would hardly use the words 'poor and pitiful' to describe Kate Yardley. I dare say she'd cringe at that description. I only wish I had her confidence. It's true. Kate does seem to have feelings for Dash, but I believe he's made it clear to her that they are only friends. So we can't heap all the blame for that on Dash."

"You're probably right about all of it. I just don't want them to start dating. I don't need a starry-eyed young woman drifting around the bakery, daydreaming about Dashwood Vanhouten."

"Your niece seems far more sensible than that."

Elsie got up to pour the coffee. "I've known plenty of girls who are perfectly sensible until a handsome man pops into their life. Our Lola, for instance." She stopped halfway back with the coffee. "Scratch that. Bad example. Our Lola has never spent one day being sensible."

We had a good laugh as she set the coffee down and dropped back onto the chair.

Elsie took a long sip and sighed. "Well, this talk has helped me. I should pay you like a therapist."

I picked up a second scone. "Oh trust me, I've been rewarded handsomely for being your friend and therapist."

Elsie picked up a scone too. "So tell me, how was your date with James?"

"Do you have a few hours?"

CHAPTER 26

The crisp fall air smelled of apples and maple or at least it seemed it should have. I pulled on my favorite comfy, over-sized sweater and walked out to the front porch to watch the wind tease the leaves from the trees. I carried out the Rockmore yearbook and the remainder of my morning coffee.

Nevermore joined me, spending the first few minutes rubbing himself along the back of my sweater, creating a good storm of static charges with his fur. Kingston had marched out of the house in a snit when Elsie and I were saying good-bye. I was sure he hadn't gone far, but I was equally sure he was still brooding about the morning.

The phone rang and my heart did its usual skippity-do when I saw who it was. "Did you oversleep too? How's your head?" I asked before Briggs could say a word.

"My head is still attached, but it feels as if it's carrying marbles instead of brains this morning. It was definitely a struggle getting out of bed. I'm at the station right now. I'm heading over to the hotel soon. I want to get there for the brunch and catch a few people before they leave. Nate's office is sending over Riley Morrison's clothes. I thought you might come by the station and give them a sniff."

320

"Absolutely. And I'm sure I don't need to say this, but I'd love to go with you to the hotel."

"I figured you'd want to tag along. In fact, if you can drive, then I can pick up my motorcycle."

"Darn, I guess that means no ride back for me. You're going to owe me."

"Somehow, in my daze, I wrote that in my notebook." I heard paper shuffling. "Here it is. You owe Lacey a ride on the bike."

"I'm not sure if I believe you, but that's all right. I'll be reminding you daily. I'll be there soon. I just want to glance through the Rockmore yearbook. See if I can find anything significant."

"All right. The clothes should be here in the next twenty minutes. The brunch starts in an hour."

"See you soon." I put down the phone and perused the pages of the yearbook, not terribly sure what I was looking for. Grady Ramone seemed to be far more involved in school activities than Clive, Riley and Dane. Grady had wavy hair and wore shirts with Star Wars characters and Einstein. I glanced through the various clubs and noticed that he was the president of the debate club, the math club and a club called the Sherlock Holmes Club. The yearbook staff had taken the time to write a description and major accomplishments of each club. It seemed the Sherlock Holmes Club was a group of students who plotted and acted out murder mysteries. They met one weekend a month at a club member's house to create and solve murder mysteries. I went back to the picture. There were an impressive ten people in the club, and each had shown up for the photo wearing a plaid deerstalker hat like the one Holmes wore.

I ran my finger along the list of names. Jessica Trumbo's name jumped out at me. I moved my finger up and found her. She was standing right next to Grady with a plaid scarf wrapped loosely around her neck. The way she had her arm resting on his shoulder made it seem that they had been good friends in high school.

There were a few more nice pictures of Jessica Trumbo sitting at a piano and leading an auditorium in a holiday sing along. Debra had mentioned that Jessica was a musician and her dream was to become a concert pianist.

I turned the pages to get to the senior class. There were no comments or good-byes scrawled in the copy I was holding, leading me to conclude that it had been an extra, one that never belonged to a student. It would have been interesting to see a copy with personal notes and friend's comments.

Dane Caputo's hair was cropped close to his head. He was wearing a smirk that made him look entirely unlikeable. It wasn't a nice thought about a dead man, but it was the first thing that came to mind. Riley Morrison's deep set eyes made him look mean rather than mysterious and Clive Jergens was still wearing his thick mop of hair in the same middle parted hairstyle that he wore in high school. We'd been so busy in our hunt for evidence and witnesses, I realized that we hadn't seen or heard from Clive since his alleged attack in the hallway. He'd seemed shaken enough by the incident that it wasn't surprising he'd stayed locked in his room for the rest of the night.

Grady had his hair combed neatly to the side for his senior portrait. He looked like someone I would have wanted to be friends with in high school, someone always full of cool information and good ideas.

Nevermore rubbed against my hand, causing a few of the pages to flip forward. The book fell open to Jessica Trumbo's picture. I stared at Jessica's gently smiling face. Something about her looked oddly familiar. Nevermore shoved his head against my hand again, causing me to lose the page. "Darn it."

I stood up. I didn't have time to linger on the porch. I had to get to the station and lend my nose to the murder investigation.

CHAPTER 27

*B*riggs came out of his office as I entered the station. Officer Chinmoor was on call at the front desk. Chinmoor always smiled at the both of us as if he knew some big secret, even though everyone in town knew we were dating.

"Come in to the office, Lacey. Then I'll take you back to the evidence room. The clothes just arrived." Briggs wore a stern, businesslike expression as he ushered me past him into his office. He snapped the door shut behind us.

I turned back to him, ready to ask what was wrong when he grabbed my hand and pulled me toward him for a kiss.

I smiled up at him, enjoying the strength of his arms around me. "That was well worth the trip down to the station."

"I'm glad. We were on such a nice date and then it morphed into a long night of twists and turns. We didn't get a good night kiss, and I really needed it."

I reached up and touched his face. "Me too. So how is your head? Did you get some sleep?"

Reluctantly, he lowered his arms. "I did once the aspirin kicked in. I want to fill you in on a few things before we head over to the evidence room." He walked to his desk. "Preliminary coroner's report confirms that Dane died by strangulation. There was no other sign of struggle, which again, makes me think his attacker knew him. Riley died from head trauma when his skull hit the pavement. Blood tests showed he had been drinking but was well below the level of legally drunk. That goes for Dane too. Time of death for Riley was obvious since there was a witness. He fell around eight thirty. It seems that Dane was strangled just after eight."

"I suppose that still gives one person plenty of time to get from Dane's room to Riley's room in the separate wing of the hotel."

"Yes it does. And I have the short list of people who were not present for their group photos between eight and nine. I let the hotel know who I needed to still talk to. I told them to contact me if any of them were checking out early. I got a call around seven from the hotel clerk that Emma Sanders, a woman on the list, was checking out with her two daughters and mother. They put her on the phone. Emma had brought her family with her for the trip. They had planned to do some sightseeing at the Pickford Lighthouse. That's why they were checking out early. Her family could also corroborate her alibi that she left the party early to join them for a movie in the room. She mentioned she'd had enough of the reunion and preferred to spend the time with her kids. Terry Brickman checked out just after Emma. He was nice enough to stop by the station to talk to me. It turned out he left the reunion to meet with friends at a restaurant in town. He gave me names and numbers to check out his story."

Briggs leaned against the front of his desk and braced his hands on it. I could still see the long night and the blow to the head in his face. He had dark circles under his eyes.

"That narrows down the list considerably," I noted.

"Except that list only contains the names of people who attended the reunion. We don't know if there was someone else staying at the hotel with a connection to the victims. Cross referencing that is going to take some time. Then there are the many employees of the hotel and of course, the caterer, Katrina Jessup and her team. Frankly, she's the most intriguing person so far because she was presumably the last person to see Dane alive. But the motive is weak and it doesn't explain why she'd push Riley off a balcony."

"Or *how* she'd do it," I added. "She doesn't look big enough to push a grown man to his death."

Briggs pushed off his desk and walked toward me. "You never know. Some women have power that you can't see." He tapped the end of my nose. "Let's go put your hidden power to use in the evidence room, then we'll head over to the hotel."

CHAPTER 28

*R*iley's clothes, a nice sweater and slacks, were folded into evidence bags. The sweater had a great deal of dried blood. Briggs handed me latex gloves and pulled some on himself before taking the sweater from the bag. Aside from the bitter smell of blood, Riley's aftershave wafted up from the sweater. It was the same fragrance I'd smelled in the hotel bathroom when I examined the zombie mask.

Briggs laid the garment out on the table as if it was a delicate fabric and not a cotton and wool blend. I lowered my face to the sweater and closed my eyes. It helped me concentrate on each smell as it wafted toward my olfactory cells.

I had to stop to rub a potential sneeze from my nose. "Sorry, it seems Riley liked to wear a lot of fragrance." I passed my nose closer, trying to pick up anything apart from the blood and aftershave cologne. I was just about to give up when I smelled something familiar, or at least something I'd smelled before. I drew my nose along the fabric once more and straightened.

"That's strange." I lowered my nose again to be certain. "Yes, there it is."

"Please tell me it's a scent that will lead us straight to the killer."

"I could do that if I knew what the familiar yet strange scent was on his sweater. I picked up the same smell on the phone cord. It's something that contains oil, something cosmetic."

"Like foundation or hand lotion?"

I lowered my nose one last time and gave the sweater sleeves a thorough sniff. There were traces of the scent near the bottoms of the sleeves. "No, it's not anything I can put a name to. It seems someone had it on their hands, and they transferred it to Riley's sweater when he tried to fight them off."

Briggs looked at the bag with the trousers. "I'll spare you the task of smelling his pants." He returned the sweater to the evidence bag. "Then the list of evidence grows but nothing matches up or connects. It's like trying to put together a puzzle without building the frame first. And we still haven't found the jester's hat. I have the entire hotel staff on high alert for it, but no word yet that it has turned up."

Briggs placed the clothes back on the appropriate shelf and turned off the lights as we walked out of the room.

"That oily smell is the first thing that might actually connect the two murders. If we can find the source of it, that might lead us in the right direction. I'll send it out for analysis first thing tomorrow. In the meantime, I want to get back to the hotel. The front desk hasn't called to let me know that Grady was checking out, so I'm hoping I'll be able to talk to him before he leaves. Other than the picture of a shadow and the possible motive of revenge, there is little to hold Grady on. His room was searched thoroughly, and there was no sign of the jester's hat. It seemed he was telling the truth about someone stealing it."

Officer Chinmoor looked up from paperwork as we walked out to the front office. "Are you heading out to Chesterton?" he asked.

"Yes, we'll be at the Chesterton Regency Hotel. Call if you need me, but try not to need me," Briggs added.

Chinmoor nodded with a smile. "How is the lump?" he asked.

Briggs reached back lightly and winced as he touched it. "Still the size of a ping pong ball."

"Do you still think that it was someone's fist?" I asked.

"Yes. A hard object would have probably cracked my skull or at the very least drawn blood. It was just enough of a blow to knock me momentarily senseless and give me a terrible headache."

"Maybe that's what we need to look for," I suggested. "It seems probable that the person who hit you was involved in the murder. They were trying to get something from Riley's room and were surprised to find us inside. Rather than get caught, they took the extreme measure of hiding in a closet to attack you. They know they're in big trouble, and they're probably not thinking rationally."

"You just need to find someone who is not acting rationally," Chinmoor said confidently, proud he'd come up with the theory.

"Right," I said with a twist of my mouth, annoyed my theory had been stolen. "Of course first we have to decide the definition for irrational behavior. Every person has their quirks."

Briggs smiled at both of us. "Or we could just look for someone with bruised knuckles because my skull is telling me it gave as good as it got."

"Yes," I said, feeling somewhat deflated, "or that too. Might be simpler."

"Might be," Briggs mused. "Let's head over to the hotel. On the way, I'll tell you about information I've found on Clive Jergens that may or may not be significant."

I turned my car onto Culpepper Road.

"Looks like clouds are moving toward shore." Briggs lowered his head to get a clearer view of the coastline. "The seagulls are doing what I like to call their nervous rain dance over the water. I need to get my bike in the garage."

It was rare for me to be driving Briggs through town and it felt odd to be in the driver's seat.

I glanced out at the ocean. Heavy gray dollops of clouds hung low over the horizon. Just as Briggs had noted, the seagulls were darting back and forth, seemingly raising the alarm that the breakfast fish hunt would soon be over.

The thought of a bitter cold rainstorm made me instinctively pull the panels of my coat shut. "Not sure if I'm ready for winter yet.

Which is ridiculous because during the summer heat wave I was constantly saying, 'I can't wait for cold weather'. Now that it's looming out on the horizon and making my bones ache, I yearn for warm sunlight and an August breeze."

"I don't know," Briggs smiled over at me. "I'm looking forward to bonfires on the beach and hot cocoa in front of a roaring hearth."

"With marshmallows?" I asked.

"If that's what it takes to make your cocoa experience complete, then marshmallows it is."

"You're right. Why am I complaining? I can't wait for weather that encourages coziness. Especially this year when I have a coziness partner."

"Nevermore?" Briggs asked with a laugh.

I reached over the console and shucked him on the shoulder. "Although, I must say, the cat is quite the bed warmer in winter. If I could figure out a way for Never to wrap himself around my feet without scratching or tripping me, I'd replace my slippers with him." I peeked up in my rearview. There were few cars on the road. "What did you find out about Clive, and does it mean you're considering him a suspect?"

"It's hard to put him in the suspect category since he alleges that he was also a victim. But I'm still thinking about that expensive watch that went missing from Dane's wrist. Rolex watches catch a pretty penny on the black market. While nothing else about the murders points to robbery as the motive, the missing watch can't be ignored. And from the preliminary research I did on Clive Jergens, he is in financial trouble. His construction company was sued, and he didn't have enough insurance coverage. He had to claim bankruptcy. Whereas, his two friends, who were not so lucky this weekend, had been considerably more lucky in business."

"Yes, Debra told me they made it big with some real estate venture." I reached forward to turn the heat up.

"Apparently, Riley and Dane bought some land for cheap because they knew the locations were going to be worth something because of a new freeway project. They sold it to developers for huge profits. It seemed they had the golden touch. Everything they invested in turned a nice profit."

"And they came from money," I added and kept back a smile when I realized I'd told him something new.

"Did that come from Debra or have you been researching their finances too?"

"From Debra. No time for research. First, I overslept. Then I had to placate an angry crow because I overslept. Then I had to eat delicious fresh baked scones with Elsie."

He glanced my direction. "Had to?"

"Yes, I was being a good friend. Elsie had some stuff on her mind, and I listened. And the scones were a bonus. But I did glance through the Rockmore yearbook. More on that in a second. Do you think Clive might have killed Dane to steal his watch?"

"People have killed for less. However, that doesn't explain Riley's death. Aside from the overturned table on the balcony, the room appeared untouched. And his wallet was inside the pocket of his pants when he fell. I made a point of asking Nate if there was an imprint of a watch on his wrist. No evidence of a wristwatch."

I turned onto Highway 48, the two lane road that connected Port Danby to the town of Chesterton. There was rarely any heavy traffic on the highway. Sunday morning was exceptionally quiet.

Briggs scooted down and rested his head back. "It's kind of nice being in the passenger seat for a change. Especially with the way my head is feeling. I hadn't gone deep enough into their pasts to discover that the two victims came from money. I wasn't involved in telling the next of kin either. I haven't heard from the parents yet. I expect that'll happen today sometime."

I glanced over and felt pity for the man as he gazed out the window.

"I guess that's the hardest part of your job, huh?" I asked.

"It is. Another hard part is when I have a scattered murder investigation like this one. I can't tell if I'm just off my game because of the blow to my head or if I'm just looking in the wrong places."

"It'll get solved, James. I'm sure the lump on your head isn't helping matters, but this will get sorted out. You'll see."

"Wish I had your optimism." He sat up straighter as we neared the hotel. "Can you remember anything else Debra might have told you about the three friends, other than they were bullies?"

"She did mention the money thing and that Clive had gotten sort of left behind because Riley and Dane had become so successful. Something Debra noted as unfair considering how awful they were in high school. Of course, I guess that's sort of a moot point now considering..."

I turned onto the street where the Chesterton Regency's tall facade loomed over the sidewalk. "Debra insinuated that Clive was kind of a third wheel. Riley and Dane hung out with him, but he was always the *third* member of the group, if you know what I mean. That might have been because Clive didn't come from money like the other two."

Briggs pulled out his regular notepad. He caught me eyeing it with amusement. "Yes, I moved my scribbles from the tiny notebook to my official notes. That's when I realized how disjointed the case was so far." He wrote down what I'd told him about Clive being the third wheel and not from money like his friends. "You mentioned you were looking in the yearbook."

"Yes, but it seems kind of silly to even bring up."

"Nothing's too silly when you have little to go on."

I turned into the parking lot of the hotel. Aside from a news van parked outside of the guest lot, all seemed quiet. It was hard to believe there had been a double murder in the hotel the night before.

"It's just that Grady Ramone was part of a club called the Sherlock Holmes Club. Apparently the group plotted and acted out murder mysteries." I parked and looked at him. He hadn't written anything down. "See, I told you it was silly."

"Not silly but probably not too important. Anything else?"

"Not really. Although, I saw quite a few pictures of Jessica Trumbo, the girl Clive and his friends liked to tease. The one who died in the car accident after high school. Something about her looked familiar but that's about it. Sorry I don't have more."

We climbed out of the car. Ronald Sexton, the hotel manager, was talking to the reporters by the news van. He didn't look too pleased about the attention his hotel was getting. It was hard to blame him.

"Whoever said any publicity is good publicity didn't have two people murdered in their hotel," Briggs quipped.

"Yeah, he's going to have a rough few months. That's for sure."

Briggs opened the door for me. "Especially if I don't catch the killer."

CHAPTER 29

The brunch was well enough attended considering the circumstances. Debra waved to me from her table where she sat with four other women eating French toast piled high with berry compote. Being the type of person who never did things half way, Debra had taken the time to set the tables with nice royal blue linens. There were even goodie bags waiting for the guests to take on their way out. Some people lingered in the hallway outside the room, sipping coffee and nibbling pastries. There was definitely a gloom in the air.

"I'm going to go in and look around for Grady. I want to ask him a few questions," Briggs said.

I stopped him before we entered the room. "I have an idea. I'm going to head to the kitchen and see if I can find out what kind of hand lotion they use. Maybe it will be our mystery smell. If I could pick up the lemon and garlic scent, it makes sense that I'd find traces of hand lotion. People who cook and wash a lot of pots and pans always use some kind of hand cream to heal chapped and dry skin. Hopefully there will be just enough chaos in the kitchen for people to take little notice of the snooping investigator."

"That's a good idea. If you can't find anything out, come get me. I don't mind point blank asking to see what they use. With any luck, it'll be a match."

"Then I have my orders, sir." I winked and turned sharply on my heels toward the caterer's kitchen.

Two of the kitchen helpers pushed out the door just as I reached for it. I stepped out of the way as they rolled a cart with a coffee urn, cream and sugar out the door. They were both concentrating on their task and neither paid any attention to the woman they almost ran down with their coffee. I stopped the door before it shut completely and slipped into the kitchen.

Warm, fragrant steam filled the kitchen, causing my stomach to grumble with hunger. With brunch mostly served, the food prep stations were being cleaned. Chef Anne was still cooking eggs on the stove. Her back was to me. None of the other helpers seemed to care that a stranger was walking through the kitchen.

The dishwashing room was at the far side of the kitchen. Tiny iridescent bubbles floated around the entrance to the dishwashing area, assuring me the brunch cleanup was already under way.

I straightened my posture, smoothed my coat and walked confidently toward the dishwashing room. As I passed a small hallway, I noticed an office. The door was open and classical music floated out of it. I ducked into the hallway and peeked into the office through the open door. Katrina Jessup was looking over some receipts. She was moving her head in rhythm to the music while she read the numbers. Her hands rested on each side of the pile of receipts, and her fingers moved along the desk as if on a keyboard, instead of oak.

Right then, Katrina sensed someone watching her and looked up. She reached up to her laptop and turned off the music. "You again. For a florist, you sure get around. Can I help you?" she asked. I'd already been caught sneaking around, I decided to just ask my question.

I stepped into the office. "Yes, as you mentioned for a florist I get around. Well, it happens that I have a particular talent for picking up faint scents. It's called hyperosmia but that doesn't matter right now. Detective Briggs takes me on cases when he needs some fragrance expertise." Just mentioning Detective Briggs seemed to agitate her.

"I've already talked to the detective," she said curtly.

"Yes, of course. I just needed to ask if there's a particular hand lotion or cream your employees use to relieve chapped hands."

She stared up at me in confusion and a notion sparked in my head, a wild, inconceivable notion. I needed to get to a computer. I was just about to make my apologies and exit, forgoing the hand cream, when she pulled open her drawer and tossed a tube onto her desk. "This is the one most of us use. It's fragrance free and works great on dry hands."

My mind was still rolling with my new theory. "I see." I pointed to the tube, asking her if I could try some.

"Knock yourself out. I buy it by the dozen. We go through a lot of it."

I hadn't missed the phrase fragrance free, but I also knew that sometimes a product was fragrance free for regular noses. I could usually pick up hints of various substances.

Katrina watched with keen interest as I dabbed a tiny bit on my wrist, rubbed it in and lifted it to my nose.

"I told you it was fragrance free." She leaned back on her chair.

I could smell a few of the usual ingredients I'd expect in moisturizer like glycerin and shea butter. They were scents light enough to be invisible to a regular sense of smell. It wasn't the oily smell I was looking for, but I was sure I'd fallen onto something else that might solve the case.

I had one more question for Katrina, but it wasn't something I could just blurt out without seeming rude and nosy. I pointed to my chin. "Let me guess, you got those scars running through a back door screen. I did that when I was ten." I lifted the curls from my forehead to expose a small scar that was mostly covered by hair. "I went forehead first instead of chin first."

Her mouth tightened. It seemed I'd worn out my welcome. "I didn't run through a screen. Now if you're through with your *investigation*," she said the word with a good slap of sarcasm. "I've got work to do."

"Absolutely. Thank you for your time." I hurried out of the office and through the kitchen.

I walked past the banquet room where people were finishing brunch. Briggs was nowhere in sight. I headed straight to the front desk. I was certain a big hotel would have a complimentary computer with wifi somewhere in the lobby. I needed to get online and do some research. If my hunch turned out to be right, it would add an incredible twist to the investigation.

CHAPTER 30

$\mathcal{T}$he complimentary computer station was for guests only, but once I explained to the woman at the front desk that I was working with Detective Briggs, she handed me the pass code for the hotel's guest wifi.

My fingers flew ahead of my thoughts as I typed in the words Jessica Trumbo and accident into the search bar. The top entry was for, of all things, an accident lawyer named Jessica Trumbo. There was no similarity with the picture of Jessica Trumbo in the Rockmore yearbook so I moved on. The next few entries were about other women named Jessica Trumbo that just happened to have the word accident somewhere on the page. I moved down the list and found one about a car accident. I clicked on the page. Jessica's senior portrait came up as part of the article.

I skimmed the page. Apparently, Jessica's car had slid off an icy road. A truck coming the opposite direction couldn't stop in time. Jessica's car wasn't struck head on because the truck driver swerved. But he wasn't able to miss her car completely. The truck clipped Jessica's car sending it into the air. It rolled several times before landing in a ditch on the side of the road. "Jessica was taken to the Westville Hospital in critical condition," I read to myself. "She suffered broken bones and multiple lacerations to face and hands when she was thrown against the side window from impact. She was a budding concert pianist with a big future, her grandfather, Jerome Trumbo told reporters." The next quote from her grandmother, Pamela Trumbo, nearly made me jump from the chair. "Now our only concern is getting Jessica well again." There was no mention of Jessica dying in the accident. It was entirely possible that she eventually died of the injuries, but there was no indication of it in the article.

I sat back and stared at the entry and at Jessica's picture. A familiar pair of eyes were gazing back at me. It was crazy, I reminded myself. How could someone completely reinvent themselves without notice?

I typed in the name Katrina Jessup. There were far less people with that name than Jessica Trumbo. Naturally, Katrina's Elegant Edibles took up most of the first entries. One write-up in a culinary magazine talked about her life as a caterer and wife of a prominent plastic surgeon, Dr. Calvin Jessup. The next sentence sent a rush of adrenaline through me. 'The couple met after Katrina was injured in a car accident. She required multiple surgeries on her face and Dr. Jessup was her doctor. He admired her spirit and she fell in love with the man who saved her face.'

My phone buzzed, nearly sending me straight up to the ceiling. I pulled it out.

Briggs texted, "where are you at?"

I glanced around to see exactly where I was sitting and noticed Clive Jergens walk past the complimentary computers. He headed out a side exit that was meant for hotel employees. His phone was pressed to his ear and he looked agitated.

"I'll find you in a minute, I'm hot on the trail of something," I texted back.

My phone rang. I knew it would. I answered it.

"Lacey, what are you up to? Don't do anything dangerous. I'm just heading to Clive's room. He never came down to brunch. The hotel tried calling him, but he's not responding."

"Well, he's not in danger, if that's what you're thinking." I headed down the hallway to the employee exit. "He just walked past me out the employee exit on the west side of the ground floor." I opened the door and poked my head outside. The exit led to three trash bins and maintenance only parking spots. Clive was just disappearing around the back of the building. "I'll call you back, James." I hung up before he could protest. He wasn't going to be happy but I was on a mission and I didn't have time to fret over it.

CHAPTER 31

Once Clive was out of sight, I walked cautiously to the corner of the building and stopped at the edge, staying hidden. I pressed close to the wall and listened carefully to his conversation.

"Look, I'm stuck here because my friends were both killed last night. In fact, the same person tried to kill me. Some big shot detective is making the rounds this morning, and I'm sure I'll have to answer some questions. I'll get the money to you tomorrow. I just have to sell something first."

My mind went straight to the Rolex watch. It was obvious Clive's financial troubles went much deeper than bankruptcy. It sounded as if he was in debt to someone far more dangerous than a bank. He might have had more motive than we realized. But then my mind flashed back to what I'd just learned about Katrina Jessup. If it was true, then the caterer might have had motive too.

Clive's footsteps drew closer, ripping me from my thoughts. I raced back toward the door but feared I wouldn't make it inside in time. I ducked behind the trash bins. Clive hung up the phone call. He marched back toward the employee door and disappeared inside.

I circled around the trash bin. The large black lids were propped open, and the overwhelming odor of garbage sent a wave of nausea through me. I covered my nose and turned away from the bin. As my gaze traveled past it, a splash of bright purple caught my eye. I lifted my sweater up over my nose as a mask and hopped up on my toes to peer inside the bin. Buried deep beneath stuffed trash bags was Grady's jester hat. It was my second shot of adrenaline for the morning.

I scooted back to the side of the bin, holding my breath and working hard to ignore the harsh odors wafting up from the piles of garbage. I stepped on the narrow ledge around the bottom of the bin and hoisted myself up. I leaned my upper body into the can and stretched my arm out as far as I could. My fingertips brushed the hat, but I couldn't get a firm grasp on it.

"Lacey." Briggs' loud voice pitched me forward. I closed my eyes and braced myself for a fall into the garbage when Briggs grabbed my legs and stopped my momentum.

"Lacey, what are you doing?" He reached for my waist and helped me back off the lip of the bin.

"The hat," I said excitedly. I was still feeling the rush of excitement and my sentences were coming out in spurts. "It's there in the garbage. I found the hat. And I think Katrina Jessup is actually Jessica Trumbo. There was an accident. She didn't die and she got a nice husband out of it all."

Briggs placed his hands on each side of my face. "Slow down, Lacey. None of this is making sense."

He lowered his hands. "Start with your plummet into the trash bin."

I nodded and took a deep breath. "The jester hat is sitting right inside this bin. That's what I was digging for, only my arms were too short."

Briggs walked up to the bin and looked inside. "Well, there it is in full color. I'll have to talk to Officer Clark. He assured me his team searched trash cans for the jester's hat." He stepped up on the ledge and repeated my acrobatics act. Only his arms were long enough to reach the hat without toppling forward. He dropped back down and held the hat up high on his hand, being careful not to touch much of the fabric. The bright swaths of fabric were stained with grease and other stinky substances. Several pieces of paper were stuck to it. Briggs pulled them free.

"Do you think you'll be able to smell anything after it's been sitting in the garbage?" he asked.

"Not here by these trash bins. Let's walk it over to some fresher air. Then I can get my olfactory cells in order."

Briggs smiled at my comment. "Thank goodness for those olfactory cells and thank goodness you're so observant. A team of trained officers didn't notice the brightly colored hat sitting at the bottom of the bin."

"Maybe the trash moved around and exposed it enough for the purple to catch my eye," I offered in defense of the investigating officers.

"Or maybe none of them wanted to dig around in the disgusting trash to actually do a proper search," he countered.

"Guess that might explain it too."

We reached the corner where I'd eavesdropped on Clive. There was still so much to tell Briggs, but at the moment, I needed to focus on my sense of smell.

Briggs looked at the hat in its sorry state after a night in the trash. "I'm not quite sure if there'll be anything significant on the hat. But if it's not too disgusting . . ." He held it up to me.

"What a shame it was tossed out. It's such a nicely made hat."

"It seems someone was trying to cover their tracks."

I moved my face toward the hat and closed my eyes. I twitched my nose back and forth to wave off some of the unpleasant odors. "Why are bananas so delicious in cereal and so disgusting in the trash can?" I continued my nasal inspection, all the while trying to discern between the expected trash odors and anything different that might be evidence. It took me several passes over the fabric until a smell didn't just pop out at me but smacked in the nose, metaphorically speaking.

I looked wide-eyed at Briggs over the top of the hat. "That oily smell, the one I can't figure out—it's on the hat."

"Are you sure?" he asked.

I raised a brow at him. "I'll double check just to make sure," I said wryly.

"Right. Guess I should never question Samantha's expertise."

I lowered my face again and picked up traces of the smell on different sections of the hat. As I passed closer to the bottom of the hat, where it would have sat on Grady's head, the scent grew stronger. "James, turn the hat sideways so I can get a better angle on it."

Briggs tilted the hat. I lowered my nose to the inside rim where it would have rested against hair. The scent was strongest in the rim. I straightened. "It must be a hair product because I can smell it along the entire inside where the fabric would have touched hair. We need to find out what hair care products Grady uses," I said.

"Seems like you just sniffed together a connection to each of the murders as well as the attempted attack in the hallway."

"Wait, didn't you just talk to Grady? Were there bruises on his knuckles?" I asked.

"No but then I'm only halfway certain it was a fist. Grady's still standing by his story that the hat was stolen. But maybe that doesn't matter. If the same substance on Grady's hat is found on both victims, that could be the evidence we need. Let's get back inside. We need to find Grady before he leaves." He lifted the hat. "This needs to go to evidence. I don't want to walk through the hotel with it and tip off our murderer. Let's put it in your trunk before we go back inside."

CHAPTER 32

*W*e weren't ten feet inside when Briggs stopped me in the empty hallway. "Wait, Lacey, what were you saying about Katrina Jessup really being Jessica Trumbo?"

I tapped the side of my head. "I nearly forgot all about that after finding the hat. It was sort of crazy at first and my theory seemed thin but then pieces started fitting in the holes."

"Lace—"

"Right, I'm getting to it. I was looking at Jessica's senior portrait and something about her looked familiar. Later, I realized what it was. Jessica had pretty almond-shaped, hazel eyes that looked remarkably similar to Katrina's eyes. Jessica had dreams of becoming a concert pianist. That's when my wild notion really started to gel."

"I don't understand," Briggs said, looking rightfully perplexed. (The man even made confusion look good.)

"Earlier, when I walked past Katrina's office, I caught her pretending to play piano on her desk while she was looking at paperwork. There was classical music playing on her computer. Even though it was just pretend, it looked as if she knew what she was doing on her invisible keyboard. By the way, the hand cream they use in the kitchen doesn't match up to the oily smell. Anyhow, after I caught her playing air piano, I headed straight out to the hotel guest computer and did a little research. Everyone at the reunion thought Jessica Trumbo had died in the car accident. Even Grady Ramone, her good friend." I snapped my fingers. "Or did he?" I asked.

Still somewhat baffled, Briggs waited for me to answer my own question.

"Maybe Grady knew all along that Katrina was really Jessica Trumbo. Maybe they killed both men for revenge because of how badly they'd been teased in high school." Brainstorming out loud wasn't helping to convince me though. My enthusiastic posture, one that would have made my third grade teacher proud, crumpled. "But then they are both so successful. Why would they throw that all away? Then the bullies would have won anyhow."

"You mean the dead bullies?" Briggs asked.

"Well, I meant won in the virtual sense because if it's true that Grady and Jessica, I mean Katrina, murdered Riley and Dane, they haven't won at all. They'd be going straight to jail."

"Yes, they would. If that's where the evidence leads." Briggs rubbed his chin. "I don't get it. If Katrina is Jessica, how come no one recognizes her? Ten years isn't such a long time."

"That's where the story gets good enough for a Hollywood movie," I said excitedly. I had never untangled something so complicated, and I was feeling pretty good about my investigative skills. "Jessica was in a terrible accident. Her car flipped and she was thrown into the driver's side window, injuring her face and hands. I suppose that's why she gave up the piano. The doctor who helped heal her and saved her face was a plastic surgeon named Dr. Calvin Jessup."

"So they fell in love while she was his patient," Briggs said. The pieces were coming together for him too. "I wonder why she never told anyone she was Jessica. She's obviously done well for herself. Unless, she came here for a specific reason," he added darkly.

"Exactly. When Debra and I were setting up flowers, Debra mentioned how lucky she was to get Elegant Edibles as the caterer for the reunion. But it wasn't luck or coincidence because Katrina reached out to her when she saw a post online about the reunion."

"Well then, it seems we need to talk to both Grady and Jessi —Katrina."

CHAPTER 33

*M*ore people were lingering in the hallway, chatting and saying their farewells when we got back to the room where brunch was nearing conclusion. We looked around but didn't see Grady. Clive was filling his plate with eggs.

"There's Clive," Briggs said. "Looks like he'll be here eating for awhile. Let's go talk to Katrina first. When I spoke with Grady earlier, he was going to work on his laptop while waiting for a two o'clock flight."

We headed straight to the caterer's kitchen. I was feeling a rush of nerves about confronting Katrina. She was going to be more than shocked when we revealed to her that we knew her true identity. Then an explosion of nerves hit me. I grabbed Briggs' arm just before he reached for the door.

"What if I'm wrong?" I asked. "I'm confident about my nose but what if I'm wrong about this?"

He winked. "You forget who you're with. I'm not going to just walk in there and blurt out an accusation."

He swung open the door and I followed him into the kitchen. The catering team was moving slower than the day before. I couldn't blame them. Three straight days of cooking and serving seemed exhausting. The lingering aroma of brunch swirled around us.

We found Katrina sitting in her office. Just like an hour earlier, she was more than surprised to see me, especially when she saw Briggs with me. "My goodness, I can't believe I'm still part of this investigation." Her words were light but her tone was harsh.

"Yes, I'm sure you didn't expect us back," Briggs said. "I know work is almost done here, so, Jessica, if you don't mind, I thought I'd ask you a few more questions." He glided so smoothly over the name, she didn't even notice.

Katrina clicked out of her computer screen and sat back. "Ask away. I've got nothing to hide," she said rather confidently for someone who was hiding a heck of a lot.

"So it is Jessica then?" Briggs asked.

Her face blanched white. Her eyes darted around the room as if she was looking for some magical escape exit, or, at the very least, making sure none of her employees were around to hear the conversation.

"No, I'm Katrina," she said brusquely. "I wasn't paying attention to what you said. I thought you said Katrina."

"No, I said Jessica and you didn't even flinch. Which leads me to believe that you're used to being called Jessica when you're at home with the family. Katrina is just your business name," Briggs continued undaunted by the look of shock on her face.

She sat forward. "What is it you want, Detective?" It seemed she was no longer putting up a fight about her true identity. I gave myself a virtual pat on the back for a job well done.

"I suppose my first question would be—why haven't you revealed yourself to your classmates? They all think Jessica is dead."

"That wasn't my fault. Someone heard a rumor that I'd died and they posted about it. The accident happened out of state, and I hadn't kept in contact with anyone from high school. As far as I'm concerned they can go right on thinking I'm dead. In a way, that awkward girl from high school is dead. I'm a different person now. I want nothing to do with those high school years."

"Except you sought out this catering job," Briggs pointed out.

Again, she was stunned by what he knew. She stared up at him for a long moment, then reached for her purse. "If you want to hear all about my diabolical plan of revenge—here it is." She dug deep inside for a few seconds pulling out sunglasses, another tube of the hand cream, and a tin of mints before finding what she was looking for. Her hand emerged with a box of what appeared to be an over the counter laxative.

Katrina slapped it on the desk. Briggs and I stared down at it, both wondering why she felt the need to expose her personal digestion issues.

"Yes, I saw the post about the reunion and sought out the job. I figured those three bums would show up to let everyone see just how little they'd changed. And I was right about that," she said with a head shake of disbelief. "Dane didn't even realize he was trying to flirt with the girl he used to call Dumbo." She pushed her hair back, exposing two nice ears. "My husband pinned them back for me. It was painful but not nearly as painful as the taunts I endured when they stuck out nearly perpendicular from my head. When I heard Dane's name called out in the hospitality kitchen, the idea to confront him outweighed my common sense. I walked into his room to tell him off, and he had the nerve to grab for me. I pushed him away and told him he wasn't worth the dirt on the bottom of his shoe. Then I ran from the room, mad at myself for bothering to challenge him."

As she spoke my empathy grew for her. The torture she must have endured in high school, bullying so rough she actually showed up to her own reunion as a completely different person.

"I knew all three of them had flown into town. I thought an uncomfortable plane ride would be a nice slice of revenge for the agony they caused me. My plan was to grind up these laxatives and put a heaping bunch in their breakfasts. Then Debra changed her mind to a buffet style brunch, so my plans went out the window."

Briggs cleared his throat. "Actually, I think your plans were out the window anyhow considering two of them are dead."

"Yes, and I'm not sorry about it either," Katrina confessed easily. "In fact, I came close to revealing my true self to Grady Ramone just so we could have a private smile about it. But I decided to keep to myself. I can tell you this, while I haven't shed a tear for either of them, I certainly didn't kill them. In high school, I pictured it often, though. Getting some kind of horrible revenge on them. I have everything I want now, a good husband, a successful business, ears that no longer serve as wind flaps," she added with a light laugh. "Why would I throw all that away? Then the bullies would win again, just like they always did in high school."

I peeked over at Briggs, who seemed to be feeling the same way as me. While she had good motive, Katrina didn't kill Riley and Dane. He nodded. "Thank you. We won't take up any more of your time, Mrs. Jessup."

We walked out of the kitchen and into the hallway.

"Penny for your thoughts," I said, elbowing him lightly.

"They aren't worth that much, I'm afraid. I was just replaying what she said in there about not throwing her successful life away on the men who bullied her."

We stopped and I looked at him. "And that has you thinking about Grady?" I asked

His charming crooked smile appeared. "Are you sure that nose of yours is the only thing with super power? Sometimes I think you can look right into my head and read my thoughts."

"Or do we just think alike?" We headed toward the elevator. "Are we still going to talk to Grady?"

"Yes, but first I want to talk to Clive. I think there's more to his story."

I stopped so fast, I could almost hear my shoes squeal like a car's tires. "With the hat and the whole thing with Katrina and Jessica or is it Katrina *or* Jessica—" I waved my hand. "Anyhow, in all the excitement, I forgot to tell you why I was outside near the garbage cans."

Briggs looked stunned with himself that he'd not asked the same question. "That's right. You just reminded me of our phone conversation where I was warning you not to do anything dangerous, and you were ignoring me."

"Yes, well, not purposefully, just out of necessity. Clive walked out that back door. I waited for him to turn the corner," I added quickly, letting him know just how cautious I'd been. His brow lift assured me he wasn't buying it. "Anyhow, I walked to the corner. Clive has one of those deep, from the barrel kind of voices so I could easily eaves—" I cleared my throat. "Overhear his conversation. He was pleading with someone to give him more time and that he'd have the money as soon as he sold something."

Briggs' brown eyes lit up. "Like a Rolex watch?"

"That's the first thing that popped into my mind. See, we really do think alike."

CHAPTER 34

*B*riggs motioned for us to continue to the elevator. "I was heading toward Clive as a person of interest. What you *overheard* adds weight to my suspicions." He pulled out his phone as we waited for the elevator. "I wasn't up to it last night, but this morning I looked at that jester's hat picture again and something doesn't seem right." He held it up for me to look at it with him. "The angle is so odd, like Clive went out of his way to make sure no head or shoulders were caught in the shadow."

"Do you think Clive stole it himself? He did seem to know about that employee exit, the one leading to the trash bins."

"Good point," Briggs said as he put the phone away. "All I know is the picture just seems too staged for someone who, on the spur of the moment, decided to snap a photo of a shadow." Briggs looked over at me as we exited the elevator on the fourth floor. "When was the last time you snapped a photo of a shadow? Then the whole story about Grady running off before he could spin around and confront him didn't hold much water either." He stopped to illustrate his point. He held up his camera snapped a picture of me and spun around quickly. "Not much time there for someone to make a clear escape, especially not in a jester's costume." He glanced down at his feet. "I didn't see the full costume, but I'm assuming since the hat was such high quality that Grady was wearing the long, pointy jester shoes."

I thought back to the previous night when the guests were streaming into the party in their costumes. "Yes, I think you're right. Grady was dressed head to toe. It really was a spectacular costume. I would have noticed if he was wearing sneakers."

"So, if Grady had snuck up on Dane, planning to hurt him, he would have had to run very fast, not just around the corner but to the nearest stairwell to disappear without being seen. And his attire would have made that a much harder task."

We turned down the hallway. The housekeeper's cart was sitting in the hallway outside Room 420. The door was propped open. Inside the room, a vacuum cleaner was hissing and spewing out a musty carpet smell.

Briggs picked up his pace and I followed suit. The housekeeper's eyes rounded when she saw us in the doorway. She turned off the noisy vacuum.

"I hate to stop your work but did the guest staying in this room check out?"Briggs asked.

"I haven't seen him, but his suitcase is still here," she motioned to the closet. Clive's bag was sitting on the suitcase rack. It was locked up and tagged for the airport.

The shower in the bathroom turned off, and a second housekeeper was followed out by a steamy cloud of bathroom cleaners. Carrying a trash can, she smiled politely as I stepped out of her way. My gaze dropped to the contents in the trash can as she brushed past.

"Hold on," I said.

The woman turned back to me. "Yes?"

"I just need to check something." I reached inside the can for my second garbage dig of the day. Without touching too much, I grasped the mostly empty tube of hair gel. The outside of the tube had a picture of a vampire. It was the cheap kind of hair gel you could get at a costume shop. Clive had used the entire tube, even rolling it up like a toothpaste tube to get every bit out. Fortunately, there was still plenty of product left for my nose.

Briggs had noticed what I was up to. He walked over and waited as I gave the crumpled tube a sniff. I gave it a good once over and nodded. "Yep, that's the oily smell I found on the phone cord, Riley's sweater and the jester's hat. When Clive came down to the party, his hair was slicked back with this stuff to go with his vampire costume."

Just then, Clive showed up in the doorway to his room. "What's this about?" he asked sharply.

Briggs walked toward him. "Mr. Jergens, may I see your knuckles?"

That was all it took. Clive's face smoothed with fright. He grabbed the room door and swung it shut, closing us into the room.

"Stay here, Lacey." Briggs dashed toward the door and raced out.

Naturally, I ran to the hallway. Briggs hadn't pulled his gun but he had his hand close to his holster as he turned the corner of the hallway. I scooted to the edge of the corner and peered around it. The door to the stairwell was just closing. Briggs grabbed it and gave chase down the stairs. On his way through the door, I heard him on his phone calling in back up units to the Chesterton Regency. It seemed the hotel was about to add to its weekend of bad publicity.

My heart thumped in worry. Clive had nearly knocked Briggs out with one punch to the head. He was obviously as strong as he was mean. Still clutching the incriminating tube of hair gel, I ran to the stairway door and looked through the narrow vertical window. A flurry of moving shadows splashed on the wall one flight down. I couldn't stop myself. If Briggs was in trouble, I'd never forgive myself for just watching from a tiny window.

I pulled open the door and raced to the edge of the landing on the fourth floor. As I looked down over the handrail, Clive flew up against the hard wall of the stairwell. His nose dripped blood as he sank to his knees with a groan.

Seconds later, Briggs stepped into view. My deep sigh of relief echoed through the stairs.

Briggs' attention was on the suspect, but he still managed a curt lecture. "You never listen," he said.

"I was worried about you," I said meekly in my defense.

"Take the elevator down. I'm taking him down through the stairs.

See if you can find the hotel manager at the desk. Tell him I need Room 420 secured now. No one can enter and that includes the housekeeping staff."

I hurried back onto the floor and ran to the elevator. It just so happened the manager, Ronald Sexton, was stepping out of it. The employees must have alerted the front desk that something was up. His face bunched with worry when he saw me.

"Mr. Sexton, Detective Briggs has caught the murder suspect. He's taking him down the stairwell. More units will be arriving soon if you could tell the housekeeping staff not to touch anything else and secure the room."

"When will this nightmare be over?" he muttered as he headed toward Room 420.

I caught the elevator before it left the fourth floor and jumped inside. Earlier my heart was thumping in fear, now it was dancing with adrenaline. Police work was exciting stuff, especially when the bad guys got caught. As the elevator dropped down to the bottom floor, I stared at the half rolled tube of hair gel in my hand. Clive's hideous plot was betrayed by a five dollar tube of vampire hair gel.

Briggs managed the entire scene outside with minimal chaos. He had his suspect, a man who'd apparently acted alone and out of envy. His two best friends had left him out of a successful real estate venture, and apparently, Clive couldn't forgive them. The remaining reunion guests, including Debra and Grady, huddled outside in a chilly mist to watch their former classmate get searched and placed into a squad car. Katrina stood next to Grady. From the look on his face, it seemed Katrina had confessed her secret to her old friend.

I joined them. Debra greeted me first. "What a wild weekend, eh? Not exactly what I envisioned, but now I'm just glad it's over. Thank you for all your help, Lacey. And be sure to thank Detective Briggs for us."

"I'm just glad the murderer has been caught." I smiled tentatively at Grady and Katrina. "Is the cat out of the bag?" I asked Katrina.

"Yes." She placed her arm around Grady's. "I'm actually glad we got a chance to talk. We had a lot of catching up to do."

Grady nodded. "Let's just say this weekend has far surpassed my expectations."

Debra laughed. "Praise indeed coming from a man who builds rocket ships."

The three watched as the police car drove away with Clive. "In high school," Grady said quietly, "I always wondered when Dane, Riley and Clive would finally get what they deserved. It never happened. They barreled right through those years being as mean and unlikeable and inexplicably popular as ever. They seemed to have everything. But I guess in the end, it caught up to them."

"With all the times I imagined myself getting revenge on those three," Katrina said. "I never would have expected this kind of an ending."

One of the officers carried Clive's suitcase out of the hotel. He walked it over to the squad car where Briggs was talking to two officers.

I nodded politely at the three friends. "Hope you all have a safe trip home. I think I'll join Detective Briggs to hear more details on the case."

"Good-bye, Lacey. And thanks again," Debra called as I walked away.

Briggs opened the suitcase just as I reached him. A small amount of digging produced the shiny gold watch. Briggs dropped it into an evidence bag.

"Did he confess to anything?" I asked.

"Not a full confession. He tried to deny it at first but then I asked him how his knuckles got bruised and he started spilling details. Turns out he had taken Riley's room key card after he shoved him off the balcony. He was planning to come back after the excitement had died down and search his things for anything of value. He was also on the hunt for a phone cord. Apparently strangling his friend with his own cord had left him with the inconvenience of a dying phone."

"What about the jester's hat picture?" I asked.

"When Clive saw it sitting in the lounge of the men's restroom, he decided to use it to his advantage. He thought if he made himself look like a victim too, then the police wouldn't look at him as a suspect. What he didn't know was that the police had a secret weapon." He leaned forward and rubbed my nose with his.

"Samantha was definitely on point today."

"Definitely." Briggs pushed a newly forming curl off my forehead. "This weather is wet and miserable. I think I owe you a hot lunch at Franki's."

"I was just going to suggest the same thing."

CHAPTER 35

$\mathscr{I}$ crossed my arms against the chill as I waited for Briggs to climb out of his car. Bear galumphed out behind him and loped toward the porch when he saw me. A leash stopped his progress, so I walked down the stairs to greet them.

I rubbed Bear's soft ears and hugged his big warm head. The dog had almost grown into his magnificent paws, but it seemed he might still get bigger. I glanced back to my house. The front window was open a few inches, but Nevermore was not in sight.

I turned back to Briggs. He was looking handsome in a dark green flannel shirt over a black t-shirt. "To tell you the truth, James, I'm not sure if this plan will work. Nevermore usually jumps right to the windowsill if I open it, no matter what the weather. I think he knows something is up. He's been hanging back, away from the window."

"We'll give him some time. It's the best way I can think of to get that darn elephant out of the room." Briggs patted his dog's head. "On the way over here, Bear and I had a long talk about decorum, polite society, cats and their sensitivities and not acting like a slobbering fool. I think he was listening to at least part of it. I also told him that if he didn't straighten up and learn to behave around Nevermore, he'd find himself stuck in the dog house. Literally."

I leaned down to the dog. "You can do it, can't you, Bear?" He licked my nose.

"Hey, watch it, buddy, that's a million dollar nose," Briggs mused as we headed up the porch. We sat on the bench near the front window. Briggs' plan for our pet problem was to introduce them slowly, like through a window screen. It seemed like a good plan as long as Nevermore could work up the courage to come to the window screen while Bear was on the other side of it.

I reached down and picked up the thermos of hot chocolate I'd made for our time on the porch. I handed Briggs a cup and poured in the cocoa. "I've got some mini marshmallows inside," I suggested.

He sipped his cocoa. "Nope, this is fine."

Dash's front door opened and shut. He was dressed nicely, and his usually wild hair was combed back. He didn't notice us sitting on the porch as he climbed into his truck and drove off.

"Vanhouten looks polished up," Briggs said dryly. He was still never overjoyed to see Dash. He never brought him up in conversation, but he was able to at least say his name now without getting red in the face.

"I think he might have a date with Elsie's niece, Britney. Elsie is not in love with the idea of them dating."

"I don't blame her," Briggs said into his cup before taking a sip.

"I think Dash is lonely. This will be good for him. As long as he doesn't break her heart," I added. "Otherwise, he'll be sorry because Elsie might just bake him into gingerbread cookies."

Briggs enjoyed that idea. He dropped his arm around my shoulder and tugged me closer. "I have to say, even though Dash and I were sort of what I guess might be considered big men on campus back in high school, neither of us ever bullied people. There were plenty of mean kids in our school, but I guess we were raised right."

I rested my head against his shoulder. "That's the kindest thing I've ever heard you say about Dash."

"Yeah but don't get too used to it."

A low meow sounded behind us. Bear popped right to his feet. Briggs pointed at him. "What did we talk about in the car, buddy.

Nobody likes a slobbering fool." As if the big dog had understood every word, he lowered his ears and his tail and walked politely to the window. Nevermore's hair went straight up, but he stayed on the windowsill. Eventually, the cat relaxed enough to press his nose against the screen. Bear pushed back with his nose, and the two animals sniffed each other civilly.

"See, one elephant successfully removed from the room," Briggs said confidently.

I rested back under Briggs' protective arm. "Or at least put behind the screen. But I think if we're patient, they'll be fine."

Briggs squeezed me to him. "They have no choice."

WALNUT DATE SCONES

View online at: www.londonlovett.com/recipe-box/

Walnut Date
SCONES

Ingredients:

2 3/4 cup all-purpose flour
2 Tbsp brown sugar
1 Tbsp baking powder
1/4 tsp salt
1/2 cup butter, cold and cut in cubes
2 eggs, lightly beaten
2/3 cup buttermilk
1 cup walnuts, chopped
1 cup pitted dates, chopped (about 14 dates)

Maple Glaze:
3/4 cup powdered sugar
2 Tbsp maple syrup
1/2 tsp vanilla
1 Tbsp milk

Directions:

1. Preheat oven to 375°

2. Whisk together dry ingredients: flour, brown sugar, baking powder, salt.

3. Use pastry cutter or food processor to incorporate butter into dry mixture until it resembles coarse crumbs.

4. Mix together eggs and buttermilk. Pour wet ingredients into the dry mixture. Stir until moisture is distributed evenly.

5. Fold in the chopped walnuts and dates.

6. Turn dough out onto a floured surface (You'll need around 1/4 cup extra flour for this step.)

7. Pat dough into an 8 inch square, and then cut int 9 squares. Cut each square on the diagonal so that you end up with 18 small scones.

8. Place scones on a baking sheet lined with parchment paper and bake for 12-14 minutes or until lightly golden in color.

9. Allow scones to cool and prepare the maple glaze.

10. Whisk together maple glaze ingredients until combined and drizzle over scones. Or you can use it as a dipping sauce on the side.

11. Enjoy your scone with a cup of your favorite tea or coffee!

LONDON LOVETT

CROCUSES AND CRIME

CHAPTER 1

A few warmer than average days had melted the early January snow and rivers of ice cold water rushed along the Harbor Lane gutters toward the coast. The crisp morning air still prompted me to push my coat collar up higher to hug my ears. Normally, the chill would have prompted Kingston to trot quickly toward the flower shop door, but Elsie's newest endeavor, a seating area for people with dogs, pulled my always hungry bird toward the bakery. On a long winter jog around town, a new, bold idea popped into Elsie's head. (She insisted she always did her best thinking when she was out on a run. I told her I'd be happy to test her theory as long as it didn't require me to actually run.) Her brilliant, new plan, hatched on pops of endorphins, was to start baking dog treats. Naturally, as with everything Elsie created, the peanut butter pup biscuits were a huge success. It wasn't until last week that Elsie decided her new furry customers needed a place in the sidewalk seating area to enjoy their goodies.

Elsie had squeezed together her overly elegant sidewalk tables to make room for three curved benches, painted a bright blue. Whimsical yellow paw prints were hand stenciled along the backs of each bench. A large swath of fake grass acted as the outdoor rug beneath the benches. Silver water bowls sat at the end of each bench so that her newest customers had something to wash down the peanut butter biscuit.

Kingston had quickly discovered that the green Astroturf rug was the perfect catchall for biscuit crumbs. He'd taken it upon himself to 'tidy-up' the place every morning. His sharp black beak disappeared between the thin green blades of fake grass as he quickly rid the area of messy tidbits.

Elsie saw me waiting for Kingston. Dressed in a pale green apron that was stained with what appeared to be blueberry she hurried around the counter. On her way to the door, she grabbed a bone shaped dog biscuit. She waved it in the air as she stepped outside. Kingston's head shot straight up and he waddled quickly toward the cookie. Elsie leaned over to offer the crow his goodie.

"You're such a good boy, coming by each morning to clean up after those silly, slobbery pups that you deserve a reward." She cooed to Kingston in a tiny, cartoonish voice as if she was talking to a baby. Elsie wasn't my crow's first true love, (Lola held that prestigious title) but her newest marketing idea could eventually win her the crown. I wondered when I would win it, considering I was the one who boiled him eggs every morning and kept his perch and cage clean.

Elsie looked up and smiled. Her gray streaked, toffee colored hair was swept back into a neat bun, which meant she was engaged in some serious baking. The stains on her apron were proof of that too. "I'm making some sweet cherry and blueberry tarts. They have a pecan shortbread crust. Come by later if you want to sample them."

I walked toward her. "You know you only have to ask me once. Actually, you don't even have to ask once. The aromas drifting through my shop wall are the only invite I need. Aren't sweet cherries a summer fruit?"

Elsie's lips rolled in shyly. "Yes. Don't tell anyone but I had to resort to frozen cherries."

I feigned a dramatic gasp. "Shocking. But your secret is safe with me mostly because my unsophisticated pallet can't discern between fresh and frozen. And because I like anything that comes out of your oven."

"I had no choice since fresh cherries are months away. I just thought we needed a little summer sweetness during this long, dreary winter."

"Like I said, I'm not here to judge . . . just taste."

Kingston had finished his treat and was busy collecting up his own crumbs. "Thanks for making my bird happy. Guess I should open up for business." I turned to head to the flower shop.

"If you have time later," Elsie said, "I need to talk." Her expression soured into a frown as she motioned with her head toward the bakery. From the look on her face, I knew we wouldn't be discussing baked goods. Elsie's twenty-five-year-old niece, Britney, had arrived in town a few months earlier. She was a budding baker with great talent. She was skilled and hardworking and extremely pretty. She'd also caught the eye of the town's most eligible bachelor, Dashwood Vanhouten, my neighbor and friend.

"Uh oh, trouble in paradise?" I asked.

Elsie rolled her eyes. "I'll say. Come by later. Some of the tarts will be ready."

I managed to lure Kingston away from the bakery tables. Once inside the shop, Kingston flew to his window perch and I headed to the office. I'd only just put away my purse in my desk drawer when the bell rang. The smell of coffee energized me as I headed to the front of the shop. Lester was pacing the floor, clutching a cup of coffee in his hand. His face was scrunched up, signaling he was either deep in thought or distressed.

"Les, is everything all right?"

My voice startled him as if he hadn't expected to see and hear me in my own shop. "Oh, yes, uh, here." He walked forward with the coffee. "It's hazelnut with extra whipped cream. Your favorite."

I took hold of the cup and breathed in the rich, nutty aroma. "Between you and Elsie, I'm going to be too wide to fit through my front door. But, thank you." I took a sip. The hot earthy liquid was cooled just enough by the delicate cream. "Heaven in a cup. This was very thoughtful of you, Les." During the warmer months, Les wore brightly colored Hawaiian shirts and sandals. Even with the white cloud of hair on top of his head, his dark blue winter sweater made him look much more somber. His serious brow only added to the uncharacteristically gloomy look.

"What's up, Les? You don't seem your usual cheery self."

His mound of white hair tossed about as he shook his head. "It's that sister of mine. She's really gone off the deep end with that dog park in front of her bakery."

I should have guessed that his glum mood would have something to do with what I amusingly referred to as the Great Table War. Ever since I'd moved into the store between Elsie's bakery and Les's coffee shop, the two had been in a brutal and expensive competition to outdo each other on their sidewalk table arrangements. Because of my neighbors, Port Danby was home to some of the fanciest sidewalk eating areas in the country. For months they tried to one up each other with lush seat cushions, misting fans, heating lamps and free goodies. I thought they'd both exhausted their creative ideas and their pocket books because the war seemed to have fizzled to an occasional sparring. But Elsie's newest venture into dog bakery treats seemed to have sparked a new battle.

Lester rubbed the gray stubble on his chin as he sat on a stool at the counter. "What am I supposed to serve on my side to entice dog owners to sit in front of the coffee shop?" The most comical part about the entire thing, aside from a brief scandal with a cardboard Mr. Darcy, was that customers generally bought from both Les and Elsie when they came for a treat. There was no better compliment to Elsie's baked goods than one of Lester's rich, aromatic coffees and vice versa. The table war wasn't really a competition for business more than it was a popularity contest. People sitting in front, filling up tables and chairs, made the place look popular. But no matter how I tried to explain to each of them that they both had reason to be proud of their shops, I couldn't get past the stubborn wall of sibling rivalry.

"I wish I had some suggestion for you, Les, but I just don't think dogs will go for coffee lattes. Although, my cat, Nevermore, would be happy to help with the whipped cream." I took another sip and licked the cream off my lip. "Yum. So good." I could see our chat was not helping his mood. "Look, Les, if it makes you feel any better—" I leaned closer. "And this is just between the two of us. Not a word to your sister."

Les's blue-gray eyes sparkled with anticipation. "My lips are sealed."

"I'm not sure how long Elsie will put up with the dog area. Yesterday, as I was locking up, I heard her over there muttering to herself about someone letting their dog lift its leg on the bench. She was tossing a bucket of water on the bench to clean it. You know how particular Elsie is about everything."

He chuckled wryly. "I grew up with the woman. I know too well." Les hopped down off the stool. "You might be right, Lacey. I hadn't thought about the possible drawbacks to her plan. I guess I should just go back to my place and do what I do best—make coffee. Sorry to take up part of your morning with my silliness."

I held up the cup of coffee. "If anything, you made my morning brighter. I think it's a good start to what I'm sure will be a wonderful week and all because you came in and treated me with my favorite hazelnut coffee."

Under the mop of white hair, the crinkle of lines next to his blue eyes made me think of Santa. Only we were well past Santa season, and Les never had more than a few gray stubbles on his chin.

Les walked over to pat Kingston on the head. "Is it me or is this crow getting fat?"

I cleared my throat. "He prefers to be called husky, and yes, that has something to do with Elsie's new dog treats too."

Les shook his head. "That woman," he muttered as he headed toward the door. "Just when I think she's going to finally start slowing down, she finds more energy."

"I just wish she could find some way to bottle whatever magic she's using," I called. I raised up my coffee in a thank you toast as Les waved and walked out.

CHAPTER 2

"I think I have a new favorite flower," I announced to Ryder as I stuck the lavender crocus into the white vase. I stepped back to admire the casual cluster of long stemmed crocuses. Thick, soft petals cupped around fuzzy, bright yellow stigmata made them look like the more relaxed, easy going cousin of tulips. I ran my fingers along the lush petals of a bright yellow blossom. "And their colors remind of me of Easter eggs. Just what is needed to offset the bland, monochromatic winter landscape."

Ryder walked up to the work island. "They are stunning." He rubbed his finger across the stigma of a purple bloom. "Crocus sativus. Saffron comes from this type."

I nodded. "I actually knew that . . . for a change," I said from the side of my mouth. Ryder was a veritable treasure chest of information, especially when it came to horticulture. I'd learned a great deal from my assistant. "I've never cooked with saffron. Not even sure I'd know what to do with it. Plus the exorbitant price tag makes it one of those ingredients I can only dream about—like caviar and truffles. Not that I'd know what to do with them either."

"Fish eggs, fungus that grows underground and flower stigmata," Ryder laughed. "It's almost as if someone somewhere said 'hey, look at these slimy fish eggs. We'll slap a high price on them and people will think they are something special when in reality they are just fish eggs'."

"Oh my gosh, wouldn't that be funny if all this time caviar was just a big prank someone was pulling?" My phone beeped with a text. I picked it up off the counter.

"Cherry tarts are done if you're interested."

"Oh, I'm interested," I texted back. "Elsie desperately needs my taste testing abilities, and I hate to let her down. So, off I go. I'll bring you back a cherry tart."

"I'll hold down the fort," he called as I headed out the door.

The rich fragrance of butter and brown sugar tiptoed between the tart, sweet aroma of cherries. "The thermometer would, no doubt, argue the point, but I smell summer in the air," I practically sang as I walked into the bakery.

Elsie came out from her kitchen with a plate of tarts, flakey golden crusts flecked with pecans tenderly cradling a bubbling mix of deep purple fruit.

"See, Pink, you get me. My goal with these was to bake a little sunshine and warmth into these dreary winter days." Elsie lowered the plate of tarts onto her gleaming white counter. She baked all day like a mad woman and still managed to keep her bakery as clean as a hospital. It made me more than certain about what I'd told Lester this morning to ease his anguish about the dog benches.

Elsie moved a tart onto a plate and handed it to me. It was still warm as I gently picked it up. The fragrant steam nearly overwhelmed my super power nose, but that didn't stop me from taking the first bite. A carnival of flavors and textures filled my mouth. The hot fruit filling was just sour enough to be pleasantly complimented by the sugary crust.

"Hmm, my friend, you have done it." I held up the tart. "This is a summer picnic in a grassy meadow all mixed together in pastry perfection. I hadn't realized how badly I needed a taste of sunshine until this moment."

"Wonderful. Goal accomplished. I'm going to draw a picture of the sun on my sidewalk chalkboard, and underneath, it will say stop in for a bite of summer."

"Genius." I took another bite of the tart and was certain I'd finish every crumb in one long taste test. I was so absorbed in my treat, I hadn't noticed that Elsie's expression had drooped some. She stretched up and looked past me out the front window.

"Are you expecting someone?" I asked.

"Just Britney. I sent her to the Corner Market for some lemons. I wanted to have a few minutes alone to talk to you." Even though we were completely alone, she pushed the tarts aside and leaned closer. "Dash hasn't called her in over a week. She's texted him a few times but only got short, clipped responses back." A flush of color darkened her cheeks. "I knew he was like this. I should never have let her date him in the first place. Now, she's so distracted, she had to throw out an entire batch of cookies when she absently grabbed the salt instead of sugar."

I crinkled my nose at the thought of that unfortunate mix up. "That's not good. I'm sure Dash has just been too busy down at the marina." I'd fretted more than once that I'd somehow end up in the middle of the Britney and Dash relationship. Frankly, I didn't need to be sandwiched in another tumultuous pairing. I was already the unwilling referee, confidante and makeshift therapist in the center of Ryder and Lola's tenuous teaming. Although, that was more my fault because I spent the good part of six months persuading the two of them that they'd make a great couple. Great turned out to be a slight misjudgment on my part. Interesting might have been a better adjective to use. It was certainly never dull in Ryder's and Lola's world of romance. But I just didn't think I could be the buffering zone or sounding board for another couple. Dash had figured that out early enough that he never brought up his relationship with Britney when we chatted. We tended to keep our conversations light, airy and far from anything serious, and I liked it that way.

Elsie picked up a white cloth from the hook at the end of the counter and started wiping down her cash register. Elsie had a tendency to clean and tidy up things that didn't need it when she was angry. I attributed the habit to having an abundance of energy and needing to release it whenever it built up. When she was upset, she needed to blow off steam immediately. She buffed away on the chrome register even though I could already see my reflection in it.

"He's got some nerve messing up that girl's head. Britney was doing an outstanding job. I thought I'd finally found an assistant who could live up to my standards." She vigorously rubbed the top of the register and then moved to the stapler sitting next to it.

Elsie had searched for an assistant for months, never finding anyone suited to the task. When Britney arrived, bursting with enthusiasm and talent, Elsie worried that Britney would outshine her, but the two had settled into a nice working relationship. Elsie finally had some much needed help in the bakery. I hoped that Dash hadn't ruined the whole thing.

"Maybe Britney just needs to give him some space," I suggested lamely. "I know it's cliché," I added quickly before Elsie could arch a brow at me. "Dash has been a bachelor for a long time, and we both know there has never been a shortage of women interested in landing him."

Elsie laughed wryly. "Kate Yardley is evidence of that. Britney made the mistake of walking into the Mod Frock to buy a skirt. Kate was so rude, Britney left empty handed."

"Kate *does* let everyone know what she's thinking." I finished the last bite of tart, but the conversation was putting a dimmer on the sunshine switch. I could see I wasn't being much support to Elsie, as evidenced by the vigorous way she buffed her stapler.

I reached over to stop her manic moment with a dust cloth. My hand clamped over hers. She lowered the stapler. "Sorry, you know how I get when I'm upset."

"Yes, but I think you need to let this take its course. Just keep an eye on the salt and try not to worry about it, Elsie. Britney is a beautiful girl with so much to offer. And she's so young."

Elsie huffed loudly. "That she is. She is so confident about everything else, I sometimes forget that she is still only in her mid-twenties. She is so talented. I only wish I had that much talent."

I tilted my head with a brow lift. "Really? I just vacuumed down that tart, one that was still a few degrees too hot, as if my life depended on it. I think your talent is still uncontested in this part of the world." I'd been debating offering to talk to Dash and was just about to mention it when Britney walked into the bakery with a bag of lemons.

She'd recently had her shiny brown hair cut with layers and long bangs. They highlighted her almond shaped brown eyes, making her look even prettier, if that was possible. "Hello, Lacey," she said sweetly. "Auntie, this was the last bag of lemons." She squeezed one of them. "They have thin peels, so they should have plenty of juice. Do you want me to get started on the lemon-lavender cupcakes?"

"Yes, please."

Britney smiled politely before pulling her phone out of her jacket. She stared at it as she disappeared into the kitchen with the fruit. She definitely wasn't herself.

I looked questioningly at Elsie. "Lemon and lavender? More summer?"

Elsie shrugged. "You know how it is when I shoot off on a tangent."

"No complaints here. That tart makes me want to go home and pull out my beach umbrella and swimsuit. Anyhow, I need to get back. Oh and I promised one for Ryder." I picked up a tart. I hated to think I was leaving the bakery, satiated with a summer tart but leaving my friend still distraught about her niece and Dash. Without giving it more thought, I leaned toward her and dropped my tone to a whisper. "If I see Dash, I'll ask how things are going and see what I can find out."

Elsie mouthed the words 'thank you'.

I turned to leave. Elsie's voice returned to its normal volume. "I forgot to ask, how is that handsome detective of yours? He hasn't been in lately for his usual breakfast pastry."

I laughed. "He insisted he was getting a paunch around his belt line from eating too many baked goods. But everything with *my* detective is just fine. Thanks again for the tarts, Elsie."

CHAPTER 3

*R*yder helped me finish the five other bouquets of crocuses. A customer had ordered them for a special retirement party. The lavender, yellow and white clusters added a rainbow of delight to the shop.

I turned one vase around to examine it on all sides. "I stand by my earlier statement. Crocuses are my new favorite."

"They are definitely showy," Ryder noted. "There's a really cool heirloom crocus called Pickwick that works great in pots." He pulled out his phone and found a picture of some large blooms with light purple petals that were pinstriped with a deep plum color.

"Oh wow," I gushed. "I love those. They'd be gorgeous with some bright yellow roses." I quickly walked to the notepad on my work table and wrote down heirloom Pickwick crocus and yellow roses. "I even love their name. When I have spare time and some extra funds to experiment, I'm going to order some different species of crocuses and do some arranging."

"Sounds fun. Sort of like a test kitchen but with nothing edible. We could take some pictures of the new bouquets so you can create a new catalog of crocus arrangements."

"Excellent idea. What a team," I cheered. My phone buzzed. I sensed even before looking at it that it was Briggs.

"How about a hot dog on the pier?" Briggs texted.

"Absolutely. One hour?" I texted back.

"Sounds good. Looking forward to seeing you."

I sent back a pair of lips for a virtual kiss. Our relationship had entered the emoji stage where I felt free sending him little symbols like kisses and hearts. He wasn't quite as apt to send off a smiley face, but he didn't seem to mind getting mine.

I put the phone down. "James and I are getting lunch on the pier in an hour. Do you want to take your break right now? Or are you waiting for Lola?"

Ryder glanced through the front window, across the street toward Lola's Antiques. "Lola is on some secret mission, or at least that's what she called it when I asked her about lunch." He put down the spool of white ribbon. "Do you happen to know anything about this secret mission?"

"Secret mission?" I asked, not sure I'd heard him correctly even though he'd said it twice. "I haven't heard a thing about it. I talked to her last night, but there was no mention of anything secret." Ryder's face fell some as I spoke. "Maybe she's buying a new rock star t-shirt or a hat?" I suggested weakly. "Or maybe she's buying you something new which is why it's secret."

Ryder returned to his work. "She does like to keep me on my toes." He gave a weak shake of his head.

"You know Lola. She likes to add mystery to her life." I picked up the broom to sweep flower scraps. "Maybe she's getting a tattoo," I suggested. I was starting to feel a touch hurt myself that she hadn't even mentioned the secret mission. She usually shared everything with me.

I'd only dragged the broom across the floor once when the bell clanged and the mystery of Lola's secret mission was solved. Lola smoothed down her newly straightened hair. A long fringe of red bangs hung across her forehead. Aside from the hair color, the whole look was suspiciously similar to Britney's new hairstyle. Lola had instantly grown green with envy about Britney's natural beauty. And in true Lola fashion, she'd immediately decided that Ryder would fall in love with Britney and never once look back. She was wrong, of course but Lola was expert at holding onto her insecurities.

"What happened to your curls?" Ryder asked, apparently forgetting to hide the disappointment in his tone. (This was not going to help with the insecurity thing.)

Lola picked up on it immediately. She lifted her chin. "I'm tired of wearing hats to hold down my clown curls."

I cleared my throat and patted my own puffy cloud of curls.

"Your curls are much less comical, and they aren't red," she added with a huff.

"But you love those hats." Ryder put down the flowers he was holding and walked closer to her but seemed to be rethinking his approach as he neared. "I love those hats. They're sexy. They make you different than everyone else." His voice smoothed and grew quieter. He'd opted for a romantic style over the earlier disappointed tone.

I rested my broom against the work counter. "I think I've got a thing to do on my computer or something." I stumbled over my words before finally getting smart and sealing my mouth shut. I nearly made good my escape to the office.

"Oh no you don't," Lola snapped. "Get back here, cowardly best friend. I need to hear your opinion. I think Ryder's already given me his assessment. He'd prefer I remain hidden under hats and caps and a puff of red curls."

"I never said anything like that." Ryder backed up a few steps. "You came in here without letting me know ahead of time that you were changing your hair. It's taking me a few minutes to adjust to it. I like it. The bangs look great."

Ryder had still not figured out all the best ways to move ahead of an argument. I knew he'd said the wrong thing, and it showed in Lola's face. Her mouth pursed and her chin swished side to side as her hands braced firmly on her hips. "Excuse me, I didn't know I had to get your permission to change my hair. I was thinking of trying a new color lipstick. Should I send you a photo of it before I put it on?"

"Again"—I pointed with my thumb over my shoulder—"Just got a thing to do on the computer. Big thing. Important thing for the business." I backed up as I sputtered out my excuse.

"Stop right there!" Lola said sharply.

I stopped just past the doorway and pointed to my chest. "Who me?"

"No, I'm talking to the crow," Lola said with a wave toward Kingston. Then we all looked toward Kingston's perch, and a moment of truce fell over us. It dawned on all of us at the same time that Kingston hadn't made his usual fuss, the cooing sounds and perch dance, he made anytime Lola, his sweetheart, walked through the door. Instead, he was standing on the tray below his perch shuffling around for unopened peanuts like a chicken scratching in the dirt.

Lola threw up her arms. "Great, Kingston, my one true admirer doesn't even recognize me without my curls."

Her pointed statement mentioning that Kingston was her one true admirer was all Ryder needed to hear.

"Hey, boss, I know you wanted me to take my lunch break, so I'll head out right now." He walked toward the coat hook.

Lola watched him gather his things with a puzzled brow. Her confusion only grew as he swept past both of us and out the door without another word.

Her brown eyes rounded beneath the curtain of bangs. "What did I say?"

"Seriously? You just referred to a crow as your one true admirer. Directly in front of the man who actually is an admirer. Or at least he would be if you'd let him do it without all the drama."

"How am I in the wrong here?" Lola flipped her straight hair back. "I've always wanted to do that. You can't flip hair when it's curly. It just sort of bounces and stays in place."

"Again, friend, you are preaching to the choir. I didn't just wake up with this pile of ringlets this morning. They've pretty much been following me around since I was two. But how on earth did your hair stay so straight after you walked outside in the coastal air? I gave my collection of flat irons and other medieval torture instruments to the thrift shop three weeks after moving into frizz town, U.S.A..

Lola pulled out her phone to use the camera like a mirror. She tucked a strand behind her ear and ran her fingers across her sleek bangs. "I had a straightening treatment. It'll last a few months, but I'll still have to work to keep it this straight. You should try it. The stylist is this talented woman, Gina, over at Coco's Salon in Chesterton. She's awesome." She finally stopped with the hair information and looked toward the door. "I guess he's really mad," she said with a deflated sigh. "I just thought he'd be more excited about my new look."

I wondered just how much Britney had to do with Lola's new look. Knowing how much Ryder adored Lola made it extra aggravating that she'd worry at all about Elsie's niece. Lola frowned and looked a touch miserable.

I walked over and took her hand. "If you like your new look, that's all that matters, Lola. It's beautiful. Really. I'm not just saying that. I'm someone who dreams in straight hair."

Lola half grinned. "Does that mean—"

"Yes, when I'm in my dreams, I have long, luxurious straight hair. So straight you can see yourself in it."

"You poor curly haired misfit." Lola gave me a quick hug. "I'll see if I can catch up to him and apologize. Catch you later. Just let me know if you want Gina's number." She made a show of flipping her straight locks back off her shoulder as she sashayed out the door.

CHAPTER 4

*A*fter the morning tart tasting, I readily volunteered to walk to the station to meet Briggs. I needed the exercise and the fresh salty air helped revive me after a long morning of friend therapy. Lola managed to smooth things over after the rough start with her new look. Ryder was in a much better mood after he returned from lunch.

Briggs stepped out of the station just as I reached it. He'd pulled on a black overcoat and the blue scarf I gave him for Christmas. "I was going to walk and meet you halfway, but you must have been skating along today."

"I needed to burn some calories so I took quick, jaunty steps. My new boots are super comfortable. They make me want to glide along like a ballerina." I reached up and straightened the collar of his coat. "Have I mentioned that I love this black coat? Makes you look extra serious and a touch dangerous."

His brown eyes smiled. "You have mentioned it a few times. Dangerous wasn't the look I was going for, but now that you mention it—" He pulled on the end of the coat sleeve to straighten it. "I'm feeling kind of menacing. Might have to keep wearing it. Although it might get a tad warm in summer."

We started walking. I wrapped my hand around his arm. "So you were hankering for hot dogs today?" I asked.

"We could get something else, if you prefer."

"No, a walk on the pier sounds nice. There is just enough blue sky to make it feel like spring or fall, my preferred seasons."

He peered sideways at me. "What about summer?"

"I love summer, but it's not spring or fall. Hey, I've got a question."

"Summer," he answered.

"No, not that. But summer is overrated. We can debate that another time." We turned the corner onto Pickford Way, the road that ran parallel with the beach. Seagulls dotted the sand, hunkered down near the water and trying to avoid the brisk breeze while they napped off their morning catch. The temperature had dropped a few degrees, and I snuggled closer.

He chuckled. "What's that about summer being overrated?"

"Yes, a few notches up on the thermometer would be nice. But I was wondering, what would you think if I got my hair straightened?"

"Straightened? My mom used to go to the salon for a perm so that her hair would curl. I didn't realize they could do the opposite."

"Scientists had some time on their hands. They already put a man on the moon, figured out how to trade human organs around and connected everyone in the world with fiber optics. Straightening curly hair was next on their list."

"Smarty pants," Briggs muttered.

"You never answered my question." I stopped and primped up my curls for a visual. "Should I say goodbye to all this clutter and go for something sleek and shiny?"

Briggs reached for my hand and pulled me to him. "You can get a crew cut and dye it green as long as I can keep kissing you." He finished his declaration with a kiss that did a way better job of keeping me warm than my thick winter coat.

After a brief, wonderful snuggle, we continued walking. "Green is not really my color but a crew cut would make it much easier to get out the door each morning."

We reached the pier. It was a January Monday. All the glittery trimmings and strings of holiday lights had been cleared away, leaving behind the bald pier in its naturally rustic, coastal state. It was somewhat drab and lifeless in the winter, when people opted to stay inland rather than venture out to the beach. A few diehard beachcombers hiked along the sand. Otherwise, the Port Danby coastline was deserted from Pickford Lighthouse all the way to the bend where the sandy beaches gave way to steep rocks and craggy coves.

The sun had slipped temporarily behind a cloud, casting a cold shadow over the entire marina. I released my hold on Briggs long enough to prop my coat collar up higher around my ears.

Briggs glanced my direction and smiled. "You look like a baby bear trying to hibernate in a puffy parka."

"It's chilly near the water. No wonder the seagulls are all bunched up like fuzzy balls down there. Did I tell you that Kingston has apparently decided he'd prefer to be a gull than a crow?"

Briggs' short laugh produced a puff of white air. "Did he just wake up one morning and say, hey, I think I'm switching species?"

"No, actually, I think he gave it more thought than that. Instead of hanging out in the trees around the shop or at the town square, where all his kin like to loiter, he's been heading straight down to the shore. I've caught him watching the seagulls with great interest, as if he was taking mental notes about their behavior. Just a theory, and one based only on the expertise I've gained from living with my pretentious bird, I think he prefers the gulls' cocky, bold attitudes as compared to the boorish Port Danby crows."

"Seagulls are bold?" Briggs asked.

"What other animal will walk right up to your beach towel and snatch away a bag of potato chips without a second thought?"

"Uh, I can name at least two. The pretentious bird you referred to earlier and a large, uncouth, and apparently *bold* dog named Bear."

"Yes, but they don't count because they are spoiled pets."

We reached the Harbor Hot Dog stand. There were several people in line in front of us, which gave me time to decide on toppings. Briggs and I stared up at the blue sign above the order window. As we perused the list, the intense, earthy smell of cigar smoke circled through the normally briny sea air. I waved my hand in front of my face to wipe it clear, but the cigar smoke was persistent and intrusive. My gaze followed the thin stream of the pungent smoke to its source. A man was sitting on a nearby bench, hunched down in a blue raincoat. His face was mostly hidden by an olive green bucket hat pushed down low over his head. His fishing rod was arched over the side of the pier. The line disappeared into the choppy water below. The fat cigar jutted from the side of his mouth, its red glowing tip fizzling in the cold mist.

"What toppings do you want?" Briggs asked.

I turned my attention to the list again. With my olfactory senses being overwhelmed by the tobacco scent, nothing on the list sounded good. I scrunched up my nose, hoping to clear away some of the aroma. No luck. Cigar smoke was like that. It stuck to everything, including sinuses.

"What's wrong? Do you want to eat something else?" Briggs asked. We stepped forward to the counter.

"No, it's just that I can't figure out what my taste buds are craving because cigar smoke is coating my tongue. Just get me mustard and pickle relish. I'm going simple today."

"Mustard and pickle relish," Gracie, the woman who ran the hot dog stand during the week, checked off her order pad. She always wore her hair in two long braids. I wondered if she had the same curl curse as Lola and me. The yellow and red striped cap on her head matched the yellow and red striped awning hanging over the stand. Today Gracie was wearing her purple contacts, which were always slightly disconcerting. They almost made her eyes glow.

"I'll have the same but with a scoop of chili," Briggs said as he pulled out his wallet. His nose crinkled too. "Guess we'll eat these downwind from that cigar."

"Isn't it awful?" Gracie piped up as she finished taking down the order. She leaned her head out to see past the edge of the stand. "Yep, same guy. He's been here every day for the past seven days, smoking those smelly cigars and tossing his line into the waves. I don't think he's even caught one fish."

Briggs looked over at the man on the bench. His face was still mostly hidden by the hat and raincoat, but he was a good-sized guy with a big shoulder span and thick neck.

Briggs turned back to Gracie. "I don't recognize him. Is he local?"

Gracie's braids swung like pendulums as she shook her head. "Never seen him before but I sure wish he'd move away from the stand. People are getting turned off by the aroma. When they walk up here they expect to smell hot dogs, ketchup and onions. Not bitter cigar smoke." She made a face. "Reminds me of my Uncle Ralph, the guy no one wants to invite to Thanksgiving because he smokes yucky cigars."

"Would you like me to ask him to move farther down? "Briggs asked.

Gracie spooned chili on a hot dog. "No, thank you, Detective Briggs. I'm hoping since the fish aren't biting, he'll give up the quest and leave." She handed us our hot dogs. "I don't want to start any trouble."

Briggs nodded. "Then, for your sake, we'll hope his hook stays empty."

We turned and scanned the pier for a place to eat upstream from the cigar. "We could sit at the marina and admire all the boats that we can't afford," Briggs suggested.

"Sounds good to me."

CHAPTER 5

Four persistent pigeons had been circling us like groupies around a rock star for our entire meal. I ate my hot dog strategically so that a large chunk of the bun was left behind and all without getting a drop of mustard on my coat.

The birds perked up when they saw me tearing the chunk of bread into bits.

"You had that planned all along, didn't you?" Briggs noted. "I thought you were being awfully dainty with that bun, nibbling around the parts that were free of mustard and pickle."

"Mustard is an acquired taste. I'm sure they'd prefer plain bread. And they provided us with such nice cooing sounds for our lunch, I thought they deserved a little tip."

I tossed the crumbs out. The four birds quickly multiplied to ten, each one frantically flapping wings around to grab hold of their prize.

Briggs ducked when two pigeons swooped down close enough over his head to ruffle hairs. "Now you've done it. It's going to look like the set of a Hitchcock movie in a second." Just as he said it, a large white gull dropped in like a helicopter, hovering for a minute and kicking up a good wind with his wings, until finally landing smack dab in the middle of the bread crumbs. The pigeons scattered.

"I see what you mean about those cocky gulls," Briggs said. "I should get back to the office."

"Yep, I need to get back to my flowers."

We threw away our trash and headed back across the pier.

"Wish I was going back to flowers instead of paperwork." Briggs took hold of my hand. My fingers warmed instantly.

"Working on anything interesting?" I asked.

"Nothing too noteworthy. Trying to zero in on a gambling ring in the area. They are not a terribly nice group. Let's just say, you don't want to fall short on your debts with them."

"Wow, that sounds scandalous and seedy and . . . interesting."

"I thought you might say that. This one is definitely a big, fat scandalous no to my partner and her nose. Too dangerous."

I smiled up at him. "Guess I'll leave the really sketchy stuff up to the menacing detective in his black coat."

We traveled back past the hot dog stand. The man in the raincoat was still attempting to fish, but it seemed he'd grown weary of his cigar. The scent of it still lingered heavily in the air or, at least, heavily for my nose.

"This weekend is supposed to be clear skies and a full moon." Briggs squeezed my hand, then let it go to check his phone. He put it back into his pocket. "Maybe we should have a moonlight picnic on the beach."

We started down the pier steps. "I like your way of thinking, Detective Briggs." This time it was my phone buzzing. I stopped to answer Ryder's text regarding the whereabouts of the potting soil. Briggs hadn't noticed me pause. He was several steps ahead when someone's shoulder bumped mine hard enough for me to lose a grip on my phone and, very nearly, a grip on the step.

My surprised chirp caught Briggs' attention. He swung back around. Brilliant man that he was, he managed to catch my airborne phone, saving it from damage. His brow lowered and his brown eyes darkened. "Theodore Hall, right?" Briggs barked at the sixty something man with round shoulders and an angry scowl who was stomping past me.

The man looked up, somewhat surprised at Briggs' tone. He'd been so preoccupied, he hadn't noticed that he nearly launched me off the steps. Briggs hadn't seen the full collision, which was probably a good thing because his expression reminded me of a dragon about to breathe fire.

The man, Theodore Hall, as Briggs noted, barely hesitated until Briggs stepped right in front of him to block his progress. "Mr. Hall, it seems you owe Miss Pinkerton an apology. You nearly knocked her down these steps."

The man turned back to me. His ashen gray skin nearly matched the gray in his goatee and thick eyebrows. His gaze streaked right past me. He quickly scanned the pier behind us before looking at me. "I'm sorry. I was in a hurry, and I didn't see you." He surveyed the pier once more in an agitated, frightened manner.

Briggs stepped closer. Some of the anger had washed away from his expression. It had been replaced by curiosity. "Is anything the matter, Hall? You seem upset about something."

The man shook his head and muttered something.

"What's that?" Briggs asked.

"I'm just mad at that useless boat mechanic, Vanhouten." Hall waved back with his thick arm in the general direction of the boats, in case we hadn't noticed the large marina in the middle of the pier.

My ears perked forward at the mention of Dash.

"Well, if this is a business matter between you and Vanhouten, I'll leave it at that," Briggs said. "Just watch where you're going. You almost hurt someone." Briggs reached his arm out to me. I placed my hand in his. We were just about to continue on our way when Hall started up again.

"Everyone's trying to get my money," he blurted angrily enough that spittle flew out with the words. "I asked him to fix the boat, but it's still making a funny sound. But he's got his hand out for the five hundred bucks just like everyone else."

Briggs waited politely for him to finish his rant. It seemed he had to let some steam off, and it was probably better that he did it in front of a neutral party than face to face with Dash and all these other money grabbers. I was having a hard time believing that Dash was insisting on payment if he hadn't solved the problem.

Hall's gaze shot back up to the pier. He did a quick check of the area before turning back to Briggs. "I mean no one should have to pay for something that didn't get done right. I'm not paying," he said emphatically. "I'm tired of handing out money to people who don't deserve it."

Several people reached the steps. Their voices drew Hall's attention away from his rant. He quickly lost interest in them. They obviously weren't the people he was looking for so urgently on the pier.

"I'll let you get on with your day," Briggs said again. He was done listening to Hall's complaints. A business squabble wasn't exactly police business.

Hall's triangular beard flicked back and forth as he moved his jaw side to side. "Yes, good day," he grumbled and continued on, at a fast clip, checking his surroundings as he went.

Briggs wrapped his hand around mine. "That was strange." We watched as Hall crossed the street and disappeared into Franki's Diner but not before glancing back over his shoulder twice.

"Do you know him well?" I was worried about Dash. The man seemed to be slightly unhinged. Instead of feeling even the tiniest bit contrite about nearly pitching me headlong off the pier steps, he exploded directly into an angry tirade about money he owed Dash.

"Not really. He's a retired banker who did pretty well for himself. He owns that sweet luxury fishing boat, *Windsong*."

We continued along Pickford Way. A late afternoon fog was rolling in from the ocean. My curly hair sprang to life with just the scent of the salty mist.

"Is he always so gruff and grouchy?" I asked.

We stopped in front of the police station. Briggs turned to me with a sly grin. "Why? Are you worried about Dash? I'm pretty sure he can take care of himself."

"I'm not worried about him," I lied. "Maybe a bit. It's just I can't imagine that Dash did shoddy work. He's not the kind of guy to do something halfway."

"I'm sure it'll all get sorted out." We'd reached a new understanding about my friendship with Dash, and I was greatly relieved. I could now mention his name without Briggs' jaw clamping shut. (Baby steps.)

Briggs took hold of my arms, brought me to him and kissed my forehead. "I've got to get back inside. Hilda hasn't had lunch yet, and Chinmoor is out on patrol."

I wasn't quite finished with my inquiry. "Was it me or was Hall acting as if someone was following him? He kept looking around as if he expected someone to jump out at him and yell 'gotcha'."

"Nothing gets past you, Investigator Pinkerton." He pushed a curl off my cheek. "On second thought, no crew cut. I'd miss these curls too much. They always end up in places they shouldn't be, giving me an excuse to touch them. And yes, Hall was acting strange. Maybe he thought Dash was going to come after him with his tool belt."

"Stop teasing." I shucked him on the shoulder. "I'm heading back to my flowers. Thank you for the hot dog. My pigeon friends thank you too."

CHAPTER 6

$\mathcal{I}$ watched the two women, a mother and daughter, head out the door. They had come to a fairly quick consensus about flower choice and budget, which was rare for a wedding order.

"Another April wedding. That makes three," I said to Ryder as I put away the notebooks that were filled with examples. "I hope we can get it all done."

"I think the floral dream team can handle three weddings in a month." Ryder was arranging a fiery mix of yellow, orange and red roses that were well past bloom. They were no longer viable for bouquets, but they were plenty fragrant. January was never a great month for roses. People were waiting for the big rose month of February.

I picked up my order pad. "What are you doing with those past-their-prime roses?"

Ryder tucked a bright yellow rose in the center of the bouquet. "I hope you don't mind. After the rocky start to the day with Lola's new look, I decided to give her some flowers."

"Well, aren't you a smooth operator?" I'd been with the wedding customers for more than an hour and hadn't noticed that Kingston's perch was still empty. "Kingston didn't come back?" I walked toward the front door.

Ryder's face popped up. "Gosh no. I'm sorry. I should have looked out for him while you were with the customers." He leaned into the front display window to get a good look at the trees in front of the shop. "I don't see him. Should I go out and look for him?" There was just enough panic in his voice to make me anxious too. Kingston rarely left for more than an hour. He'd been gone over three.

I opened the front door. A blast of late afternoon cool air hit my face, making my eyes and nose water. I stepped out onto the sidewalk. The winter sun was just starting its descent, but there was still more than an hour of daylight left. I whistled a few times and called his name, but Kingston must have been out of hearing range.

Lola walked out of her shop to pull in the two rocking chairs she had sitting on the sidewalk as part of a two for one special. She waved. "Are you looking for Kingston?"

"Yes, have you seen him?"

Lola looked up and down her side of the sidewalk and then stepped out a few feet and hopped up on tiptoes to get a view of her roof. She turned back around. "I don't see him."

"You try calling him," I suggested. "Maybe he'll come soaring in when he hears your voice." Ryder joined me on the sidewalk.

"Kingston, King, my handsome boy, where are you?" Lola sang. Two women were strolling past as Lola unabashedly made flirtatious calls for her 'pretty boy'. They stared at her and hurried their pace to get past the crazy antique seller. Lola just smiled politely and sang into the air for her missing love.

Ryder chuckled. "And that is why I adore the woman. She couldn't care less what anyone thinks."

It was my turn to chuckle. I peered up at him. "With the exception of her boyfriend, who she immediately felt slighted by when he didn't shower her with admiration and sappy poetry about her new hairstyle."

Ryder had no response, but a smile was lurking behind his expression.

393

"Which says just how much she adores you," I added. His smile broke free.

"Should I walk down the street and look for Kingston?" Ryder asked.

"That would be great." I crinkled my nose. "I hate to ask but you could take a quick walk around the town square. The trees are mostly bald, so he should be easy to spot. Take a peanut butter treat with you just in case he's mixed in with a bunch of other crows. Then it becomes a case of Where's Waldo, only none of the birds are wearing a red and white hat."

Ryder straightened his posture and saluted. "I will carry out my mission with courage and honor." He lowered his hand. "That is, after I put on my coat and scarf." He shivered. "It's cold as the Arctic out here."

Ryder took off to look for Kingston, and I started cleaning up the work table. The front door opened and Britney walked in. Her full lips were rounded in a pout. I was certain I would have noticed a few more details about her gloomy expression, but my gaze and mind went directly to the tasty looking croissant tucked in a napkin. The lively and always welcome scent of almond drifted toward me.

"Hey, Lacey," she said without any of her usual brightness. She handed me the napkin. "I brought you an almond croissant. Aunt Elsie said you love almond and croissants and . . . well, there was an entire list when I asked her what I could bring you for a visit."

"Yes, I'm easy to please. And it's very nice of you to visit." Britney and I were friendly, but it was rare for her to stop by and chat. My intuition, coupled with the pained look on her face, assured me that the conversation was about to turn to Dash.

"I gobbled up a hot dog at lunch, so I'll save a yummy treat for this evening when I'm at home with a hot cup of tea." I wrapped the croissant up and set it next to my order pad.

Britney had her hair pulled back in a bun for baking. Even her long bangs were clipped back. The hairdo would normally be considered severe, but it only highlighted her flawless olive skin and large eyes. She reminded me of a young deer in the woods when she blinked her long lashes.

"Lacey, I hope you don't mind me asking—" She paused.

"Not at all. What would you like to know?" Inside, I was chanting please let it be a question about flowers or even my extra sensory nose.

"I know you're friends with Dash and you live next door to him," she started, the hopeful breath I'd been holding fluttered out.

"Yes, it's true. We are friends and neighbors." I waited for her to continue and was quickly trying to anticipate what she might say or ask next. Somehow, I was once again the sounding board for relationship problems. It was humorous, considering some of my track record. With the exception of my current relationship. At least things were going smoothly with Briggs and me. I'd hate to be surrounded with all the drama and be mired in my own soap opera.

Britney hoisted herself onto one of the stools. It seemed we were going to have a long chat. "I'm not spying on him, mind you—" I'd found anytime a person pointed out that they *weren't* doing something, the opposite was true. "I was just wondering if you've seen him with any other women. You know—has he brought anyone home lately?"

"Oh." I was taken aback by her direct question. "Naturally, I don't know everything that's going on with Dash, but I can't recall him bringing home any new friends. He's been very busy," I added. "That I know for certain. Just last week he complained that his business slows to a crawl during the holiday season and then explodes as soon as the new year starts. He said people immediately see it as a downhill slide to spring and summer. They are anxious to get their boats ready for the warmer weather. And when he's not working at the marina, he's busy hammering and sawing away on that house of his. I swear I don't know when that man has time to sleep." I laughed lightly, hoping my speech would appease her worries.

Her lip was still jutting out in a pouty frown. "I'm sure he's busy, although taking the time to text or call and say hello doesn't take too big a chunk out of the day."

"True." I decided on a different tact. "Britney, when I first met you, I marveled at how confident you were. You stepped into a new situation, a new town and all with an aunt, who is a spectacular person, but, let's face it, she's tough to impress. But Elsie is thrilled to have you here. Don't let one man erase any of that confidence. And if you'd like my opinion on it—"

"Yes," she said excitedly. "I would. I love Aunt Elsie, but I can't talk to her about this. She immediately spins off into a diatribe about how Dash isn't good enough for me and how he's never going to settle down."

I scooted closer. "I don't pretend to know the inner workings of Dash's mind, or any man's mind, for that matter. They are so different than us women, but I think if you stick to being that self-assured woman who showed up in town back in October, it will catch his attention. Make yourself a little less available if he calls. Show him you're far too independent to be waiting for his attention."

Britney mulled over my suggestion a second and then hopped off the stool with a snap of her fingers. "Yes, that's a great plan. I'm going to be nonchalant and lukewarm when he calls." She hugged me. "Thanks, this is the pep talk I needed. Now I've got to help Elsie measure ingredients for tomorrow morning's cinnamon rolls and pastries." She hurried to the door. "Enjoy the croissant."

"I can't wait to eat it."

As she walked out, Ryder held the door for her. He stepped inside. I leaned to the side and looked past him, hoping my feathered friend would follow in behind him but he was alone.

"No sign of him?" I asked.

"Sorry. I went around the town square twice. Didn't see any crows at all, only a few seagulls picking at the garbage can."

"Seagulls. That's it." I tapped the side of my head. "I should have thought of this earlier. He's been obsessed with seagulls lately."

Ryder squinted. "Is this like that weird crush he developed on the Fruit Loops' toucan?"

"No, and thankfully he got over that odd phase quickly. He seems to have decided, somewhere in that wild, smart little brain of his, that seagulls are much cooler than crows. I'll bet he's down at the pier."

"Do you want me to go down there?" Ryder asked.

I pulled out my phone to text Lola. "Nope, I'll go this time." I grabbed my coat off the hook. "And I'm taking my secret weapon —Lola."

CHAPTER 7

$\mathcal{I}$ had more than just Kingston on my mind when I asked Lola along for the search. I was absorbing everyone's woes, and I needed to unload some of it on my best friend. (Even if she was occasionally the *woe* giver.)

The sun was getting lower in the sky and shadows stretched long on the sidewalk. The notion of Kingston staying out all night on his own made me pick up my pace. Lola started skipping to keep up.

"Whoa, I volunteered to help you look for King. There was no mention of a sprint."

"Sorry, I'm just a little panicked about the idea of Kingston staying out all night. Alone." My breaths were shortening and shooting out in puffs of white air. "Now I know why my mom was always in a lather if I got home from the park or a friend's house after dark."

"All the other crows seem to manage it all right. He's not a timid bunny or kitten. I'm pretty sure he'd be fine. Although, he probably wouldn't look at you for a month to make you suffer for neglecting him."

"I know it's the same town without sunlight, but I always imagine dark is when all the evil, terrifying creatures come out from their hiding places."

Lola skipped a few steps to keep up. She stared over at me as we made our way to the pier. "Sometimes, my friend, you are more warped than I give you credit for. Evil and terrifying? Do crows even have any natural enemies? Aside from fast moving vehicles and really clean windows?"

I peered sideways at her. "You're not helping much. I needed some friendly support, but I'm questioning my decision to invite you along."

"He'll be fine. Like you said, he's probably just on the pier admiring the seagulls."

"I'm sure that's where we'll find him, but that wasn't the only support I needed." We reached the steps of the pier. I flew up them. Lola trotted behind and caught up to me.

"Ugh, there's a fog," she groaned. "The hair straightening treatment is supposed to withstand moisture, but Port Danby fog is so dense." She pulled her coat hood up over her hair. "So what kind of support do you need this afternoon? The doctor is in."

I was just about to ramble on about my day when the main subject appeared through the mist hovering over the pier. Dash had his coat zipped up and, like Lola, his hood over his head. He had his hands snuggly in his coat pockets. He stared down at the ground as his heavy footsteps rattled the wood planks. Even with his curled, almost angry posture, there was no way he could have missed Lola and me as we walked toward him. But he marched past as if we were invisible.

Lola and I stopped to watch him disappear back into the haze as he headed toward the steps. "That was strange," Lola said. "Did you two have an argument?"

"Not that I know of. He was definitely not himself. But it might have to do with what I was just about to say before he emerged from the fog. Somehow, I've found myself caught in the middle of the Dash and Britney thing."

Lola's face perked up. "Are they broken up? Does that mean Britney is single again?"

I stared back at her. "Seriously? You're going that route again? Ryder only has eyes for you. Besides, I asked you along to hear my problems, not to add to the drama."

Lola pulled the drawstrings on her hood. It tightened around her head, leaving only her face in view. "Just want to keep out that dastardly fog. Go ahead. I'm listening. No more drama."

"That's basically it. I'm stuck in the center of this whole thing." I grabbed her arm to stop our progress. There, sitting on the pier, looking sadly alone, was my bird. He was staring out at the sand where the seagulls were just settling in for the evening.

"See, that's where crows belong. Out here in the open. That one is nicely behaved too, unlike yours," Mayor Price's snide tone shot over our shoulders. His cheeks were stained red from the cold as his thick fingers curled around the cup of coffee in his hand.

"Evening, Mayor Price," I said extra sweetly.

He grunted in return. I had yet to discover why Mayor Price had taken an instant disliking to me, but I was determined not to make things worse. He'd made one failed attempt to get a law passed that crows were not allowed inside local businesses, but by then, Kingston had won the hearts of most everyone in town and the city council voted the ordinance down.

"Kingston," I said in a sing-song voice. Kingston turned around. He was happy to see me, mostly because I had Lola at my side. He lifted off the railing and flew over to my shoulder.

I smiled brightly at Mayor Price. "Thank you for saying my bird is nicely behaved."

Mayor Price sputtered and coughed out his sip of coffee before stomping away.

"Wow, Price just adores you," Lola quipped. Her gaze landed on the hot dog stand. "Yay, Gracie hasn't closed up yet. I think I'll get a hot dog. My fridge is empty at home." She stopped. "Wait, I forgot. We were talking about you being thrown into the center of the Britney, Dash thing."

"Yes, we were. I feel like my loyalty to two dear friends, Elsie and Dash, is going to be pulled in opposite directions." We made our way toward the hot dog stand. The fisherman with the stinky cigar had finally given up his quest. The bench was empty.

"Elsie?" Lola asked. "How did Elsie get into this?"

"How could she not be? Britney is her niece, and she's—well, she's Elsie."

"That's true. The woman does like to keep control of situations. I'll bet she's mad at Dash." That was Lola's last comment before I lost her to the long list of possible topping choices at the hot dog stand.

CHAPTER 8

ingston grew bored of Lola's lengthy hot dog decision. He returned to the railing to watch his newest obsession, the seagulls. After five cold minutes of reflection over the hot dog toppings, Lola settled on mustard and ketchup. Hardly a selection that required so much thought, but that was how she rolled. Lola leaned her arm along the counter edge of the hot dog stand. She hadn't released the drawstring on her hood. It was hard not to chuckle about her serious, thoughtful expression with just her face showing through the opening.

"You remind me of the Oompa Loompas when Mike Teevee shrank himself in the television room. You just need an orange curl of hair right here." I reached for her forehead but she swept my hand away.

"I'm sitting here, contemplating your dilemma, and you're comparing me to the Willy Wonka work force. Do you think he paid them well?" she asked with all seriousness.

"There was a river of chocolate in the middle of the factory and a room made completely of candy. Don't think salary would be an issue. At least not for me."

Gracie was having a good giggle over our conversation as she waited for Lola's hot dog to heat up.

"Maybe Dash marched past us without a word because he is so distraught over his relationship with Britney." Lola was a master at switching topics. "You should probably talk to him and find out what's going on."

"I suppose. Although, what we saw just a few minutes ago didn't look like despair. He looked angry." I clapped once. "That's right. Briggs and I came here for lunch, and by here, I mean right here at the hot dog stand."

Gracie's face popped our direction. "Did you enjoy the hot dogs?"

"Yes, delicious as always." I turned back to Lola. "James and I were walking back. I stopped on the steps to check my phone, and a man plowed into me. James snatched my phone midair, saving it from sure death," I added just to brag. "The man's name was Hall, Theodore Hall, I think. Anyhow, he's a boat owner and he was grousing about Dash not fixing his boat right."

Gracie handed Lola her hot dog. "That would explain the loud shouting match Theo and Dash had out on the marina. Their voices carried all the way over here."

Her words alarmed me. I'd only seen Dash get extremely angry once and that involved Briggs . . . and me, unfortunately. They were close to throwing fists until I intervened.

"Did it get physical?" I asked.

Gracie shook her head. "Couldn't see from here but it doesn't seem like Dash. Theo is a good-sized man, but he's much older, and Dash, well, he's got those extra broad shoulders," she gushed and even took a second, apparently, to visualize those shoulders. "He's much too nice to hit an old guy like Theo, even if Theo is a grouch." She shrugged. "You'd be surprised how much you learn about people just by sitting in this hot dog stand watching the day go by."

"I'll bet there's never a dull moment around here," I said. "Have a good evening."

Lola took a bite of hot dog before we even took two steps. "Yep, this hits the spot."

"It sure seems like Dash is going through a rough patch," I said as we started on our way back.

"I'm sure it'll pass." Lola took another bite.

I didn't need to call Kingston this time. His favorite human, Lola, was eating a fragrant hot dog. No coaxing needed. He hopped off the railing and fluttered onto my shoulder. He nearly clawed through my puffy coat in his excitement to get to the piece of hot dog Lola kindly handed him.

"One of you should get an eye patch," Lola quipped between bites. "Port Danby's version of a pirate girl and her odd looking parrot."

CHAPTER 9

ingston flew instantly to his perch to rest from his long afternoon adventure. Ryder had finished cleaning up as I reached the shop. He grabbed his coat and scarf. "Hope you don't mind if I cut out early." He walked to the refrigerator and pulled out the colorful bouquet of roses he'd arranged for Lola. "Think I'll see if Lola wants to head to Chesterton later for some Italian food."

"Not too sure about that. She just ate a hot dog on our walk back to the shop."

"Did she?" He glanced at his phone. "Must have been her four o'clock snack. Knowing Lola, she'll probably be hungry in an hour for dinner. See you tomorrow."

"Thanks for cleaning up."

Ryder opened the door. The sound of sirens shattered the early evening air. An ambulance raced past the shop with red lights flashing and horn blaring. Ryder leaned back inside. "Looks like something's happening at the marina. Briggs is heading that direction too."

I'd only just hung up my coat, but I grabbed it back off the hook. "Think I'll head down there."

"Should I wait here?" Ryder asked.

"No, I'll close up early." I flipped the sign and locked the door.

The sun was at that low point in the sky where the light was blinding. It was especially harsh through the fog. I shielded my eyes with my hand and headed down Harbor Lane toward the coast. Even with the sun's glare, I could see the paramedics heading toward the moored boats with their equipment. Briggs had pulled out his light. It blinked red on top of his car.

Franki and a few of the customers had gathered in the front windows of the diner to watch the events unfolding across the way. I waved to her as I hurried past and turned onto Pickford Way. By the time I reached the steps down to the boat slips, Officer Chinmoor was at the landing turning curious spectators away and asking people to stay back from the marina so emergency personnel could do their work. It was a signal that something very serious was happening.

Chinmoor was just about to hold out his long arm, stopping me from continuing, then he saw who it was under the puffy coat. "Oh, Miss Pinkerton, it's you. I suppose I can let you cross."

"Thanks." I scurried past a sizeable group of people who must have managed to enter the marina before the police barrier. A milky haze had settled around them as more fog rolled in from the ocean. They huddled at the entrance to the boat slips, but someone had put up a makeshift barrier of caution tape to keep them from traveling closer to the scene.

Gracie was standing amongst them, stretching her neck up to see over the heads. I came up next to her. "What's going on?" I asked.

She looked over to see who was addressing her. "Hey, Lacey. You've sure been out here a lot today. And I see your boyfriend has made several trips too." She winked at me. "He always looks extra hot when he's working on a case."

"Is this a case?" I asked, genuinely surprised. "I thought it might be a heart attack or accident. Is someone hurt?"

"Might have been an accident, but from the rumblings I'm hearing coming through the crowd, one of the boat owners is dead."

"How can they be certain? I saw the paramedics cross with their equipment," I added.

"You didn't see them bring up a gurney, did you?" she asked.

"That doesn't necessarily mean anything. I'll see if I can find out what's happening."

There were a few grumbling complaints from the others as I stepped over the caution tape. A woman in the crowd, a voice I didn't recognize, quickly explained, with some derision, that I was Detective Briggs' girlfriend. I smiled at hearing the phrase, a phrase I was still getting used to. I only hoped my detective boyfriend wouldn't be angry that I'd crossed the caution tape.

I raced down the walkway to the boat where the emergency personnel were gathered. It was a small fishing yacht with a lovely white paint job and teak deck. My eyes traveled to the stern. The dark blue and silver lettering spelled the name *Windsong*. It took me a second to recall where I'd heard the name before. *Windsong* belonged to Theodore Hall, the man who smacked into me on the steps.

Briggs was standing on deck wearing his black coat. He'd pulled a black fedora on to keep his head warm. I couldn't see what he was looking at but I had my suspicions.

I knew I'd been to enough of these scenes when even the medical crew recognized me as someone Briggs allowed past the police barriers. I walked right by them and over the gangplank someone had lowered from the vessel. I stepped onto deck and rounded the wheelhouse. An almost ghostly seeming fog hovered above and nestled into the nooks and corners on the boat. I quickly found that my suspicion was right. Theodore Hall's lifeless body was stretched out on the polished teakwood deck. A puddle of blood pooled beneath his head.

Briggs looked up at the sound of footsteps. "Lace—" he cleared his throat. "Miss Pinkerton," he said more officially. "I guess I shouldn't be surprised to see you."

"I saw the commotion from the flower shop." I looked down at the victim. A grotesque dent in Mr. Hall's skull revealed the obvious cause of death. "Did you find the weapon?"

"As a matter of fact . . ." Briggs held up his hand. He was holding an evidence bag containing a large socket wrench smeared with blood. His phone buzzed with a text. He read it and looked at the paramedics still standing by with their gear. "Thanks, everyone. Doesn't look like we'll need you tonight. The coroner is on his way."

The emergency crew lugged their unwieldy bags and equipment off the boat, leaving just Briggs and me on board. Briggs stooped down next to the body. I crouched down on the other side.

"A visual inspection doesn't show any sign of a struggle, but Nate will know more when he gets him on the table." Briggs fell silent for a second. His dark brows furrowed in serious thought.

"What is it?" I asked. "Do you know something?"

"No." He shook his head once. "It's a fairly sparse crime scene. It seems the perpetrator walked up to him and hit him once on the head with the tool. The blood splatters seem contained to just this area, so he fell where he was struck. Of course this fog, the waning sunlight and the dark teakwood deck make it hard to know for certain. There might be blood elsewhere. I've got some portable work lights coming, so we can do an evidence search." He rubbed his chin in thought.

"You must have something more on your mind because you keep dropping into a pensive frown and you haven't asked me to use my sniffer for evidence."

"It's nothing."

"James," I said sternly.

It took him a second to look me in the eye. "I was just thinking back to our run in with Theodore this afternoon. When he plowed into you on the steps."

"I remember it well, but I promise I didn't come back here and crown him on the head with a socket wrench."

His mouth twisted angrily at my sarcastic response. "Never mind."

"No, you're right. I'm being silly. What is it? What are you thinking?"

He shook his head and stayed silent.

"Let me fill in the blanks for you," I said. "You're thinking about how Mr. Hall went on an angry rant about Dash not fixing his boat correctly."

He stared at me with no response. I fretted as a few seconds of the old animosity between Dash and James splashed across his face. And it never helped when I sided with Dash, so I decided to keep my opinion to myself. But there was no denying that the air between Briggs and me had grown a bit colder. Only it had nothing to do with the weather.

CHAPTER 10

The sun had nearly vanished, and the fog was like a thick cloak of wet wool. Briggs and I had put the tense moment behind us. He helped Nate's team set up the battery operated lights while I set to work sniffing for clues.

I had a few minutes before Nate would get to work with his initial inspection of the body. I knelt down next to the victim. The harsh light being set up for Nate's exam brought the whole gory scene into sharp focus. Theodore Hall was on his back, but the wound was on the side of his skull, just above the temple. The round edge of the wrench had made a perfect circle, like a cookie cutter on dough. Blood smeared the entire side of his face and head as if he'd fallen first on his side and then rolled onto his back. He was a large man with big features, a bulbous nose and a wide mouth. His gray goatee and brows were stained dark by the blood.

As was usually the case when the victim suffered significant blood loss, my investigator's tool, my nose, was having an impossible time finding any odor past the strong scent of blood. The dense, wet air wasn't helping matters much either. The cold condensation covering the deck quickly seeped into the knees of my jeans as I ran my nose over Theodore's coat and sweater. There were hints of cologne on the sweater, near the collar, which no doubt meant Theodore had put on cologne this morning. I moved down his arm to the only part of his body exposed, his hands. The faint scent of onion drifted up from his right hand, most likely signaling he'd eaten something with onions for lunch or dinner.

A shadow passed in front of the light. Briggs' deep voice rained down over my head. "Any luck?" he asked.

I drew my nose along his coat one last time and straightened. I lifted my hand. Briggs' fingers wrapped around mine, temporarily warming them as he helped me to my feet. Cold, wet spots stained both of my knees. I shook my legs to peel the damp fabric from my skin.

"Just blood, aftershave and onion. The air is too thick with ocean moisture. It's hard to smell anything past the briny odor."

I surveyed the deck. Less of it was visible than just ten minutes ago. The harsh lights had burned off the moisture in the space around the murder site, but the rest of the boat was obscured by the fog.

A shiver rattled me briefly as the pervasive moisture seeped into my bones.

"You're cold, Lacey." Briggs reached for my hand. "Why don't I have one of the officers take you back to the shop."

"I won't need a ride. I can walk."

Before he could protest, Officer Chinmoor interrupted our conversation. "Sir, I've been asking around for possible witnesses."

Briggs turned around to face him. "Any luck?"

Officer Chinmoor stood up straight as if he had very significant news to report. "No witnesses," he said with an official tone. Chinmoor always took himself quite seriously. At first, I considered him somewhat of a character, with his gangly build and stern brow, but I'd come to respect him. He wasn't stellar at his job, but he always performed it with great enthusiasm, an admirable quality.

Briggs looked at him and waited for more. "Is that all?"

Chinmoor cleared his throat, his gaze flashed my direction for a second but he pulled it away quickly.

"Officer Chinmoor? Is that all?" Briggs repeated.

"Sir, it's only that some of the people I talked to had the same story." He ended with that and flashed his eyes my direction again.

I was being thick, but I finally got the hint. "I think I'll walk around the deck and see if there is anything else my nose can pick up." I pointed out my nose, in case they hadn't noticed it sitting there in the center of my face. "I'll just go over here." I followed that up with an unnecessary point as well. I wandered away from the conversation but worked hard to keep an ear turned their direction. It seemed Chinmoor had something significant to say that he didn't want me to hear.

The activity on board the *Windsong* had started to pick up as Nate got to work taking pictures and examining the body. There was too much clamor for me to get a clear shot at listening in on Briggs' conversation with Chinmoor. I relaxed, knowing Briggs would fill me in if it was anything of note. I decided to take the opportunity to walk around the deck and look for anything that might seem out of place.

Theodore kept a tidy ship, literally. The wood and steel and fiber-glass was all polished to a glistening shine. Ropes were stacked neatly, gear was stored away and there wasn't one piece of debris floating about. It almost looked as if the boat had just come off the showroom floor, if there was such a thing for boats.

One trip around led me to absolutely nothing. This was going to be a tough case unless the wrench provided some valuable clues. I headed back to Briggs. He was watching Nate do his examination. Chinmoor was no longer on the boat.

I came up next to Briggs. "What did Chinmoor say?"

Briggs peered sideways at me but then returned his focus to the scene in front of him.

"You're not going to tell me, are you?" I asked.

"Lacey," he started, which meant he was stalling.

"That's all right. Your hesitation is a major clue. I think I know what he had to say. He told you about the fight that Dash had with Theodore Hall."

Briggs stared at me, blinking only once. "You knew about it?"

"Yes. Lola and I walked down to the pier just an hour ago to look for Kingston. Lola decided to get a hot dog, and Gracie mentioned that the two men had an argument, lots of loud yelling, apparently." I shrugged nonchalantly. "We already knew about their disagreement."

Briggs' mouth pulled firm, a sure sign that he wasn't too pleased. "Why didn't you bring it up when I showed you the wrench?"

I made a loud enough harrumph sound to blow the fog away from my face. "Please, James, you can't possibly think that Dash had something to do with this. You're being ridiculous, and I think your general ill-will toward Dash is making you jump to conclusions." Apparently my words were being picked up by some of the surrounding personnel.

Briggs took hold of my arm and moved me brusquely over the gangplank and out of earshot of the others. The warm cocoa color of his eyes turned to dark roast coffee. I'd never seen him look so angry. Even though adrenaline was preparing my defenses for a fight, a terrible lump formed in my throat. It seemed we were heading for our first serious spat, and I wasn't ready for it.

"Lacey, I'm going to insist you remove yourself from this case. I won't need your assistance anymore." His tone was dry and harsh. "I'm going to have someone drive you back to the shop." He hadn't realized he was still holding my arm until I snapped it free.

"No, thank you. I'll walk." I blinked fast to make sure not one tear dropped. It was the last thing I wanted him to see.

"What's going on?" a deep voice sounded next to us.

Dash had the hood of his coat up over his head. He looked genuinely distraught. His eyes landed on me first, then he quickly shifted his attention to Briggs. "I was over at the diner, and I saw the commotion. Is it true? Theo Hall is dead?"

I turned to Briggs, waiting to hear his response.

His jaw was tight. He was still angry at me. "Yes, it's true." Briggs shot me a cold glance. It was all I could do not to crumple in despair. "Actually, Dash, we need to talk." Briggs looked at me, expectantly.

I crossed my arms to let him know I wasn't leaving.

With a grunt of frustration, Briggs reached into his coat and pulled out the evidence bag with the wrench. He held it up in the glow coming off the lights on deck. "Does this look familiar?"

Dash stared at Briggs in confusion, then leaned down to squint at the blood smeared bag. He straightened again. "Tru-lock, that's the brand I use, but mine are in my toolbox on the deck of the boat I'm working on." He motioned farther down the marina. "Tom Colton's twenty footer." He focused a hard green gaze on Briggs. "What's this about?"

Briggs returned the hard gaze. It felt as if any of the progress we'd made toward the two of them being civil toward each other had been erased in a few seconds time.

"I'll need to see your toolbox."

CHAPTER 11

*B*riggs had made it clear that he wanted me to go, but with the change in events, I made it equally clear that I wasn't leaving. He was technically in charge of the situation and could have ordered me from the scene in an official capacity, but he knew that would put a rift between us that might never be repaired. I nearly buckled in relief when he decided to ignore me tagging along. It was only fair. He'd asked me to assist him on other cases. It wouldn't be right for him to dismiss me on this one just because it involved a friend.

I tagged along, my chin high, letting Briggs know I was going to *nose* in on the investigation even if he didn't like it. The tension between us grew tighter with each step along the dock. The bobbing vessels looked like giant, tethered beasts in the dense fog. It was probably my dark mood, but everything about the scene made me feel gloomy. It was all a touch surreal, walking through a cloudy, movie set quality mist behind the two men I knew best in Port Danby. There was enough heated tension between them to melt some of the haze. I could see the hard tension in both sets of shoulders. It was hard to tell who was angrier, but given my stubborn insistence on tagging along, I was going to guess Briggs. Dash, on the other hand, didn't seem the least bit bothered about me being there.

There was no gangplank set up on Tom Colton's boat. Dash pulled one of the mooring ropes to bring the vessel closer, then he swung himself on board. Briggs followed easily, but I was left on the dock. I caught a triumphant glimpse of a smile on Briggs' face after he realized my tagging along had just been cut short. That was all I needed to hurl myself toward the railing. I caught it and was just about to throw a leg over when the boat floated away from the dock. I lost my footing and chirped a cry of distress as I clung to the boat. My feet dangled over the cold, choppy water. Both men lunged for me. They each grabbed an arm and lifted me over the railing. I landed clumsily in Briggs' arms. He held me for longer than necessary. It felt almost possessive as if he was angry that Dash had helped at all. (Sometimes men were the silliest creatures on Earth.)

Dash led us to the stern of the boat where the engine compartment was located. He opened the hatch and disappeared a few steps below deck. He returned with a heavy metal box. His fingers were white with tension as he gripped the handle and heaved it onto the deck. The solid, straight mouthed expression on his face reminded me of the uncharacteristically bitter expression he was wearing when he marched past Lola and me without a word. That whole unusual scene was coming back to me in frightening detail. Why had he been acting so strangely?

Dash opened the latch on the box and tossed back the heavy metal lid. The box scraped the deck as he spun it around to let Briggs see inside. "The socket wrenches are on the bottom, all lined up in order of size." The confident way Dash was showing the inside of his toolbox had to assure Briggs he had absolutely nothing to hide. Yet the tension between them was still as thick as tar.

Briggs crouched down next to the box. I peered over his shoulder. It was dark on the boat with only the sparse yellow lights strung between posts on the dock to illuminate the deck. Dash lifted the top tray of tools out to reveal the bottom where the socket wrenches were snug in their holders, all lined up in order of ascending size. Briggs pulled out his keys and shined his pen light into the box. "Where's the ratchet and the one inch socket?"

Dash's face blanched white. He spun the box back around to face him and reached inside to search for the tools. "They were here when I put my tools away." He pushed things around in the box, searching through the loose tools for the missing ratchet and socket. He lifted his face. His fretful expression made my chest tighten. He seemed genuinely puzzled about the missing tool. Briggs and I usually had the same instincts when it came to reading people. I only hoped he could look past his bitter feelings toward Dash and see what I saw—an innocent man. Or was I letting my favorable view and friendship with Dash cloud my perception?

The day had started out just fine with sweet cherry tarts and colorful crocuses, but it had quickly disintegrated into an ugly, dismal, foggy mess.

Briggs straightened. His jaw moved side to side, something he did when he was deep in thought or conflicted. He reached into his pocket, pulled out his phone and took several pictures of the box and its contents. The whole process made Dash curls his fists and tighten his jaw. Briggs finally stuck his phone back into his pocket. I hadn't realized I was holding my breath until it showed up in front of my mouth in a white cloud.

Dash lifted his shoulders and stood taller, coming face to face with Briggs. "Briggs, I swear to you that socket wrench was inside the box. I didn't even use it today. It never came out once."

Briggs didn't respond. He glanced down at Dash's jeans. "You usually wear coveralls when you're down in the engine compartment, right?"

"Yeah, unless it's too hot outside. I was wearing them today." He disappeared back down into the engine compartment. A long period of silence followed. The only sounds were the slightly brusque slapping of the water against the hull and the occasional clang of a pulley on one of the moored boats. I realized then, the thick as tar tension I'd sensed between the two men was equally sticky between Briggs and me. That realization sent a dull ache through my head and chest.

Lately, our relationship had grown stronger than ever but it was suddenly at risk. I briefly considered walking away, letting this play out without me, but the look of despair on Dash's face as he'd disappeared back into the engine compartment kept me in place. (Along with the notion that there was not going to be any graceful way to leave the boat, thus ending the possibility of a succinct, dramatic exit.)

Dash reappeared, looking as if someone had just stolen his lunch box from his cubby. His head shook as he climbed up on deck. "It's not there."

"Maybe you took it home to wash it," I suggested weakly.

"Why would I do that?" Dash asked sharply.

Again, I was being thick. I was going to blame it on the horrendous end to the day and the ghastly fog. "No, I didn't mean it like that. I didn't mean you took it home to wash away evidence." My voice trailed off as both men stared at me waiting for me to climb out of the tangle I'd put myself in. I was really starting to regret even walking down to the scene. I shrugged as much as my thick winter coat would allow. "I just meant maybe you took it home to wash out the grease and dirt."

Dash's expression softened. "Yes, I'm sorry, Lacey. I shouldn't have jumped on you like that. It's a logical question." His brows lowered again as he turned back to Briggs. "I swear to you, Briggs, I took those coveralls off, folded them up and left them next to the toolbox for work tomorrow. Then I went to dinner at Franki's. You can ask her. She waited on my table."

Briggs nodded. "I still don't have a timeframe for the murder, but I'll follow up on that if necessary."

Dash leaned down to close the lid on his toolbox.

"Wait, don't touch it. I'm going to need to take that toolbox for a forensic exam. We need to match up the sockets with the ratchet in the evidence bag to see if it came from this set."

"Now, wait a minute," Dash started. I braced for a big blow up, but Briggs diffused it with his usual cool expertise.

"Look, Dash, if the tools match, then the surest way I can help you is to look for someone else's fingerprints on this box. We might even find other evidence like a hair or fiber of clothing that doesn't match yours."

Dash's rigid posture relaxed some. I was certain it was more from the idea that Briggs believed him and was already considering that someone stole the tool and coveralls.

"How am I going to work without my set of tools?"

"I'll get forensics to go through the toolbox first thing in the morning. You can swing by the station and pick it up after ten. Hopefully that won't set your day back too much."

Considering the seriousness of the entire situation, I was absurdly glad the conversation had grown more civil. Dash accepted the fact that he was going to have to give up his toolbox for examination, and Briggs seemed to believe Dash. At least, for now, it seemed he wasn't going to bring Dash in for questioning.

No more words were exchanged between the two men, or with me, for that matter, as we walked back to the railing.

"I'll hop onto the dock and hold the boat so Lacey can climb over," Dash volunteered. Before any other plan could be offered, Dash hoisted himself up and over the railing. He leapt onto the dock and reached down to pull the boat closer.

Briggs helped me up and over the railing. I stepped onto the dock and waited for Briggs to follow. His gaze never met mine once, which made it impossible for me to sense what he was thinking. His lack of eye contact meant he was either still upset with me, or he was thinking about something that wouldn't make me happy. I knew Dash was still a person of interest, but I hoped Briggs had already concluded that Dash was not the killer.

The three of us walked in silence back to the boat where Nate Blankenship was preparing Theodore Hall's body for transport to the morgue.

The night sky was totally hidden by a dreary, gray fog. Even the stars weren't burning bright enough to twinkle through the haze. Briggs and I stopped at the *Windsong*, but Dash continued on, anxious to get home from a bad day at the marina.

The last few hours had left me with a solid knot in my stomach. I knew I wouldn't be hungry for dinner or anything else. I predicted a long, fretful night ahead with plenty of tossing and turning in bed.

Something told me Briggs wasn't going to have an easy rest either. There was no anger in his face as he turned to look at me, but I was pretty sure I wasn't going to get an impromptu kiss either.

"You don't think he did it either." It was the first thing I could think of, but I regretted not giving it more thought before blurting it out.

"And that's why I need you to take yourself off this case," he said calmly, but there was a slight storm in his eyes.

"If this is some latent jealousy thing—" The cold and the strain of the last few hours was getting to me. I tended to *let go* too much when I was stressed. "I like Dash. He's a good friend."

"Yes, you've mentioned that far more than I need to hear." The bitter aftertaste of his words stung.

My eyes watered. "James," I started, not terribly sure which way to go.

He took hold of my hands and looked down at them. "Your hands are freezing." He pressed my hands between his to warm them. It was a gesture that should have given me some comfort, but I was only feeling angst about the whole evening.

Briggs looked at me. "You can't be on this case because you are too emotionally involved. Yes, I know. He's just a friend," he added before I could protest. "But I'm just going to say it once more, and you need to listen." His brown gaze held mine before he spoke. For a brief few seconds we were back to that nice, warm, wonderful place we were just a few hours earlier when we ate hot dogs on the pier. "You have to stay off this case." His order cleaved the nice fuzzy feeling in two. I pulled my hand free of his.

"Fine," I said with a haughty shrug. "You just keep this case all to yourself, and we'll see how Samantha and I feel about helping with the next one." My childish threat backfired.

"That's probably not a bad idea."

"What do you mean?" My voice wavered.

"It's not safe or even proper protocol that I include you in my investigations."

"No, that's not what I meant. I love working on the cases. Please don't take that away."

He noticed the stupid, traitorous tear that had broken free, and he wiped it off my cheek. He leaned forward and kissed my forehead. "And you're the best partner I've ever had. But, Lacey, please leave this one alone. Now come on. It's cold. I'm going to get someone to drive you back to the shop. Just wait over by Chinmoor's squad car, and I'll find him. I need to get back to the scene."

I nodded but didn't have anything else to say, especially because nothing helpful was spilling from my lips this evening. I could feel Briggs watching me as I headed along the dock to the squad cars parked below on Pickford Way.

I reached the car and looked back to make sure I was out of view, then I kept walking. I needed the brisk hike back to the shop to clear my head.

CHAPTER 12

*K*ingston and I both trudged dejectedly inside. He was envisioning himself soaring with the seagulls, and I was dreaming of better times, like earlier in the day when Briggs kissed me for no other reason except that I said mustard was an underappreciated condiment.

Nevermore was sitting like a sentry in front of his food dish, in case I had any ideas about not feeding him. I filled his bowl and got Kingston settled in for the night. He'd had a long day. I couldn't remember the last time he'd spent so much time outside on his own. Kingston's long afternoon adventure reminded me again of how strangely Dash was acting when he walked past Lola and me on the pier. I was feeling a good dose of guilt about not mentioning anything to Briggs. Under any other circumstance, in other words, if it had been anyone but Dash, I would have brought it up. But Briggs had made it clear he wanted me off the case, so I felt free to keep the information to myself. I could only assume Dash's unusual behavior had to do with the argument he'd had with Theodore. That conclusion brought my mood even lower. Apparently, the disagreement had been loud and rambunctious enough for others to hear it. That was another strike against Dash. If the murder weapon matched up with the missing wrench from his toolbox, that was going to be a major blow. But no matter how much evidence piled up, I was firm in my belief that Dash was not the killer. And I was certain Briggs felt the same way. He was just following protocol, or at least that was what I was going to tell myself to help me get through the evening.

I was hungry but nothing sounded good. I swung open the pantry cupboard and contemplated which tea might boost my mood. It seemed not even chamomile or dandelion were going to help tonight. I closed the cupboard and walked back to the coat hook near the door.

The Chesterton Library stayed open until eight during the week-nights to allow the high school kids to do homework. I laughed to myself as I recalled my own high school days doing *homework* in the town library. Two things were as wrong with the term then as I was sure they were now. My friends and I were not at *home*, which was the point, and very little *work* ever got done.

Just thinking about Tilly Stratton's charming, peaceful and brightly lit library with its stacks of colorful books made me feel better. I hadn't looked into the Hawksworth murders for a good month. There was sure to be more newspaper articles from the time period that would give me some clues. I just needed to switch to a different murder case to lighten my mood. (And, yes, that sounded disturbing in my head too.)

I grabbed my keys and headed out to the car. Dash's truck was in the driveway. I nearly walked over to knock on his door but thought better of it. I was sure he wouldn't be in a mood to chat. I climbed into the car and headed to the Chesterton Library.

The library parking lot was surprisingly crowded considering there was less than a half hour until closing. Fortunately, I was heading into the research room at the back of the library where they kept the entire collection of local newspapers from the last century. People rarely used the room. With any luck, I'd have the room to myself. I wasn't in the mood for company tonight.

A young woman with bright red glasses and blue eye shadow was sitting behind the front desk when I walked in. "Hello, we close in twenty-eight minutes."

"Thanks," I said and smiled about her knowing the exact amount of minutes until closing. I walked through and decided, on my rush through the main library, that I might save some time by going through the microfiche files in the research room. Tilly had mentioned them on a previous visit. At the time, we'd had a good chuckle about the antiquated system that used to be considered advanced technology. Tilly mentioned that the files were well organized by date. Tonight, they might save me some precious time. The newspapers required gloves and careful handling. The microfiche files would be more convenient.

I walked up to the circulation desk in the non-fiction section. The young man behind the desk looked up from his computer screen.

"Hello, I'd like to use the research room," I said.

He looked at the clock. It seemed everyone was anxious to go home for the night. "It's—'

"Twenty-eight minutes until closing." I glanced back at the clock on the wall. "Pardon me, it's twenty-seven minutes until closing. I promise not to make a mess. I'll be out in twenty minutes. Tilly knows me."

My name dropping of the head librarian did the trick. He reached into the drawer and pulled out a key. We walked across the room to the door. "Where is Tilly tonight?" I asked.

"We had two librarians out in the children's reading room so she had to take over." He opened the door. "Then you know about the gloves and not putting the papers back. Tilly likes to put them back herself."

I smiled at him. "Yes, I know all that. Thank you and I'll be out in twenty." I lifted my phone to show him that I'd be keeping track of the time.

As predicted, I had the entire room to myself. It always took me a second to adjust to the overwhelming odor of old ink and newspaper. It was a dense, chemical kind of smell, at least to my nose. I was sure no one else noticed it when they walked into the room.

I headed to the massive four drawer file with the microfiche sheets. I decided to look at the year 1906. The Hawksworth family was murdered on October 7, 1906, but I thought it might be interesting to see what was going on in Port Danby between the abrupt cancellation of Bertram Hawksworth's shipyard project and his tragic death. The sheets were filed by month and year. I pulled out June and July, for no other reason except they were summer months and would likely show lots of town activity because of the nicer weather. Tonight's cold, dreary weather might have prodded me toward the summer months too.

Someone had kindly written out easy to follow directions for using the microfiche reader. The machine itself looked like a large, clunky computer from the nineties. It was surprisingly easy to load in the first sheet for June. A six by five array of newspaper front pages popped up on the screen. The images were somewhat grainy and yellowish in tone. I pulled out my reading glasses and leaned forward to scan the headlines and pictures. It was easy to get sidetracked by stories about a traveling carnival coming to town and an argument at the town hall over property taxes, but according to my phone, I had sixteen minutes left for research. If nothing else, the trip to the library had pulled my mind off tonight's unfortunate events. Naturally, just as that notion flashed through my head, my phone buzzed with a text from Briggs.

"Did you get home all right? Why didn't you wait for the ride?"

I texted back a simple, 'yes, I'm home'. I didn't feel the need to explain myself about anything else. I pushed the phone away. I didn't have time for a text conversation, and somehow, just exchanging a few typed words seemed wholly insufficient considering the trying evening we'd just experienced.

Turned out I hadn't needed to push the phone away. My succinct answer had apparently clued him in that I wasn't in the mood to chat. There was no response from his end. I was glad and slightly miffed all at the same time. We had, after all, had a very contentious evening. Things were definitely not all cotton candy and balloons at the moment. (Apparently my mind was still stuck on the traveling carnival story.)

It took some willpower but I dragged my mind away from Briggs and focused on the small grainy pictures in front of me. Much simpler times produced almost comical headlines, considering they were the front page news of the day. One headline read "Mrs. Robert Moore's Sunday Social Ends Early Due to Rain". Another discussed the absurd two cent price increase on canning jars. There had also apparently been a problem with feral rabbits eating garden flowers. Who knew bunnies could be feral?

My eyes skimmed past a few more of what I termed 'quaint' headlines until the name Mayor Price caught my attention. I'd found no direct connection between Mayor Price and the murders, but he did have an important hand in the end of the Hawksworth Shipyard project. That alone seemed significant enough to make me pause at the Price name. The headline read "Mayor Harvard Price Wins Again". A picture took up a good third of the front page. Even with the poor quality of the photo, the size of it allowed me to see many details. Mayor Price, the current mayor's great-grandfather, was sitting imperiously behind a massive mahogany desk. His expression was slightly less gruff than our Mayor Price, but the family resemblance could not be missed. The great-grandfather did a much better job at looking pleasant.

The photographer must have been standing so that the angle of the photo gave me a clear view of the desk. Since there was no technology back then to clutter up a desk top, it was mostly empty. An ornate silver ink well and pen set sat on the top corner. Mayor Price's big hands were folded neatly on the desk, directly behind the leather bound Port Danby town ledger. I stared at the ledger for a second as something came to me. The beautifully handcrafted ledger sitting in front of the mayor had silver plating on the corners. The name Port Danby had been embossed across the top. It was the second photo I'd seen taken in Mayor Price's office, and the ledger was in both pictures. The first photo was from an earlier edition of the paper, and the ledger was being held by a Miss Jane Price, Harvard Price's daughter from a first marriage. That ledger was leather bound but not nearly as ornate, and there were no silver embellishments.

I sat back and considered some reasons for the difference in ledgers. The simple but far less intriguing one was that the town had purchased a new, fancier ledger. It seemed a frivolous waste of taxpayer dollars, but then priorities and appearances were probably different back then. The second, far more riveting, explanation might be that Mayor Harvard Price had two sets of books, the real one and one that gave a much rosier but entirely false picture of the town budget. Maybe that was why Jane Price left town. She didn't want to be a part of the scandal.

I chuckled to myself for letting my imagination run wild with the possibilities of corruption and intrigue. No doubt, some of that wishful thinking came from my own unpleasant relationship with the current mayor.

The young man who'd unlocked the door, poked his head into the room to let me know it was getting close to closing.

I pulled the microfiche sheet from the machine. It was certainly faster to use the microfiche reader than to browse through the brittle newspapers on the shelf. I pulled out my phone and opened the reminders tab. I typed in what I'd noted about the two different ledgers before shutting down the machine. That would be the extent of my sleuthing for the night. I was exhausted from the emotional afternoon. Hopefully exhausted enough that I would fall into a nice deep sleep once my head hit the pillow.

CHAPTER 13

$\mathcal{M}$y plan to go straight inside, grab a cup of tea and climb into bed with a book until my lids dropped shut was abruptly interrupted when I found Dash sitting on my front porch as I pulled into the driveway. He looked like a boy who'd dropped the fly ball and lost the game.

I climbed out of the car and headed toward the porch. He pushed the gray hood off his head as I reached the steps. "Hope you don't mind me lurking on your front steps. I walked over hoping for a chat but you weren't home." He waved his arm toward the car. "But you obviously knew that because you just pulled into your driveway." He raked his hair back from his face. "Sorry, I sound like a crazy man."

"No, you don't, Dash. You sound like a man who has had a very bad day."

He pushed to his feet. "See, that's why I needed to chat. I figured, if nothing else, you'd understand and listen and more importantly make me smile."

I walked up the steps with my keys ready. "The good news is I've got a new box of cocoa inside. The bad news is that I forgot to buy marshmallows." I peered back at him as I clicked open the lock. "So, if

428

you can stand the thought of marshmallow-less cocoa, I'll heat some up."

His signature, Hollywood leading man smile made a quick appearance. "I think I can bear it."

We walked inside, and Kingston stood up and shook himself off from his sleepy state. Nevermore hopped off the couch and ran for the bedroom, but I was sure he'd return once he realized it was Dash.

Dash walked over and stroked Kingston's head while I took off my coat and scarf. I pulled my phone out of the pocket and checked it discretely. No message from Briggs. Once again, I was torn between relief and irritation.

I walked into the kitchen to make the cocoa.

"I think Briggs is going to arrest me for murder." Dash's alarming statement made me spill some of the cocoa mix.

"What on earth makes you think that?" I grabbed a wet towel to wipe it up.

"First of all, it's Briggs," he said as he sat at my small dining table. "He would love to find an excuse to ruin my life and now he has it."

I spun around and scowled at him. "No, don't do that, Dash. That's not even in your character. You're just upset. You know that James has too much integrity to use his badge for his own gain."

He nodded, still looking like the kid who'd dropped the fly ball. "You're right. Sorry. I'm just in a bad mood. In high school, Jimmy was always the guy who did the right thing. He was honest to a fault. It was actually kind of annoying waiting for him to take a wrong step. It never happened."

"Jimmy," I said through a grin, "I've never heard you call him that." I poured hot milk into the mugs.

"That's what we all called him back in school." He sat back. "When we were still friends or, at least, before I betrayed him. I'm sure if I called him that now, he'd throw a fist at my nose."

"Again, not the James Briggs I know, but you're not yourself tonight." I placed the cocoa in front of him.

He stared down at the cup.

"I know, it's boring without the pillowy little mallows bobbing in the froth."

He chuckled as I sat down across from him. He lifted his face "It's not the cocoa. It's just everything else and by everything, I mean my whole life. I've got a house that seems to be trying to gaslight me. I fix or improve one thing and another five things pop up that need repairs. The boat owners, who are generally way better off financially than the rest of folks, are also the cheapest group of people on earth, or, should I say, the sea. I fixed Theodore Halls' boat just fine, but the fool motored right into a sandbar. Then, instead of using oars to push it out, he kept firing the engine up so that it filled with sand and rocks. He thought he could pull a fast one and insist I never fixed it, but it was easy to tell what happened. From now on, I'm taking half up front or I'm not stepping a foot on deck." He sat back with a sigh and took hold of his cocoa. "There, I feel better already, and I haven't had one sip. Guess it was worth the hour long wait on your front porch."

"You were out there for an hour? We must have just missed each other."

"What did he say about the case?" Dash asked.

I peered at him over the rim of my cup as I took a drink. "Who? James? I wasn't with him. I left right after you. I went to the Chesterton Library for a little relaxation and mind clearing." I put the cup down and rested my arms on the table as I leaned forward. "Dash, I was on the pier with Lola late this afternoon, just as the fog rolled in. Kingston hadn't come back from his outing, and I was worried about him so we walked to the pier."

He waited for me to continue, somewhat puzzled at where I was heading with my Kingston story.

"You walked right past Lola and me, and I have to say, you were wearing a really sour expression. You were in such a distressed state, you didn't even notice us. You just stomped right by."

"Did I? I apologize. I'd probably just had the big blowout fight with Theodore down on the *Windsong*. I took a brisk walk along the pier to cool my head. He really angered me. When I confronted him about the sand in the engine, he called me a liar. Told me I was a worthless mechanic and that he wouldn't pay me one dime. I spent a good three days on his boat, fixing it and making it purr like a kitten, just so he could run it into a sandbar."

I warmed my hands around the cup. The chill from the dreary fog still hadn't left my bones. "I figured it had something to do with the argument."

Dash frowned. "Did you think it was because I'd just committed murder?"

"No, of course not." I reached across and touched his hand. "Dash, I haven't for one second considered you a suspect."

"That leaves one of you."

"Briggs knows it wasn't you. He just has to do his job. Other people on the dock heard you two arguing just before Theo was murdered."

"Then my socket wrench ends up as the murder weapon." He rubbed his face. "How the heck did this happen?"

"Someone must have stolen the wrench from your box."

"But who? It was down in the engine compartment with those missing coveralls." His green eyes widened. "It had to be someone who was watching me work."

"Think about the day. Was there anyone hanging around the dock?"

Dash sat back in thought for a second. "No one. But then I wasn't really watching out for anyone. I was mostly below deck." He lifted the cup but then set it down. "Let's change topics. This one is making my stomach feel as if I just downed two breakfast burritos with extra hot sauce."

"Do you need something? I have antacid."

"No, I'll be fine." But the release of breath that followed made that hard to believe.

"What else is bothering you? Or should I guess?" I added.

Dash tilted his head as he gazed at me across the table. "Why can't everyone be this easy to talk to?" he asked.

"Does that comment have something to do with Britney?" Dash

seemed to have a lot to get off his chest. In turn, I might get some insight into his relationship with Britney. Since I'd been involuntarily pulled into the middle of it, I'd be better off knowing all sides of the story.

"I suppose Elsie has already given you an earful about terrible Dash and his bad manners toward her niece." Nevermore had returned to dance around Dash's legs. Dash reached down to scratch the cat's chin.

"Elsie might have mentioned something about it." I pushed aside the cup of cocoa. "This cocoa is sorely lacking without the marshmallows. I have to say, I'm somewhat surprised. Britney is such an amazing woman, beautiful, talented, smart," I started the list.

"Sort of boring," he added lightly as if that might soften the words. He sat forward fast enough to make my shabby kitchen chair creak. "Britney is all the things you mentioned. She's special in every way, but I'm not sure she's for me. This is going to sound shallow, but she doesn't make me laugh. Equally shallow, she doesn't seem to get my humor at all, which means either I'm not nearly as funny as I thought or we just don't click. You need to be able to laugh with someone to click. That was why things never worked between Kate and me. You probably noticed, but Kate Yardley takes herself very seriously. Stern is her middle name."

I cleared my throat quietly. "I might have noticed that about Kate, yes. But Britney doesn't seem anything like Kate."

"And she's not but—" He shrugged. "Maybe it's just me and my commitment issues." He smiled. "I can see you agree with that assessment."

"I didn't say a word," I said far too abruptly. His fear of commitment had instantly crossed my mind but then that was always the go to excuse for men who didn't want to be tied down.

"You don't have to say a word. I can always read everything you're thinking on that perfectly adorable face of yours."

My cheeks warmed at the compliment. While Dash and I had started our friendship with some occasional flirting, that had come to an abrupt end when I made it clear that I chose Briggs. It felt wrong now too, only I was just angry enough with Briggs to easily tamp down any guilt.

"I seem to be far more readable than I intend to be. James always knows exactly what I'm thinking too." I decided a quick reminder of my boyfriend wouldn't hurt . . . for either of us.

"I hope tonight's scene didn't cause any problems between you two. I genuinely want you to both be happy." He tilted his head side to side. "Well let's say I want you to be happy, but if Briggs is required for that then I can live with it."

"Well, thank you." I replayed his last few words in my head. "I think. And don't worry about us. We've hit rough patches before." Just none quite so rough, I thought but didn't say aloud. "The truth is, even though James has accepted that you and I are going to remain friends, regardless of what has passed between you, he still has a hard time of it. Especially when I'm defending you as a possible suspect." I covered my mouth. "Oops, you didn't want to talk about that anymore."

"No, that's all right. Somehow, it doesn't feel as daunting and hopeless coming from you. Hopefully Briggs will find the real killer soon, and I won't have to give it another thought. Although, it looks as if I'm going to be out three day's pay, either way."

I arched a brow at him.

"Yeah, that's bad. The guy is barely cold, and I'm fretting over money." He lightly slapped the table with his hand. It sent Nevermore scurrying out from under the table. "Sorry about that, Never." Dash stood up from the table. "I've bent your ear enough for one night. Thanks for inviting me in. I needed someone to talk to. Captain had no interest in my rant. He just lifted his big head, looked at me with droopy eyes, and dropped his head back onto the pillow."

"I have found that the animals are much more willing to play the part of therapist if you hold a treat up while you spill out your story."

Dash laughed. "See, that's all that I'm looking for. Why is it so hard to find a person to click with?"

"Dash," I said as I walked him to the door. "If you aren't going to take this any further with Britney, then you need to let her know. Don't just stop calling. That way she can move on."

"Right again, oh clever one." He smiled down at me. "That Briggs was always the lucky one in high school too," he said before opening the door and walking out.

CHAPTER 14

I sat back against the pillows I'd propped up against the headboard and tucked the plush comforter around my legs. I was sure I wouldn't read more than three lines of my book before falling asleep. Nevermore curled himself up next to me to give his paws a good grooming. I stroked his soft fur, and his purr machine rumbled to life.

"Never, would you like to switch places for awhile? That way I could lay here all day in a marathon cat nap, waking only occasionally to stretch, or nibble food, or lick my paws. A completely stress-free existence." The cat stopped his licking and rubbed his head against my hand for some extra strokes.

The ringtone on my phone made his ears and mine perk up. It was nearly ten o'clock. I reached for it. While relieved to see it wasn't Mom or Dad calling with some emergency or bad news at a late hour, my pulse raced even faster when I saw it was Briggs. I hesitated only for a second before answering it.

"Hello," I said in my most non-committal tone, as if I was just answering a sales call.

"Hello," he said back with a much warmer voice. "Just wanted to make sure you were all right."

"I'm tucked in bed with a book and my most loyal companion, Nevermore. I'm just fine."

"Thought Kingston was your most loyal companion." We were already off on a silly tangent just to avoid real stuff.

"He's my companion but loyal? Not so much. He'd take off to live with Lola in an instant if she just asked."

"Silly bird. He doesn't know how good he has it with you. Which brings me to my reason for calling." A long pause followed. "I'm sorry if I upset you tonight, Lacey. It wasn't my intention. You've been a brilliant assistant on cases, and you've been an even more brilliant girlfriend. I don't want anything to get in the way of our relationship."

My throat tightened as he spoke. I suddenly realized how badly I needed to hear his voice before I fell asleep. "I don't want anything to get in the way either."

"I hope you understand why I took you off this particular case." He turned the wrong corner in a conversation that seemed to be heading in the right direction. Sometimes, I wished a tech genius would create a GPS system that helped you navigate a smooth journey in a relationship. I decided to take my own wrong turn, and I wasn't sure if any rerouting would get us back to the right place.

"I don't really understand why. I could see if Dash was actually involved or a serious person of interest, but surely you know he had nothing to do with Theo's death. I spoke to him tonight. He was horribly upset about the whole thing." The last part wasn't just a wrong turn but an irreparable detour.

"You spoke to him about the case?" he said sharply. "That proves my point. You can't be part of a case when you're totally blinded by your friendship with a susp—the person in question."

I sat forward so quickly, Nevermore hopped up and moved to a less turbulent corner of the bed. "You were just about to call him a suspect."

"No, I meant—He's not a suspect. Not yet."

I could hear my own disgusted sigh come back to me through the phone. "Not yet. It seems to me you're in the same boat as me. I'm defending him because he's my friend, and you've already charged and convicted him because he betrayed you."

"No, Lacey, I'm not. I wouldn't be able to do my job if I couldn't keep my feelings and emotions out of it."

"But are you?" I asked. "Are you looking at this totally like a detective who has absolutely no connection to the case?"

The silence on the other end was as loud as a drumbeat. Or that might have been my heart thumping wildly in my chest. It seemed we were having our second significant fight and all in the space of five hours.

"I don't know what bothers me more—" he said quietly. "That you're questioning my integrity as an investigator or that you're willing to sabotage what we have to defend Dash."

"That's not true. I'm siding with a friend, that's all. It should have nothing to do with us. You're the one connecting it to our relationship." I turned my face away from the phone to hide my first sniffle, but I was sure he already heard it in my wavering voice. "I think I just need to sleep now, James. It's been a long day."

"Yes, right. Well, I'll let you go." It felt as if a raw, taut string had been broken between us. It made me feel as if I was just flailing in space with nothing to hold onto.

"Good night, James," I said through tears.

"Good night, Lacey."

I hung up and hugged the extra pillow to my stomach. Suddenly, I was a brokenhearted teenager again. I had an urge for milk, cookies and a Mom chat. I looked at the phone, the purveyor of both good and bad conversations. This one definitely fell in the latter category. I released my death grip on my pillow and scrunched down under the covers.

Just this morning I was thanking my lucky stars that James and I weren't having any troubles like everyone else. Now those darn stars had deserted me.

CHAPTER 15

"**W**ant to talk about it, boss?" Ryder asked as he finished carrying the last order of new flowers to the cooler.

"Talk about what?" I asked airily as I pushed another rosemary plant into a tiny plastic pot.

"Oh, I don't know, possibly about the fact that you walked in here like a zombie, without a word or glance at anyone, including the two customers at the counter. And that you left your purse on the hook." He pointed at my purse swinging on the coat hook. "And you tried to shove your puffy coat in the desk drawer. And that Elsie left some molasses cookies and you haven't so much as sniffed their direction. And then there's—"

"All right. Point made." I knew I sounded gruff but couldn't seem to stop myself. I picked up another stem of rosemary. "Sorry." I rubbed my forehead. "I didn't get much sleep."

"Then I can add that to the list of reasons you might have something to talk about." He took the rosemary that I was nearly crushing from my fingers.

"Why don't you let me finish the herb plants. You said you've been wanting to draw a new chalkboard sign for the shop. You should do that. Creativity always helps clear a foggy head. We've got a lot of roses that are almost past prime. We should sell them at half price. That would be great for the sign."

"Maybe you're right." I washed the potting soil from my hands and headed over to the island in the center of the shop. I pulled out my tub of colored chalk and a piece of paper and pencil to scratch out a design before putting it on the board.

"Also, I'm here to listen. Just like you do for me and Lola and Elsie and it seems just about everyone in town. I wouldn't mind returning the favor."

I took a deep breath. "Thanks but I'm not really sure what to say. And some of it has to do with the murder case James is working on so I can't say much about it. Then again, I'm not on the case, so maybe I don't have to worry about protocol. After all, I'm not part of the police force." I started sketching a large, ugly rose with pencil strokes deep enough to rip the paper. "Boy, but he sure does use my olfactory skills when they are needed. And I'm happy to do it, but one case that involves a friend and suddenly, I'm off the team. No nose needed. Not that there was much in the way of scented evidence anyhow. But who does he think he is just picking and choosing when I can help out or not. And if he thinks he's going into this with an unbiased investigator's eye, then he needs to look in the mirror and take a good long look at himself." I looked over at Ryder, who was staring my direction with a slightly open mouth and a pot of basil in his hand. He had no apparent response. But I didn't need one. I knew just what I wanted to do, and this time, I wasn't going to let even one silly tear escape. I slammed down my pencil. "Thanks for the talk, Ryder."

"You're welcome?" he said, questioningly.

"If you don't mind captaining the ship for a few minutes, I need to walk down to the police station." I headed to my coat and pulled it on.

"Sure thing. Go get 'em, boss," he cheered as I walked out the door.

My fast, sure-footed steps lightened and grew far less confident as I neared the station. Briggs' car was out front, which meant he was in the office. I'd briefly hoped that he wouldn't be, then I'd have an excuse to turn around and head back to the shop. I stopped a few feet from the large tinted front windows of the station. There were no rules that said I had to finish what I'd started. I could just spin around, go back to the flower shop and keep brooding while doing absent-minded things like squeezing the life out of helpless rosemary plants.

Or I could let Briggs know how unfair this all was.

"Yep, get this off your chest, Lacey, or you'll never forgive yourself." I took a deep breath, marched to the door and swung it open.

Hilda, the wonderfully sweet woman who ran the front office, peeked up over the chin-height counter. "Lacey, there you are." She popped up from her chair waving a piece of paper. "Just this morning I asked Detective Briggs when you'd be stopping by, but he just grunted in response." She lowered her voice when I reached the counter. Her nose crinkled. "Just to warn you, he's in a terrible mood." Her smile returned and her nose unfolded as she slapped a hand-written paper down on the counter. "I wrote out my recipe for that pimento cheese casserole you liked so much at the town Christmas potluck."

"Oh, that's wonderful." My forced smile was nothing to the feigned enthusiasm in my voice. In truth, the casserole tasted terrible, but Hilda was so proud of it and she kept asking if I'd tried it yet. I finally put a spoonful on my plate and forced myself to eat it. I raved about it for the rest of the night. Now, it seemed I'd earned the privilege of knowing the secret recipe. Hilda had even taken the time to write a little note to me about how excited she was that I loved the casserole.

Her smile nearly split her face in two as she grinned at me over the counter. She pointed to the paper. "I even wrote down a few substitutions in case you don't have all the ingredients."

"This is so kind of you, Hilda. I can't wait to bake it at home." I reached for the paper, but she took hold of my hand.

A serious brow met me across the counter. "Now, don't forget. This recipe is not to be shared with just anybody. The few of us who have it in our possession need to keep it top secret. Otherwise, it's no longer special. Plus, other people start tweaking the ingredients and the directions and then it's no longer in its truest, purest form." She patted my hand and released me. The pact had been sealed. I was now entrusted with the secret of the pimento cheese casserole for life. The entire scene had quickly dissolved the resolute anger I'd built up since my rant about Briggs began back in the shop. Hilda was such a fun, dear person. She easily lifted my dark mood.

I folded the recipe as if it were a map to a priceless treasure. "Your secret is safe with me, Hilda." I stuck the recipe in my pocket and decided to slink back out, without a word to Briggs.

"Where are you going?" Hilda asked. "I was just going to let him know you were here."

"That's all right. I've got to get back to work." I pointed back over my shoulder and spun around to make a fast exit.

I heard a door open behind me. "Lacey." Briggs' voice coasted over my shoulder.

I froze and contemplated just making a run for it, explaining later that I hadn't heard him. But I knew that was absurd. I swiveled back around and smiled meekly at him. There were dark rings under his eyes. Seemingly, I wasn't the only one who tossed and turned the night before.

"Come on into the office." His warm, cocoa brown eyes pleaded just enough to break me. One foot dropped in front of the other, and before I knew it we were standing in his office, face to face, alone.

I would have preferred if he sat down, putting his big metal desk between us. Instead, he leaned against the front of it. I had no such luxury of being able to brace myself, even though I was certain my knees were more wobbly than his. He had his shirt sleeves rolled up, a look I always found very pleasing. It made him look strong and official all at once. My gaze lingered on his strong, muscular forearms as he rested his hands back along the edge of the desk.

I finally worked up the courage to lift my face to his. "I came to say a few things," I said in an usually hushed tone. "But I can't really think of what they were anymore." I patted my coat pocket. "Hilda gave me the prized recipe for her pimento casserole."

His mouth pulled in a straight line. He, too, had been prodded into eating it at the potluck, and he, too, had gone overboard in his praise of it. "You mean *the* pimento casserole," he whispered.

I giggled behind my hand and nodded. "She was so sweet and hand wrote the whole thing. Then there was this sort of secret pimento cheese club hand squeeze. Anyhow, she reminded me how much fun life can be if you don't take yourself too seriously."

Briggs was a *picture* when he was serious, and the way he gazed at me right then turned my wobbly knees to butter. "I couldn't sleep at all last night, Lacey." He stepped forward. My heartbeat sputtered into overdrive as my lips waited for a kiss.

Before his hand could take hold of mine, an urgent knock interrupted us. Officer Chinmoor came in without being invited. His cheeks turned pink in embarrassment. "I'm sorry, sir, Hilda wasn't at her desk. I just assumed you were alone." He was doing that same glancing at me and pulling his gaze away thing that he'd done the day before at the murder scene.

"What is it, Chinmoor?" Briggs asked impatiently.

"Just thought you'd like to know that we found—" He flicked his eyes my direction again and cleared his throat. "We found the coveralls." He fidgeted with his gun belt. "We found a pair of work coveralls in the trash can behind the fish cleaning station. This was in the pocket." He held out a business card, which I recognized instantly as one of the sea foam green cards Dash handed out to customers.

Briggs took the card and glanced at it briefly. "The garment was stashed in a trash can?"

Chinmoor nodded and cleared his throat again. Of course, leaving would have been the proper thing for me to do but I stayed.

"They were splattered with what appears to be blood," Chinmoor continued after an awkward pause. "I've sent them to forensics to be tested."

Briggs avoided looking my direction. "Thank you, Chinmoor. Let me know as soon as you get those results."

Chinmoor backed out of the room, looking more than relieved to get out of the office.

Briggs stared down at the business card on his palm. He tossed it back and forth once, for no other reason, it seemed, except he didn't know what to say. For a magical moment, I thought we'd patched things up, but we were really just glossing over the problem with sweet, idol chat.

I couldn't stop myself from breaking up the tense silence that followed. "Dash said his coveralls were missing. We were both there when he went into the engine compartment to find them. We were both—"

Briggs lifted his focus from the business card and looked at me. "I should get back to work. I've got a lot to do."

I swallowed to relieve the dryness in my throat. I hated everything about his last comment, the words, the dismissive, dry tone, the formal expression on his face.

"Yes, fine. I need to get back to the shop." I rushed out of his office and out of the station without looking back.

CHAPTER 16

*T*he morning had taken the wind out of my sails. I was
thankful for the post holiday lull in business. Ryder
puttered at the potting table with a few succulents. Like Elsie, occasionally, when I was frustrated or upset, I moved into cleaning mode.
A habit I obviously inherited from my mom, who would notoriously
arm herself with a mop and bucket after every argument with my dad.

I climbed into the front display window with a bottle of glass
cleaner and a rag. I stepped gingerly over the wintry display of white
and blue carnations Ryder had arranged in silver vases. The flowers
were starting to look tired and altogether less crisp.

I freely sprayed the cleaning solution on the window in the
cramped space, somehow forgetting my nose. I folded over into a
sneezing fit. By the time I recovered, I found my ever-wonderful
assistant leaning into the window with a box of tissues.

I plucked a few out and sneezed once more for good measure.
"Why do cleaners have to smell so strong?"

"I think it's to give people the sense that their windows are very
clean. I could do that, if you like. I'm getting bored with potting." As
he spoke, his gaze was drawn to the window behind me. He leaned his
head. At the right angle, we could see a short section of the coast. An

ocean view was what the real estate agent for the shop had boasted on the listing, but it was more of an ocean glimpse and only if you were at the right height and leaning or standing in the display window.

"Looks like something is happening down by the water," Ryder said.

I twisted around and looked down toward the shore. Briggs' car and another squad car were parked at the entrance to the marina.

"Oh no, no, no. It can't be." I reached for Ryder, and he gave me his hand to help me out of the window.

His eyes were wide with alarm. "What is it? What's happening?"

I raced to the coat hook. "I'm not sure. I just hope it's not what I think." I pulled on my coat as I headed toward the door. "I'll know for sure soon." With that cryptic explanation, I flew out of the shop and headed quickly down the street toward the beach.

The closer I got to Pickford Way, the more my fears were realized. The activity was down at the marina, right in front of the boat that Dash had been working on the day before.

Officer Chinmoor made a half-hearted attempt to stop me from crossing the barrier he'd made with a few cones. It seemed Briggs had at least taken the trouble of keeping the entire town away from the scene, saving Dash the humiliation.

I reached the twenty foot vessel where Dash had stored his toolbox for the week's work. This time, the gangplank had been lowered. Briggs was walking Dash off the boat. I was relieved almost to tears when I saw that Dash was not in handcuffs. Maybe he was just being brought in for questioning, I told myself quickly. But then why the police barrier? Briggs would have just asked him to come in for questioning. He wouldn't have gone to his work site and walked him personally off the boat.

Both men spotted me the second they stepped onto the dock. A more somber pair of expressions could not have greeted me. I was relieved to see that Briggs seemed equally upset by it all. If he had felt nothing then I was certain it would've changed my view of him forever.

Briggs gazed at me but seemed unable to speak.

"Lacey," Dash said urgently, "please, take care of Captain for me. The spare key I gave you works best on the back door." Dash and I had exchanged keys in case of an emergency, like this.

The mention of me having Dash's spare key broke Briggs' otherwise stony expression. His brows raised ever so slightly, but he knew that the worst thing he could do at that moment was question why I had a spare key. I pushed the disappointment over his reaction out of my head. It seemed whenever I'd convinced myself that Briggs was no longer upset about my friendship with Dash, he did something to smash that confidence. But that was a topic for another day.

I looked at Briggs. "I don't understand. How did this move so quickly?"

Briggs was hesitant to explain. "Lacey, this is police business. I need you to exit the area."

I stared so hard at him it was almost as if I was giving him a slap with just my eyes. He flinched as if he felt it good.

"My coveralls were found. They were splattered with Theo's blood." Dash had no problem explaining. "I was framed." He looked over at Briggs. "But Detective Briggs, who just happens to hate me, has found what he considers enough evidence to make an arrest."

Briggs looked sharply at him. "I chose not to walk you down this dock, in front of everyone, in handcuffs. I can change my mind on that."

Dash stared just as sharply back. "You know I'm right. You know there is more to this than a murder and some evidence. You've finally got your chance for revenge. Lacey chose you, not me. Isn't that sweet enough for you?"

This time it was my turn to flinch. They were the last words I'd expected to hear from Dash, especially at a time like this. Briggs could only flash a glance my direction. The tiny muscle spasm in his cheek that made its appearance only when he was particularly upset was flickering like crazy. I'd made a tense scene even worse, but I stuck by them as Briggs walked Dash along the dock.

A cold Tuesday morning had thankfully left the marina mostly deserted, but the few folks who had braved the grim weather turned to watch the unusual spectacle of Detective Briggs walking a sullen looking Dash Vanhouten toward the police car on Pickford Way. They stared unabashedly and began murmuring behind their hands. It could almost have been just a normal group of friends out for a stroll, if not for the morose expressions on our faces and the police cars at the end of it all.

The journey seemed to stretch on forever. Not one word was spoken, but invisible thought bubbles above our heads were filled with words. My stomach churned with everything that had gone wrong for each of us in the last twenty-four hours. But Dash was suffering the most. How terrifying it would be to be accused of murder, especially if you knew you were innocent. And I had no doubt of that. Briggs might have ordered me off the case, but he had no control over what I did in my spare time. I was thin on ideas or a plan at the moment, but I had every intention of finding the real killer. It would surely cause an even bigger rip in our relationship, possibly even one that was too tattered to mend, but I couldn't stand by and do nothing.

We finally reached the steps. Both men plodded with heavy, angry footsteps.

"Don't worry about, Captain," I said to Dash as Briggs opened the back door on his car.

Dash's green eyes glinted with anguish as he nodded his thanks toward me.

"Let me know if I can do anything else," I called out as he lowered himself into the backseat.

Briggs stared down at the ground, avoiding eye contact with me as he circled around the back of his car. It took all my courage to step in front of him, forcing him to finally look at me.

"James," I said pleadingly.

Standing face to face with him weakened my courage.

"Obviously, there is evidence or you wouldn't have just put Dash in the car, but remember to self-reflect on your own motives. Make sure every decision you make is unbiased." His cheek muscle was still dancing. "Put the past behind you with this." I should have stopped but

I tended to blather on when I was nervous. "Like Dash said, I chose you."

His gaze locked with mine. "Are you sure about that?"

He dragged his gaze away and walked around to the driver's side, leaving me standing alone and stunned and feeling as if the wind had just been knocked out of me.

CHAPTER 17

$\mathcal{I}$ reached the shop and stood outside for a few minutes, pacing back and forth, trying to catch my breath and regain my composure. Ryder kept a close watch on me over the heads of the two women he was helping. I couldn't stay outside on the sidewalk, marching back and forth like Kingston waiting for a treat. Lola was sure to spot me, and I wasn't ready to talk about anything yet.

I took a steadying breath and walked into the store. "Morning," I said with fake cheer to the two customers before disappearing into my office and closing the door.

I sat down at my desk and stared at my computer and the summery beach scene Ryder had downloaded as a screensaver to 'keep away the winter doldrums'. How badly I wished for those 'doldrums' to come back. I much preferred a slow, listless winter to this.

A tentative knock sounded on the door. "Boss? Lacey, is there something I can do?"

"You can come in, Ryder. I think I'm finished with my meltdown."

He opened the door as hesitantly as he'd knocked. It made me chuckle.

Ryder seemed relieved to see me smiling. "Oh good, for a moment I thought something terrible had happened."

"It has. My giggle was one of those ill-timed laughs, borne more out of quiet hysteria than humor."

Ryder pulled up the extra chair and sat across from the desk. "So it's true? Dash was arrested?"

My eyes rounded. "Jeez, news in this town travels at the speed of light. How on earth did you find out?"

"Lola texted me just as the customers walked out. She said a customer who came into the antique shop saw the whole thing down at the marina."

"Oh boy, then it's only a matter of time before Elsie and Britney hear the news." I'd barely finished the last word when the goat bell clanged. "That's probably Elsie right now."

Soft, sputtering sobs rolled down the hallway before I reached the shop front, letting me know it wasn't Elsie. I paused. Ryder was close on my heels. I mouthed the word *Britney* to him.

Britney was standing in the center of the flower shop wearing an apron that was stained with pink icing. She must have flown out of the bakery the second she heard.

She ran over and hugged me. "Is it true?" she muttered between sobs. "Did they really arrest Dash for murder?"

I patted her back a second until she caught her breath and released me. She even managed to look pretty crying. "He couldn't have done it. Dash isn't capable of murder." She sniffled.

"I know he's not. And I'm sure everything will get cleared up soon. For now, we have to keep our wits about us." The last part was more for me than Britney.

"I'm sure you're right. I wish I could talk to Dash and let him know that I'm here to support him." She wiped a tear away.

I thought back to the conversation I'd had with Dash about his relationship with Britney. Now, more than ever, I wished I hadn't helped it along or convinced Elsie it would be a good thing. Britney seemed more than just a little smitten with Dash, but it seemed he didn't have quite as strong of feelings about her. That was always a recipe for disaster. From now on, I'd keep my nose out of relationships. Anyhow, it seemed I wasn't exactly an expert when it came to keeping them running smoothly. That thought pushed against my chest like a wet bag of sand. I managed to mess things up even more this morning. It wasn't going to be easy, but I needed to push Briggs out of my head and focus on helping Dash.

The bell clanged and Lola walked inside. I was still getting used to her hatless, straight red hair look. If not for the Beatles t-shirt under her sweatshirt, I might not have recognized her at all. She looked surprised to see Britney, in tears, and obviously counting on me for comfort. Ryder motioned for her to follow him down the hallway to the office to let Britney and I finish.

"Everything will sort itself out, Britney." I walked toward the door, hoping she would follow. She stopped short before exiting. Her button nose was pink from crying. It made her look even younger than twenty-five, almost like a little girl. "I don't know what to do," she said. "Should I try and call him?"

"I don't think you'll get through to him right now." I patted her arm. "Give him some time. I've always found that I can handle calamities much better when I keep myself busy. Go back to the bakery and create one of your magnificent desserts. That will help take your mind off of everything. This is going to take some time, but I know everything will work out right in the end." Again, the words were more for me, but they were true. My intuition told me everything would turn out fine in the end. At least as far as Dash's predicament. I only wished I could be so sure about Briggs and me working everything out.

Britney hugged me quickly and hurried back toward the bakery. Lola and Ryder came out from the office at the sound of the bell.

"Boy, she was distraught," Lola said rather callously. Obviously, her unwarranted jealousy toward Britney was deeper than I realized.

"Well, it's kind of a big deal." I walked around the work island to start organizing ribbons and cards. I decided to heed my own advice and keep busy.

Lola hopped up on a stool, but I wasn't much in the talking mood. "Did James really haul Dash into jail?"

Ryder didn't seem any more pleased with Lola's comments than me.

"Uh, I think you're watching too many crime shows, Lola," Ryder said curtly and headed back to the planting station to work on his newest project—succulents. Lola stared after him for a second, seemingly baffled by what she'd done to deserve his brusque response. I was busy with the card display, but I could sense her staring at me with the same question.

"Come on," she said. "I'm upset too. I like Dash. I think I'm not getting overwrought by the whole thing because there is no way he did it. I mean Dash could never kill someone."

I looked at her. "I agree. There's no way this will stand."

Lola's mouth twisted around in thought. "Although, he was acting strange yesterday when he plowed right past us on the pier."

I shook my head at her and returned to my task of straightening the cards.

Lola tapped the counter. "No, I still don't think he did it." Kingston heard the slightly desperate sound in her voice and immediately flew down from his perch, marched across the floor and fluttered up to the counter to sit with her.

She stroked his head. "At least you still like me, no matter what comes out of this big mouth."

"Dash already explained his behavior to me. He was angry after he'd argued with Theodore Hall," I said.

"So he fought with the victim," she reminded me.

"You are not scoring best friend points this morning," I noted. "Yes, he happened to have had a largely noticed argument with the victim not long before his murder, which looks bad but—"

Lola held up her hands. "You don't have to defend Dash to me. But if I know you, and I think I do, you've been defending him to a certain detective, and I imagine that has caused a certain amount of tension between you and the aforementioned detective."

The mention of Briggs made me drop the stack of tiny note cards I was holding. They fluttered to the ground like leaves. Lola hopped off the stool and circled around to help me pick them up.

"I'm sure James will figure out quickly that Dash is innocent," Lola said as she swept up a pile of cards and handed it to me. "If you ask me, Theo's ex-wife did it. She was complaining up a storm about him when I got my hair straightened. It took four hours, so, trust me, I learned everything about every stylist in that salon while I was sitting there waiting for the curls to go."

I straightened the collection of cards. "His ex-wife?" Lola had my full attention. I wasn't sure how to start my own investigation of the murder without much information to go on. I knew little about the victim, but it seemed I'd found my first lead.

"What did she say about Theodore?"

Lola was pleased to have landed on the right topic after her first few missteps. "She mentioned that even though he made good money, he was always in debt. She said he couldn't stop betting on the horses and on fights. She said something about him having the knack of always picking the loser."

"So he had a gambling problem?" I rubbed my chin. "Coincidentally enough, Theodore Hall ran into me yesterday when James and I were heading back from the pier after lunch." That pleasant, flirty lunch date seemed so far away now. I tamped down the emotions that were stirred by the thought. "Theodore was really angry and distracted. That's why he nearly pushed me off the steps. He kept looking around as if waiting for someone to jump out at him." I snapped my fingers. "Aside from mentioning the dispute with Dash, he muttered something about everyone trying to take his money. It wasn't specific to just Dash. He must have been in financial trouble with other people or he wouldn't have used the word *everyone*."

Lola's face brightened. "Like an ex-wife. She was probably trying to squeeze money out of him too. Maybe he refused or fought her in court, and she was mad enough to kill him." She slapped the counter after her enthusiastic theory. "Woo hoo! I can see why you like this investigative stuff. It's kind of a rush. Maybe I should help you."

Ryder's laugh reached our side of the room.

Lola put her hands on her hips. "What are you chuckling at? I just solved a murder."

"Well, it's not solved yet," I noted. "In fact, far from it. There is more to finding a killer than finding motives. But I could use your help."

Lola's eyes rounded. "Sure. When do we start? Ooh, I've got one of those deerstalker hats like Sherlock Holmes wears."

"I just need the name and number of your stylist. I might go in for a haircut and see if I can find out more about Theo's ex-wife."

Lola's posture deflated. "Guess I won't need a hat for that. I've got a business card back at the shop. Why don't you have her straighten your hair?" Lola flipped her hair back. "Then you can do this too." Lola flipped her hair back again. "We could be twins. Sort of."

"Don't think I have the patience for a four hour process. A haircut and style should be enough."

"I'll bring the card by later." She skipped over and kissed Ryder, then headed for the door. Kingston made a gurgling sound to get her attention. "Aw, I nearly forgot my King." She scurried back over and patted him on the head a few times. "By the way," Lola added, "I don't think Elsie is too happy with her new dog area. One lady sat down on the bench with her three tiny dogs. She didn't even buy anything. She was just sitting there to rest, only those three dogs just kept chirping and barking. I think they smelled the bakery goods and were mad they didn't get a treat. Anyhow, Elsie finally poked her head out the door and said something to the lady. She got up and marched off with her three yappy dogs in tow."

"I had a feeling she might come to regret that decision. Poor Elsie. And now she has a weepy, mopey baking assistant to add to her troubles."

CHAPTER 18

Somehow the news that Theodore had an ex-wife, who clearly disliked him, helped me get through the rest of the work day. Ryder left early to take his mom to visit his grandma, so aside from a few customers, I had the shop mostly to myself. Lola hadn't returned with the business card, but I planned to get it from her soon.

I'd spent most of the day cleaning shelves and racks that badly needed it. The arduous task along with the feeling of accomplishment helped ease the nerves and tension of the day. It was an hour before closing. I decided to use the time to work on purchase orders for Valentine's Day.

The bell rang just as I headed to the office. I turned back around. My heart skipped a beat as I stepped out of the hallway.

Briggs was fidgeting with the hat in his hands. "I came here to let you know that I've taken myself off the case." He blurted it so quickly, it took me a second to comprehend.

"I don't understand. Who'll be working on it?"

"Officer Chinmoor needs more responsibility. I never give him enough opportunity to improve his investigative skills."

I curled my hands to hide the fact that my fingers were shaky. I hadn't expected to see him, and they were taking a second to calm down. "Officer Chinmoor is a very nice, enthusiastic police officer, but I can't picture him leading an investigation." It dawned on me that I'd made a mistake insisting that Briggs wasn't going into the investigation with a clear, unbiased view. Now he was putting Chinmoor in charge.

"I thought you'd be pleased. You were the one who made it clear that I shouldn't handle this case. Dash pointed it out more than once too. And you were both right. Deep down, I know I would have put aside any of my feelings about Dash and done the professional job I always do." He looked pointedly at me. There was no missing the hurt in his expression at my doubting him. "But I knew it would look bad to everyone else, so I took myself off the case. I've got several other important investigations I'm working on, so, frankly, I'm glad to have one less on my case load. Chinmoor is going to be working with a veteran from the Mayfield precinct, so I'm not just throwing him out there to sink or swim."

"No, I don't think this is a good idea. I shouldn't have said anything. Of course you would be professional." I was back pedaling as fast as I could, wanting to kick myself as the words sputtered out. "We need to find who killed Theodore. It wasn't Dash. Like he said, someone was trying to frame him." I moved closer, but we were still more than an arm's distance apart. "James, stay on the case. There can't be any mistakes."

He shook his head. "I've handed it off. Chinmoor will be fine. Anything I do will be questioned and scrutinized." He had a difficult time looking at me as he spoke. "Just stay clear of the investigation, Lacey."

My muscles went rigid, and I jumped into defense mode. "You can't stop me from finding out more information about Theodore Hall. For instance, did you know he has an ex-wife? And she has plenty to complain about. Apparently he was always in debt." I realized as I finished that I hadn't mentioned anything new. My posture sank. "Of course, you probably already knew that."

"It's part of the job." He stepped closer. For a second, the warmth that always passed between us when we were in touching distance, curled around me. But there was too much cold on the edges to melt us together. "Lacey," he started, but I turned away before he could say anything else about letting the police do their job.

"I've got some paperwork to do, James. Thanks for stopping by." Dismissing him coldly was the hardest thing I'd done since I moved to Port Danby. I forced a weak smile and turned back to him. "Good luck with your other cases."

It would have been much easier if he'd just turned and walked out. Instead, he gazed at me long and hard with those mesmerizing brown eyes. There was a mix of emotions in his face. I didn't need to see my reflection to know my expression mirrored his. He dragged his gaze away, pushed his hat down on his head and walked out the door.

I stumbled back as if he'd been holding me with a taut tether and it had been cut in two. I didn't want to even consider that this was the end between us. I'd been too happy. Maybe that was the problem. I'd been too happy. It was a brutal fact of life that when things were going too smoothly, you could always count on a bump in the road. Only this didn't just feel like a bump. It was more like a mountain, a giant, jagged, impassible mountain.

CHAPTER 19

J sat in my office chair, still trying to recuperate from the scene with Briggs when the shop bell rang. He was back. My heart went right back into overdrive. I immediately searched for words that might erase some of the negativity of the last few minutes. I pinched my cheeks for no other reason except that was what women sometimes did in movies when about to face the man they loved. And that was what it was for me. If nothing else, the last twenty-four hours had solidified that in my head and my heart. It took these last few horrid conversations with Briggs to assure me that I was wild about the man. Otherwise, these curt arguments wouldn't have made me feel as if I'd been wrung out like a wet dishtowel. Nothing felt right when Briggs and I were apart.

I took a steadying breath and stepped out of the hallway. The rush of adrenaline that had gained steam as I walked down the hall dissipated with one long release of breath.

"Les, good to see you." My voice sounded as strained as the smile felt on my face. Les's grin, on the other hand, couldn't have been more natural.

"Lacey, I wondered if you'd left and forgot to lock up."

"No, I was just in the office. But I am going to close up soon. You look pleased with yourself about something."

"Do I?" he asked cheerily. He walked over to Kingston's perch and stroked the bird's back. "I suppose it's not nice of me to feel this way." He pulled his hand away from Kingston and turned back to me. "I think Elsie's going to shut down the dog area in front of the bakery. Too much mess for my very neat and tidy sister."

I raised a brow at him. "You two and that darn sibling rivalry. Look what it's done to the absolute nicest man in town." I waved my hand at him. "You're smiling about something that is probably making Elsie miserable."

His face dropped. "Guess that makes me a heel."

"Nonsense. You're already so many points ahead in niceness, this won't set you back much. But you might offer to help her take away the benches."

"That's a great idea." He walked over and hopped up on the stool. "Now let's discuss how to make you feel better."

I walked around to the other side of the island and started stacking notepads and receipts. "What do you mean, Les? I feel fine."

"Uh huh, that almost sounded convincing. But it doesn't explain why you walked out of the hallway looking tense and distraught and most assuredly not like the Lacey I know. And as I was leaving my shop to come visit, an equally tense and distraught version of James Briggs walked past. He didn't even notice me or say hello." He patted the stool next to him. "Leave those receipts alone and come sit, Lacey."

I walked over with heavy feet and droopy shoulders and climbed onto the stool next to Les. He always smelled like rich, aromatic coffee.

Les rested one arm along the edge of the island. "I assume this has something to do with Detective Briggs arresting Dash."

"Yes, which in itself is highly distressing. James has the wrong man. There's no way Dash killed Theodore Hall."

"You'll get no argument here," Les said. "I'm sure that will get straightened out soon enough."

"I hope you're right. It almost seems as if someone framed Dash."

"So, there's been a rift between you and James because you've been defending Dash?" His gray brows bunched in question.

"You are a wise man, Les. Yes, my vehement defense of Dash made James angry." I scrunched my nose up. "And I sort of made things worse by accusing James of being biased and not seeing things clearly because of their bitter past."

"Ouch. That probably stung."

"Like a swarm of bees. Now James has taken himself off the case and left it in the hands of Officer Chinmoor."

Les had a great belly laugh, one that nearly shook him off the seat. "Oh, I shouldn't laugh, but giving such responsibility to Chinmoor—well, it would be comical if this weren't all so serious. Poor Dash."

"I know. I tried to convince James to get back on the case, but it seems Dash has also accused him of judging him based on the past. So James has decided it's for the best that he stays away from the investigation."

"And what about his unofficial partner?" He winked at me.

"Oh, I intend to get my nose into all of this. Without crossing paths with the police, of course. I don't need to make James any angrier than he already is." I slumped down. "I'm afraid I've made a terrible mess of things, Les. I'm worried James and I are through. I don't see a way out of this."

Les reached over and patted my knee. "Love is a roller coaster. Lots of ups and downs and crazy turns, but if it's true, it will endure all those unexpected twists. I know you'll probably not rest until you've figured this case out, but stay out of danger. You usually have James right there with you."

"It wouldn't be the first time I got myself into trouble on one of these investigations, but don't worry. I'll be careful. In fact, I think I'll close up the shop and head down to the beach and have a look around the marina."

Les nodded. "And I'll go next door and see if Elsie needs help with her benches. I'll try not to gloat while I'm asking her, but it won't be easy."

We both hopped off the stools. "Maybe you should wait until she comes to you for help?" I suggested. "This might be premature. Elsie might see that you're too anxious for the dog area to close and take that as a sign she should keep the benches."

Les put his hands on his hips. "Sometimes I think you know my sister better than me. Good thinking. I'll wait. I've got beans to grind for tomorrow morning anyhow. Thanks for the chat."

CHAPTER 20

$\mathcal{I}$ had an hour of light left when I grabbed my coat and scarf. I left Kingston napping on his perch and headed toward the beach. Normally, I would cross the street and walk past the police station, possibly even stopping in to say hello, but today I walked with long, fast strides along the opposite side of the street. I'd pulled my hood over my head to cover my easy to spot curls. The last thing I wanted was Briggs to see me heading toward the marina. I had to steer clear of any police activity and keep my own investigation secret.

It seemed there would be no heavy, dreary fog to cloud the beach this evening. That worked both for and against me. I would be easily seen, but it would also give me a clearer view of the marina.

Gracie was unlocking her bicycle from the bike rack below the pier.

I headed toward her. "Closing down for the day?" I asked.

"Yes, I ran out of buns and not many people are interested in bun-less hot dogs. Business picked up again because the man with the stinky cigars never showed."

"That's good to hear. Maybe he's given up since the fish weren't biting."

"I sure hope so." Gracie frowned. "How is poor Dash? Do you think he's the killer? I can't imagine it."

"I haven't spoken to him, but I agree, he couldn't be the killer." I was anxious to break free from the topic. "I closed down early too because I needed a walk. I better get going before it gets dark. See you later, Gracie."

"Yep, I'll be thrilled to get home before dark for a change. Have a good walk."

Once I reached the marina, I relaxed and pulled my hood back. It was much easier to get lost and move unnoticed among the moored boats. One strand of yellow caution tape dangled from a cleat on the dock near Theo's boat, *Windsong*. The strand of yellow plastic waved in the wind, beckoning me to come closer. On the walk over, I'd debated whether or not to board the *Windsong* and have a proper search around. It was a daring and possibly crazy plot, but once I arrived at the boat, I knew I had to have a look around. I wasn't going to be able to help Dash if I didn't even have the guts to climb onto the boat for a search of the crime scene.

The weather was in my favor. There was only a slight breeze so the water around the marina was calm. Gentle, flat waves rolled in toward the dock, most hardly strong enough to move the boats.

I stood next to Theodore's sleek, shiny *Windsong*. It looked almost sad and lonely as if it knew its captain was gone. A few men were having a chat on the fishing boat several slips down, and there were the usual feathery characters, two seagulls and a few pigeons. Otherwise, the marina was quiet, which made sense with the sun setting and the gloom of winter still hovering over the beach.

I waited for my opportunity to pull myself aboard. The frightening moment when I had to cling to the railing until Briggs and Dash pulled me over was still fresh in my mind. The water looked less choppy and dangerous, but it would certainly be cold. And I had no idea what would happen if I fell between the large, unforgiving hull of the boat and the equally hard dock. A shiver raced through me as that tiny nightmarish scenario took hold. I shook it away. This was no time for cowardice.

A few minutes passed as I waited for the tide to push the boat close enough for me to grab hold and pull myself aboard. I glanced around at the other boats and slips. The boat Dash had been working on was empty, no doubt still in the middle of repairs. The boat owners would feel Dash's absence. Nothing about any of this made sense. It certainly wasn't the first time Dash had had a difference of opinion with one of his clients. He'd told me that the more expensive the boat, the cheaper the owner. He'd had difficulty getting payments on more than one occasion, and it didn't drive him to murder.

I was mired deep in thought when the dock beneath my feet vibrated. Theodore's boat had pushed up against it. I grabbed hold of the side, leaned over the railing and clumsily pulled myself onto deck. The men chatting down the dock were too deep in conversation to notice.

Just to make sure no one would spot me prowling around, I crouched down low and walked frog like across the slick teak decking. Aside from the dark stain of blood in the center of the stern sitting area, the boat was spotless. I'd noticed the same thing the day of the murder. Theodore kept his boat pristine, so pristine it would be easy to spot if something was out of place.

After a few minutes of a crouch walk that produced not one molecule of evidence, my legs cramped up. I sighed with relief as I straightened and stretched. I sat down on the cushioned bench that ran along the stern. From that position, I could keep my head below the railing and still survey the entire deck. Disappointment set in fairly quickly when it grew apparent that nothing was out of place. I stared at the grim spot in the middle of the deck. It seemed likely, by the grotesque wound in Theodore's head, that he was struck and fell right where he stood. It was probably a useless and somewhat painful plan but I dropped forward onto my hands and knees and crawled on all fours to the place where Theo died. I swept my gaze from side to side, hoping to find something, anything that might not belong on the otherwise immaculate boat.

My knees and my enthusiasm were both about to give up when my eyes drifted over something blue beneath the edge of a folded up chaise lounge on the railing across from the blood stain. I crawled over to the chaise. A matchbook was jammed beneath the chrome leg of the lounge. I reached into my pocket for my stash of tissue and pulled one free. I used the tissue to pick up the matchbook. The cover art was a vintage pinup style drawing of a mermaid. She had big curls of auburn hair which doubled as a bathing suit top, heavily painted red lips and a shimmery blue tail. The matches were from the Blue Mermaid Pub in Mayfield. Someone had circled the word Mermaid with a blue pen.

Using the tissue, I opened the book of matches. The same blue pen was used to scribble down a phone number. The person hadn't written any other information, just the phone number. I closed the matchbook and wrapped it in the tissue before tucking it safely in my pocket.

I crawled around for a few more minutes or as long as my knees would allow. It seemed the matchbook was going to be the only find for the day. I was happy I wasn't leaving empty handed. The match-book had been mostly hidden beneath the lounge, but finding it by merely dropping to my knees did not give me much confidence in Officer Chinmoor's investigation.

Still on my knees, I stretched up just enough to peer over the railing and along the dock. The coast was clear. I rose up to my feet and hurried to the side. The vessel had drifted a good three feet from the dock. I considered waiting for the tide to move the boat closer again, but voices at the end of the marina signaled more people were heading my way. I had to make a jump for it.

My pulse raced as I climbed onto one of the seats. I looked both ways. The two men down the dock had moved their conversation below deck. I could no longer see them. The people heading toward the marina had stopped to take a few pictures. It was my chance. I climbed onto the railing and gasped as the boat moved even farther from the dock. I pushed off and landed first on my feet and then my knees.

I got to my feet and brushed off my pants. I was going to feel this little venture tomorrow, but it was a small price to pay. In the hour when I was still Briggs' assistant, I was able to smell the victim's clothing and hands. There wasn't even the slightest trace of tobacco or smoke, making me fairly certain that he wasn't a smoker. The matches didn't belong to Theodore. I patted my pocket and grinned with satisfaction. My intuition told me that I'd just made a brilliant discovery.

CHAPTER 21

*C*aptain lifted his big head and his ears perked forward as a car drove along Loveland Terrace. He dropped it back down with a big doggie sigh when he concluded it wasn't Dash. I rested my arm on him and scratched the back of his neck. The two of us had eaten a sad dinner of chicken and rice and then settled on my couch to mope. Captain was such a slow moving, non-menacing kind of dog that Nevermore had no problem curling up right next to him.

For all of five seconds, I'd considered taking the matchbook to the station to let them know they'd missed it in their evidence sweep, but I was sure I would earn a lecture from Briggs. I'd both disobeyed his order to stay off the case, and, if I was honest with myself, I had trespassed on Theodore's boat. I came to the conclusion, after I swept right past the station with my piece of evidence, that I was an independent investigator on this case and that meant I was on my own. I'd find the killer with no help from the police. That would prove to Briggs just how skilled I was at a murder investigation. Or, at least, that was the pep talk I gave myself as I rushed past the station and back to the shop. Once I'd gotten home and invited poor, depressed Captain over to share dinner with me, my confidence waned and I wondered if there was any possible way I could do this alone. After all, I wouldn't have access to the usual insider information like the coroner's report, the autopsy results and the evidence collected at the site, other than the matchbook.

My phone buzzed, startling me from my thoughts. A temporary rush of nerves hit me as I reached for it thinking it might be Briggs. Maybe someone saw me on the boat and reported it. I sat brusquely forward causing both animals to lift their heads. I was relieved to see a text from Lola.

"I've got a bottle of wine left over from Christmas," she wrote. "Should I bring it over?"

"Yes, yes, yes," I texted back. I rarely had a drink on a work night, but it seemed I had a good excuse. It was only Tuesday night, and it had already been a whirlwind of a week.

My mood brightened knowing Lola would be dropping by. I hadn't had a chance to talk to her about the terrible time Briggs and I were having. I hadn't realized how badly I needed to just hang out and talk to her.

I popped some slice and bake cookies in the oven, also a leftover from Christmas. The premade cookies were disappointing for someone who was an official taste tester of Elsie's wonderful creations, but they'd do in a pinch. And they were the perfect accompaniment to a bottle of wine.

Lola's car pulled into the driveway giving Captain another moment of hope that Dash was back home. He walked dejectedly to the door to give Lola a half-hearted greeting before plodding back to the couch.

"He looks so sad," Lola said as she handed me the wine and pulled off her coat. "Any word on when Dash will be out?"

"I don't know anything." I carried the bottle to the kitchen. "I'm out of the loop. I assume he'll be arraigned tomorrow. I think that has to happen by tomorrow." I stopped and looked at her, blinking back tears. "I don't even know if he's gotten hold of a lawyer. I've been so busy thinking about my own emotional turmoil that I hadn't given it much thought. What a terrible friend I am."

Lola walked into the kitchen and hugged me. "You're not a terrible friend. Dash's dog is curled up on your couch, looking depressed but content. And if I know you, you haven't been sitting back doing nothing. You've been working on the case." She pointed at me. "See, you're biting your lip, which means it's true."

"I might have done a little boat hopping today to look for evidence," I said sheepishly. I searched through my 'everything but the kitchen sink' drawer for a corkscrew. It had been a long while since I needed it.

"What are you looking for?"

"That darn corkscrew. It's not as if it's a small, demure little tool."

"Don't waste your time." Lola grabbed the bottle, unwrapped the top and twisted it off. "I always buy the good stuff."

"Obviously." I pulled two glasses down from the cupboard. "I think I'll skip pulling out the stemware, what with the twist off cap and all. I wouldn't want the wine to feel self-conscious."

We poured the pretty pink wine with what my uneducated nose deemed a pleasant bouquet. I took a sip and nodded. "Tastes good to me."

"Might give you a headache in the morning, but it'll do the trick tonight." Lola lifted her nose and crinkled it. "Do I smell cookies?"

"Cut and bake sugar cookies. I had every intention of rolling, cutting and decorating them at Christmas but then, even with the premade dough, the whole thing seemed daunting. The entire scenario of me creating dazzling holiday sugar cookies seemed much more wonderful in my head." I picked up my oven mitt. "I'll pull them out now so they're still a little gooey."

"Good idea. My motto, when it comes to cut and bake cookies, is that under baked is always better than over baked."

"And that is yet another reason why we are friends." I lifted my glass for a toast. "I'm glad you came. I'm already feeling better."

I carried my glass of wine back to the couch. Captain lifted his nose and wiggled it back and forth but quickly surmised that he was not interested in my drink.

"Almost forgot," Lola reached into the pocket of her jeans. "I brought you Gina's business card." She handed me the card and sat down on the chair adjacent to the couch.

The card was bright pink with gold embossed lettering. Absently, I ran my thumb over the lettering. "I wonder if Theodore's ex-wife will be at work. If she was married to him for a long time, divorce or not, she'd probably be broken up about his death."

"Unless she killed him," Lola said airily.

"True but she'd still want to make it look as if she was distraught about his death."

Lola took a sip of wine and pursed her lips from the taste. "I'm wondering if twist off top wine was not the way to go. Anyhow, you should make an appointment." She smoothed her hands over her shiny, straight hair. "Even if you're not going to take the plunge into living a straighter less curly life. Just get a haircut or style. Gina loves to talk, and she knows everything about everyone. You could pry a lot of juicy information out of her while you're in that chair."

"That's good to know. I'll make an appointment. Besides, maybe an hour of pampering myself with a new haircut will do me good."

"Uh oh." Lola sat forward. "That sounded like a momentary pity party. What's up? Other than the obvious."

I drank a few good gulps of wine and placed the mostly empty glass on the coffee table.

"That's another uh oh," Lola said. "She's putting down the glass first, which means she is heading toward unloading a lot of bottled up feelings."

I chuckled. "You sound like a sports announcer narrating a golf game. And I'm not too sure my feelings are all that bottled up. I've been letting them flow pretty freely these last two days. James is angry at me for defending Dash."

Lola tilted her head side to side. "Understandable. Of course, that's coming from someone who is hopelessly jealous." She scooted farther forward. "I was doing some research, and I think it comes from my own inferiority complex." She waved her hand in front of her face. "Obviously I've got a self-centered thing going on too because this is about you, not me. Continue. Did James forbid you to work on the case?"

"Bingo and that's not all. I put up a big fuss, insinuating that he was going into this case with a biased view of the suspect."

Lola straightened sharply. "Ouch. Bet that hurt."

"Yes, and I was being silly. I know James well enough. He would never let his own emotions influence a case. But now, me and my big mouth—" I shook my head. "James took himself off the case. He decided it would look bad."

Lola got up to get a plate of cookies. "Who's taking over?" She laughed dryly. "He didn't put goofy Officer Chinmoor in charge, did he?"

"Yes, as a matter of fact he did."

Lola returned with a plate of cookies. She set it on the coffee table and plucked one up for herself. "Poor Dash. He's doomed."

"Don't say that, Lola." I leaned over and placed my hands over Captain's ears. He decided I was just going for a nice scratch session and tilted his head to the side to accommodate me. I scratched behind his ears. "Who am I kidding? I don't want to hear it because it makes my stomach ball up in a knot. Dash did not kill Theodore Hall."

"You don't have to convince me," Lola said relaxing back with her cookie. "How did it come this far? What was the evidence, other than they had a disagreement just before Theo was found dead?" She crinkled her nose. "That sure doesn't put a good light on it, does it?"

"No, the argument, which was witnessed by a lot of people at the marina, was certainly the catalyst. But there's more." I paused, deciding whether or not it was my place to tell Lola. Then I remembered I was not technically involved with the case so who was I to keep it under lock and key.

Lola nibbled on her cookie and waited.

"Don't tell anyone else this, all right? The murder weapon was a socket wrench, more specifically, Dash's socket wrench. Theodore's killer stole it from the Dash's toolbox, along with his work coveralls. The coveralls were found in the trash can on the pier. They were splattered with the victim's blood."

Lola pulled the cookie from her mouth. The pink in her cheeks faded some. "Wow, that doesn't sound good for Dash at all. It's as if someone was trying to frame him. Where were his toolbox and coveralls that they were so easy to access?"

"Dash had them stowed in the engine compartment a few boats down."

Lola's brows twitched. "That's weird. So they weren't even out in the open, easy prey for a killing thief. How would they know the tools were down in the engine compartment?"

It was a good question and one I should have already asked myself. Here I was accusing Briggs of cloudy judgment in the case when I was letting my own emotions get in the way. I was going to have to go at this in a different direction. I was moving ahead so certain that Dash had nothing to do with this that I was pushing aside all the real evidence.

"You are brilliant, Lola," I said.

She shrugged. "Yes, well, that's been established. What did I say that was so brilliant?"

"I've got to start about this in a different way. Instead of just pulling a wild card out of a hat to find the killer, I need to figure out just how the person managed to frame Dash. It had to be someone who was hanging out at some point near the boats. The person had to know not only that there was tension between Dash and Theodore but they had to know which vessel Dash was working on and where he was keeping his tools and coveralls." I finished with an enthusiastic clap that startled Nevermore off the couch.

"How are you going to do that?" Lola asked, bringing me back down to earth.

"I'm not sure. But I think I'll start with a hair appointment to see what I can find out about Theodore's personal life. That might lead to other people who had a beef with Theodore. After all, when he nearly knocked me down, he claimed everyone was after his money."

I leaned forward and picked up a cookie. "I need to find out just who *everyone* is."

CHAPTER 22

$\mathcal{L}$ ola had predicted correctly. The cheap wine left me with a miserable headache, my punishment for drinking on a work night. Fortunately, two aspirins and two cups of coffee revived me enough to face my first customers of the day, Edna and Tracy. The two sisters were planning a surprise engagement party for a young niece, and being sisters, they had their share of similar tastes and major differences of opinion.

I'd made the fabulous decision long ago to create notebooks displaying various bouquets that were perfect for each occasion. An engagement party wasn't my usual event, but the bridal shower notebook had pages of pretty, colorful bouquets perfect for an early spring party. I left Edna and Tracy alone to peruse the book and busied myself with a new order of vases that came in. Ryder had taken it upon himself to clean out the fresh flower cooler.

Naturally, my mind was on the murder investigation more than on my work. I'd called Coco's Salon first thing in the morning. Gina had a two o'clock appointment available. I had no real plan except to casually lead Gina into a conversation about Theodore's wife. With any luck, the woman would be working and possibly even spilling details on her own. But I wasn't holding out much hope that she'd be back at work right after Theodore's murder.

The two sisters had thumbed through the pictures three times. Edna looked a few years older than Tracy. She had a slight hunch in her shoulders. Her silver-gray hair was cut in a short, stylish bob. Kingston's cooing sound grabbed her attention away from the notebook. She walked across the room to the perch. Kingston sat up tall, his go to move whenever a stranger approached him in the shop.

"Such a beautiful bird, although crows are quite the stinkers when I'm feeding the sparrows in my garden." Edna turned back to me. "They just won't let the poor little things eat."

"Crows do love food," I said. "Kingston prefers waffles and eggs to bird seed but then he also prefers to be driven home in a car."

Edna's laugh was soft and charming. "What an extraordinary companion he must be."

Tracy was more serious than Edna. Her thin brows furrowed. "Edie, are we going to make a decision or not? Jennifer will be married and off on her honeymoon at this rate."

Edna padded quickly back to the island. "I've already told you, I like the pink ranunculus with the white baby's breath. I'm just waiting for you to realize I'm right."

Tracy huffed. "Fine, I suppose we'll go with your choice."

"Great." I grabbed my order book from under the counter. "Let's write it up." I picked up a pen and wrote their names at the top of the form.

"Wasn't that terrible about Theodore Hall?" Edna asked her sister. "I can't believe it. And right here in Port Danby."

I glanced up from the order form. Edna looked as if she could be fairly close in age to Theodore. "Did you know Mr. Hall?" I asked casually.

"Somewhat. He lived down the street from my husband and me," Edna said. "He was the financial advisor at the bank when my husband started his business. Theo had been there a long time and worked his way up to the top." Her mouth pulled down at the corners.

"But I think he was having money troubles. You can't be a successful financial advisor if your own finances are in disarray."

"Now, Edna," Tracy said. "There you go gossiping like a busy hen again." Tracy rolled her eyes and shook her head. "If you get this one started, she won't stop until she tells you what her neighbors had for breakfast and who the mailman is dating."

"Oh, but I'm interested," I said too abruptly, causing both women to look at me with rounded eyes. "Well, he was murdered and that means a killer might be on the loose. Better safe than sorry," I added weakly.

Edna's smile reminded me of my sixth grade teacher, Mrs. Strayer. "You don't have to worry about that, dear. My neighbor, Susan, told me that her cousin heard they'd already arrested someone. In fact, I still can't believe it. It's that handsome young man who fixes the boats. I don't understand it. He's such a charming man, always friendly and polite." A blush of pink colored her cheeks. "And that smile."

Tracy clucked her tongue to scold her sister. "Edie, you are always taken in by handsome looks and a great smile. Charming or not, the man is a murderer."

"No he's not." Again my delivery was abrupt enough to surprise them. I shrugged. "What's the saying? Innocent until proven guilty." I decided to disregard Tracy's warning about Edna's propensity to gossip and press further. "How did you know Mr. Hall was in financial trouble? Have you talked to his wife?"

"Ex-wife," Edna corrected. "No, I don't know Marissa well, but Fran from the yardage store told me that she left Theodore because of money problems. And then there was that morning when a tow truck rolled down the street. It picked up Theodore's new Mercedes and took it away for good."

"So his car was repossessed?" I asked.

"Well, Theodore was yelling at the tow truck driver the whole time, so I don't think it was going in for repairs. And we never saw it again." Edna got sidetracked by a picture in the notebook. "You know, I think I've changed my mind. Let's do something with yellow roses."

She started turning the pages of the book to apparently start over with the flower choice.

Tracy groaned in frustration. "I knew we'd be here forever. Remember, Edie, dear, the wedding is in June. The engagement party should be before that."

CHAPTER 23

*R*yder took Lola to lunch early so I could make my two o'clock hair appointment. After Edna's visit, I now had more evidence that Theodore was in financial trouble and that kind of trouble, especially if it involved big money, was always an ingredient for murder. With any luck, I'd find out even more at the salon.

Elsie burst in with her usual energy and spirit. Only, on this occasion, she looked more energy than spirit. "I'll tell you what, Pink," she said sternly as she stopped in the center of the store. She placed her fists on her hips to go along with the tone. "I need a restart to the new year because if this week is any indication of the months to come, I'm buying a grass hut on a remote island and retiring."

"I'm packing up and heading to that grass hut with you. And you have my vote for a new year restart."

Elsie marched to the potting table where I was finishing with a few house plants. "What's happening in your world? Aside from the obvious problem." Her mouth turned down and she shook her head. "Poor Dash." Her face popped up. "Although, I'm also angry at him. He should never have started with Britney. She's absolutely useless. This morning she spent an hour decorating a special order birthday cake, and she used the wrong pink for the roses."

I lifted a brow at her. "Elsie, that's hardly a reason to call her absolutely useless."

"Possibly, but she's not herself. I blame that all on Dash. Of course, now, I suppose he has bigger things to worry about."

"You think?" I adored Elsie but occasionally she dipped into being just a touch too self-centered.

I lowered a fern into a pot and pressed down the soil around it. "I assume Britney's not the only reason you need a restart on the year. The dog area?" I said as a question.

She grunted. "Me and my big, silly ideas. The dog biscuit business is fine. They are easy to make, and the customers always add them on to their own orders so they sell out quickly. But having them bring their dogs to the bakery to eat, well that's just not working out."

"That's an easy fix then, Elsie. Just take out the dog area and set the table area back to the way it was. No one will notice or care. If anyone asks, you tell them there was a problem with city codes. Or just say it didn't work out."

"Yes, that's what I'll do. Boy, that brother of mine will be smirking and smiling about my idea going south so quickly." She tapped her chin. "Maybe I should add a few cushioned settees and one of those neat tables that has a fire pit right in the middle."

"Yes, you should," I said, pretending to be right along with her on the crazy plan. She sat up straighter with excitement. "However," I continued. "I'm not sure how your pastries and cakes will taste with all that smoke drifting in through the windows from the fire pit."

"You and your practicality issues. But you're right. It'd be different if I was running a barbecue and grill restaurant, but my delicate cream filled petit fours would not be tasty coated in smoke. I'll just remove the dog area and go back to the way it was last month."

I nodded. "Good plan."

Elsie hopped off the stool. "See, my new year is already improving."

"Wish mine was," I muttered to myself. Elsie and her super ears heard me.

She scrunched up her face. "Are things bad with James? Because of the Dash arrest?"

"Bad isn't the right word. Calamitous. That's closer."

Elsie walked to me and took hold of my hands. "Don't fret about it. James is nuts about you. It'll all smooth over soon."

I squeezed her hands. "Thanks, Elsie, but I'm not too sure about anything smoothing over."

She hugged me. "I'll bring you some of my toffee cupcakes later. That should help."

"Can't hurt, that's for sure."

Elsie walked with much lighter steps on her way out.

I had some free time and the shop was empty. I headed into the office. I decided the only way to find out about the number on the matchbook was to call it. With any luck, it might open up a clue into the case, or with a bigger dose of luck, it might connect me to the real killer.

My phone rang as I sat at my desk. I picked it up and answered quickly when Dash's name showed up on the screen.

"Dash? Where are you?"

"Hey, Lacey, I'm at home. I wanted to let you know. Thank you for taking good care of Captain. He looks a little disappointed that I'm back. I think he figured you'd adopted him."

I laughed lightly. "I would in a heartbeat. He's such a doll. But he was very depressed without you. So what's going on? I've been cut off from everything having to do with the case."

"Yeah, I sort of gathered that when Briggs said he took himself off of it. My dad's here. He hired a good friend who is an excellent lawyer. She got me out with a few mild threats that they had a weak case and that they were going to be sorry they jumped the gun on the arrest. But she did advise me to stay in town and be ready in case they come at me again. For now, I'm a free man. I'm also an innocent man, but they are short on other possible suspects. And with Chinmoor in charge . . ."

"Yes, that's mostly my fault. I pushed James too hard about there being bad history between you two. He took himself off the case. As soon as he told me, I knew it had been a mistake to even bring it up. I'm sorry."

"No, it wasn't just you. I told him the same thing. And I regret it as well. I'd much rather have Briggs investigating the murder than Chinmoor. Even though I'm out right now, my reputation is ruined until they find the real killer."

I opened the drawer and pulled out the matchbook wrapped in tissue. "Don't you worry about at thing, Vanhouten. Lacey Pinkerton is on the case. I won't rest until the real culprit is behind bars." I sat forward. "But you can't tell anyone. James gave me strict orders to keep out of it."

"Your secret is safe with me," Dash said. "Just don't do anything dangerous. I think Theodore might have been burdened with gambling debt. That means he might have been doing business with some shady characters."

"I'm slowly peeling away those layers." I opened the matchbook cover and wrote the number on a separate piece of paper. "I've heard he was in financial trouble. The gambling problem is high on my radar too."

A deep voice in the background mentioned there was no milk in the fridge. "As you know, Dad, I haven't been around to shop for milk," Dash said away from the phone.

"How long is he in town for?" I asked. I'd met Dashwood Vanhouten the second, more formally known as Darren Vooten, the real family name, only once. He was as charming as his son but with a certain salesman style quality.

"He's here just for a few days. I'll let you go, Lacey. I know you're busy at work. And it seems I need to go out and buy milk."

"All right and I'm glad you had a clever lawyer. I have every intention of finding the real killer, so your ordeal will be over soon."

He laughed quietly. "I feel better just knowing you are on the case. Bye, Lacey."

"Bye." I hung up and clapped quickly several times. "Yay. Now to get down to the business of solving a murder."

I dialed the number from the matchbook. It rang several times, then a woman answered. "Park Street Laundry."

I was thrown off by getting an actual person and not a voicemail message. I was equally unprepared to learn it was a business number. It took me a second to respond, and when I did, it was rather unimpressive in sleuthing terms. "Hello, yes, Park Street Laundry?" I asked.

"Yes," the woman sounded clearly annoyed.

"I was just wondering where you are located?" My second attempt was not much better than the first.

And she was even more annoyed. "We're on Park Street."

"Yes, of course. Duh. Makes sense with the name and all. And you're in the town of . . ." I left the blank hoping she'd fill it in.

"Park Street in Mayfield. We're open twenty-four hours. A dollar a load and no more than three machines at a time per person. We sell detergent here or you can bring your own brand."

"Thank you. That tells me all I need to know. Goodbye." I hung up and leaned back in my chair. A laundromat was hardly exciting or intriguing.

It was sure going to be harder solving a murder from outside the official investigation, but it was far too soon to get discouraged. Hopefully, the visit to the salon would be more productive.

CHAPTER 24

*C*oco's Salon was a charming mix of glam and frill. White brick walls were punctuated by floor to ceiling gold framed mirrors. The lavender salon chairs worked perfectly with the crystal sconces between the mirrors and the glass pendants hanging down the center of the salon.

A twenty something woman with straight black hair and long bangs called from across the salon. "Are you Lacey? I'm all ready for you." She grabbed the top of the lavender chair and spun it toward me. Her thin forearms were covered in contrasting tattoos, a silver and green cobra on the right and a much cheerier bouncy Tigger on the left.

I sat in the chair and she twirled me to face the mirror, reminding me why I hated salon visits—way too much time staring at myself and finding every flaw. She immediately started fluffing up my curls.

"I love the natural wave in your hair. It's gorgeous," she gushed as she stared at me in the mirror.

"You need to tell that to my sixteen-year-old self," I quipped.

Her smile was somewhat hidden because it was hard to look past her bright orange lipstick. "Everyone with curly hair always wants straight and vice versa. In fact, you mentioned your friend Lola gave you my card. I'll have to send her a discount coupon for the referral. How is she liking the straight look?"

"Considering she doesn't stop flipping her hair back to remind me how straight it is, I'd say she is thrilled."

Gina laughed. "I can see why you two are such good friends. She made me laugh too. Now what are we going to do today? You aren't thinking about erasing all this beautiful curl, are you?"

"No, I gave up that battle after I moved to Port Danby. I've grown used to it curly. Maybe just a trim."

"All right. I've got a wonderful coconut hair masque that will leave it feeling soft and lush. Would you like to try it?"

"Sure."

"Perfect. I'll be right back." Gina sauntered away on very tall boots. I took a moment to glance around the salon. A young man was working three chairs down putting highlights in a woman's hair. Another stylist was at the other end of the chairs talking on the phone as she straightened up her station. The three other stations were empty. My eyes trailed along to the gold name plates sitting under each mirror. The name Marissa was two mirrors down. Just as I'd predicted, Theodore's wife was not at work.

Gina returned. "Let's go over to the sink area so I can wash your hair and put on the coconut treatment." I got up and followed her to the line of chrome sinks at the back of the shop. I sat in the chair and leaned onto the uncomfortable neck rest so Gina could wash my hair.

"Is the salon always this quiet?" I asked over the rush of water.

She rinsed my hair. "No. Two stylists are out sick with a cold. And one is out because her husband died."

"Oh, that's too bad. Was he sick?"

The water turned off as Gina paused to massage shampoo through my hair. "No." She lowered her voice but not much. "He was murdered on his boat."

"That was her husband? My flower shop is near the marina, so I saw all the police activity."

"Yeah, far as I know they caught the guy." She picked up the water sprayer and talked loudly over it, not seeming to care who heard.

"Marissa wasn't too surprised by his death. They were divorced," she added by way of an explanation.

"Still, even divorced, surely she would be shocked to hear her ex was murdered. Why wasn't she surprised?"

The water turned off again. Gina opened a jar. The fragrance of coconut filled the steamy cloud hovering over us. Not knowing anything about my special nose, Gina lowered the jar so I could get a good whiff of it. The scent was so strong it made me sneeze.

"Oops, bless you." Gina grabbed a tissue and handed it to me. "Are you allergic to coconut? I could find a different conditioner."

"No, no it's fine. I just have a sensitive nose. It smells wonderful. I'm going to feel like an Almond Joy bar for the rest of the day."

Gina chuckled. "You'll definitely be smelling coconut after this treatment." The aroma was nice but a bit overwhelming as she piled the cream into my hair.

I needed to get our conversation back on track. "So you were saying something about Marissa not being surprised about the murder?"

"You can sit up now." She wrapped a towel around the back of my neck and we walked back to her chair. I fretted she'd forgotten about my question again and debated whether it would be awkward to bring it up once more when she answered on her own.

"We complain and gripe to each other about significant others all the time in here. But Marissa was positively disgusted with Theo. When they were still married, she used to get calls all the time from creditors and people looking to collect money from her husband. Marissa was sure he was dealing with some terrible people. She thought he'd either end up dead or in prison."

"That's awful. I suppose she's out making sure all the arrangements are taken care of."

"Probably." Gina smiled. "But if I know Marissa, she's also doing some shopping."

It was such a strange statement, I wasn't sure I'd heard her correctly. "Did you say shopping?"

Gina laughed dryly. "I know that sounds terrible. But she really despised him. He made her life miserable. She hasn't shed too many tears over it all. About a year before she filed for divorce, Marissa took out a life insurance policy on Theo. She was sure something would happen to him, and she didn't want to be left with all his debt, being hounded by creditors and collection agencies. It was a big one too." She mouthed the words a million in the mirror reflection.

"Wow, that is a big one. But if they're divorced?" I said.

"Far as I know, she never cancelled the policy. I'm expecting her to saunter in here any day, sweep up her scissors and her brushes and wave ta ta as she heads out to her new million dollar life."

My mind was spinning. It seemed I'd landed on someone who not only despised the victim but who would make out very well from his death, a million dollars well, in fact. I wondered how much Officer Chinmoor knew about Theodore's ex-wife. It sure seemed as if she had motive, but was there anything to place her at the marina on Monday afternoon? There was only one way to find out.

I reached up and wiped dripping coconut cream from my forehead. "I suppose Marissa was probably standing right there at her station on Monday when she got the call about the murder."

"No, I'm not sure where Marissa was that day. The salon is closed on Monday. But I could ask Nell. They hang out sometimes on their day off. Hey, Nell," Gina called across to the other stylist, an older woman with a rather out of date hairstyle. "Were you with Marissa on Monday?"

Nell shook her head. "No, I had that dentist appointment, remember?"

Gina lowered her voice so only I could hear. "Sure do. She told me every gross detail of her root canal."

"Why are you asking?" Nell called back.

"We were just wondering if you were with her when she got the call about Theodore."

"No, I wasn't but I doubt she was too broken up by the news," Nell added. "I think she told me she was cleaning house when she got the call."

"There you go, then. Marissa lives alone. They never had kids.

Something with Marissa's *plumbing*." Gina circled her hand in front of her belly in case I didn't understand the plumbing analogy. "Doesn't seem as if anyone was with Marissa when she found out the news." Gina pulled a pair of scissors and a comb out of the drawer. "Now then, if you're done smelling like a candy bar, we can rinse you out and give those curly locks a trim."

"Great." My mind was no longer on the haircut. I'd stumbled onto a person of interest. Marissa had what seemed like good reason to hate Theodore. She also had good motive to kill him. And from what I gathered, she'd been alone at home. That meant no one knew for sure where Marissa was at the time of the murder.

CHAPTER 25

The coconut fragrance was probably pleasant to a normal nose, but I felt lightheaded from the aroma. Ryder noticed my misery and volunteered to close up for the night so I could go home and rinse my hair. It had been my fault. When Gina put the jar of conditioner in front of my nose, I should have known it would be too strong for my super nose. But I'd been so focused on the case, it hadn't even occurred to me.

It turned out an extra long, hot shower was just what I needed to revive my spirit and wash the coconut fragrance from my hair. I could still smell a hint of it, but it was at a far more tolerable level. I pulled on fresh jeans and a sweater and headed to the kitchen to dig up something for dinner. It was nearly time for my weekly shopping trip. I was down to cans of soup, boxes of macaroni and cheese and a few frozen entrees that looked tasty in the store but looked unappealing now, even with my stomach growling. I went to my old standby, toast and jam. Not much of a dinner but then my appetite was not great. The toffee cupcake Elsie delivered an hour before I left the shop might have had more to do with that than my mood.

A knock on the door startled me. My mind went straight to Briggs. Was he coming by to apologize or to tell me he caught the real killer and that as he arrested the person he realized he couldn't live without me? Nope. Dash was at the door.

His green eyes and smile weren't sparkly. He was still in a funk. I could hardly blame him.

"Hey, Lacey, my dad and I ordered pizza. I let him do the online order. He somehow managed to order five medium pizzas instead of the one large. It'd be great if you came over and helped us eat the pizza tower."

"Sure, I guess I could help out with the pizza tower. You actually saved me from a few sorry pieces of toast. Let me just get my sweatshirt." I motioned him inside. He headed straight over to Kingston's cage. The crow had finished his dinner and was settling into a long session of preening. Kingston always had time to greet Dash.

I hurried into the bedroom and pulled on my sweatshirt. "Hope this isn't too casual for eating dinner with Dashwood Vanhouten the second and third." I held out my arms.

"We Vanhoutens aren't big on formalities." He pointed to his own faded jeans. "You'll fit right in."

I grabbed my keys and locked the door on my way out. I decided the short journey to Dash's house would be a good time to fill him in on my progress, not that there was much to brag about yet.

"I snuck onto Theodore's boat," I blurted quickly, hoping he'd slow his long legged pace. It worked. He came to a near stop.

"I told you not to do anything dangerous, Lacey."

"It wasn't. Not really. The water was calm and it was surprisingly easy. Anyhow, I snooped around. His boat is immaculate."

"Yes, he had it detailed after I fixed it. He was planning to sell it to pay off some debts. At least that's what Chuck, the boat owner in the next slip, told me. Guess you didn't find anything."

We stopped at the bottom of his porch steps to finish the conversation. "It took some crouching and crawling, but I stumbled upon a matchbook. It was jammed under a chaise lounge. Do you happen to know if Theodore smoked?"

Dash shrugged. "I never saw him smoke, but I can't say for sure."

"The matches were from a pub called the Blue Mermaid."

Dash wrinkled his nose in distaste. "That place is a dive. There's no way Theodore Hall would have gone there. He was a big snob. The matches must have belonged to someone else."

"That's what I figured. There was a phone number written on the inside cover. I called it but it turned out to be a laundromat. I also found out something interesting about his ex-wife."

"Marissa Hall?" Dash asked.

"Yes, do you know her?"

"Not really. I know they had a bitter divorce only because I once overheard Theodore on the phone complaining to someone that his wife had cleaned out his pockets in the divorce and then came back to pick his bones more by taking the expensive furniture."

"I think she picked his bones and then some. According to her coworker, Marissa took out a million dollar life insurance policy on Theo before the divorce."

Dash's brows lifted. "Million bucks. Sounds like she made out pretty sweet from his death."

"Pizza's not getting any younger and neither am I," Dash's dad called from the front door. He was smaller in stature than Dash, but he was handsome with the same green eyes. A gray moustache hid most of what I was sure was an equally engaging smile. "Good to see you, Lacey." He waved and turned back inside.

Dash and I started up the steps. "It seems you've been busy with the investigation. I'm sure you're big steps ahead of Officer Chinmoor."

We walked inside. Dash's house was always in transition from old and dilapidated to new and improved. He had been patching the plaster on the ceiling in the front room before the recent upheaval in his life. The ladder and supplies were still piled on a large canvas tarp. Protective plastic had been pulled back from the couch and easy chair.

"Pizza party is in the kitchen," Dash said. "As you can see, the front room is hardly inviting for guests at the moment. Obviously, I wasn't expecting my dad to have to fly to Port Danby."

"What can I get you to drink, Lacey?" Dash's dad said from the refrigerator. "We've got milk, orange juice and beer."

"I'll just have a glass of water, thanks, Mr. Vanhouten."

"Please call me, Big Dash." His laugh seemed big in the small kitchen.

Dash pulled out a chair for me at his round wooden table. "But please do not call me Little Dash," he added as I sat down.

"Darn, that name was just forming in my head, and I was hoping to try it out." I grabbed a napkin and plate. Captain came trotting into the kitchen. He sat next to me, rested his head on my lap, and stared up at me with big, brown eyes. "Well hello, roomie. Nevermore and I are going to miss you tonight."

"Told you he looked disappointed to see me," Dash said. "He was ready to pack up his pillows and dog toys and the million bones he has buried all over the yard and move in with you."

I stroked Captain's head. "Anytime, buddy." I lowered my voice to a whisper. "But I think your daddy needs you right now."

"I think this will all be over soon," Big Dash said. "Briggs will get it all straightened out. I never liked James Briggs. He's hardheaded but he's smart."

"Dad," Dash snapped. "I told you this more than once, but you never listen. James and Lacey are dating. And we don't need to talk about him at all because he took himself off the case."

Big Dash's green eyes flicked disapprovingly my direction and an awkward moment followed. I busied myself with selecting a pizza.

"Well, I don't need to apologize," Big Dash reached for a slice. "If she's dating him, then she knows he's hardheaded." He looked pointedly at Dash. "And if you had let me finish, I was going to say he was probably a great detective because one thing can always be said about that kid, he never failed at anything."

Dash shook his head with a laugh. "That kid," he repeated. "In your mind, we're still playing on the football team together."

"No, it's just my age. To me, everyone thirty and under is a kid." He took a bite and struggled with a long piece of melted cheese for a second. "Why is he off the case?" he asked after swallowing.

"Told you this too, Dad. I told him I wasn't sure I'd get a fair shake with him doing the investigation. I was angry and upset and feeling more than a little sorry for myself."

"Rightly so," I said. "Who wouldn't in that circumstance? And I pushed too, so don't blame yourself." The pizza was slightly cold, and I wasn't terribly hungry. I picked at the pieces of olive and onion on top.

"If you don't like that kind, there are plenty more to choose from." Big Dash opened the next box to reveal a sausage and green pepper pizza.

"No, this is fine. I ate a cupcake an hour ago. I guess that's why Moms don't let kids have dessert first." I picked up the slice. "But it's good. Thank you for inviting me."

"No, thank you for helping put a dent in our pizza mishap." Dash looked wryly at his dad. "I guess that explains why you occasionally send the same email three times in a row. You're click happy."

"I'm not click happy. That darn computer of yours is just sensitive." Big Dash winked at me across the table.

"Yes, the computer was feeling sensitive so it ordered five pizzas." Dash turned to me. "They're fun, aren't they? Parents, I mean."

I smiled. "I think it's fun sitting in the same room with Big Dash and Little Dash."

"You were working for a way to toss that one about, weren't you? Very smooth, Pinkerton." Dash put down the slice of pizza he was holding. "Lacey, if you don't mind, could you ask Briggs to get back on the case. I want them to find the killer soon. My life won't be back to normal until this is over."

"I tried once but I can give it another whirl. The truth is, we're not really talking right now."

"Told you James was hardheaded," Big Dash said before his next bite.

"Enough commentary, Dad. Just eat your fifty slices of pizza." Dash turned back to me. "Don't do it if you're not comfortable asking."

I smiled weakly. "I guess you read that easily in my expression. Our last couple of conversations ended pretty badly. I'm not sure if I have the nerve to call him right now." Just the thought of it coupled with the worry that he might be disappointed to hear from me wiped out the little appetite I had left.

"I won't flatter myself into thinking that the trouble is all because of me, but don't get yourself in any deeper. I know you two have something special together, and I don't want to be in the middle of it."

"You're not. Technically. I think we were just overdue for a rough patch. Things had been going pretty smoothly, unusually smooth for my life. But I promise, if he calls me, I'll bring it up."

Dash shook his head. "No, don't worry about it. I'm sure Chinmoor will eventually solve the case." His shoulders dropped some. "Hopefully."

"Hey," I said with some pep. "Don't forget about me. I've got a few tricks up my sleeve. And I'm going to find out more about Marissa Hall. She had good motive."

Dash reached over and squeezed my hand. "I haven't forgotten that the world's greatest detective and her super nose are on the case."

That comment yanked Big Dash's attention away from the pizza. "Did you just tell this lovely lady that she had a super nose? It's as small as a button," he added.

"It's small but it's powerful," Dash said. "Lacey has—" He squinted at me as he attempted to pronounce the scientific word for my sense of smell. "Hi—per—rose—mia. Was that close?"

"Very close."

"She can smell the tiniest bit of scent and even separate aromas out of a mix of things," Dash continued. "That button nose has solved a few crimes in town."

"No kidding," Big Dash said with a laugh. "Well, who knew? Never even heard of hyper—-hyper—" He pointed at Dash. "What he said."

"It's a blessing and a curse," I noted. "I went to the salon today, the one Marissa Hall works at," I added.

"I thought your hair looked shorter," Dash said. "Looks very nice."

"Please, it's still just a big head of curls. But the stylist talked me into a coconut hair treatment. I was dizzy from coconut fragrance for the rest of the afternoon. I had to come home early to wash it out. So far, the Hall murder case hasn't given me any nasal clues, but I'm holding out hope there's still something to connect the dots. In the meantime—"

"Remember what I told you, don't do anything dangerous," Dash said.

I tapped my forehead with a sudden thought. "Oh my gosh, you know Marissa Hall. Or at least you know her well enough to recognize her, right?"

"Yes, she's easy to pick out of a crowd. She's quite tall with short, white blonde hair. The few times I saw her she had on large, shiny earrings."

"That's even better. Dash, I need you to think back to Monday. I'm sure you'd rather wash it from your mind for good but think hard. Did you see Marissa Hall at the marina or anywhere near the boats?"

"Hmm." Dash sat back and rubbed his chin. "Monday is such a blur now, but there weren't a lot of people at the marina. That pea soup fog had been lingering out on the water all day, waiting to come on shore, so no one took out boats." He sat forward. "No, I don't remember seeing her at any point. She rarely came down to the marina after the divorce, only once or twice to yell at Theo or toss some unpaid bill his way."

"So no sign of Marissa on the dock?"

Dash shook his head.

"It was the ex-wife," Big Dash interjected, taking a few second break from his pizza feast. His plate was piled high with pizza crusts. "It's always the ex. And with a million dollar life insurance policy—" A confident puff of air blew his moustache around.

Dash looked at me. "There you have it. Crime solved and all from behind a pizza box."

I laughed. "If only it were so easy. But I do think Marissa is a person of interest. It would help though if I could place her at the scene of the crime."

"Well, I might have missed her. I'll ask Gracie at the hot dog stand tomorrow when I head back to work. She sees everything and everyone," Dash said.

"That's a good idea. Gracie does know everything that's happening. So you're heading back to work tomorrow?" I asked.

He swept his eyes out to his half-patched living room. "This glamorous mansion isn't going to pay for itself. I've got to work. But I'm not looking forward to the suspicious stares and curious glances. I should pull on a disguise, maybe a black hood and sunglasses and a scarf around the bottom of my face."

"Yes, a creepy disguise. I'm sure that won't make people think of you as a killer at all. Just be yourself. Soon enough, people will forget this whole episode. You know Port Danby. Gossip and rumors change as quickly as the weather."

"That's the problem with small town living," Big Dash said.

Dash looked at him. "Said the man who has always lived in a small town."

"Sure, small towns have their problems, but big cities have bigger problems. City sized problems." Big Dash grinned at his play on words. "I'll have to write that little nugget of wisdom down."

Dash laughed. "Maybe you could publish the Big Dash Book of Useless Nuggets." He took a deep breath. "I'm feeling so much better than I did at the beginning of the week. I just hope this ends soon so everything can get back to normal."

CHAPTER 26

*T*he dinner with Dash and his dad helped my mood. I decided a cup of hot herbal tea and a good book would send me off to a peaceful sleep. But as usual, my plans were sent into disarray when the phone rang. I stared at the name James on the screen for a second. I contemplated not answering, knowing it was only going to make me toss and turn all night. But *not* answering would probably produce the same result. Besides, I missed the man. Darn it.

"Hello."

"Hey, Lacey." He paused. A few seconds felt like an eternity. Normally, I would have hopped right up to fill in the gap with small or flirty talk, but I was stuck on pause too. In the back of my mind, the promise I made to Dash to ask Briggs to get back on the case was on replay.

The phenomenon that always struck after an awkward pause followed. Both of us spoke up at the same time.

"Sorry. You go," I said.

"I just was just calling to see how you were doing. Bear was worried that he hadn't seen you in a few days."

"Oh, he was? Well, give him a big hug for me." My face warmed

495

with a smile. It had been our first *nice* conversation in two days. I was so pleased, I didn't want to throw cold water on it by bringing up Dash's request.

"So what's happening in the world of Detective Briggs? Are you working on anything exciting?"

"Just the usual gritty stuff, gambling rings and bad people doing things they shouldn't be doing." I realized how just the sound of his voice sent a rush of excitement through me. I knew I was crazy about him, but it'd taken this turmoil and a few harsh exchanges to help me understand just how much I counted on him being a part of my life. "What about you?" he asked.

"Just doing the flower thing. Oh, and I think I might be onto something with the murder case."

"Lacey," he said sternly.

"No, not that murder case. After all, you told me to stay clear of that one."

"Yes, that's my worry."

I decided to get off the topic before it spiraled down into an argument. "I'm talking about the Hawksworth murders. I went to the library and looked at some old newspapers on the microfiche machine."

He chuckled. It was deep and smooth and music to my ears. "Glad to see the Chesterton Library is floating right along into the mid twentieth century. Where did they get a microfiche? Did a time capsule wash up on shore?"

"If you're through with the stand up jokes, I'll have you know it's a much quicker way to look at a lot of headlines without having to sift through the stacks of old, brittle papers." Suddenly, it felt right between us, as if the past few days had never happened and we were back to ourselves. The warm familiarity of it helped me relax back into my pillows.

"What did the microfiche tell you?"

"It's just a little detail and might mean nothing at all, but I've found that little details all added together can sometimes add up to something big. And this *something big* involves Mayor Price's great grandfather, Harvard Price."

"That should endear you to the man even more," he quipped. "What did you find out?"

"Again, nothing definite but I think there might have been some funny business going on with the Port Danby account ledgers back then. I found one picture where Harvard Price was sitting at his desk. Jane Price, his adult daughter from his first marriage, was standing at his side holding the town ledger in her arms. Apparently, she was the Port Danby treasurer until she left town. And that seems to be a part of the story too, but I don't know enough yet to say for sure. But I found another picture of Harvard Price sitting as his desk. It was taken following his reelection. The Port Danby ledger was sitting in the middle of his big desk. Only this ledger was more intricate and with fancy silver plated corners. It was definitely not the same ledger I saw in Jane's hands."

"Maybe they just ordered a new book for the new term?"

"Yes, that's possible," I said with disappointment.

"Or maybe there were two sets of books, the real one and one where money was being siphoned off for personal gain," he added.

I sat up excitedly. "That's what I was thinking. Guess I'm not too far out there with my thinking if the highly respected Detective Briggs came to the same theory."

"Not too sure if the *highly respected* phrase works anymore. I'm feeling pretty out of sorts about everything that happened this week."

"You and me both. But you were just doing your job, James."

"Yeah? Dash's lawyer made me wonder if I'd jumped to conclusions too fast. I'm glad I made the decision to pull myself off the case."

I slumped back with a sigh. "Then, I guess I won't bother to ask you to get back on it. I'm worried it's not going to get solved, and Dash is going to be stuck under suspicion by the entire town." I knew bringing up Dash's raw deal in all of this was probably not going to go over well, but Briggs had brought it up first. And it was true. Without a proper closure to the case, Dash's life would never get back to normal.

"I'm staying off it." His tone was already sharper. I wanted to erase my last sentence. "Lacey, you have to understand, Dash is still a person of interest. Every piece of evidence and the witness accounts of the argument with Hall make a fairly solid case against him. The sharp talking lawyer knew it too, she just found enough loopholes to get him out."

The warm, fuzzy feeling was melting away. It seemed we just couldn't bring up the subject without getting angry.

"James, you know he didn't do it. Why do you keep insisting on talking about it as if you know Dash is guilty?"

"I'm not, Lacey. I'm just trying to make you understand this is far from over for Dash. Until another credible suspect emerges, Dash will be at the top of the list. I can assure you he's been told not to leave town."

"Well, maybe if you put someone more qualified in charge of the case, you could find that more credible suspect. For instance, has Chinmoor interviewed Marissa Hall? Not only did they go through a bitter divorce, but she took out a million dollar life insurance policy on Theodore before they split up."

His low sigh came loud and clear through the phone. "So much for you staying off the case."

"Someone has to find the killer since the main detective is not interested in discovering the truth."

There was a long, cold stretch of silence. I quickly replayed my last words in my head. They were harsh. It was surprising he didn't just hang up. At least I didn't start crying this time, but I was wringing the edge of my blanket pretty roughly between my fingers.

"That's not fair, Lacey. You're accusing me of not doing my job. First, you broadsided me with the accusation that I was too biased to run the investigation fairly. I ended up second guessing my own integrity. So I removed myself from the case, and now you're accusing me of shirking my duty." The hurt in his tone poured through the phone.

"No, you're right. I shouldn't have said that. I should never question your integrity, James. No one has more of it than you." I pulled the covers up higher. "Why can't we get past one conversation without ending up like this? Angry and upset and hurt?"

"I don't know, Lacey. It's like something has been thrown out of alignment, and we're just not clicking." His words made my throat ache. Dash had said the same thing about his relationship with Britney.

"Well, alignment problems are easy to fix, right?" I asked with a forced airy tone.

"I'm not sure. I'll let you go. It's late. Good night, Lacey."

"Good night." My voice was so weak I could barely hear it. I put the phone on the nightstand, flopped back on the pillows and drew the blanket up and over my head. It was going to be another long night of tossing and turning.

CHAPTER 27

*a*fter a long morning at work, with a few customers and a lot of time in between to stew about Briggs' phone call, I headed out for a lunch break. Only I wasn't going to have time to eat. Occasionally, a sleepless night led me to new ideas and plans. Sometimes those plans ended up seeming crazy once I climbed out of bed in the morning, like the idea to learn how to sky dive or the one where I decided to start a travel blog on YouTube. I pictured myself in all kinds of exotic locations, sipping bright colored drinks and chatting amiably with the locals. The idea came to me after watching a travel show where the lucky woman yachted between the Greek Isles and stayed in one charming place after another. By the time I stepped out of bed after that elaborate middle of the night, insomnia induced fantasy, I remembered that I had no extra money for travel and I wasn't all that fond of flying. But last night's middle of night epiphany was still solid. Mostly because instead of traveling around the world it only required a quick trip to Mayfield, more specifically, to Park Street Laundry.

I turned the corner to head into Mayfield. My stomach rumbled, reminding me that it was supposed to be the center of attention on a lunch break. Breakfast had consisted of charred toast and coffee, not nearly enough to get me through the rest of the workday. With any luck, there would be a sandwich shop or hamburger stand along the way.

My phone was directing me to travel miles ahead to Park Street. Mayfield was a much larger and more heavily populated town than Port Danby, but it was far from being categorized as a city. Most of the businesses were centered together a good few miles from the coast. Park Street was at the end of a long stretch of city buildings. At my phone's insistence, I turned right four hundred feet ahead and was instantly at my destination. At least according to the phone.

I turned into a small shopping center and drove slowly past each store, including a bakery. I almost considered stopping for a muffin or scone or other quick bite, but I was sure Elsie would somehow know that I'd stopped and ate a bakery item that did not come from her ovens. I had enough problems. I didn't need to start one with Elsie. I was probably too spoiled by her goodies anyhow.

A dog washing center was tucked in between a nail salon and a dentist office. The one thing I didn't see was a laundromat. I reached the end of the string of shops and was just about to pull out and try the other side of the street when I saw a woman carrying what looked like a large quilt across the parking lot.

I headed in her direction past the main buildings. There, sitting in the back, behind the shiny shop fronts, was a dilapidated building with peeling paint and a flat roof. The words Park Street Laundry had been painted on the window by someone who was not particularly skilled at lettering. The only parking spot in front of the building was one marked for handicapped people.

I parked in the main lot. I wasn't sure what I expected from my excursion, but it was the only thing that came to me in the middle of the night. I hadn't been inside a laundromat since college, but the smells, sights and sounds were exactly what I expected. Industrial sized washers ran along one side of the rectangular room. Dryers lined the back wall and long metal tables filled the center. A few uncomfortable looking benches had been set throughout the room for people to sit and wait for their laundry. A vending machine with sample sized pouches of detergent and softener stood in the corner next to a counter that had been painted a sickly pale green. The washer and dryer rates along with some rules were posted on a sign that was taped to the front of the green counter.

A man sat on one of the back benches listening to his headphones with his feet propped up on an overturned laundry basket. The woman with the quilt was shoving the large blanket into a washer.

The phone rang and a door behind the counter area opened up. A woman, who might have been thirty or forty, her thick, unruly hair covered a good portion of her face making it hard to guess her age, emerged. A few voices rolled out from the back room before she snapped the door shut.

She answered the phone brusquely. "Park Street Laundry." I easily recognized the snide tone. It was the same woman who answered when I called the number on the matchbook. She dashed off the prices for the machines and hung up. Her scrutinizing gaze landed directly on me.

"Did you need something?" she asked. She was absolutely not the kind of person who should have a receptionist job, but I supposed it worked for a laundromat.

"Me?" I quickly realized that I was standing in a laundromat with no laundry. I wanted to stay a few minutes longer, just to see if anything popped out as odd. I had to come up with a good excuse other than invisible laundry. "No, actually, I hope it's all right. I'm doing a favor for a friend. She was in here a few days ago, and she lost a sock. You know those wayward little buggers never like to stay with their twin. It's kind of a special sock that her—uh, her great grandma knit with her own two ninety-year-old gnarled fingers." I lifted my knuckles for a visual. "So I was heading over to the dentist office, and I told her I'd stop in to look for it."

"What does it look like?" she asked.

"Look like? Uh, of course. It has the usual sock shape, you know like the ones we draw in elementary school at Christmas time?" She was losing patience fast, something I'd already learned about the woman in our two short encounters. "Green and pink," I blurted. "It's green with pink stripes or pink with green stripes depending on which way you see it. It's the whole zebra question, I suppose. Who knew it could be applied to socks?"

The woman stared at me as if my hair was on fire and rightly so. I held my breath wondering if she was going to ask me to leave. Instead, she leaned over and pulled a large gray laundry basket out from under the counter. She dropped it on the counter.

"You can look through these lost items. But take it to the folding table. I have work to do here."

"Thank you." I hurried over and picked up the basket. My wondrous nose instantly alerted me to the unpleasant fact that not all the items in the basket had actually made it to the washer. I held my breath, forced a smile and carried the basket to the table.

I gingerly picked through a mishmash of clothes, working hard to avoid the underwear. I shook the basket around to make it appear as if I was really looking for the pink and green sock. The woman headed to the door that led to some sort of back room. Again, I heard a few voices as the door opened and shut, but I couldn't make out the words. I looked up at the ceiling and tried to estimate how much of the building was dedicated to the laundry area and how much was used for the back room. It was hard to figure out just why a laundry would need a backroom. I was sifting through some ideas, storage, counting quarters, rolling up the quarters in those cute finger tubes from the bank, when the phone rang again.

The door opened and shut. The woman returned, looking annoyed at the interruption. "Park Street Laundry," she said curtly. I waited for her to dash off the hours or prices again but not this time. "Why did you call on this line?" She sounded even harsher than usual, which was saying a lot.

I kept my ear toward the counter and watched the woman's reflection in the dusty front window. She was rummaging around under the counter. She pulled out a pad of paper and pen. Her scowl shot my direction. I lowered my eyes so she couldn't see me watching her and returned my focus to the basket.

"Yeah, got it. Tonight. And don't call on this line again." She smacked down the phone, ripped the paper off the notepad and rushed into the backroom. There was something not right about Park Street Laundry.

I'd had enough of the stinky laundry. I carried the basket back to the counter. The woman hadn't returned. An idea caused a surge of adrenaline to race through me. I certainly didn't want to be caught snooping by the most unfriendly laundromat owner in the world, but I leaned over the notepad to see if I could read the indentation left behind by her hasty scrawl across the paper. I could make out the number two hundred followed by some initials and numbers that looked like a code of some kind. I pulled out my phone and was just about to type in the code when the door flew open.

I patted the basket. "No luck on the sock. Thanks anyway." I hurried out of the building and stepped off the curb but stopped short and faltered back when a car sped around from the back of the building. The windows were tinted so darkly I couldn't see the driver, and considering the way he nearly ran me down, I wondered if he could see me. I watched the luxury sedan race without caution through the parking lot. It was one of those high end cars, expensive with all the bells and whistles. And it seemed totally out of place coming from behind the laundromat.

Curiosity made me turn toward the back of the building. I walked along the side and peered around the corner to the rear of the laundromat. A large trash bin was pushed up against the building adjacent to a back door. Another expensive looking car, shiny with silver paint and fancy wheels, was parked a few feet away from the door. The only explanation I could think of, and it was fairly plausible, was that the laundromat was owned by rich people. Perhaps they owned a chain of them and they were checking in on the business.

I headed back toward my car feeling a little dejected. I was grasping for something, anything to lead me to a killer, but it was starting to feel somewhat like the proverbial needle in the haystack. Being on the outside of the case and no longer privy to the police and coroner evidence made finding a suspect much harder. I considered more than once handing over the matchbook that they had clumsily overlooked but then I would be admitting to trespassing on Theodore's boat. Briggs would be so angry he'd probably never forgive me. I wasn't even sure now if we'd get past this but learning that I'd snuck on the boat would surely be the final straw. It probably didn't matter anyhow. The matchbook wasn't connecting any dots. In fact, if anything, it threw the dots into disarray.

I decided to get back to my original plan and focus on Marissa Hall. I pulled out my phone and sent Ryder a text.

"Is it all right if I take an extra long lunch? I've got some snooping to do."

"Sure thing, boss. King and I are just chillin'. It's a slow day."

"Great. See you in an hour."

CHAPTER 28

$\mathcal{I}$ had no appointment at Coco's Salon but came up with a reason to go inside. The coconut hair treatment had been far too fragrant for me, but I had to admit, even after rinsing it out a second time, it left my hair feeling luxuriously soft. I decided to buy one for a home treatment. I'd probably never eat coconut again, but my hair would be pretty.

It would be hard to linger and make small talk since I didn't know Gina that well. I wasn't sitting for a haircut but, I could be pushy with my prodding if I really worked at it. I was probably wasting my time again, but the ex-wife was still my only real person of interest.

I was mentally crossing fingers and toes as I walked into the salon. It worked. A woman with short white hair and big dangling earrings was standing at the stylist station with Marissa's name plate. It seemed I'd stumbled onto the woman herself. Gina was standing with her, staring down at what appeared to be a box of scissors. I spent the walk across the room strategizing on my approach but hadn't come up with anything solid by the time Gina looked up and noticed me. I was going to have to wing it.

"Hello, Lacey," Gina said cheerily. Then her smile fell. "Uh oh, did you not like the cut?"

I primped my curls on each side of my face. "No, I love it. But your coconut treatment was so amazing, I had to come back and buy one for home. Do you sell them?"

"Yes, of course. Isn't that stuff magical?"

"It is." I smiled and nodded politely at Marissa. She was an attractive woman with high cheek bones and full lips, features that looked high fashion with the short white haircut.

"Lacey, this is Marissa." She shot me a secret wink to let me know it was the same Marissa we'd discussed the day before.

"Hello, I'm sorry to hear about your husband," I said quickly before Gina could sweep me away to the hair product counter.

"Thank you. It was quite the shock," she said with no indication of shock or even emotion, for that matter.

I decided to do a little namedropping. I couldn't think of any other way to keep the conversation going with someone who was a complete stranger. "My boyfriend is Detective Briggs. I know they are working round the clock to find the killer."

Gina's eyes rounded. She looked at Marissa. "Didn't you tell me they caught the killer?"

Marissa didn't seem the least bit interested in discussing Theodore's murder. She shrugged. "They did but I think they had to release him. Obviously, they aren't doing a great job with the investigation." Considering I'd just told her I was dating Briggs, she had no qualms voicing her negative opinion. I was already sizing her up as someone perfectly capable of murder.

"I'll let you help the customer," Marissa said. "If I see anything else you might need while I'm cleaning out my station, I'll put it on your counter."

"Thanks," Gina said. She was smiling ear to ear as we headed to the hair product shelves. She leaned her head closer and lowered her voice to a whisper. "Told you she'd be quitting the salon now that she has all that money. She's moving to Florida."

"That was fast," I whispered back. We reached the shelves of hair products at the back of the salon. We were far enough away from the chairs to not be overheard. "It's almost as if she had the whole thing planned." Gina seemed somewhat stunned by my words. "I mean, the move to Florida, of course," I corrected abruptly, even though I was thinking about the murder when I said it.

Gina glanced back toward Marissa. She was busy cleaning out her drawers. Gina leaned in closer. "Between you and me, I think she's trying to get out of town fast. She says Theo owed a lot of people money. They've already been calling her to get their debts repaid."

I'd learned one important thing during my time as an investigator —there was nothing better than finding someone close to a suspect who loved to gossip. I was going to need to take Lola to lunch for pointing me in Gina's direction. My next question was ready to go. It was one way to find out what Officer Chinmoor was up to. "Is Marissa leaving before they solve the murder? It seems like the police would want her around, you know, in case they find a suspect. After all, it could have been someone they both knew. Maybe even one of those people calling her for money. Did she talk to the police at all?"

Gina bit her lip in thought. It seemed she wasn't entirely sure. It was possible Marissa kept some details from her. I certainly would if I knew how freely Gina talked about other people.

"Come to think of it, she did complain about having to sit down for an interview at the station yesterday. They just asked her about Theo's possible enemies and when she saw him last. You know general stuff like that. That's all she said about it, so I guess it wasn't a big deal." Gina reached up to the top shelf and pulled out a jar of the coconut conditioner. "Here you go."

I nearly dropped the jar when I saw the thirty dollar price tag on top. "Oh wow, it's a little more than I wanted to spend."

"Are you sure? This jar will be good for at least three treatments."

I handed it back to her. "You know what, I'll come buy it another time. My bank account is still in mourning after the holidays. Thanks for your time."

"No problem. And trust me, I understand about the bank account thing. Mine is as dry and empty as the desert. I have five siblings and four cousins. My shopping list was a mile long. By the way, we have a buy one get one free promotion in February. You might want to wait until then."

"That's exactly what I'll do. Thanks." I glanced in Marissa's direction as I walked through the salon. She was emptying her last drawer. I wondered if Officer Chinmoor had any idea the victim's ex-wife was leaving town on the pot of gold she'd earned from his death.

CHAPTER 29

$\mathcal{I}$ parked in my usual spot just down the block from the flower shop. Ryder was standing out front moving succulent pots around on the cart we'd pulled out in the morning to display our plants. Lola was sitting on the bench under the front window sipping a coffee and talking animatedly about something. Whatever it was, Ryder was enjoying the company. His grin stretched from ear to ear.

"Hey, boss," he said as I walked up. "Have a good lunch?"

"Oops, lunch," I said to myself. "Forgot to grab a bite to eat."

Lola hopped up from the bench. "Isn't that the goal of a lunch break?"

"Yes, I suppose it is. It's just my head is flooded with too many things right now."

Lola put her arm around my shoulder. "Like trying to show up your boyfriend when it comes to murder investigations?"

I pulled away to look at her. "That's not what I'm doing. I'm helping Dash." Lola always knew exactly what to say to get the gears spinning in my head. Was it possible my drive to find a suspect and clear Dash's name was more to prove to Briggs that I could do it without his help?

And as usual Lola was reading my mind. She pointed at me, cup still in hand. "Ah ha, I sparked a little self-reflection there, didn't I?"

"Don't you have old, dusty stuff to sell?" I asked as I headed into the shop.

"I have the stuff to sell. I just don't have the customers to sell it to," she followed me inside.

"Business is slow on that side of the street too, eh?" I pulled off my coat.

"Typical after holiday slow down." Kingston cooed to her. She walked over to pet him. "I guess only the Port Danby Police Department is busy. I saw Briggs zip past in his official car just a few seconds before you pulled up. His jaw and brow were both jutted forward with grit and determination. I think he was off to capture some bad guys. Or maybe the serious, stern expression is permanent since he and his cute assistant have hit a cold spell."

I stopped and stared at her. "For someone who is halfway to drama town when one little thing goes wrong with her boyfriend, you sure could do a better job at showing empathy when I'm in drama town."

She flounced over, put her coffee down and gave me a big hug. "I'm sorry. Is this better?"

"No, because it's all on my suggestion and you smell like—" I wriggled my nose and sniffed her sweater. "You smell like old cinnamon and oranges."

"You sure are good with that nose. I found an old bag of potpourri in a vintage dresser someone dropped off. Guess what it was made of?"

"I don't have to. You're wearing it." The mention of Briggs driving past was still in my head. "Did you say James drove past just a few minutes ago?"

Ryder walked inside as I asked the question.

"Yeah, he looked like he was on an important mission," Ryder added.

"Are you going to text him to find out where he's going?" Lola asked.

I reached for my coat again. "Actually, that's the last thing on my mind. Ryder, I'll be back in twenty minutes." I pulled on my coat, hurried out the door and turned left toward the police station.

Officer Chinmoor and I had struck up a fairly nice friendship since Briggs and I started dating. If Briggs was out on a call, then I had a chance to talk to Chinmoor alone. But I wasn't just going into the station to pry details out of Chinmoor. I had information about Marissa Hall to give him. From what I saw at the salon, Marissa was anxious to get out of town with her chunk of money. Just as Gina had reasoned, it could be that she was trying desperately to avoid the people Theo owed money. It was just as possible that she was running because she was guilty of murder.

I pulled my coat closer around me to keep out the chill and marched full speed ahead to the station. I hoped once I told Chinmoor what I learned about Marissa, he'd be softened up enough to let me run my nose past some of the evidence, namely Dash's coveralls. I hadn't had a chance to examine them yet.

Hilda peeked up over the counter as I walked inside. I paused in the doorway when I saw her hand go to her mouth.

My pulse raced as I surveyed the room for a possible assailant or something that would cause her stunned expression. Before I could take even one step farther, Hilda burst out from behind the security gate and ran to me. "Lacey, I'm so glad to see you." She hugged me so hard, when she let go her perfume was on my coat. She held my shoulders and leaned back to get a look at me. "I was worried I'd never see you again. Briggs is not himself. I do hope whatever is going on between you will be worked out soon. He doesn't say anything, of course, but I know that something is amiss."

I hadn't planned for this kind of greeting from Hilda. I assumed she wouldn't know anything was wrong. I secretly took a little pleasure in knowing Briggs was out of sorts.

"It's good to see you too, Hilda. I'm sure things will be fine." (There was that dreadful, vacuous sentence I seemed to be saying a lot lately.)

"Well, you missed Briggs. He left about ten minutes ago. He's working on a big case in Mayfield. He might not be back for a few hours."

"Perfect." I hadn't meant to say the word out loud. Hilda's brows bunched up.

"No, I mean, I wasn't here to see James. I was hoping to see Officer Chinmoor. I see the squad car out front."

The bunched brows were joined by a bunched forehead. "Chinmoor? I see. He's just down in the evidence room. I'll let him know you're here." She was rightfully puzzled. I'd walked into the station many times, but I'd never asked for Officer Chinmoor.

Hilda walked back behind the counter and headed down to the evidence room. I'd expected her to just pick up her two way radio to let him know. I could only assume she wanted a few private minutes to let him know that I was out there waiting to talk to him. Chinmoor would probably have the same stunned reaction when he heard.

I waited at the counter, lightly drumming my fingers and staring longingly at Briggs' office door. How badly I wanted to be on the other side of it having a fun, flirtatious chat with the man behind the desk. Footsteps plodding along the hallway pulled my attention away from the office door.

Officer Chimoor was well past his growing stage, but he seemed to get taller and thinner every time I saw him. "Miss Pinkerton, Hilda mentioned you wanted to see me?"

"Yes, if you have a moment."

"Sure." He buzzed me through the gate and pointed out a chair next to his desk. We both sat. He fidgeted with a few items on his desk that didn't need fidgeting with but gave him some time to compose himself.

He cleared his throat. "How can I help you?"

"First of all, I need to ask a favor."

"Miss Pinkerton," he started.

"Please, like I've said many times before, call me Lacey."

Hilda walked back out and pretended to busy herself at her desk.

"Actually, now that Hilda is here, I need to ask this of both of you," I said. "Could you please not mention my visit to Detective Briggs."

Hilda looked stricken at my request. "But why?"

I turned back to Chinmoor. "I've got a bit of information about the case you're working on and James— Briggs told me not to get involved."

Chinmoor was the one to look stricken next. He sat back and crossed his arms, making his thin shoulders stick out like points. "I'm working hard on the case, Miss Pinkerton. I don't need your assistance. If Detective Briggs asked you not to get involved—"

I decided to go for it, hoping my information would soften his stance. "Marissa Hall, the victim's ex-wife, just cashed in on a million dollar life insurance policy. She is, at this moment, packing up to leave town. She says she's moving to Florida." I knew I was feeding him new information because with each statement his straight posture slumped more.

"Well, Mrs. Hall is not a suspect," he said hesitantly.

"Why is that?" I asked.

He was about to tell me but shook his head. "I'm afraid that's police business. I can't tell you those details, but I can tell you she's not a suspect."

"A million dollars is pretty good motive, don't you think? And then with her leaving town so quickly—"

"She has an alibi," he blurted. "Marissa Hall has an alibi. She wasn't anywhere near the marina at the time of the murder because she was having coffee with two neighbors. The neighbors already confirmed it. And if you'd do the same favor for me and not mention to Briggs that I told you about the case, I'd appreciate it."

It was a double blow. First, I'd lost my main person of interest, and it seemed Briggs had told Chinmoor not to give me any information.

I couldn't hide the waver in my voice. "Briggs asked you specifically not to tell me anything?"

Some of the color blanched out of his cheeks. "No, I mean, not specifically." He fidgeted with paperwork on his desk to avoid direct eye contact. He knew he'd just stepped on something tender and was working hard to make it less hurtful. "He just meant, in general, not to let out details of the case. You know I'm a stickler for protocol," he added with a forced grin. "I need to get out on patrol." He stood up to let me know we were done with the conversation.

"Yes, sorry to keep you." I pushed up to my feet. The visit had been a disaster, but I thought I might be able to leave with one triumph. It was a long shot but I had to ask. "Officer Chinmoor, I don't suppose you'd let me run my nose over the coveralls that were found in the trash." His refusal was on its way, so I added something to my defense. "Don't forget how many murders this nose has helped solve. I could help you find the killer. You could take full credit. I wouldn't say a word about my visit to the evidence room." I offered one last sweet, pleading smile.

For a second, I thought it had worked. Chinmoor shook his head. "I couldn't do that. It's against—"

"Protocol," I finished for him. "Thank you for your time and good luck with the case."

CHAPTER 30

*a*fter my visit to the station, I was out of sorts enough to talk myself into a brisk walk along the pier to clear my head. The shop was slow, and I had no doubt Lola was still hanging around keeping Ryder company.

A dreary mist was once again floating in from the sea, carrying with it the strong scent of the ocean, which could be good or bad. Today, I was going with the latter, but that might have had more to do with my mood than the actual smell.

It was late afternoon. With the exception of the birds, the pier was mostly empty. My footsteps felt weighted by the disappointment of losing the only person of interest on my list. Finding out that Marissa had an alibi also showed me how difficult my task was without the benefit of being on the inside and working alongside Briggs. I'd learned that Marissa had been home house cleaning on the day of the murder, but I wasn't privy to any interviews and I couldn't conduct any myself, other than the nosy questions I asked in an informal chat.

I was back to the proverbial square one, and at this point, I couldn't see a square two. I was out of ideas.

I walked briskly along the pier hoping the salty breeze would sweep my gloomy mood away. A familiar voice called my name.

I spun back around. Gracie was sitting on one of the benches alongside the pier. She was huddled down in a parka eating a salad. She wasn't wearing the purple contacts, and she'd left her striped hat at the hot dog stand. She used her plastic fork to wave me over.

I looked pointedly at the salad in her hands. "I see the hot dog vendor eats healthier than her customers. That explains why you're in such good shape for someone who spends her day slinging chili and cheese on hot dog buns."

She scooted over to invite me to sit down. I sat next to her.

"I think selling the hot dogs makes me eat healthier. After smelling that rich food all day, all I can think about is something fresh." She stabbed a tomato slice and pushed it into her mouth. She washed it down with her bottle of water. "I don't usually see you out here at this time of day, unless you're with hunky Detective Briggs. Come to think of it, I haven't seen him much either. I thought I would, what with the murder and all."

"I think Detective Briggs is working on another case."

She laughed lightly. "You think? It sounds like you two don't talk much about work when you're together. I heard Dash was out. I still can't believe he's capable of murder. He's such a nice guy."

"I agree." My gaze swept across the way to the hot dog stand. There was a closed for break sign sitting on the counter. My eyes rolled past the stand and landed on the bench adjacent to the stand. A pigeon was busy picking up crumbs under the empty bench. "Has Mr. Cigar left for good? I'll bet you're relieved."

"So relieved. I swear he was there from morning till night every day for a week. Like he was staking out the hot dog stand. Aside from the cigar scent intruding on the hot dogs, he was kind of creeping me out. But I haven't seen him since Monday. Hope I never see him again."

I listened carefully, absorbing everything she said. Her words were adding up to a jackpot of a notion. I looked at her as she rummaged through the boring greens on her salad for an olive. I let her finish the bite before continuing.

"So he sat there every day for a week, smoking that cigar and fishing?"

"Yeah, but he never caught one fish. At least not that I saw. I don't even think he knew what he was doing. I didn't see any bait bucket or tackle box. He just showed up with his pole and cigar and a bag of donuts. That's a health regimen, eh? Cigars and donuts. I think that just made him seem more unsavory. Usually the fishermen show up with a thermos of soup or coffee and a breakfast sandwich. Maybe he hasn't returned because he landed in the hospital with a heart attack from donuts and cigars."

I smiled and pretended to be listening, but my mind was dashing in every direction. Internally, I had to remind myself not to get too excited. There was nothing connecting the cigar smoking stranger to the murder other than the fact he was on the pier that day. He'd been there for a week casting his line into the ocean and smoking his cigar. Then he just happened to disappear after the murder. It could all be coincidence, or it could be something more. Unfortunately, my theory had an obvious setback. I had no idea who the stranger was or where he went.

"Gracie, you don't happen to recall seeing that man talking to anyone else on the pier? Did you possibly hear anyone call him by name?"

She snapped the container lid shut on her salad. "Not that I recall. About the only interaction I heard between him and anyone on the pier was when someone walking by commented on the smoke. He did occasionally walk away from the bench, but he was usually back after an hour or so, right back to stinking up the place."

"Can you remember which way he went? Is it possible he went— say, to Franki's or the Corner Market?" If he had shown up at some of the familiar places in town, I might be able to find more information out about the man.

"Gosh, I didn't really notice. I was just always relieved when he left. I think he walked down to the beach and the marina." Gracie seemed genuinely baffled by my questions. "Why are you so curious about him?" Her eyes rounded. "Do you think he's the killer? Do you mean

I've been selling hot dogs just fifteen feet away from a cold blooded murderer?"

"No, no. I'm just thinking aloud really. He was probably just some retired guy who came to town for a week to fish and now he's back home, wherever that might be." The last thing I needed was to start rumors and tall tales, and Gracie talked to a lot of people.

Gracie seemed to relax at my suggestion about the retired man. We both stood up. "Well, I hope they find the person soon," she said. "But at least it's nice to have Dash back on the marina. He's sort of a permanent fixture out here, a tall, handsome fixture." She giggled as she lightly elbowed me.

"Is Dash over at the marina?" I'd forgotten that he'd mentioned heading back to work.

"Far as I know." Gracie headed across to the hot dog stand. "Thanks for keeping me company on my break," she called.

"My pleasure." I waved to her and turned toward the marina. If the cigar man had been lurking around the marina, then Dash would certainly have seen him.

CHAPTER 31

he piece of yellow caution tape was still dangling from the cleats where Theodore's boat was moored. Apparently, Officer Chinmoor and whoever was supposed to be helping had not bothered to revisit the scene of the crime since the first night.

A few boats down, Dash's tall head appeared above the railing on the boat he'd been working on at the time of the murder. I watched him for a second while he reorganized some pieces in his toolbox. It seemed he was cleaning up for the night.

"How did your day go?" I asked.

Dash twisted around. "Hey, Lacey, didn't hear you walk up. My day went fine." He walked to the railing. "I spent most of it below deck in the engine compartment, so I didn't face too many suspicious glares or scrutinizing scowls."

"What's your dad up to?"

"He needed to get back home, so he caught an early flight out. Just when you think you don't need your parents anymore, you find out that you do. I don't know what I would have done without him this week." He gazed at me. "Or you. Thanks for being a friend at a time when I really needed it."

"It didn't take much effort. I know you'd do the same for me."

He nodded. "I would but I advise you not to get arrested for murder. It's scary stuff."

"I can only imagine. Can I come on board? I wanted to ask you a few questions."

"Sure, let me lower the gangplank so you don't have to make a jump for it." He walked over and opened a section of the railing. He pressed a button and the gangplank lowered to the dock.

Dash offered me his hand and helped me on deck. "Much easier than climbing over the railing. I don't want to keep you. It looked like you were cleaning up."

"Yeah, I finished the job. I had two more lined up for next week, but they were mysteriously cancelled." He snapped shut the cover on the toolbox.

"I'm sorry to hear that, Dash. But they'll be calling you again as soon as they find the person who killed Theodore. After all, it's a big marina, and you're the best boat mechanic on this coast. At least that's what I hear since I don't actually own a boat." The water was choppy enough to cause me to grasp the railing to catch my balance. "Guess I wouldn't make a great sailor. My sea legs are like wet noodles."

Dash laughed. "I have the opposite problem. After I've been on deck a long time, I get back on solid land but the waves keep rolling beneath me." He walked over and picked his coat up from a pile of rigging.

"I'm sure you're anxious to get home, so I'll get right to my questions. For a week before the murder, a middle aged man had been fishing on the pier every day. All day, in fact, according to Gracie."

My mention of Gracie stirred his memory. "Yeah, the guy with the smelly cigar. I'd never seen him before." He pulled on his coat. "He wasn't much of a fisherman either. I saw his line in the water, but I never saw him reel anything in."

"That's exactly what Gracie said. She was annoyed with him because the scent of his cigar kept seeping into the hot dog stand. She also mentioned that she hadn't seen him since Monday, the day of the murder," I added to see if he caught the direction I was heading.

Dash stopped the zipper on his coat halfway and looked up at me.

"That's interesting. He was a shady looking guy too. Every once in awhile, I'd catch him hanging out here between the boats. I could swear he looked away when I glanced his direction, as if he was watching me and didn't want me to notice. Heck, Lacey, you might be onto something. Maybe you should tell Briggs."

I scrunched up my nose. "Not sure if that's a good idea. I'm not supposed to have anything to do with the case. I asked him to consider putting himself back in charge, but he wasn't convinced."

"That seems counterproductive to the investigation. You're out here finding real clues, while I haven't seen Chinmoor out here once since the night of the murder. They never even cleaned up the yellow caution tape. I found a strand of it on this boat when I climbed on board this morning." Dash's tone was filled with irritation. "Maybe Briggs doesn't care if it gets solved."

I gave him my *seriously* look. "He's lead detective. Of course he wants a successful investigation."

"Then you should be able to walk right into that station and tell them what you just figured out."

"That makes sense to me too, but since this is only a theory right now, I'm going to keep it to myself. I have a few ideas on where to go next to find out more about the stranger on the pier. You didn't happen to hear his name or see him talking to anyone?"

"Not that I remember. I wasn't paying that much attention I guess. Wish I had been now."

Dash picked up the toolbox. "What are you going to do? Remember, if this guy was the killer, he's dangerous. If Theodore was having money problems, he might have gotten involved with some bad people."

"Believe me, I have no intention of confronting or even getting close to the guy. I probably won't be able to find him. But I promise if I can't make any more headway with my theory, I'll tell James everything I know."

CHAPTER 32

$\mathcal{I}$ pulled out the matchbook and turned it over to get the address of the Blue Mermaid Pub. I typed the address into my phone, put the matches back in my pocket and dropped my phone into the cup holder on the console. It was probably one of my crazier ideas, especially after Dash mentioned it was a crummy place, but I had no other options. The man from the pier had disappeared into thin air, and the only possible clue I had was the book of matches. It would make sense that a cigar smoker would carry matches, and since the matchbook was a promotional tool from the Blue Mermaid Pub, it was easy to reason that the person who dropped the matches had visited the pub at least once. It was also easy to reason that it might very well be that person's favorite drinking hole.

I turned off of Myrtle Place and headed toward Mayfield. The sun had set. Front porches were lit and kitchens were glowing warm with activity. I'd taken extra care to eat a very bready sandwich for dinner. After my striped sock performance at the laundry, when I got caught off guard by the woman behind the counter, I needed a better plan. I decided to order a glass of wine so as not to draw attention to myself. I'd briefly considered inviting Lola along for the adventure, but she would surely tell Ryder and then it would be a whole thing because

Elsie and Les would know and I'd be hearing lectures from every direction.

My stomach was a hurricane of nerves as I drove along the dimly lit street my phone had directed me to. After the map lady told me three times I'd reached my destination, I finally spotted a small building with black tinted windows and a glowing *open* sign over the door. I wouldn't have known it was the right place if not for the neon blue mermaid floating above the sign.

I found a parking spot not too far from the bar. I checked my face in the mirror, although I wasn't exactly sure what I was looking for. I suppose I was just making sure I didn't look too much like a scared rabbit.

The low rumble of music rolled out from the place as I reached the corner of the building. I hesitated just long enough to consider heading home and waiting until morning to hand over the matches to Chinmoor. But he had been so clear that he wasn't going to let me in on the investigation, I wasn't sure he'd even see me. Then there was the little voice in my head reminding me that I'd trespassed on the boat after being told to stay away from the case. If Briggs found out, it would just be more fuel added to an already roaring fire. I was in a pickle, and I felt very alone in the jar. There was no one to turn to. I'd always been rather proud of my independence. I needed to assert that now.

I took a deep breath, put on my brave rabbit face and headed to the door. One glass of wine and a look around and I'd head back home.

The window on the front door was also tinted nearly black, but someone had scratched through the tint with a sharp object to etch out a few cuss words. No one had bothered to remove them.

The door was heavy, almost immovable as I pulled on it. A moment of comedy followed when after pulling it with all my weight, I discovered that after the halfway point, the door opened easily, so easily that I stumbled backward. A chirpy sound shot from my mouth as I caught myself by hanging tightly onto the door handle.

I stepped inside the dimly lit room. The clumsy entrance had gotten everyone's attention. All eyes were on me, including the gruff looking man behind the bar.

I chuckled lightly and pointed back to the door with my thumb. "Guess you only oiled the hinges halfway."

No one in the room seemed amused. Fortunately, they were also no longer interested in the odd woman bundled in winter gear. I hopped up on a stool that was covered in ripped blue vinyl. The weak overhead lights were so covered in dust, I could smell it burning with the glow of the bulbs. And dust burning was the most pleasant odor in the place. There was enough cigar and cigarette smoke floating around the room to make it seem as if a flock of ghosts were floating above the tables and chairs. Three people sat at the long oak counter, a couple and a lone man. The mirror behind the bar gave me a partial view of the tables and chairs behind me. There were a surprising amount of people sitting at the tables. Billiard balls click clacked in the next room.

It was Thursday night, which some people liked to call Friday eve. It was a popular night to go out and celebrate the near end of the work week. I couldn't see the entire room or all the faces clearly, but I didn't see the cigar man from the pier. Or at least I didn't think I saw him. I never got a clear look at his face, only his thick build. What if I couldn't recognize the man? Why was I just thinking about this now? In my head I had a clear picture of a broad shouldered, thick-necked man in a raincoat, but I never saw much of his face. I glanced around. Several of the patrons had relatively the same physique as the mystery cigar man. This was starting to feel like another failed mission.

A napkin dropped in front of me. A mermaid, the same mermaid as on the front of the matchbook, smiled up at me. "What can I get you?" The brusque looking bartender, complete with scruffy beard and a plethora of tattoos, had a surprisingly polite, pleasant tone.

"A glass of white wine, please."

He nodded and walked away. I peered around, using some of my curls as shields to keep my scrutiny hidden. The couple who'd sat on the bar stools farther down picked up their drinks and headed to a booth. A waitress carried an empty beer pitcher to the bar. She had a bright blue headband holding back brunette hair. Her t-shirt was emblazoned with the mermaid logo. Her apron was decorated in rhinestone hearts, which drew my attention as I immediately considered decorating my work apron with rhinestone flowers. But I was a realist. As I learned in my teens, when I insisted on decorating my new pair of jeans with rhinestone peace signs, bedazzling was a long, arduous process. Just like with the peace signs, I'd never make it past the first flower.

I was lost in my rhinestone thoughts as the bartender placed a glass of wine in front of me. The waitress slapped the bar. "Wayne, can I get a refill for Harkey?" She pushed the empty pitcher his direction.

The barkeep, Wayne, apparently, lifted his head and looked toward the back of the room. I nearly slipped off the stool as he bellowed across the room. "Harkey, you need to clear your tab before I refill this pitcher. It's been two weeks."

"Yeah, yeah, I've got your money," a hoarse voice said from a dark, deep corner.

I picked up the glass and sipped the wine. It wasn't too bad but then I wasn't exactly an expert. I was far more skilled at tasting baked goods. I lifted the glass for a second sip as footsteps plodded from behind. I glanced sideways at the man, Harkey, who had come up to clear his tab. Just like several of the other patrons, he had approximately the same build as the cigar man. I was feeling fairly silly for setting out on the adventure and not really knowing what I was looking for. It seemed my entire investigation so far had been based on hunches and little else. I was hoping to show Briggs just how good of a detective I was on my own. Instead, I'd proved to myself just how hard murder cases were without being privy to police information.

Deciding I might as well hang out a bit longer, I lifted the glass to my lips. Just then, the fruity fragrance of the wine mingled with cigar smoke. Not just any cigar smoke, *his* cigar smoke. My nose was sure of it. I glanced over at Harkey as he pulled his wallet from his coat. There was a nice wad of cash tucked into the money fold. While he fished out the bills he needed, he kept his lit cigar in the corner of his mouth.

The smoke streamed my direction. I caught another whiff of it. I was certain I was looking at the man from the pier.

And he was looking at me.

I pulled my gaze away and focused back on the glass of wine in my hands. My fingers trembled some and my tummy did a nervous bounce. I could likely be just five feet away from a cold blooded murderer. The dots were being connected. A stranger sat on the pier all week, pretending to fish, and lurking around the marina. He disappeared after the murder. The out of place matchbook at the crime scene just happened to be from a place the man frequented, as made clear by the fact that he ran a big tab, a tab he'd left unpaid for two weeks until now when his wallet was overflowing with cash. Was he a hit man? Did someone who Theodore owed money hire Harkey to kill Theodore? The day Theodore ran into me on the pier, just hours before someone clobbered him on the head with Dash's socket wrench, he grumbled about everyone wanting his money. More importantly, he kept glancing around in paranoid fashion as if he worried someone was following him. And someone was. The man standing next to me with the fragrant cigar. His name was Harkey. It sounded like a surname, but it could have just as easily been a first name or a nickname.

I had my person of interest. Now what?

I pulled out my money and left it on the counter. There was nothing more I could do tonight. I needed to go home and strategize how to find more evidence to prove my person of interest was the perpetrator. I didn't want to accuse someone only to have it fall apart, much like I did with Marissa Hall. I needed to be certain. I had some ideas on how to do just that.

CHAPTER 33

I glanced at the clock. It was close to noon. The morning had been excruciatingly slow. My mind was on the case and what I considered significant developments in my investigation. I was using that official sounding word because I was proud of how much I'd discovered, and all on my own without the help of my usual partner. (Although I missed him terribly.)

Despite being chilly, it was a bright and sunny day. Ryder had set himself the task of assembling a sidewalk sale of tiny potted succulents and herbs. He'd spent most of the morning finishing his potting while I helped a handful of customers. Since his sidewalk sale would be all afternoon, he took an early lunch so he could set up the tables and plants when he returned.

While I waited for Ryder to get back from his break, I finished the chalkboard sign listing the prices for Ryder's sale. My mind was swirling with plans for my next investigative move. There was one piece of evidence that I badly wanted to get my nose near. Dash's coveralls might very well connect Harkey, the man from the pub, to the murder. I considered telling Briggs that I was sure I'd found the killer and that I just needed a whiff of the coveralls, but I wasn't supposed to be working on the case. Besides, my pride kept me from telling him. What if I was wrong? It would be humiliating. I had to be sure.

I glanced up as the bell rang. Officer Chinmoor's squad car drove past just as Ryder stepped inside. The car was heading away from the station. "Ryder, did you happen to see if Detective Briggs' car was at the station on your way back from Franki's?"

"Not sure." Ryder stopped, turned and leaned out the door to look down the street. "I don't see it."

I raced for the coat hook. "Perfect. I'm taking my lunch now if that's all right."

"Sure thing."

He watched with curiosity as I scurried past him, struggling to put my coat on in my haste.

"Whoa, boss, where's the fire? Franki made extra chili and corn-bread. She's got plenty for the Friday lunch crowd today."

I smiled back at him. "No time for chili today. I've got a murder to solve. I'll be back soon."

I headed straight down to the station. Both Chinmoor and Briggs were out of the office, which left only my good friend, Hilda. I had no idea if I could convince her to let me into the evidence room but I had to try. Hilda was my only chance.

Hilda was on the phone when I walked inside. She peered up over the counter and waved when she saw me. She finished her call and hung up with a disgruntled sigh.

"Uh oh, problems in the neighborhood?" I asked.

"Mildred Fitch out on Dawson Grove is constantly squabbling with her neighbor Harry Linton. Her cat, Tiger, is missing, and she thinks Harry did something to the cat. I told her Tiger is probably in some tree or harassing the chickens at Peggy Wright's coop. Tiger is kind of a neighborhood bully. Enough of that." She smiled broadly. "James left an hour ago. Have you two made nice yet? He's been so busy on a case, I've hardly seen or talked to him. I won't be happy again until I know you two have kissed and made up."

"I wish I had better news on that front, Hilda."

Her round shoulders curled forward with disappointment. "What can I do to help it along?"

I perked up at her offer. "Well, there is one thing."

She hopped up from her chair and came to the counter with conspiratorial excitement glittering in her eyes. "Should I drop hints about seeing you with another man at the diner?"

"What? No, no, not that." I held back a grin. "No, I've never been one to play games or work the jealousy angle. I'm hoping for a much more practical and less scandalous solution."

She leaned closer. "I'm all ears. Although, I think my solution would be much faster."

"Not sure if it would be effective at this point, Hilda. Things are pretty cold between us. Our last few conversations were pretty rough."

She reached over the counter and took my hand. "Nonsense. James is crazy about you. This is just a pothole in the road. Now what can I do to fill in that hole?"

"Hear me out first. All the trouble between James and me is a result of Theodore Hall's murder and Dash's arrest."

Her cheeks puffed with a grin. "Lacey, dear, I figured that out right from the start. I know you are friends with Dash, and I know James is *not* friends with Dash." She sucked in a sharp breath. "I could tell him that I saw you at the diner with Dash. That should rile him up enough to put on his suit of armor and fight for his lady."

"No, Hilda, that would only push him farther away. Now back to my much more practical solution."

"Right, sorry. I'm listening. Just let me know what you need me to do." She added in a cute military salute to prove her dedication to the cause.

"I need you to let me into the evidence room."

Her puffy cheeks deflated. "Oh, I don't know about that, Lacey."

"I'll just be in there for a minute, I promise. I'll put everything back where it belongs. I know all the protocol for handling and storing the evidence. James has taken me into the room many times. Please, Hilda. I'll be forever grateful."

She looked around as if there might be someone listening, even though we were entirely alone. "I suppose a fast trip down to evidence." She pointed a finger. "One minute and no more. But if it will help bring you two back together, it's worth the risk." She pushed the button to allow me through the counter gate.

I turned to her. "I can't promise anything about James and me, but you and I are hoping for the same happy ending."

We padded lightly down the hallway to the evidence room as if we were sneaking through a crowded building instead of an empty police station. "How is the investigation going for Chinmoor?" I asked in a low voice.

She shook her head. "He doesn't say much to me, but I gather not too well considering his bewildered expression every time he sits down with the file folder. I think he's convinced they already had their man."

"You mean Dash? He's just looking for an easy end to the case." Chinmoor was quickly losing some of the respect I had recently gained for him. "He's not thinking of arresting him again, is he?"

"I think he's afraid of that lawyer. He's looking for ways to make the case against Dash more solid."

"He's going to be out of luck on that front."

"I think so too." We reached the evidence room. Hilda's keys clinkered as she fidgeted with the lock on the door.

She looked back at me. "One minute. I'll wait out here and listen for the front door. The last thing either of us needs is for Detective Briggs to find us snooping about down here."

"Thank you so much for doing this, Hilda. I'll be right out." I slipped into the stark, cold evidence room. Most of the shelves were empty. Evidence from solved cases was stored in the basement of the station. It was easy to spot the bag with the coveralls. I pulled two latex gloves out of the box and lifted the bag off the shelf.

Dash's logo, a vintage motor boat, was embroidered on the pocket of the coveralls. Blood was splattered across the right arm and front panels of the garment. I pulled it carefully out of the bag and placed it on the examination table. I gave my nose a good wriggle and closed my eyes to concentrate. I leaned down over the table planning to give the coveralls a thorough nasal exam, but it turned out that wasn't needed.

"Cigar smoke," I muttered to myself. I could smell it even through the garbage odors the fabric absorbed in the trash. It was there as clear as the nose on my face, and thanks to that nose, I'd solved the murder.

My excitement was dampened when Hilda burst into the room looking as if she'd seen a ghost. "Lacey, you've got to get out," she whispered so loudly it caused the veins on the side of her neck to bulge. "Officer Chinmoor is here." She motioned for me to get out.

My adrenaline kicked into overdrive. I swiftly folded the coveralls, slid them back into the bag and nearly tossed them onto the shelf. I hurried to the door. Hilda stopped me and pointed frantically at the gloves on my hands.

I pulled them off and shoved them into my pockets.

"What shall I tell him? How do I explain why you're down here with me?"

The last thing I wanted to do was get Hilda in trouble, especially after she'd taken the risk to help me. "Is there an emergency exit?"

She snapped her fingers. "Yes, the alarm will trip, but I'll tell him I set it off on accident." She motioned for me to follow her. We turned right toward the back of the station.

"Hilda," Chinmoor called from the front of the office. "Are you in the lunch room?"

His voice faded as we made it to the back door. Hilda lifted her shoulders in preparation for the earsplitting alarm. "Here goes," she whispered as she pushed on the door handle. The alarm clanged so loud it left a ring in my ears as I raced out. I headed behind the back of the building so I wouldn't have to pass by the front windows. The alarm stopped by the time I reached the sidewalk.

With the new evidence, I walked confidently back to the flower shop to plan my next move. Along the way, I developed a good dose of irritation at everything that had happened. If Briggs or Chinmoor would have just let me smell the coveralls on the day they were removed from the trash, I could have solved the case right then and spared Dash and the Port Danby Police Department the embarrassment of a false arrest.

I had the real murderer, but it seemed the person officially in charge of the case had not gotten farther than the first big mistake in the investigation. The cigar smoke was good evidence, but I needed more. I wanted to make certain I had everything I needed when I went to Briggs to let him know I'd solved the case. And yes, there would be some gloating because I deserved it.

The motive piece of the murder was the only thing that was a little hazy. I was sure Harkey was some kind of hit man. By all accounts, Theodore had gotten himself in deep financial trouble. Easy to do if someone had a gambling problem. I still needed to connect Harkey with Theodore.

I reached into my pocket, past the latex gloves, and felt for the tissue wrapped matchbook. It was just a tiny piece of cardboard filled with matches but so far it had been the key to everything.

CHAPTER 34

Several hours after Ryder had carried the tables and plants outside for his sidewalk sale, the blue sky turned an ominous gray and the temperature dropped enough to threaten snow. I helped him carry everything back inside, and we cleaned up for the afternoon. The incoming storm had basically cleared Harbor Lane of shoppers, so we decided to close up early. It was an easy decision to make because I was anxious to further my investigation. I was so close to the climactic end, I could feel it in the air. Or that might have been the frosty weather looming ahead, either way I was giddy from my new knowledge about the case.

Once the plants were put away, Ryder took off to help his mom with a few home projects. Kingston had decided not to play the flower shop mascot this morning and opted for a quiet day at home on his perch. I was free to continue my plan. I was going to head to Park Street Laundry for one more snoop around. The phone number inside the matchbook had to somehow be connected to Harkey. That was what I needed to find out.

This time, I decided to take the precaution of letting someone know where I was. Not that I expected anything to happen, but with the snow about to fall, I figured it couldn't hurt to let my best friend know that I'd be traveling over to the next town.

I pulled on my coat and flipped the hood up over my head as I crossed the street to Lola's Antiques.

"I'll be right with you," she called from somewhere in the store as I walked inside. Late Bloomer left his pillow long enough to trot over and greet me, then he made a sharp turn and headed right back.

"It's just me." I walked to her counter and grabbed a piece of paper and pen. I wrote down the words Park Street Laundry on the paper.

Lola emerged from behind a stately looking walnut dresser with a feather duster in one hand and an antique ice skate in the other.

"I can't tell if you were dusting or considering a twirl around the ice."

She lifted the skate. "Somehow this old leather topped ice skate ended up behind the dresser." She looked pointedly at Bloomer, who stared back with innocent brown eyes. "Ryder told me you guys were closing up early. I think I'm going to do the same. I want to get home before the snow falls. My tires are as bald as eagles." She looked at me. "Are they really bald though? Because it seems like the feathers should count."

"Contemplation for another day," I said. "I'm off. I just dropped by to let you know—" I tapped the paper on the counter where I'd written the name of the laundry. "If you don't hear from me in two hours, this is where I went."

Her forehead puckered with worry. "What are you up to, Miss Pinkerton?" she asked sternly.

"Nothing much. Just solving a murder, I hope."

Lola walked over and picked up the paper. "You're going to a laundromat to solve a murder?"

"Not solve it but with any luck, I'll pick up some new information to help me paint a clear picture of Theodore Halls' death."

"Should I be worried?" she asked. "You've never left me a cryptic note with a warning about not hearing from you in two hours."

"That's because I'm usually doing this stuff with James. I'm on my own, so I thought I should let you know. Especially with the bad weather coming in. I'm not doing anything dangerous, just a little snooping." I headed toward the door before she could ask any more questions or, worse, make me rethink the whole escapade.

"Call me in two hours, or I'm sending out the Calvary," she called as I walked out the door.

I hurried across to my car and climbed inside. Light snowflakes, the kind that melted the second they landed on the windshield, had started to cascade from the gray sky. The whole scene outside the car and the fact that I was off to find a killer's connection to a crime felt a little surreal, like I was in a movie. Only I wasn't, and the flutters in my stomach assured me it was all too real.

Traffic had slowed because of the weather, but I managed to get to the parking lot where Park Street Laundry was stashed in the back corner. I came a little more prepared for this visit. I reached into the backseat and pulled out the two wool throw blankets I'd tossed in before leaving the house. Even before I'd made the profound discovery of cigar smoke on the coveralls, I'd decided I needed to check out the laundry business once more. The woman behind the counter had been abrupt and rude. Then there was the phone call where she chewed someone out for calling on the wrong phone. Something seemed off about the place.

I pulled the blankets out, yanked my hood up and headed across the lot to the laundry. Two young women were in the back talking and giggling while folding up their baskets of clothes.

The unfriendly woman was nowhere in sight. I dropped my two blankets into the washer and walked to the vending machine to buy some detergent. I pulled some quarters out of my coat pocket and accidentally pulled out the tissue with the matchbook. The matches fell to the floor before I could catch them. I stooped down with the tissue and picked it up. I stared at the front cover for a second. I'd forgotten about the ink circle around the word *mermaid*. Was it significant, a password or a code word? I stuck the matchbook back into my pocket and purchased my soap.

"You're back," the woman snapped. "I thought you couldn't find the sock."

I'd been so absorbed in my thoughts, I hadn't heard her walk out from the back room.

"No, no sock." I'd been caught off guard again, and I stumbled over my words. I lifted the foil pouch of detergent. "I'm here to wash a few blankets." She had dark firm brows that were intimidating when she scowled. She had really perfected her glower.

I had her attention, so I saw it as my chance. "But my friend did also ask me to look for a t-shirt she lost." I laughed lightly. "She's obviously not great at keeping track of her clothes. It's yellow and it has a mermaid on the front."

The second the word *mermaid* left my mouth her expression smoothed to cold marble. She skewered me with a suspicious glare. "What did you say?"

Her tone and expression made my throat dry. "A yellow t-shirt with a mermaid," I said with a crackly voice.

"Wait here." She turned sharply on her heels and disappeared into the back. The earlier stomach flutters now felt like marbles ricocheting around inside of me. I briefly considered making a run for it, but she returned almost instantly. "Come with me, I have your shirt."

I was stunned. It felt as if all the blood rushed from my head to my feet. I grabbed the edge of the counter to steady myself. The two women were still folding laundry behind me.

"Come," the woman grinned, her creepy attempt at being friendly.

I tapped the side of my head. "You know what, I just remembered that I left the fabric softener in my car. I don't want my blankets to feel rough. I'll just go get it." I raced out the door but didn't get three steps before someone took hold of my arm. A hand went around my mouth before I could scream. My captor held it so tightly, I couldn't move my lips enough to bite him, the only line of defense I could think of. He moved me brusquely around the back of the building and knocked three times on the door.

"It's me. I've got her."

The door opened. The rotund man who had opened it waddled back to his chair at a table that contained a few notebooks, a laptop and a phone. His face was more jowls and chins than eyes and nose.

537

He looked almost like a cartoon character or a creature you might see in a Star Wars movie.

I couldn't get a good look at the man holding my arm and mouth but his thick, callused fingers were digging into my skin. He walked me roughly over to the table and let go of my mouth. I gasped for breath. The scream was lodged in my throat, and the thick cement walls of the room made it clear it was useless to even try. I was sure my captors would find a way to silence me permanently if I dared to cry out for help.

The big man in the chair leaned back and nodded to the man holding my arm. He released me and circled around to get a look at me. I sucked in a breath, and my skin went clammy with fear. It was Harkey, the killer. He had cold gray eyes and leathery skin. Stale cigar smoke circled him like a cloud.

"Yeah, that's the little bird who's been following me." Without warning, he rudely patted me down, apparently looking for weapons. I held my breath until he finished.

It took all my courage to find my voice. "I haven't been following anyone. I just came here to wash some blankets."

Harkey sat on the edge of the table and crossed his arms. "You were at the Blue Mermaid last night."

I shrugged. "Is there a problem with a grown woman going out for a glass of wine?"

"Let's just say you don't look like the Blue Mermaid type."

"I saw an advertisement for the pub, and I thought it sounded like a fun place." My voice sounded feathery and frail.

"Was it fun?" The big man asked. He leaned back and the chair creaked as if it was on its last breath.

"Yes. It was very nice. Now, if I could just go get my blankets, I'll be out of your hair."

The phone rang. I was wound so tight with fear, the sound of it nearly sent me straight into the ceiling like a rocket. (If only I had a rocket right then.)

His pillowy hand picked it up. "Yeah. Nope, you're too late. Call earlier next time." He smacked the phone down. "Did you find your pink and green sock?" the big man asked.

I was in such a state of alarm, it took me a second to figure out what he was asking. "The sock?" I decided to play dumb. "I don't know what you're talking about."

He kept his beady eyes on me as he opened the laptop. He hit a few keys and spun the computer around to show me a security camera taping of the laundry area. A few seconds in, I walked into the camera's view with my ridiculous green and pink sock story.

I smiled weakly. "You know how those darn socks are always going rogue."

"Yeah but that's not the best part of the video." He spun the computer around hit a few keys and turned it back. There I was, stealthy investigator extraordinaire, checking out the imprint the woman had left on the notebook in direct view of the security cameras.

"I didn't see anything on that pad. And as far as I'm concerned I didn't see this room or this laundry. You can even keep the blankets. I'll just forget I was here." I backed up a few steps and found, to my surprise and terror, that there was another man in the room. He was built like a steel wall.

"Did that detective send you?" Harkey sneered.

I felt the blood drain from my head again and swayed on my feet. I took a deep breath to steady myself. "There's no detective. I told you, I was here to wash blankets. You have the wrong person if you think I'm some kind of police officer. Not that there's anything illegal about running a laundry business," I added quickly.

"You were with him on the pier eating hot dogs," Harkey sneered. "Seems like you two were pretty cozy."

"Nope not cozy. He's an acquaintance, and we decided to get hot dogs. I have no connection with any investigation." Another amateur move on my part.

Big man sat forward, torturing the chair beneath him even more. "Who said anything about an investigation?"

"Oh, I just thought—Well, you brought up the detective. I don't know what any of this is about. I'm sorry I glanced at the notepad, but it's hardly worth all this trouble. Just let me be on my way. I promise you won't see me in the laundromat again."

The men shot looks at each other as if they were considering my offer. But that was wishful thinking, which became frighteningly clear when the three men burst out with a round of laughter. My knees turned to jelly at the sound of it. But I had to hold myself together. Crumpling into a weak, scared mess wasn't going to do me any good. Not with these rotten characters.

"Tie her to that chair over there until I figure out what to do with her," the big man ordered.

Harkey took rough hold of my arm and led me to a metal chair in the corner of the room. "You don't need to tie me up. I mean it's three big guys against one small woman. What am I going to do, pummel you with my tiny fists?"

"You're a clever little bird, aren't you?" Harkey said as he pointed for me to sit. The third man with a jaw that looked as if he chewed nails for breakfast brought over a spool of fishing string.

"Guess you guys are prepared for anything," I quipped. I tended to get far more talkative when I was nervous, and I had passed nervous long ago. "I'm definitely leaving a one star review for Park Street Laundry on Yelp."

The big man's jowl wobbled as spoke from his chair. "Joe'll be here soon with the haul. We can count it and leave." He scowled at me. "It seems our front has been blown." He floated his scowl toward Harkey. "That's on you. It seems you left too big of a trail behind."

Harkey tensed at being told off by the boss. He turned to me with wide nostrils. "How did you find me, nosy little bird?"

It seemed it was time to give up my washing blankets storyline for good. I sat up straighter, not wanting them to know how scared I was. "Let's just say you should be more careful where you drop your matches."

Harkey stared at me for a second, then he seemed to comprehend my meaning. His leathery face blanched some as it dawned on him a simple matchbook had betrayed him.

The big man slammed his phone down. "Can't reach that idiot. He's not answering. He better be here soon." He was starting to lose his earlier cool and grew increasingly more agitated. He was worried.

My heart sank knowing that he had nothing to fret about. I was out here on my own, silly, lone woman trying to catch a killer. There was no one coming in behind me to save the day.

With some effort, the big man stood from the chair. "We need to be ready to go the second he shows up."

"What about the girl?" Harkey asked as he tied my hands with the plastic string. It cut painfully into my skin.

The big man's eyes were nearly hidden by the fat in his cheeks, but I could see them skewering me from across the room. "What do you think, fool? We need to get rid of her."

CHAPTER 35

*M*y mind darted from terror to survival mode and back to terror again. Just moving my hands made the tight fishing sting carve lines into my skin. Short of hopping out on the chair, a move that I was sure wouldn't go unnoticed, I had no way out. I was sullenly sinking into that mindset where you start mentally listing things you never got do in your short life, like climbing Everest, sky diving, scuba diving in the deep sea. Or at least that was what a more adventurous person would list. I was more of a take a luxury cruise to the Bahamas type. With the exception of stumbling into trouble with my three captors, my regrets were short, which made the possibility of leaving this life that much worse. I was in the midst of my gloomy thoughts when three quick hard knocks on the door startled me.

"About time." The big man wasn't inclined to make the short journey to the door to answer it. "Greeley, get that. And hurry up. We need to get out of here."

My heart was slamming a wild beat in my chest as I watched the man called Greeley unlock the door. Before he could pull the door handle, it flew open fast enough to knock the large man off his feet.

"Down on your knees. Hands on your heads," the voice was familiar, but I'd never heard it sound so stern or urgent.

Briggs held his gun in both hands out in front of him. He was followed immediately by four other officers. All of them were clad in bullet proof vests. The three men were outnumbered and outgunned. Weapons scraped across the floor toward the police. Greeley and Harkey dropped to their knees and put their hands on their heads. The big man couldn't get down to his knees, and it was entirely likely that once he was down, it would take the entire team to get him back to his feet.

"Just put your hands on your head, Redgrave. It's not like you're going to run for it," Briggs said wryly. His gaze swept the room and landed directly on me. Much to my shock and even a touch of chagrin, he didn't seem the least bit surprised to see me.

Briggs gave some orders to the others to keep an eye on the suspects, then hurried over. The more official expression he wore just seconds before vanished, and a look of relief, so genuine and so palpable it brought a lump to my throat, washed over his face.

"Lacey." It was all he said and frankly it was enough. The sound of it circled my heart and wrapped it in warmth.

He made quick work of the fishing line. I rubbed my wrists to get the feeling back into my hands. I pushed to my feet but swayed backward. Not all the blood had returned to my head. Briggs caught me and pulled me against him. I smacked hard into his bullet proof vest. I reached up and smoothed my hand over it, realizing it was the first time I'd ever touched body armor.

"Are these things supposed to make you look sexier?" I asked. "Cuz, I really like the way you wear this one."

He shook his head. It was the good kind of shake, not the bad one.

I pointed out Harkey. "That's the guy—"

"Who killed Theodore Hall," he finished.

"After what I just went through, you could at least let me complete the sentence. Just when I think I'm a step ahead of you," I said, "you're already there and back again. Why were you not surprised to see me?"

"If this had been ten minutes earlier, trust me, you would have seen surprise, shock, dismay, you name it. But we were on the stake out waiting for the money man to make his drop when I got an urgent call from Hilda. She said Lola came to the station to find me and told Hilda she was worried about you because you were going to the laundromat. Hilda thought it was a strange message and even laughed it off, but when I heard the word laundromat, I knew you were here and in danger. Lacey, you could have been killed. These guys are hardened criminals."

"Yep, I sort of got that from the ambience in the room and the fishing line around my hands. Then there was the big guy's comment about getting rid of me."

Briggs put his hand on my back to lead me out of the building. "We're going to have a long, hard chat about this later."

I smiled at him. "Promise?"

Another head shake. "I'm going to take her outside. Read them their rights and get them ready for transport to the Mayfield station."

It was already dark outside but the light blanket of snow had added a layer of illumination to the town. There were four squad cars parked along the side of the building. A police woman already had the rude woman in handcuffs outside the laundromat.

We reached Briggs' car. He took hold of the zipper on my coat and pulled it up higher. Then he reached behind my head and pulled the hood up. I was close enough to nuzzle my nose against his chin for warmth. The light snuggle prompted him to kiss me lightly on the lips. We were, after all, in the middle of official police business.

There were dozens of questions I needed to ask. I was sure he had a few himself.

But first I needed to make sure I hadn't messed up everything. "I know you've been working on breaking up a gambling ring."

"Yep, those were the guys."

I peered up at him and took a second to sigh in relief again. Minutes before I was in the hands of cold blooded killers. Now I was standing in front of the man who always made me feel safe and content. Sometimes my life was beyond topsy-turvy.

"Did I mess things up by making you arrest them before the money arrived?"

He pushed one of the curls off my cheek and under the hood of my coat. "No, we had him in our sights. The rest of our team apprehended him right over there." He pointed out to the parking lot of the shopping mall. Several police cars were huddled together around a black SUV. A man was sitting in the back of one of the cars.

"How did you know Harkey was the killer?" I asked.

"Oh no, now it's my turn. How did *you* know Harkey was the killer? Let me rephrase that—how on earth did you end up here, chasing an assassin, when you had nothing to work with?" His dark brow arched. "And why did you ignore my order?"

"Was it an order? I thought it was more of a suggestion."

"La—cee," he said stretching out the syllables.

I stood at attention. "May I speak freely without getting into trouble, sir?"

"I'm not sure. Depends just how far you went past my original orders not to get involved."

I held up two fingers an inch apart. "Kind of far." I opened the fingers wider. "O.K. really far. But in my defense, you'd taken yourself off the case. I was worried Chinmoor was just going to make it easy on himself and arrest Dash again."

"Ah ha, so this was all about Dash."

I released a frustrated groan. "We're not going to circle that dead horse again, are we? You know I had every reason to worry. I like Officer Chinmoor, but his investigative skills are—"

"Lacking?"

"Yeah."

He nodded and looked slightly sheepish. "I put myself back on the case yesterday when I thought there might be a connection between the gambling ring and Theodore Hall. I just didn't want to tell you and open up a whole new argument." He leaned forward and kissed my nose. "I've been miserable without you, Lacey."

I blinked back a tear. "That makes two of us."

"Back to your unofficial investigation. How did you end up here tied to a chair?"

I pulled the hood farther over my head to block my ears from the cold. "Here are cliff notes because it's kind of a long story and it's freezing out here. Trespassing on Theo's boat. Matchbook." I held up a finger. "Hold on." I fished the matchbook, still in its tissue wrapper, out of my pocket and handed it to him. "It's evidence for the case. I can show you exactly where I found it on the boat. Back to the quicker version because I think it will make me sound much more efficient and hopefully make you less scowl-y about all the stuff I did that I shouldn't have. Phone number inside the matchbook was to the laundromat. Short stake out in said laundromat on guise of missing pink sock. Quick stop for a glass of wine in seedy pub where perpetrator frequents. And the kicker, and I'll say this fast with a caveat at the end—clandestine trip into the evidence room to run my nose past the incriminating coveralls. Just a quick side note, if I'd been allowed to examine the coveralls this murder would have been solved earlier because Harkey's cigar smoke is all over them. Now the important part—I pleaded and begged and basically gave Hilda no way out of letting me inside, so please do not blame her or even mention it to her. Lastly, I came here and tossed out the code word. I didn't know for sure that it was the code word, but boy did it get their attention in that dark, cold back room."

"Code word?" he asked.

I pointed to the front of the matchbook still in his hand. "See how mermaid is circled?"

A somewhat prideful smile appeared on his face. "You could have been hurt or killed, but I've got to say, that was some amazing detective work."

"Thank you. Does that mean I'm off the hook for any future lecture about all of this?"

"Absolutely not."

"Darn. But did I mention how dangerously handsome you looked when you burst into that room? I've never seen you from that side of the crime scene. If my heart hadn't already been pounding at the prospect of a terrible death, it would have definitely been skipping and jumping at the sight of the devilishly good looking detective hard at work catching the bad guys."

"Thank you. And yet, I'm unmoved in my resolve to talk about this later. But for now—I'm just glad you're safe." He lifted my chin and pressed his mouth against mine for a kiss that warmed all the cold parts.

CHAPTER 36

I opened the door before Dash had a chance to knock. (It might have been the gold wrapped box of chocolates in his hand.) "Guess there's no missing my loud footsteps on the porch," he said with a laugh.

"That and I have a sixth sense when it comes to chocolate. Is that for me?"

"No, actually, I was just on the way to my other neighbor who risked her life to find a killer and clear my name." He held out the chocolates.

I took them with a curtsy and motioned him to come inside.

"I don't have time to stay. I'm taking Britney out to dinner."

I stopped halfway in unwrapping the box. "That's nice. Are things back on?" I shook my head. "None of my business. Never mind."

"It's your business, Lacey, because you're my friend. And I don't have as many of those as I used to. But Britney was right there for me. Like you, she knew I hadn't committed murder. I need someone like that. Someone solid and supportive. But," he said before I could say anything. "I told her we're going to take it slow. She's in agreement. Elsie is *really* in agreement. I can finally go back into the bakery and buy muffins for breakfast. Definitely missed those muffins."

I tossed aside the gold paper and opened the box to peruse my lovely choices. I went for a square. Squares were always caramel. "I think that's a wise plan. The taking it slow part, not the eating muffins for breakfast. Those things are calorie bombs." I finished my comment by taking a big bite of chewy caramel. "Hmm, so good."

Dash laughed. "I'll let you go then. It was just my lame little way of saying thank you for saving me from one of the darkest weeks of my life." His green eyes were shiny like jewels. "Really, Lacey. I can't thank you enough."

"I'm glad I could help, Dash. Have a nice dinner."

Kingston cooed angrily because I closed the door without inviting Dash inside. He marched back and forth on his perch and then dropped to the floor and walked over to wrestle around with the gold paper, apparently hoping a goodie would drop out.

Ten minutes later, my expected guest knocked on the door. My stomach was back to doing little somersaults at the thought of seeing Briggs. He'd ridden his motorcycle and was wearing his black leather jacket over his t-shirt.

"I might like this leather jacket even better than the bullet-proof vest," I quipped as I grabbed his hand and pulled him inside.

"That's good to hear because the jacket is much more comfortable to wear."

Briggs' sweet tooth could rival mine. He headed straight for the box of chocolates. Kingston joined him by fluttering up to the back of the couch so he could get a better view of the box. "These look good." He picked up a chocolate. "Who are they from?"

"Dash," I said with a grin.

He stopped the chocolate halfway to his mouth.

"Seriously, James?" I asked.

He nodded. "You're right. Sorry. It's a habit." He pushed the chocolate into his mouth. "Darn, bad choice. Coconut."

"Maybe a little karma playing its hand?" I winked. "Wait. So you don't like coconut?"

"Not at all." He walked over to me. "Is that a problem?"

"No. Just good to know when I buy hair products."

He smiled, it was that lazy half smile that made my knees weak. His arm went around me, and he pulled me against him.

I peered up at him. "James, I'm sorry I questioned your integrity. I should have known better. It won't happen again."

"And I'm sorry I let my pride and jealousy get in the way of our relationship. I know you were concerned about Dash, and you had every right to be."

I hopped up on my toes and kissed him. "And—"

"And next time I'll let you see all the evidence and I won't leave you on your own to investigate a murder because, as we know, trouble sticks to you like the caramel I taste on your lips."

His cocoa brown eyes melted my heart as he gazed at me. "Don't you have one more thing to add?" he asked.

"I suppose. I promise not to walk into seedy Mermaid themed bars or laundromats that are fronts for gambling rings."

His mouth pulled into a wry grin. "A little more specific than I was hoping for but it's a start. Just stay safe, Lacey, because I'm getting really used to having you in my arms." He pressed his mouth to mine.

SWEET CHERRY AND BLUEBERRY TARTS

View online at: www.londonlovett.com/recipe-box/

Sweet Cherry and Blueberry
TARTS

Ingredients:

Pecan Shortbread Crust:
1 3/4 cup all-purpose flour
3/4 cup confectioner's sugar
1/4 tsp salt
1/2 cup + 3 Tbsp very cold butter
1 egg yolk, beaten
3/4 cup finely chopped pecans
1-2 Tbsp cold water

Filling:
3 cups frozen sweet cherries
1 cup frozen blueberries
zest from 1 lemon
2 tsp lemon juice
1/2 cup granulated sugar
2 tsp corn starch

Directions:

1. Preheat oven to 350°

2. In a large bowl, whisk together flour, confectioner's sugar and salt. Place dry mixture into a food processor (option: you can also use a pastry cutter in a bowl).

3. Cut cold butter into cubes and add it to the dry mixture. Pulse in food processor (or cut with pastry blender) until it resembles small peas. Beat 1 Tbsp of cold water into the egg yolk and add to processor. Run the food processor until mixture gathers together into a ball. (Add more water if needed.)

4. Transfer ball of dough to a bowl and knead in the chopped pecans.

5. Grease or spray small tart pans (this recipe makes 4-5 4 inch tarts). Press dough into prepared tart pans to form the crust. (option: you can roll out a bit of the dough and cut shapes to decorate the top of the pies--see images.) Bake empty pecan shortbread crusts for 15 minutes or until just lightly golden.

6. Prepare filling: Add berries, cherries, lemon zest, lemon juice and granulated sugar to a medium saucepan. Cook over medium heat, stirring frequently. As the fruit softens add in 2 tsp of corn starch and mash with a potato masher or fork. Continue cooking until mixture thickens (approx. 12 minutes over low/medium heat).

7. Fill prebaked tart shells with berry mixture. (If you cut out some shapes of dough add them on the top here.) Bake at 350° for 12-13 minutes. Bake just until crust is golden brown on edges of tart.

8. Allow tarts to cool before serving.

9. Enjoy!

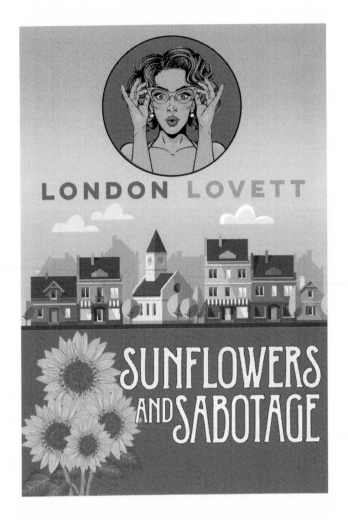

Continue the Port Danby Cozy Mystery series with Book 10, Sunflowers and Sabotage.

ABOUT THE AUTHOR

London Lovett is the author of the Port Danby, Firefly Junction and Starfire Cozy Mystery series. She loves getting caught up in a good mystery and baking delicious new treats! (The recipes from each book are available on www.londonlovett.com/recipe-box)

Subscribe to London's newsletter to never miss an update.

https://www.londonlovett.com/
londonlovettwrites@gmail.com
Follow on Instagram: @LondonLovettWrites

Manufactured by Amazon.ca
Bolton, ON

11589511R00326